Praise for
Tom Spanbauer

I Loved You More

A great read, *I Loved You More* is a brutal and beautiful book of love, sex, and friendship that begins in the impossible but totally mesmerizing decade of the 1980s and spans the next twenty years.

SAM ADAMS, Former Mayor of Portland, Oregon

A masterful novel of what becomes of us long after we've "come of age" and done all the brave things we thought would save us. Tom Spanbauer's pages pulse with life in all its messy beauty.

ARIEL GORE, Publisher of *Hip Mama* magazine
and author of *The End of Eve*

Intelligence, wit, generosity, love, wisdom, insight, humility, guts, heart-crushing truth and spirit-lifting grace – it's all there in *I Loved You More*. This is Tom Spanbauer's wrenching and beautiful masterpiece.

CHERYL STRAYED, Author of *Wild*

Tom Spanbauer's *I Loved You More* is the most important book on sexuality, love, and the lowdown of relationships that I have ever read. The brilliant language is an epic ballad so deeply rendered it killed me and resurrected me a page at a time. This book is not a love story. It guts the heart of the cliché love story and hands it back to you, beating. Love is the endless falling.

LIDIA YUKNAVITCH, Author of *Dora: A Headcase*

Faraway Places

The thing about Tom Spanbauer is – he is the real deal. [*Faraway Places*] is masterly – a near perfect book. The story is hypnotic, mesmerizing, delicately brilliant – and so well made. While you are lulled by the language and the characters, the storyline builds and then like a well-timed firework explodes – surprising, enthralling, captivating.

    A.M. HOMES, Author of *May We Be Forgiven*

A taut, brutal narrative ... that comes to hypnotize, shimmering like the brilliant sun on the alfalfa fields.

    THE NEW YORK TIMES BOOK REVIEW

Forceful and moving ... Spanbauer tells his short, brutal story with delicacy and deep respect for place and character.

    PUBLISHERS WEEKLY

The Man Who Fell in Love with the Moon

The miracle of this novel it that it obliges us to rethink our whole idea of narration and history and myth. Tom Spanbauer's wild West is the hurly-burly of the mind. He takes us into territories where few of us would ever dare to go.

    THE NEW YORK TIMES BOOK REVIEW

Haunting and earthy, this deeply felt tale of love and loss ... Spanbauer fuses raunchy dialogue, pathos, local color, heartbreak and a serious investigation of racism in this stunning narrative.

    PUBLISHERS WEEKLY

Gender and racial lines are bent out of shape in this tale of turn-of-the-century Idaho spun by a youth who is part Indian, not quite wholly homosexual, and in the grip of a powerful imagination. Spanbauer creates a pansexual West that John Wayne wouldn't have recognized.

    KIRKUS REVIEWS

A visceral, sprawling tragic-comedy ... *The Man Who Fell in Love with the Moon* is equal parts bizarre *Bildungsroman*, raucous picaresque, and hard-driving wild-West yarn.

    NEW YORK MAGAZINE

A masterful plot ... Delightfully unpredictable and compelling.

    LIBRARY JOURNAL

In The City of Shy Hunters

An expertly drawn, starkly authentic, early-1980s Manhattan provides the setting for this sprawling novel by Spanbauer. Spanbauer's rapid-fire narration and clipped sentences generate a surprising amount of tension and gritty emotion, as does his vibrant, dead-on dialogue and keen sense of place. This is a big, brazen, histrionic work of fiction, one that pays respectable, if unsentimental, homage to a devastating period in gay history.

PUBLISHERS WEEKLY

Unlike other "early AIDS" novels, this one acknowledges that AIDS touches all classes, races, religions, and sexual orientations. Excellent characters (real New Yorkers), great writing, and a new twist on an over-used plot recommend this book for most libraries, though some readers might want a more conventional ending.

LIBRARY JOURNAL

A master narrator and stylist ... *In the City of Shy Hunters* is so finely crafted, Spanbauer's characters so true to life, the New York City he remembers from the early days of the plague so exactly captures in its "unrelenting" mess and glory, you'll think you've been reading a modernist classic.

PETER KURTH, *Salon.com*

Spanbauer's genius resides even in the asides ... teas[ing] out the genuine complexity of human love.

THOMAS MCGONIGLE, *The Washington Post*

In the City of Shy Hunters has the earmarks of a literary landmark ... Its importance and originality are unmistakable.

LAURA DEMANSKI, *The Baltimore Sun*

Ambitious and compelling ... a mixture of the ghastly, the hilariousism and the curiously touching.

JOHN HARTL, *The Seattle Times*

In the City of Shy Hunters is a chronicle of deaths foretold, a journal of the plague years when AIDS swept through the city and destroyed a culture that had barely taken hold.

JEFF BAKER, *The Oregonian*

A big ambitious stylefest of a novel, in the mode of ... Edmund White's *The Farewell Symphony*, Allan Gurganus's *Plays Well with Others*, and Dale Peak's *Now It's Time to Say Goodbye* ... What distinguishes Spanbauer's novel from the rest of the pack is his hellish, distinctive voice. Longtime fans will recognize its unusual sentences, at once choppy and strangely elegant, overtly informative but weirdly surreal, tender of phrase yet cleansed of overt emotion.

DENNIS COOPER, *The Village Voice*

Tom Spanbauer breaks all the rules in his new novel *In the City of Shy Hunters* – rules of grammar, rules of social propriety, rules of sanctioned sexuality, rules that keep a novelist at a desk, on a page, in the real world.

M. L. LYKE, *Seattle Post-Intelligencer*

Mesmerizing dialogue and gritty characters immediately startle you ... The book may consist of letters typed upon a page, but those words transcend mere storytelling by nearly leaping forth and materializing into a stunning theatrical presentation. This writing as performance art ... Our beloved Spanbauer has retaken center stage. He has surpassed the art of writing dangerously to create the theater of writing dramatically.

SUSAN WICKSTORM, *Willamette Week*

In the City of Shy Hunters is near-epic in its emotional scope, a sprawling story that recalls at once the freewheeling black comedy of Ken Kesey's work, the spiritual quest at the heart of *Zen and the Art of Motorcycle Maintenance*, and some of the precise diction of Gertrude Stein. ... There is such a myriad of small truths here that the cumulative effect is overwhelming ... Fascinating and compelling.

KEN FURTADO, *Lambda Book Report*

Now Is the Hour

Publishers Weekly choice for one of the best 100 books of 2006

This author can write. You feel pulled in immediately just by the rhythms of his language. Then by his great humor, his vast heart. There is no one like Tom Spanbauer writing in America. What a terrific novel! What a huge talent.

NATALIE GOLDBERG, Author of *Writing Down the Bones*

In Tom Spanbauer's *Now Is the Hour*, white small-town America gets its cherry busted in an orgy of cigarette smoke and racism.

CHUCK PALAHNIUK, author of *Fight Club*

Copyright © 2013
Tom Spanbauer

Library of Congress
Cataloging-in-Publication Data

Hawthorne Books
& Literary Arts

Spanbauer, Tom.
I loved you more: a novel /
By Tom Spanbauer.
pages cm
ISBN 978-0-9860007-8-2
I. Title.

PS3569.P339L68 2013
813'.54–DC23

9   2201 Northeast 23rd Avenue
8   3rd Floor
7   Portland, Oregon 97212
6   hawthornebooks.com
5   *Form*:
4   Adam McIsaac/Sibley House
3
2   Printed in China
1   Set in Paperback

For Pete

I Loved You More

A Novel

Tom Spanbauer

HAWTHORNE BOOKS & LITERARY ARTS
Portland, Oregon | MMXIV

Contents

I LOVED YOU MORE

Book One
Hank & Ben

PART ONE | *Got to Go Pal*

1.

The Maroni

GOT TO GO PAL WERE THE LAST WORDS ON THE PAGE OF
the last letter I wrote Hank Christian. Soon as I wrote them down
I knew they were the words that hurt. The words that could turn
his heart against me. All those years, twenty-three of them, how
Hank and I joked back and forth, *got to go pal* now were the words
lying on the page. That old litany in this strange new place, how
it made my heart stop.

October 1, 2000. All day I sat with that letter. Wondering if
I should make it sound so final and forever, or fuck it, just take
the risk and say something more, something ridiculous at such a
ridiculous time to say it: if I should tell Hank to stop using that
Just For Men hair color because the light through his hair made
his thin hair look purple. When you say goodbye to someone you
love, maybe if you say something crazy, something true, maybe
he won't stop loving you.

I ended up not giving Hank the hair tip. So many times I've
regretted it, thought I should've said the hair thing right after
got to go pal. Maybe it would've changed the way things turned
out. If nothing else, it would have made him laugh. Hank's laugh.
That big burst from down deep coming on fast shaking him
around. But I didn't.

It wasn't long after the letter he married Ruth. In Florida,
three thousand miles away he lived, and he goes and has his
wedding three blocks from my house in Portland, Oregon. Still
don't know who his best man was.

LIKE MOST LOVE affairs, Hank and I didn't start off so good. In fact I hated his guts. Every time Jeske called on him, which was every week, Hank read his sentences out loud to the class and it never failed, Jeske always praised him as if Hank was the next Nadine Gordimer, or Louise Glück, or Harold Brodkey. Jeske even had a special name for Hank. *Maroni.* That's what he called Hank. *You've really knocked the ball out of the park this time, Maroni! You really nailed it on the head, pal! Just take a look at that, would you!*

Columbia University, winter quarter, 1985. Twelve weeks of a three-hour-long night class in a hot big bright amphitheater room. Jeske down in front of us, trim, natty, silver hair, in some kind of military hat. Skin that was flushed from too many cigarettes. Something classy about him, one of those New England guys who just stepped off his sailboat. Our eyes on him. Our eyes never left him. You never knew what he was going to do next. Every class he bragged how he went three hours without pishing. Wednesdays six to nine. Thirty-six fucking hours and Jeske never called on me. Not one time. Forty people in that class and everybody got at least one chance, but not me. A couple others in class Jeske liked besides Hank, but to my ears it was all *Maroni! Maroni! Maroni!*

Then came that class. The last class of the semester. The last part of the last hour. The last reader. Finally Thomas Jeske, Commodore Fiction himself, called on me. Fuck. My body did that separating thing where all of a sudden I'm way out there somewhere looking down at me sitting in a bright room in an amphitheater chair, the fake wood desk top flap out flat, my faraway hands trying to hold my pages still. I'm trying to find my breath, keep my asshole tight, trying to keep my chin from turning into rubber bands. All the rules I didn't know how to get right: *Never go beneath the surface. Speak with a burnt tongue. It's not writing, it's making. Take the approach that rebukes your own nature. Never explain. Never complain. Latinate Latinate Latinate.*

I took the knife, put it to my chest, punched hard in, cut down and around, pulled my throbbing heart out and laid it down on the page. But I wasn't bleeding enough. The words sounded stupid. My voice in the fluorescent amphitheater did not project, was too high, cracking like an adolescent whose balls had just dropped. Fuck. There was no getting away from it. I sounded the way I always sounded: a Catholic boy with a big apology. Then the long pause. The long piece of silence after where all there was, was my breath. A drop of sweat rolled down the inside of my arm. Everything gets bright and hot and full.

The eleventh hour! Jeske cries out, *Way to go, pal! Grunewald's pulled it out of his ass on the eleventh hour!*

Looking back on that day now, I wonder. Maybe that was the first time for Hank. That he really looked at me.

THE FIRST TIME I really looked at Hank, really stopped and looked, was during one of Jeske's classes. By then I knew who Hank was, of course. How could you not know *The Maroni*? But this one particular class I'm talking about, there was a moment that everything went away and my eyes filled up with nothing but Hank Christian.

In the middle of one of Jeske's lectures, there was a loud crash in the hall. You might think so what, a loud crash in the hall – on most college campuses that doesn't mean much. But when it's night and it's Columbia University, the hallway outside your classroom door is really a New York street. After the crash, Jeske quit talking and we in the class all looked around at each other. There was a way you could tell Jeske wanted to go to the open door and check out the situation, but he hesitated. I saw him do it. Hesitate. Something you don't figure Commodore Fiction to do. His thin body did a quick lean toward the door for a second, then stopped because he thought better. Hank saw it too. Oh! Commodore! My! Commodore! Hank saw the Commodore of the mighty ship stall. He was up and out of his seat just like that.

Hank's a big guy. Big arms, big chest. Twenty-seven to my thirty-seven years.

Thirty-seven years old. Columbia University. I've always been a late bloomer. That day, as Hank made his way through the seats and down to the doorway, Hank was holding his body that way he does. He pushes out and raises up his chest, pulls his chin down, his shoulders down, and flexes his biceps. I've seen Hank do that a lot. Usually he does that when he's trying to express something inside him that's big – as if his body is literally trying to push the thought or the feeling that's inside him out, but that day in class Hank was puffing up for another reason. He was on a mission. I've never seen Hank do anything so perfect, so true to who he was. Hank stood himself in the doorway, at the portal, at attention, elbows out touching each side of the door. Our line-backer, our protector, our bodyguard, our hero.

Immediately I was embarrassed for him. Such an obvious show of macho. I mean, what was Maroni trying to prove? That he could save our sinking ship from the big, bad pirates in the hall-way? Yet maybe there *were* pirates in the hallway! Maybe the loud crash was a street gang, or some crazy motherfucker. Maybe with a gun. Then what was Maroni going to do? Stop the bullet?

Saint Hank Christian, Guardian of the Doorway. At that moment, I had no idea what a friend, a lover, what a hero, Hank would be to me. All I could know was what I saw. His dark-brown hair down to his shoulders. Lots of hair back then, the Eighties, plus a mustache too. Almost as big as mine. Beneath his deep-set eyes – eyes with his complexion you'd figure would be blue, but weren't, were dark, almost black, under the efficient line of Roman nose, above the square jaw a bit of cleft, straight teeth, Hank's sweet smiling lips that one day no matter what I was going to kiss.

Sure made Jeske proud. Pretty soon, a bunch of other guys, but not me, were up at the door standing with Hank.

SOME MONTHS LATER, when I didn't hate Hank anymore, when I was getting to know Hank, I asked Hank what *Maroni* meant.

He said something about how *Maroni* was Italian for how guys talk to one another. Like *dude* maybe, or *buddy*, or *pal*. I never did get it exactly what *Maroni* meant. But that was just Hank. He always played his cards close to his chest, especially at the beginning. It wasn't that he had something to conceal. Hank liked to say he was a ghost. A warrior ghost. He touched the world and when he was done he left no trace. What was left of him was his sentences on the page. No wonder I fell in love with him. Seduce the laconic straight guy. Not necessarily to fuck him, but to bring him out. And not *out* like *coming out*, but *out* in the sense of *inner workings revealed*. If I could understand my father, if my father could actually be someone I could know, by knowing him, I could gauge myself against him, and discover how I was and how I was not like him.

Those first four or five weeks, though, Hank was fucking Maroni, Jeske's private ass kisser. Then it was Saint Hank Christian Guardian of the Doorway, but when it really happened big time was the night at Ursula Crohn's apartment. The first time Hank actually put his body next to me. As soon as he spoke, out of Hank's sweet lips the blow, some kind of frenzy in my heart.

Somebody who does that. Reveals you to yourself. You can't help but love.

SOMETHING I'D LIKE to say. All this I'm recalling here is not actually what happened but me remembering it. It's only now, after all the years, after all the death, after years and years of running it through running it through, there's a way that a sixty-year-old me can look at the same situation the forty-year-old looked at and see another story altogether.

It's like a photograph of two friends. Let's say me and Hank. 1988 and it's my fortieth birthday. We've just walked across the Brooklyn Bridge because we always walk across the Brooklyn Bridge on my birthday. Hank's left arm is over my shoulder. You can't see his whole left hand, just the long fingers against my blue

T-shirt, fingertips at my clavicle. My right arm is over Hank's arm because I am maybe a half-foot taller. Hank's wearing a wife-beater, a black one. His hair is shorter, mine too, because the Eighties are almost over. And a beard, gray in his beard. He's pulling his shoulders down, straightening his neck, pulling his chest up and out. I look skinny next to him. There's a Budweiser in my hand. Behind us is Manhattan and a big mustard brown cable of Brooklyn Bridge. We are smiling in a way that says that we are not like our fathers. One of us is straight and one of us is gay. We are men and we are friends and we are celebrating. We have each other's backs. We'll go to the mat. Mates the way Australians say *mate*. We're laughing hard at our joke. Instead of *cheese*, Hank has just said the thing Jeske always said, *Got to go pal*.

That photograph that back then, weeks later when we saw it, we scrutinized ourselves for what was important, what was wrong. Hank says, *Jeez I'm getting fat! Look at all the gray in my beard!* I say, *My hair never looks right. When am I going to get used to having this fucking nose?*

Now that same photograph some twenty years later, it's still just Hank Christian and Ben Grunewald, our arms around each other, on the Brooklyn Bridge. But what I can see now. The cancer that had started on Hank's cock. My viral load doubling every week. Then there's Ruth. Ruth Dearden. It won't be until 1999 and on the other side of the country in Portland, Oregon, before I introduce them, but still she's there between Hank and me. Almost as tall as me. Red hair, thick and long. Her hair looks great because I did give *her* her hair tip. *It's all in the forehead. Women like you and with a jaw like that, you should never hide your forehead.* Plus the color highlights. Blue eyes and tinted blue contacts. Dangerous beauty because her beauty wasn't given. Dangerous beauty because it's been hard won. So much like me. Larger than life, all that reckless power that somebody who has just discovered her power has.

Be careful, she's about to knock something over. Maybe it will be you.

MORE THAN LIKELY, you're like me and think that something
like this could never happen to you. That you could love a man,
then love a woman – two extraordinary people, two unique ways
of loving, from different decades, on different ends of the continent, and then somehow, through an accident of the universe,
or a destiny preordained – either way you'll never know – what's
important is that what happens is something you could never in
a million years have planned, and there you are the three of you,
dancing the ancient dance whose only rule is with three add one,
if not, subtract. If three doesn't find four, three goes back to two.
Add or subtract. That's the rule.

Myself, once I left the Catholic Church, and then my wife,
I've tried to stay away from rules. For example, I have loved men
and I have loved women. Most rule books say you can't do that.
So most of me says this rule of three is just that: somebody's rule.
Something Jung or somebody like him made up. But for Hank
and Ruth and me, I've got to say, three was not an option.

I've tried and tried but I can't figure out the fate, the destiny
part. That's where madness lies. So if I can't figure out the big
picture, then maybe I can look at the smaller one. How much of
this was Ruth. How much of this was Hank. How much of this
was me.

Mostly, I think it was Ruth's fault. But I *would* think that,
now wouldn't I? In the end she got Hank and I lost Hank. My ego's
hurt and my heart is broken, and of course, I'm going to blame
the bitch. I got to cop to it. Most of my days are spent blaming Ruth.

Those years after I got home from the hospital were the
years. Just Ruth and me. We were our own world. Funny, fucked
up, me half-dead, delusional, both of us awkward. Full of love,
so full of fear. My God, now there's a strange love affair for you.
Ruth's promise: her sole purpose in life to keep me alive, to
make me happy. No matter how much I wanted it to work, Ruth
and I didn't work. The way Ruth loved me was the way I loved
Hank. How we both thought that great a love would be enough.

Destiny, fate, fucking fortune, whatever it is, it's Christmas

Eve 1999 and Hank comes to visit me in Portland. Nearly twelve
years since we'd seen each other. The next day, Christmas day,
Hank Christian's crying in my kitchen. Hank's blind in one eye and
the doctors say his cancer's in remission. What's left of me
after AIDS. I'm fifty-one. Hank's forty-one. Two aging men who'd
stared death down, now hanging on to each other for dear life.
     The next day, I introduce him to Ruth. Hank Christian.
Straight Hank Christian. Should've known. Hank's always had a
thing for redheads.
     And Ruth, the woman scorned because I didn't love her the
way she loved me. Hell hath no fury – we've all heard that one.
But as my therapist Judith pointed out, wasn't *my* scorn every bit
as full of hell's fury? Maybe it's *hell hath no fury like a faggot
scorned*. And as Hank pointed out, the *real problem*, he said, was
that Ruth and I were *so similar*. Whatever the case may be,
when Hank entered the picture, Ruth Dearden, the over-sized
wallflower of thirty-seven years – then the sunflower that with
each passing year got deeper and stronger and skinnier, and more
and more beautiful, by the time she was forty, once she found
herself in the big piece of bright sunlight between me and Hank,
that girl *worked* it. She had the both of us by the balls. Trouble
was, only I could see it. By then Hank was in love and love is blind
but people ain't. But there I was again. Just like with my big sis,
Margaret. If I would've said anything it would've sounded like I
was just jealous. And hey! I'm here to testify. I was *fucking* jealous.
     Then I think the fault was mostly Hank's. Capricorns
always manipulate themselves to the best advantage. I believe
that about Hank even though I don't believe in astrology. Especially at the end there. Now you might say: don't we all manipulate ourselves to the best advantage? The answer is *no*. People
like Ruth and I only learned late in life how to put ourselves first.
Hank never had that problem, believe me. Hank was *the man,
Maroni,* and along with that position came his whole shtick about
men on Mars and women on Venus – please. And since Hank
found Ruth and me *so similar* – make that women and *gay men* on

Venus. Really, straight guys can be so fucking obdurate, so on Mars – especially Hank.

And something else about Hank. I'd learned a long time ago with Olga not to get between Hank and his woman. Well, I got between all right. Yet, at some point or another, each one of us was between. Maybe that's the problem with three.

Really though this was my fault. All of it. After all, I am the ex-Catholic and I introduced them. Hank was reeling from a bout with his girlfriend, who was borderline. Time was running out on Ruth's alimony check and she was facing work at Walgreens. Ruth really needed help. But by then I hated her. Not because of Hank – he hadn't quite come on the scene yet. No, I hated Ruth because she just couldn't get it, the way I got it with Hank, that I loved her, but didn't want to fuck her.

If I had it all to do over again, I wouldn't. So much pain involved. Yet all this pain wears my face. If only I could have been one of the big-spirited men who narrate my novels instead of the stink-eyed petty jealous fool that I was.

The rule of three. Her fault. His fault. My fault. Destiny, fortune, fame. All that was left unsaid.

WHEN THE DUST settled and the newlyweds left town, back to Florida, they left me here in the Portlandia rain, my mind devouring itself.

Yet even now, I've never regretted the Dear Hank letter. It's just that maybe I should have given Hank the hair tip. Made him laugh one last time. But hair tip or no hair tip, *Got to go pal* was the only way.

THERE'S SOMETHING ELSE important that happened in Jeske's class. How I made it in. After the article about him in *Vanity Fair*, he was a real celebrity. Everybody wanted a piece of him. Over a hundred people signed up for his class. There was only room for forty. So what Jeske does is he gets all hundred of us together in one big classroom, then announces that each of us has to stand up and tell the class the scariest thing about ourselves. And if it isn't scary enough he won't let us in.

In a New York minute, quiet in that room like every person sitting in the room had just stopped breathing. We don't go row by row. We don't go alphabetically. Jeske doesn't call on us. He just waits for whoever stands up. It was five minutes on the black and white clock before anybody stands up. Then two people stand up at the same time. Fuck, the tension in the room. One guy, Randy Goldblatt, who's overweight, stands up and says some damn thing and Jeske won't let him sit down until he admits that he's fat. Randy's wearing a red, white, and blue horizontal striped T-shirt. He pulls his T-shirt down over his hairy belly. He's got thick glasses and he is crying. I'm chewing on my thumbnail and then it bleeds and I get blood on my shirt. I'm a fucking wreck.

Maroni's in class that day, but the Maroni doesn't have to stand up.

David, Gary, and Lester all stand up.

Jeske rips them to shreds.

I'm one of the last people to go.

I stand up and I have no idea what keeps me standing up. Try and cover up the blood spot on my shirt. I'm in the second row in the front and most of the class is behind me. I start to speak and Jeske stops me. Tells me he can't hear. Tells me to stop mumbling. To speak up.

The scariest thing about me. That day I don't have a clue what that is. So I make up some shit about not being able to distinguish between dreams and reality.

"That's certifiable," Jeske says, "Go on."

What I say next is more bullshit and Jeske knows it and he tells me to sit the fuck down. I think I'm shafted for sure, but the next day somehow I've made it onto the class list.

WHAT I'D LIKE to do now is take the opportunity. To say what I couldn't even think that Wednesday evening in Jeske's class,

1985. The scariest thing about myself. If I were to have spoken it
out loud.

I was impotent.

By that time of my life, my thirty-seventh year – heterosexual, bisexual, homosexual, top or bottom, threesomes, orgies
with men and women, with a whip in my hand or chained to
the radiator, whatever way two or more people can get together
sexually. Drunk or stoned or otherwise fucked up. Hell, even
when it was just me alone stone cold sober.

I couldn't get it up.

Kaput. Nada. Rien. Kabisa. Zip.

Fucking limp dick.

Erectile dysfunction, man.

The shame of it.

URSULA CROHN'S INVITATION was a written invitation.
She and some other of Jeske's students were gathering together
on a Friday night to read their work to one another. I remember
holding the invitation in the bright glare of the fluorescent hallway of 211 East Fifth Street. My steel gray apartment door #1A
just past the open aluminum mailbox door. Ursula's handwriting
lilted left on blue and yellow swirled stationery with a matching
envelope and a stamp of Martin Luther King. I've always wondered
at people who have stationery and envelopes and unusual
stamps and a handy fountain pen and the address altogether so
they can quickly jot off personal notes. It takes me an hour just
to find my glasses. Forget the stamp. To coordinate all that shit and
then to have it match, like the letter itself is an invention of art,
is truly a marvel to me.

The reason why I remember the letter, though, was not
because of its bread-and-butter quality but for something else:
I wasn't used to being invited to the party. I was easily ten to
fifteen years older than the other students at Columbia. Plus,
besides being older, I was an odd duck. Always been an odd duck.
Above the toilet in my mother's bathroom is a blue and white

ceramic mother duck with three blue and white little ducks
swimming behind. They're all swimming with their beaks lined
up with their mother's in a straight line – then there's the odd
duck, the black duck with his bill tipped down.

Plus, unlike my fellow students, I had a job. Actually two
jobs. As a waiter at Café Un Deux Trois four nights a week.
And then my super job. I started out with one building, then after
I graduated Columbia there was four. So I didn't do a lot of
social gatherings. Especially literary ones. Especially after I quit
the restaurant business and was just the super. Make that
janitor. More than anything, though, what was impressive about
Ursula Crohn's letter was that it was Ursula Crohn inviting me.
She was another one of Jeske's favorites.

I had to drink a lot first, Baileys and some kind of cheap
brandy. Smoked a doobie. Then I put this big-ass Hoss Cartwright
cowboy hat on and these black high platform shoes spray-painted
with green glitter from the late Seventies – articles of clothing
I'd only wear to a costume party. But for some damn reason wore
that night. My black Peterbilt muscle-guy zippered jacket.

Ursula's address was on Maiden Lane or one of those tiny
hard to find streets in the financial district. I set off walking
from East Fifth Street, already late. I brought the bottle with me.
Clomping through those narrow streets that wind through all
those monoliths of money. It was raining. I remember because I
didn't have an umbrella, but I had the hat. My feet hurt. Finally
when I found the address there was a lot of fuss with the
intercom and pushing the right button and yelling at a wall in a
dark brick doorway. Then the formidable elevator, a freight
elevator, all the sides open, just that cross hatch between you and
the elevator shaft, the red numbers of the floor going by slow
on the back wall. On floor one thousand or something like that,
Ursula opened the gates to an industrial loft apartment like
you see in Hollywood movies that starving artists live in with a
one-eighty view of the city that takes up half the floor.

If my friends could see me now.

Friends: Ephraim, my Native brother in Fort Hall. Reuben Flores, Sal Nash, Gary Whitcombe, and Tim Tyler, my Boise, Idaho, buddies. Other than those guys, I don't know who those friends would've been. Wilbur Tucker, the owner of the Blind Lemon in Pocatello, maybe my ex-wife, Evelyn, or Bette. I didn't know him yet, otherwise, right off, I would have known who my friends were: Hank.

Really though, walking into Ursula's apartment was like sitting in a dentist's office in Bumfuck, Idaho, and opening a *New Yorker* and seeing your name listed under *Fiction*. Plus, every time I walk into a room with a bunch of people in it, I always get the feeling that they all collectively know something important about me, something wrong, that they've just been discussing.

I must have seemed ten feet tall in my hat and shoes. Plus I was probably an hour and a half late. Dripping wet. And I hate people who come late and make an entrance.

Ursula Crohn is a woman way too smart with a wicked sense of humor. Jewish. Three strikes and you're out. She's tiny, dark, and beautiful. Her hair dyed black and straightened with an iron. She'd told me that about her hair, and just the way she'd told it made me laugh like crazy. Plus, she was one of Jeske's girls. Really, you have to be careful with a woman like that. Especially when you appear to her as someone exotic.

Maroni is reading. And I've made a fuss and interrupted everything. Ursula puts her finger to her lips, shows me the pile of shoes and coats, and motions with her bright red fingernails to come into the circle and sit down. I take my Peterbilt off and my platforms, grab my pages out of my coat pocket and fold them into the back pocket of my Levi's. Leave my hat on.

There are a bunch of people crowded in the room, twelve to fifteen. Most of them from Jeske's class. Randy Goldblatt's there, and David, Gary, and Lester, too. In the middle of the room is a fireplace and in front of the fireplace a Persian carpet and on the Persian carpet is a stool. Maroni is sitting on the stool. Everybody else is sitting and lounging around on colorful pillows

and ottomans. On a long low coffee table thing is a feast of broccoli and carrots and celery and cauliflower and avocado dip
and Lay's potato chips. Jugs of red wine. Jugs of white wine. Jugs
of rosé. Entenmann's. Pepperoni pizza. The thin kind of pizza.
Real Italian pizza. My favorite kind of pizza. Not the gobbed-on
American kind of pizza with layers of sticky cheese.

I sit down cross-legged as quiet as I can, but when my ass
hits the floor, the pages in my back pocket crunch. So then I
have to take my pages out of my pocket. Then in my hands, the
pages. Fucking paper, man, can make a racket. I want to unfold
my pages to see what I've brought, but already I'm over with the
crunching paper. Besides my ears are immediately listening
hard to Hank because what Hank knows I want to know too. His
story is a story about a guy who works in a carnival. Then I notice
something I wish I'd never noticed. My right sock has a big hole
in it and there's my big toe poking out. With green glitter on it.
Then there's the smell. Wet socks and sweat from the platform
shoes. I'm sure the smell isn't half as bad as I imagine it. But still,
the rest of Hank's story, I don't hear a word because all I can
think of is the smell coming off my feet.

Funny, now that I think about it, in Portlandia that first
day I introduced Hank to Ruth, I took Hank up to her house and
we walked up to the front door and the door was open and I
called in but Ruth didn't answer. So Hank and I walked around
the side of her house and Hank stepped in a big pile of dog shit.
So when Hank first met Ruth he was scraping dog doo off his
shoes. Took me years to understand that something like that
could happen to *The Maroni*, Hank Christian. That he could be a
dork too. A Soul Brother of Outrageous Predicaments. Come to
think of it, Ruth Dearden was pretty outrageous herself.

Back in Ursula Crohn's artist's loft, twenty-three years
earlier, I'm busy trying to stuff my green glittered toe back into
my smelly sock when everybody starts clapping. Hank's sweet
lips are smiling that damn smile of his. He bows a little. Some-

thing about him, despite all the big to-do people made over him, Hank always seems humble.

That's when Ursula Crohn, Mistress of Ceremonies, gets up and says, Why don't we hear from Ben Grunewald?

Clapping. I look around. It's Randy giving me a big smile. He's waving his big fist in the air and he calls out an affectionate grunt. David and Gary and Lester say *yah!*

Fuck. I haven't even checked what I've brought to read, or even if I have all the pages. I sit my ass down on the stool on the Persian carpet in front of the fire with all those young cool Jeske *New Yorker* people looking at me. When I look down there's my big toe sticking out of my stinky sock. The green glitter. Really, the fear literally clogs up my throat and I can't think straight. Thank God I have text in front of me. Without text I'd be totally fucked.

My voice: Catholic Boy with a big apology. Trembling and shit. I read my story about the jerk-off club and the guy in the stupid underwear and the little weenie. When I finish, there is that long pause and silence again. A big turd in a crystal punch bowl. Randy, David, Gary, and Lester clap a couple of times and stop.

Ursula Crohn gets up and tells us about the avocado dip and invites us to partake of the refreshments. Randy's the first guy up to the table with a plate.

That's where I am sitting. On that stool on the Persian carpet in front of the fireplace one thousand stories up. Everybody else over at the table pouring glasses of wine, grabbing slices of pepperoni pizza. Hank walks right up to me. Big and beautiful. His chest pumping up the way he does. Maroni's body – when his body gets close to mine, it gets too close. Propinquity.

"You see what you did?" Hank says.

Some kind of mint aftershave. His eyes that should be blue but aren't, they're black. His straight Roman nose. Mustache. Those sweet lips that someday I am going to kiss.

"What?" I say.

"We had to break," Hank says, "After what you read, none of us could breathe, let alone speak."

2.

First date

SOMETIME IN THE NEXT WEEK FOLLOWING URSULA Crohn's party, Hank called me. At first, I couldn't believe it was *the Maroni*. I didn't have anything written down, so I didn't know what to say to him. I'm lost without text. Plus telephones freak me out. At a certain point, I took a deep breath and pictured myself back on that stool a thousand stories up on the Persian carpet in front of the fireplace at Ursula's artist's loft and looked right into Hank's black eyes as he spoke to me. What he had said that night had really shocked me. The fact that people couldn't speak or even breathe once I had finished reading was preposterous, and I'd looked hard into Hank's eyes for bullshit. But there was no bullshit.

Usually we have to hide a little when we risk saying something true to someone we don't know. So I looked for Hank to make himself distant, for irony, for where he would go in himself so he could say something raw like that and still have protection. Propinquity. But it wasn't only his body that was too close, the spirit inside him that made him say what he said was way close, too. It was a feeling I'd never felt before. Hank's black eyes, the way they took me in. How *looked at* I felt. Suddenly I was a child and Hank was a real old man with cataracts and mostly blind so he was unaware of himself looking, or I was a child and Hank was a child too, and since we were children we could simply look. Felt big. The way Buddha, or Jesus, or Rumi might feel.

Then less than a week later, there we were on the phone,

and Hank and I were just two awkward guys who didn't know
each other, trying to have a conversation. So I suggested he come
over to my apartment that Friday. Silence on his end of the phone. Then:

"I'll have to talk to Mythryxis," Hank said.

"Ma ... what?"

"Myth ... rix ... is," Hank said.

"Who's that?" I said.

"She's a fellow traveler of mine," he said.

MYTHRYXIS, HANK'S GIRLFRIEND. I never got her real name.
And I never met her. All's I knew was she lived in New Jersey
and she was a nurse. The whole time I knew Hank he always had
a woman, and it was always just one woman, until, that is, he
found another. For some reason, though, I got the feeling that
Mythryxis was *the* girlfriend, maybe his first love from college,
and she was waiting for Hank to marry her.

Mythryxis only lasted maybe those first six months I knew
Hank. I always tried to get Hank to talk about her, but you know
Hank. Kept his cards close to his chest. When he did talk about
her, she sounded more like a student of his – not a writing student but like somebody broken he'd taken under his wing and
was taking special care of. Then one night, after I asked, Hank
just up and said that Mythryxis had moved on. Said it like she'd
graduated. Like she was a doctor now instead of a nurse. I turned
to look at Hank when he said that, into his black eyes. By six
months, I thought we knew a lot about each other, and so when
he said that I made a special point of looking at him, because
right then I realized I didn't have a clue about him and Mythryxis.
We were sitting on the stoop of 211 East Fifth Street. The night
was muggy and from under the stairs you could smell the piss.
McSorley's was just two blocks away and the way those boys
drank they never could make it very far. The air was so thick in
the mercury vapor light you could damn near set your beer can
on it. Hank and I were brown-bagging a couple Rolling Rocks. I

had my boombox in my window and we were listening to those eighties tunes that still can stop my heart. *Sussudio*, Blondie's *Rapture*. *Every time you go away, you take a piece of me with you.* Hank is sitting on the step just above me. We're stripped down to loose fitting T-shirts and shorts, sandals. My whole body feels like crotch rot. Every once in a while, Hank's bare knee touches my bare arm and it sticks. I'm on my third or fourth beer and Hank's still nursing his second. Hank usually didn't drink more than a couple beers. He didn't get marihoochied either. That's what Hank called it, *marihoochy*.

On the stoop, when Hank said that about Mythryxis, I had to turn and look up at him, and the porch light was right there, so I had to put my hand up to shield my eyes. Hank's black eyes again. It never ceased to startle me the way he and I could look at each other. They were kind of misty, his eyes, as if the whole Mythryxis thing was a whole lot tougher than he'd ever let on.

"Are you sad about that?" I said.

Hank rolled the bottle in the brown bag around in his big hands. Looked at that bottle the same way he's looking in his author's photo on the back of his book.

"It's all sad, Gruney," Hank said. "If we let ourselves know how sad it really is, there wouldn't be anything left of us."

Just after he spoke, I swear a big gust of wind blew by. Like a semi truck on the freeway. It was *hot* wind – but still it was moving air, and it blew back our sweaty Eighties hair and then made a mess of the garbage all the way down East Fifth Street.

Sometimes I think Hank Christian, *the Maroni*, was magic. Or we were. Really, I loved that guy so much.

SOMETHING I'D LIKE you to notice, though. The Enigma of Hank Christian. When I asked Hank about Mythryxis, he did something he always did. He answered with something pithy and true and in such a way that it makes the saying beautiful, but after you think about it, he actually hadn't told me one specific thing about himself or Mythryxis or the situation he was in with her.

There are two ways I feel about this. Now that I am old and sick and Hank is dead, sometimes I wonder if I knew Hank Christian at all. Before his death, all those years we didn't speak. No deathbed reconciliation. *Nada*. Believe me, the shit that went down with Ruth could tear anything asunder.

Years passing can do other things as well. Shit that before I didn't know even existed, let alone try and understand, I'm beginning to make sense of now. Which I'm thankful for. Still, change like that ain't easy, especially when you're sixty.

Hemingway called it *the black ass*. Virginia Woolf put herself in the hospital after every one of her books. Except the last one. And the book about New York and AIDS I was writing was, on purely a physical level, only prolonging the horror of the Eighties one decade further. Once is enough with depression like that.

THE SECOND WAY I feel about the Enigma of Hank Christian is *fuck it*. So I didn't understand it all. The glorious mystery of the man who touched me in a place that wasn't there before he touched it. I want to dance my ass off in some naked-pagan-by-the-bonfire drum chant, screaming thanks at the universe for the blessing of that hole his black eyes burnt into me. So what if he didn't spill all his beans. So what if he was a persistent, obdurate, goddamn goat. I'll never be the same after Hank Christian, and thank God for it.

THAT FIRST FRIDAY night Hank came over felt like a blind date. Hank and I both were freaked. Neither one of us knew what the fuck we were going to say or do with the other. I was freaked because of what I did know. Hank because of what he didn't.

My radar for Hank – something, I figured, *that* overwhelming could only be sexual. Don't get me wrong, that was good, way good, in fact dream come true good. But dream come true good, the very perfectness of Hank Christian and his buff Italian body and black eyes, his *Maroni* status with Jeske, his beautiful sentences and the way he uttered them; instead of a dream come

true, the prospect of sitting face to face with Hank Christian in
my tiny apartment with the bed right there – I couldn't imagine.
As soon as I hung up the phone after I invited him over, I couldn't
fucking imagine. That's when the nightmare started. My body
morphed into a skinny, zitty, gawky, tongue-tied Idaho teenager.
A complete fucking flaccid fraud.

MY BROKEN DICK. Such a long sad story. It started when I was
born and just never got better. I thought after leaving my wife
things would change. And they did there for a while with Bette.
When I started walking on the other side of the street, though,
I thought that would solve the problem. I had high hopes for my
hard-on. But the Brotherhood of Homosexual Men I'd been
yearning to find turned out to be me standing solo in bars with
loud disco music. Bars with friendly names like Hell Fire, Rawhide,
or The Anvil. They were all the same. Dark with dramatic lighting
and shadows. Every man wearing the same outfit. Like we were
all straight guys on a construction crew who were having beers
after work. Or we were miners. Or we were cowboys. Nobody
talked because the music was too loud to talk and if we talked
we'd no longer be the hardwired sex machines we were posing as.

Then there was the Monster. A piano bar. The men there
didn't all look like G.I. Joe. Sitting at the crowded bar, you could
actually talk to men. But it didn't take me long to figure out it
was the cocaine. Really, I had some of the most bizarre conversa-
tions you could imagine in that place. Men making absolutely
no fucking sense at all. For example, there was this one guy one
night. He was a black guy, good looking. I introduced myself and
that quick he's talking about the night and the stars and somehow then he's talking about the trademark porcelain stamp on
the men's toilet in the bathroom, *Porcelana*, then he's talking
about Burt Reynolds's party tricks, then how the more fruit you
eat the more sour your cum tastes – all of it, all at once, spoken
in one long breathless sentence. Fuck.

The secret code. I think what being gay really means is that you understand the secret code. I never got the secret code. For example, I walk up to a guy in a bar who's carefully prepared himself to look like he's been digging fence posts all day. I say, *Hi, hello how are you* and tell him my name is Ben. More often than not this guy won't speak, he'll just look at me up and down, checking me out, what's important, what's wrong, and then he'll walk off.

Now if you know the secret code, you know to follow or not to follow. Sometimes when you follow, the guy's in the bathroom with his dick hanging out. And there's just no way in hell I'm going to kneel down in all that piss and take some dick I've never met into my mouth.

Then sometimes when you follow the guy, you aren't supposed to follow the guy, because in secret code he'd just told you to fuck off. Yet sometimes when you follow the guy who'd just somehow magically communicated to you to fuck off, that's the right thing to do. And I guess that's because that means you *want* to be told to fuck off, and if that guy is in fact a guy who gets off on telling guys to fuck off, then that's the right move to make. Otherwise it's a staredown from hell.

And that's just if you gets the balls to walk up to someone and start talking. Mostly I just stand and wait for someone to talk to me. Yah. Good luck.

Then the whole top and bottom thing. How men just know that stuff. So many times, in the bathroom, there isn't a dick hanging out waiting for you, it's a guy bent over stretching out his ass crack with his hands. I mean really, I love men's asses. I've followed men's asses all the way across Manhattan. But to just have that hairy stretched out purple crack there hanging under some bad lighting, really no matter how hard I tried, my dick just don't work that way.

Then of course, seems like every man in these friendly bars had a dick the size of Godzilla. Really what do you do with some- thing that big? It can't fit in your mouth and it certainly can't fit up your ass. So I guess the old joke is true: all you can do is throw your arms around it and weep.

HANK WAS HAVING his own troubles. The beauty of a friendship like Hank's and mine is that shit like this comes out and months later, years, and you're laughing your ass off.

Hank was freaked because he didn't know what the fuck. He knew I was gay and he figured since I was gay and since all of a sudden I was always on his mind, then he must be gay too. And that was perplexing. Gays wore tight pants that emphasized their crotches, wore rings on their pinkie fingers, had special colored hankies they wore in their back Levi's pockets, and exhibited an insatiable desire to suck cock. Personally, Hank had never even remotely experienced any of these traits in himself. He'd tried it once and couldn't even get one finger up his asshole, so what was this desire to get next to Grunewald? Maybe this was how gay started. One day you're thinking about some guy and the next day you're on your knees in a XXX sex parlor with a red handkerchief sticking out the back left pocket of your tight Levi's 501 jeans. Or was it the right pocket? Fuck.

FREAKIN' WILD THE way the city feels on a summer Friday night. Late June 1985, just before sunset, Hank Christian presses his thumb against the buzzer of apartment 1A, 211 East Fifth Street.

When I hear my buzzer, I flutter. Everything about me flutters – my hands, my fingers, the breath in my chest. I take a deep breath, look into the old, peeling mirror. *Hank Christian is buzzing my buzzer*. I unlock the locks on my apartment door, open the door, take two big steps to the front door, put my hand on the knob that always smells of the musk oil the lesbians upstairs bathe in, swing the door open. All day, the sun has baked itself into the cast iron steps. No shade, just beating down sun onto the stoop, onto the alcove of the doorway. The bright and heat blast in. The smell of the street – exhaust fumes, piss under the stairs, garbage. I blink and blink and raise my hand to block out the sun. Hank is a hazy dark object in a vat of hot bright. I go to speak, but suddenly Hank's hand pokes out into the shadows of the hallway, right at me. It is the hand of a Caravaggio and appears as if out of another dimension. I look and look and look at the hand, then grab it, Hank's hand, and I pull him in as if Hank was burning up in a cauldron out there. Both Hank and I laugh a little the way I've hauled him in. When we can see into each other's eyes, I quick pull my hand out of Hank's, and my hand falls down against my leg, fluttering.

Hank and I maneuver our bodies through the do-si-do of the front door closing, through the apartment door of 1A, then the closing and the locking of the apartment door without touching.

The apartment is a studio and right there by the door when the door is closed is one of two places in the apartment where there's room enough for two to stand. Too close really for two men. Propinquity.

Hank's black eyes assess my home, my den, where I write my abuses and murders. A writer's eyes, Hank's – must see must look must know – every detail, but careful not to get caught looking.

What I see Hank see: the fan in the window, the dark rust-colored Levolor blinds closed tight, the big red metal writing desk. No computer, not yet. A big ass typewriter that can self-erase. The lamp and the crooked shade colored with red and yellow and blue Crayolas. The exposed brick wall. Stacks of papers and books and books and books. The skinny white stove, four burners and an oven. Two white metal cupboards above the stainless steel sink. A cutting board on top on a hip-high refrigerator. In the back of the apartment, darkness, a staircase, the loft bed.

The whole time, as Hank and I speak to each other, our hands and arms move up and down, each of us on our own bodies – hands on hips, fingers in armpits, one hand on hip, a hand that pops the knuckle on the other hand, both hands hanging down at the sides, a quick cover of the crotch, then hands that wave around, fucking hands, man, two men standing too close front to front, flutter flutter, fucking arms, folding and unfolding over our cocks, over our bellies, over our hearts.

In the mirror leaning against the brick wall, its layers of silver peeling off, Hank Christian and Ben Grunewald, a dream of them, their reflections, like this story is a dream only different, standing inside in there.

My arms finally settle their flutter into a place crossed just over my nipples, my right hand up, open-palmed, rubbing the stubble of my chin. My nose is trying to sniff up the chicken and rice and garlic I'd cooked the night before. Hank's mint smell. Maybe it comes from his shampoo. I'm sucking in my gut. Hank is pushing out and raising up his chest, pulling his arms down, shoulders down, the way he does.

On our lips, smiles of course, the both of us. Our lips, what they speak. What they do not speak. How the voices inside us come up and out.

"Hank," I say, "How ya doin', man?"

"Sorry I'm late." Hank says, "Number one was running slow."

"I always take the R." I say, "Hot, ain't it?"

"Fucking hot!"

"Too hot in here," I say. "What do ya say we find some air condish and have a beer. There's a place over on Second Ave called Le Culot."

"Frenchie's always pricey," Hank says. "I'm on a budget."

"I know the bartender," I say. "The first round is free."

YOU CAN TELL a lot about a man by how he walks down the street with you. Most men don't ever have to think about shit like this, how you walk, but with me, with the father I had, I always had to be sure I knew how close or how far that guy was from me. Out of nowhere, my father's right hand could reach out and cuff me. Make my ear bleed. Or my nose. I'm a grown man now, and have been for a number of decades, and I understand that a grown man should overcome these kinds of fears. Call it what you want. Paranoia. Post-Traumatic Stress. Hypervigilance. Faggotry – for me there's always a circle my arm's length around me, and if anybody breaks into that circle, the searchlight goes on and the sirens go off.

Propinquity.

You'd think that somebody with an arm's-length rule wouldn't move to New York City. The truth is I didn't think about it. I wouldn't let myself. What I mean is I couldn't stop thinking about it.

THERE'S THIS THING I do: I call it Big Ben and Little Ben. Big Ben is the Big Voice, the authority. He makes the decisions. You don't brook Big Ben's dicta. He's the man and what he says goes.

Big Ben decided to leave my wife. Big Ben decided to leave Idaho. Big Ben decided he was going to have sex with men. The problem with Big Ben is he doesn't stick around for very long. He just drops in, pronounces how things are going to be, then he's off.

Little Ben is who's got to carry out the instructions. He's the guy who's got to do it. Little Ben is mostly who I'm stuck with.

Little Ben had to sit down with my wife in our beautiful three-bedroom home in Boise, Idaho, and tell her I didn't want to live my life with her anymore. Little Ben had to pack his shit into his used Datsun pickup and drive across the United States alone.

Little Ben had to figure out how I'm going to touch another man, when I can't even let another human being closer than an arm away.

Little Ben had to figure out how to live in a city that is a constant assault on my propinquity.

The way these three first converged – Big Ben and Little Ben and Little Ben's arm-away rule – all came together that first morning in September when I had to get on the subway to get to Columbia University. Sober.

It was late morning and I was the only guy on the bright platform. The Number One was a huge monster screaming out of darkness. It came to a stop. The doors opened and a couple people got off. Inside, there was a space, just barely, for one normal human being without propinquity problems to stand. I went to get on but couldn't move. A short Latina woman in a red scarf and gold bling looked out at me. The way she looked at me, she knew. The subway car did that subway car pushing-out-air sound and the two-toned bell ding-donged and the doors started to close. Fucking Big Ben, man.

Little Ben jumped on. The subway car lurched ahead and from all sides the arm-away rule went bust. Crushed into me were four or five people. My chest was smashed into a tall black guy's bare arm – my eyes only inches from his smallpox vaccination, somebody's suitcase was poking me in the ass, a Chinese schoolgirl with earphones on was so close I could hear the Madonna song, and the white guy in a suit was wearing Polo. Little Ben was about to pass out. My lungs were pumping overtime trying to find air. A heartbeat off the charts. I found my feet, tried to stand them square. My hand was at the silver pole and I wrapped my hand around it tight.

With each station, more people got on, then some got off, then more got on. By the time we got to 116th, I was still alive.

I may cuss him a lot, but without Big Ben I'd still be baling hay for my old man.

And by the way, yes. Little Ben's the one with the limp dick.

Big Ben says enough of this shit – all this ancient Icky Familial Catholic my mother my sister sex shame guilt. Little Ben agrees. Believe me he's trying.

SO I'M WALKING down East Fifth Street between Third Avenue and Second on a hot summer night in 1985 to Le Culot. One of the two men in my life who I could say truly loved me, Hank Christian, is walking next to me. The old Sinclair Station on Fifth and Bowery is behind us. Behind us too are the garbage cans in front of my building. We're just passing where Fish Bar's going to be, about to the corner of Second Avenue and the Greek diner where I always ordered a turkey sandwich on Thanksgiving. Hank's wearing a white T-shirt and cutoff jeans, white socks and white tennis shoes. There's something just-showered about him, even though he's been on the subway. His long hair is a charcoal color. That Roman nose. His black eyes.

THERE IS SOMETHING going on. What my arm-away rule is telling me was that something's up with this Hank Christian guy. Something about the way Hank's body is moving. I can't tell exactly what it is. I mean it isn't like Shit Sandwich Bill, a guy I dated once. Shit Sandwich Bill walked ahead a step, sometimes two, the shoulder closest to me hunched up, like I was the AIDS virus and we were in a dead heat to get the rubber on right. Who knows who was more afraid, him or me. During dinner one night, I took the chance and tried to explain to Bill about the arm-away rule, how it goes from propinquity to intimacy. I thought maybe this guy would understand. But he wouldn't have any of it.

"What do you mean afraid?" he said, "What's there to be afraid of?"

The reason I call him Shit Sandwich Bill is because two weeks later when I asked him why he hadn't called, he said, "When you know the sandwich is a shit sandwich, you don't have to taste it."

I hate to date.

Then there's Mark. When I walked down the street with him, it was like I didn't exist. He's a compact guy and darted around. He'd constantly turn and step right in front of me. As if I wasn't even there. I kept telling him to stop it. To be more considerate of me. But he never listened. So I told him the next time he stepped in front of me like that, I was going to trip him. Which I did. One day, Mark was laying in the gutter.

But with Hank Christian, walking down East Fifth Street that first Friday night, something about his body and what it was doing was tripping me out. Usually I can tell you in detail everything that's going on within the sweep of my arm. But with Hank I couldn't figure.

Later on that night, though – it was after Le Culot and we'd gone across the street to Night Birds – just as we're leaving Night Birds – was when things started to happen.

WE'VE JUST PAID the bill and I get to the door first. I open the door and hold it open for Hank. What Hank does next he does without thinking. He reaches his hand behind me and tries to get to the door so he can hold the door open for me.

It all starts to make sense. Earlier that evening as Hank and I'd walked down East Fifth Street to Le Culot, whenever the sidewalk got too narrow between the buildings and the garbage cans, Hank always stepped back and let me walk ahead. At first I thought Hank was being polite. By the end of the block, I wasn't so sure. I didn't argue, though, I just walked ahead because when it comes to two guys relating to one another on shit like this I'm fucking lost. But at Night Birds, when he won't let me hold the door for him, when his arm goes behind and grabs for the door, suddenly there isn't a force in the world strong enough to move me.

"No, you go," I say.

"No, you go," Hank says.

Hank and I could have been there all evening letting the air conditioning go out into the sweltering night. Of course, Guardian of the Doorway Hank, plus being the Capricorn goat that he is, is also determined. We stand there for some ridiculous amount of time arguing back and forth.

"No, you go."

"No, you go."

Then in a moment, I see something go off in Hank's black eyes. As soon as that happens, Hank steps out in front and lets me hold the door.

We'd walked maybe half a block when I ask:

"You all right?"

It takes several steps for Hank to answer.

"I've been doing that my whole life," Hank says. "You're the first person to call me on it."

"On what?" I say.

"It's always my fault if something goes wrong."

"Something could go wrong with the door?" I ask.

"No," Hank says. Then: "Yes, I mean it's up to me that everything goes smoothly."

"Wow," I say. "My head had a totally different story going on."

"What's that?"

"I thought you were treating me like the girl," I say.

THAT STARTED THE conversation Hank Christian and I never stopped having. Until, that is, the *got to go pal* letter and we quit speaking.

The fact that the same event happened to both of us at the same time and what Hank saw was so different from what I saw makes us both a little crazy. We are immediately right on it, trying to figure out how the other came up with what he came up with.

"I don't get it," Hank says.

"Straight guys don't get it," I say. "How ingrained they are with how they treat the other sex."

"But you're not the other sex."

"I'm one of them."

"You think that by being polite I'm treating you like a girl?" Hank says.

"Probably my own shit," I say. "But just for conversation let's say *yes*. Would you fight over who held the door with another straight guy? How do you guys figure out who goes through the door first?"

"*You guys*? Who's *you guys*?"

"Straight guys."

"Fuck if I know. It just happens."

"Do you take turns?"

"Are you making fun of me?"

"And what about you?" I say. *"It's my fault if something goes wrong – something I've been doing my whole life –* what's that about?"

"It's just a fucking door." Hank says.

"We don't live on things," I say. "We live on the meaning of things."

"You're quoting." Hank says, "Antoine de Saint-Exupery, *The Little Prince.*"

"Well, what does that door mean to you? Why were you fighting to be the one who opened it? If you give up control then the world is going to fall apart?"

"You were fighting too!"

"I had the door," I say, *"You* were trying to move *me.*"

THAT'S HOW THE whole night went, Hank and me. We started out on Second Avenue, past Love Saves The Day, Café 113, Optimo Cigars, Moishe's Home Made Kosher, B&H Dairy, Block Drugs. When we walked past Gem Spa, Hank said, *what the fuck are egg creams?*

That night, we must have walked back and forth on every street from Tenth to Houston, between Third Avenue and Avenue C, talking. Actually, it was me who did the talking. Part of it was nerves. Afraid if I didn't start talking, I never would. Part of it was Hank. I mean let's face it. I was totally crushed out on the guy. But it was more than seduction. In seduction, there's an intent, even if it's subtle. Not an iota of intent from me. In fact, I kept trying to find myself, where I started and Hank ended. There was a space, an actual place in the world that night that existed only because Hank and I existed. Stoned, mushrooms stoned, or even hashish without the paranoia. Like that. But we were sober. We were inside something in a space. Under a miracle umbrella. And we were talking – I mean I was talking, and we were side by side, walking back and forth up and down through the Lower East Side, at first Hank just a question now and then, but the way his black eyes watched, the way he turned his head, moved his ear close to listen, you could tell. Something was going on. And it wasn't just me. The way Hank described it, it was like he'd finally met his real father and his real father was me. Or we were kids playing a game the way kids out of nothing can make a whole day out of cowboys and Indians come real.

No matter how hard you try, there's no way you can make up a world like that on your own. That space, the way you get lost in it, the way you feel, takes two.

The dark heat of the night, the six-story walkups, every window open. On the stoops, jug bottles of wine, beer bottles, bottles of rum, Cokes, tubs of melting ice. People talking fast Spanish. On top of the street smell – exhaust and garbage, sweaty bodies – the thick smell of marihoochi.

Talking: how it used to feel walking next to my father. Then my mother, my sister, paper dolls, dress up. There was no getting away from them. How they fought with each other over who could pop my zits. The enemas my mother gave me – even my shit wasn't mine.

The Catholic Church. The Holy Cross nuns. Fucking Catholicism, man. What does it take to get excommunicated?

The narrow streets crowded with cars, honking taxis, loud boomboxes: Michael Jackson, Hector Lavoe, Phil Collins, Lionel Richie, Kool and the Gang. Garbage cans stacked next to scrawny trees with little cast iron fences around them.

Talking: when I was five I posed with my father's fishing pole for my sister's Brownie Instamatic. I wanted there to be concrete proof in the world that I was a boy and that my father had acknowledged I was a boy, because you see, this is *his* fishing pole and its over *my* shoulder even though he never used it.

Lumpy broken pieces of sidewalk. Piles of dog shit. Puke. You had to watch where you walked. Sidewalks so narrow only single file could walk. Now Hank was always walking through first.

We were on First Street, right where the first Dixon Place was going to be. Coming up just ahead of us was another narrow spot in the sidewalk. Hank went to step up first, but I cut in quick and stepped ahead.

"Oh no you don't!" Hank said.

Hank grabbed for my shoulder but missed.

"You'll think I'm treating you like a girl!"

"You don't always get to decide," I said. "You've spent your whole life doing it. Who made you the Grand Chooser?"

"Fuck you!"

"No, fuck you."

Deep into it. Two grown-up men pushing at each other, trying to be the one to go first. And the most amazing thing. A man is touching me and there's no searchlight going on, no sirens blaring. Hank and I are walking, I mean it's some kind of walking. More like wrestling-walking. Or dancing. My shoulder hard against Hank's. Then we roll, back against back – he almost knocks me over – neither one of us letting up, my arm pushing with everything in me against Hank's arm, then another roll and Hank and I are chest to chest. Somewhere in there we start laughing. Then a tiny moment that went by way too fast when I understand how necessary it is for men to smash and punch and wrestle and hit.

The later the night got, the more it's humid. So fucking hot. I'm out of breath, sweat running the insides of my arms. Hank's sweating, too.

"I'll buy you a soda," Hank says.

On Second Avenue, we walk into Schacht's Delicatessen. It's an hallucination. Bright fluorescence. The smell of old wood, weird cheese, and chicken soup. Hum of refrigeration. At the back aisle cooler, Hank opens the cooler door and all that cold air comes rushing out. Hank swings the door back and forth making a breeze. Christ what a relief. I lean my back against the cool glass. Hank lifts up his T-shirt and pushes his hard smooth belly inside the cooler door.

Then from inside the cooler, some guy yells: "This ain't Christmas!"

Hank jumps back, then ducks, looks inside, trying to see who's in there.

"Sorry," Hank says. ""Just trying to keep cool."

"Close the fucking door, asshole!"

Young boys. I'd say Hank and I are about ten. Hank gets a celery soda and I get a root beer.

Behind the counter at Schacht's, all you could see of the tiny woman is her head and neck. Straight gray hair parted in the middle curling up just above the brown leather of her shoulders. Crossed in front of her, on the slick wood countertop, her Florida-tanned Bingo arms. Hank's fiddling with his wallet, I'm trying to count change. Both of us about to bust a gut. As her hand, the crooked fingers, give Hank back his change, the woman tilts her head back, rolls her eyes, and hollers to the guy at the back in the cooler.

"You old fucking goat! Don't talk that way to our customer people!"

She gives Hank and me a big smile and winks, pushes her head over her arms and leans in to us. You can see where the false teeth fit her gums.

"You boys stay out of trouble tonight," she says. "Enjoy your sodas."

It's a miracle night all right, and the miracle is taking in the whole world. Skinny calico cats under the stoops, one fat yellow cat in the window on Sixth – that whole street between Second and A smelling of curry and masala. Dogs barking, a schnauzer on Ninth, Rin Tin Tin on C, a Doberman on Eighth and Second, the Toy Poodle that looks pink at the end of a leash of the huge hairy man just in boxer shorts, no jock strap, both Hank and I cross the street to avoid.

Just up from the Pyramid, the usual crowd of skinheads across from Dog Shit Park on A. Weekends, on the corner of Eighth Street is where they hang out. I should have steered us clear of that corner, but I've been too busy talking to Hank. Before we know it, we're in the middle of them. Loud scream-kill punk music blaring out of that bar. Really – the music is so loud the people in there aren't ever going to hear past forty. The skinheads are all in their Friday night finery – black leather, silver chains, spiked-out mohawks. Walking through the crowd of them – there must have been twenty or more – is like walking through a dense black leather forest with colorful windmills on top. But don't get me wrong, these guys aren't pretty. Sid was vicious. And we have to watch our step – they're all high – crack high, blasted.

Hank and I keep our heads down, keep up our pace. We must have walked a half a block when this one guy in a red, white, and blue-striped Mohawk comes up to Hank and me. His hair is sticking up tall as his arm.

"Spare a dollar, man?"

Hank doesn't look at him, keeps walking. I have to step around the guy. When we are a couple storefronts out of there, the red, white, and blue mohawk dude says, "You fags are all Republicans."

Surprised we hear him. But we do. Both Hank and I stop. Both of us turn. Both of us want to kill the skinny little fucker.

That moment.

Twenty of them and two of us. But that isn't going to stop the Capricorn goat, Guardian of the Doorway Hank. At least that's what I'm thinking when I look over at him. There's a way Hank can make his face go. It's like he can erase any feeling from it and his eyes go cold and far away and all of a sudden he's a big slab of marble staring you down. Three times I've experienced Hank look that way. One of those times he was staring at me. Made my stomach feel like it was full of ashes.

That's how Hank is looking at the skinhead dude.

Here's another place where I have no idea how a guy should act. When two guys square off and start acting like gorillas. It's like back in the day, when I still could get high enough to get hard, when I was fucking someone and they'd say, *Oh! fuck that wet hole with your big fat dick!* or something just as awful. It never failed. I got so embarrassed I had to put my pants back on. Same way with the male-to-male squaring off, the fists up, the shifting back from side to side, the chest beating, the motherfuckering – all of it – the whole scene makes me crazy, so I get myself out of there.

In that moment, though, Hank isn't about to budge. Neither is the skinhead dude. He and Hank are already in an eye lock. They're a parking meter apart, but still you can tell, this is only going lead to something brutal. At that point, I do a quick look around. That world, the miracle umbrella, where had it gone so fast? It was still Hank and me, still the same night. Hank and I were still the Indians, but the cowboys were skinheads – one skinhead in particular, and the other twenty skinheads were still back on the corner, crack high, some of them pounding down beers. None of them had noticed yet. The way things were going, though, it wasn't going to be long.

The skinhead dude smiles the way you do when you know twenty of your buddies are behind you. He pulls a cigarette from behind his ear, snaps open a silver lighter, and puts the flame to the end of the cigarette. Snaps it closed.

This moment. This long long moment.

Myself, I'm afraid and I don't know how not to show it.

I'm a sissy, all right – a fag, I know, but that doesn't mean I can't defend myself. Or my friend. My defense started when I was born, although it took me a long time to understand that I was under siege, that the story of my life was the sacred battle I was in to save my life. Finally, I left my mother, my father, my sister, my home, and the Catholic Church. Years later I left my wife. Since then, my life has been one long lesson on where to draw the line and when.

Twice in my life, well I guess three times really, Big Ben knew that this was it and I had to do it: play the gorilla, do the square-off thing, the fists up, the shifting from side to side, the chest beating, the motherfuckering, the punching, the kicking, the screaming, the gasping for air. The first two times it was a

fight for my life. Both times Little Ben was trembling and afraid
and was crying and I showed it. Both times I walked away more
alive than ever.

The first time happened way back in Idaho, the second was
just a couple months before I met Hank.

The third time was the last time I saw Hank. And I'll tell
you all about it later.

But that night, in that moment, those first two times
fighting for my life were right up close to me, inside, in my fists,
the breath in my chest. Went on forever that moment – the
adrenaline making me pop.

But I couldn't figure it out. Why was Hank taking this fight
on? The skinhead dude was an asshole but not worth a minute
of our time. Plus there was twenty of them and two of us.

Fag.

Fag. Out of that moment *fag* was what was sucking out all
the air.

THERE'S A CODE of honor among straight guys. At least for
Hank. I don't think it's as formal as that. I mean there's no rule
book. Maybe it was because he was Italian, or maybe because he
grew up in a mill town in Pennsylvania, or who knows for what
the hell reason. I never found out. For Hank Christian, though,
there was definitely a code of honor. I never understood the code,
how deep it went. For sure it has a lot to do with – after Hank
got the *got to go pal* letter – why he never spoke to me again. I've
come to understand that letter broke a couple big rules. Never
turn away from your buddy. Never let a woman come between.

The hair tip. I should have given Hank the hair tip. Made
him laugh.

Always been an odd duck. My father hardly ever spoke to
me, let alone to talk about what it means to be male, and I was
raised by women, so how could I possibly know something as
mysterious as a male code of honor. I'm just not wired that way.
I've tried, believe me. In high school, I never could go out for

sports because at home there was always so much goddamn work to do. But in college, I pledged a fraternity, twice, knew the special handshake, the secret knock, and the secret word. All that secret crap. Brothers. But that didn't stop that guy John Farrell from getting blackballed because of a birth defect that gave him a weird-looking left ear. United in a fraternal embrace, my ass. And I spent two years in ROTC. I was voted outstanding squad leader for chrissakes. The day it all crashed in for me, the reason I never went advanced ROTC was the day we had bayonet practice. We put the bayonets on the end of our rifles, lined up one squad against another, and in a hot little room in the basement of the gymnasium practiced lunging at one another in a series of three steps and bayonet thrusts while the officer yelled: *what is the spirit of the bayonet?*

There I was, the bayonet attached to the end of my M14, lunging and thrusting at Clyde Jablonski, the dorky guy who sat next to me in French class, yelling *kill! kill!*

Maybe gay guys miss out on that part of being male. I mean I understand loyalty to friends, I understand keeping your word, and I understand sticking up for what is right. But somehow it's never been enough. It's like the first rule for *Fight Club*. With a twist. If you have to talk about it then you're obviously not in it.

Male love is back to back. Female love is front to front. That's the way Hank put it. If you feel love for a guy then it's your duty to protect him against any kind of physical threat. When two guys become friends, when two guys feel love for each other, *they've got each other's backs*. They become a team, interdependent and exclusive. That exclusive team of two can expand to include a squad or a platoon, say, or other members of the playing team, or the gang. The important thing to understand is that the men unite back to back *against* something else. I mean as an outsider that's the way male love *looks*: male love unites *against* something, whether real or imagined. They can feel good feeling good with each other because there's a threat to that feeling good.

THE SCREAM-YELL-KILL-HATE MUSIC blaring out into the
street. Hank is standing there next to me in his white T-shirt,
his cutoffs, white socks and white tennis shoes, his sweaty hair, a
celery soda in his hand, staring down a skinhead dude with a
wise-ass smile who's working on the second puff of his cigarette
just ready to turn around and whistle for his leather, colorfully
topped, twenty cowboys. That moment. Sometimes you think
you've lived just to live through a moment like that. For whatever
reason – fate, personality, or shit just happens – it, whatever *it* is,
all comes together.

Then I see clear as day.

In that moment, Hank Christian had never in his life been
in this place before. Hank could've gone through his whole life
letting men call other men *fags* and while maybe he wouldn't have
agreed, or maybe he would have even found it offensive, until
that night, Hank could always have dismissed it. He had never
been in the position of ever having to defend against it. That
night, by the time the skinhead dude called us fags, though, the
bond between me and Hank was already strong. The trouble
was, neither one of us knew what kind of bond it was: the male
kind, or the female kind. Or something else altogether.

That's what Hank is doing when his eyes go cold and he's
turned to marble. Fags are what you called the guys you were
united *against*. And there he is, Hank Christian, with a friend, Ben
Grunewald: fag. Male love was being called upon to defend a
different kind of love. A love Hank didn't know anything about
except that he felt it.

So in Hank's way of thinking, since *fags* were him, he was
obliged. Hank's sense of responsibility – that I was the first one
in his life ever to call him on – had kicked in big time. Like that
first night I'd really looked at him, in Jeske's class as he stood
arms out guarding the doorway.

That's what you do when you love, you protect.

THAT MOMENT. THE skinhead dude has his lighter back in his pocket and is standing up, his back to us, waving his arms. He's yelling, trying to get the attention of his twenty skinhead cowboy dudes. That loud loud music.

I have to act fast. I step in front of Hank, up close but not too close. The normal male-to-male propinquity. I put my eyes right into Hank's eyes, the way he's making them go dead. I'm going to touch him, maybe on the shoulder, but when my hand reaches up, I put it right back down again. Big Ben starts talking:

"Hank," I say, "you don't have to smooth this out. You told me yourself – you've been doing that your whole life."

Like talking to a fence post. Hank's black eyes stare past me just over my shoulder. The dude behind me is doing something, because Hank's eyes are moving like crazy. I want to turn around but don't. I wipe the sweat out of my eyes with the butt of my hand. Take a deep breath.

"So he called us fags," I say. "The irony of it is, the guy can tell how close we are tonight. Don't let some asshole put a label on it."

Hank's eyes start coming back from the dead, but his gaze on the dude behind me never lets up. Then a sign from God, or the universe agreeing, or just something makes it all stop, and suddenly Hank raises his chest up with a quick breath of air.

"How many times you been called a fag, Ben?"

"Enough," I say.

"When's it going to stop?"

"It's not up to you to stop it, Hank," I say. "It's not your job to take this on."

I turn around quick, stand myself square next to Hank. Check out the situation. Over here, Hank and I are still the Indians. Four lunges away over there, the skinhead dude is in a torpor, facing his friends, jumping up and down yelling and screaming and waving. But his friends don't see him. They're way too fucking high. The music is way too fucking loud.

I turn my face, put my mouth close to Hank's ear.

"This guy with the red, white, and blue-striped hair in front of us here is a cocksucker. He just don't know it yet."

It's amazing all that can happen in a moment.

Hank walks the space between up to the skinhead dude, taps him on the back of the shoulder. Me, I'm right next to Hank – male code of honor, I guess. The dude thinks he's dead for sure. He jumps back, goes into a crouch. The crack-high cowboys behind him carry on into oblivion.

Hank is holding his body the way he does. His chest pushed out and up, his chin down, shoulders down, his hands made into fists, biceps flexed. The celery soda can in his hand was a wadded up piece of aluminum. I have no idea where my can of root beer has gone.

"You need to watch out!" Hank says, "Who you're calling a Republican."

LATER ON THAT night, before I go home and Hank gets on his train, on St. Mark's Place at #77, we stop at W. H. Auden's house and I read Hank out loud the poem on the plaque below the second story window. We stand there for a long time. Closer than most men would stand, but not touching. That fucking poem, man. The city's going from Friday night to Saturday morning. I think for sure I'm going to cry.

A big old smooch right on the lips, Hank gives me. Hank Christian's sweet lips on mine. He walks away and waves without turning around, the same way we'd walked away from the skinhead dude. Just move your legs and walk. Into a brand new world. It's that easy.

3.
The bullies

THE FIRST TIME BIG BEN KNEW THAT THIS WAS IT AND I had to stand my ground and fight was the end of school my senior year. The last year, the last class, the last day in high school ever. Mechanical drawing. And in mechanical drawing there was a guy named Abe Martin. For some reason, Abe Martin hated my guts. I never could figure out why Abe Martin hated me so much. Years later now, it's pretty clear.

In grade school, Abe and I were in the same 4-H club. Our club meetings were on Thursday nights. It was tough having 4-H on a Thursday night because our club jackets were green and if you wore green on Thursday that meant you were a queer. I didn't know what queer was, but I knew it wasn't good. The other boys in the club, as they started high school, stopped wearing their jackets to the meetings altogether. Myself, in eighth grade, as soon as my ass was out of Catholic school, I was out of 4-H too. Not because of the green on Thursday thing. I just wasn't no farmer. I was going to college.

Maybe that's why Abe Martin hated me.

Summer in Idaho in the 1950s, our Thursday night 4-H club meetings all pretty much went the same. After we had pledged our heads to clearer thinking, our hearts to greater loyalty, our hands to larger service, our health to better living, after we'd eaten all the cookies, cake, pie, brownies, candy, and drunk all the Kool-Aid, Cokes, Pepsis, 7-Ups, RC Colas, Shastas, and everyone ran outside jamming on sugar into the hot dry dark night and the crickets and the frogs and the mosquitoes and the stars and the crazy moon. The always-present hundred-watt lightbulb way up on top there on the yard light pole, the mess of flying bugs under the tin umbrella lampshade.

It never failed, it wasn't long and one of the boys got pantsed. *Pantsed* means that your pants and your underwear were forcibly taken off you and sometimes away from you altogether. For some reason, more often than not, it was me who got pantsed. There must have been a sign on my forehead that said: *hurt me then humiliate me I'm Catholic*. Besides my sis, Margaret, and me, everyone was Mormon.

Those last couple years I went to 4-H, the summers of my seventh and eighth grades, Abe Martin was always the one leading the troops. One time after getting pantsed, my bare ass lying on the gravel of Peter Johnson's gravel yard, Abe Martin reached down and did a quick, firm, cupping of my cock and balls. Later, when I had my pants back on, I called Abe on it. He said he was just curious to see what I was packing.

He must have liked it. During junior high and high school, Abe often drove over to my house after school. I was always out back doing the chores, feeding hay to the cows, slopping the pigs, or feeding the chickens. Abe always wanted the same thing: to jerk off with me.

It's not that I wasn't interested. Back in the 1950s on the Tyhee Flats, anything or anybody that could be construed in any way as sexual had interest. But with Abe Martin – there was just something about him. He was so desperate. Plus his sweat was sour and smelled like piss. It's always been that way for me. Sweat is what tells the tale true. If you see sweat on someone and your first impulse is to lick it off, it's a go. For example, the sweat on Hank that night at Schacht's delicatessen. If you see sweat on someone and you want to be in the next county, it's not. If they pass the sweat test, they usually pass on the other body fluids.

For example, the first time I ever saw cum, it was overflowing Abe Martin's left palm. Abe and I were sleeping out in our sleeping bags in the front yard and I'd just told Abe what Dan Rivers's father had told Dan – that pretty soon Dan was going to have a White Dream. Then I told Abe that whenever Dan and I slept out, we always tried to get to sleep as fast as we could so we could have the White Dream. Abe Martin started to laugh and pretty soon there was a bunch of commotion under Abe's sleeping bag, then a loud groan out of Abe, and then Abe was shining his flashlight onto the load of cum dripping out through his fingers.

"It ain't a *White* Dream, you dumb ass," Abe said.

White or *wet*, let's just say that what was dripping off of Abe's palm was making me wish I wasn't in Bannock County.

THE LAST YEAR, the last day, the last class of high school ever, Abe Martin had it all planned. After the bell, he and Phil Rousse and Marty Clark were going to jump me. Maybe Abe was jealous that he had to take his senior year over, maybe it was because he wanted to touch my dick, maybe he hated my guts because I was living proof that there was a time that I was the sex that he wanted. Maybe it was just his sweet way of saying goodbye. Whatever the case, Abe Martin's plan was to take me down, strip away my pants and my drawers, and leave me standing there balls out butt naked in the crowded hallways of Pocatello High School.

May 1964, the last bell of the last class on my last day in high school rang. There I was, free at last. My future ahead of me. With a college deferment, Vietnam still four years away. Four years was an eternity.

I'd just stepped out into the hallway. I could say I didn't see it coming, but I did. Propinquity, that hyperactivated sense I have. How male bodies are around me. I could feel the bullies before I saw them.

Big Ben, Little Ben. I've told you about them.

But I haven't told you about the Running Boy.

WHEN I WAS kid in the workshop with my father and my uncle Bob, I cut my index finger and the blood started pouring out.

Even though my father was standing right there, and my uncle, I started running. I felt something in my chest and I started running.

All I could do was look at the blood coming out of my finger and run. And there was no place to run to. Not to my mother, to my sister, not even to a room that was mine where I could close the door. My uncle chased me all over that farm. Really the way Uncle Bob told it, I must have run two miles here and there before he caught up to me.

At the sternum, in the middle of my chest, a lightbulb that you can see the filament flashing.

The Running Boy.

THE FILAMENT WAS flashing when Abe hit me from the side and knocked me down. I still had my books held close to my chest. Then the two other guys, Phil and Marty, landed on me. I could feel fingers down at my belt and my zipper.

That's when Big Ben stepped up. I didn't know he was Big Ben yet because that's the first time I'd ever run into him. Whoever or whatever he was, though, the message was clear. I was in a battle for my life and I'd better get my ass in gear.

The sound that came out of me was what got them off my body. Eighteen years of taking shit and sick to death of it – the sound of that – came out of my mouth. One moment I had three motherfuckers on me, then I started yelling, and the next thing I know, they're all standing around looking down at me, their mouths hanging open as if I was having some kind of fit.

It was a fit all right. A Big Ben fit. Fight or flight. Up to that day it had always been flight.

The next thing I know I'm up and standing free. Phil Rousse was the closest. His beady eyes and those glasses. The books in my hand slammed his head so hard his glasses went flying. Knocked him all the way across the hall. I guess I was still yelling because nobody – not Abe or Marty or anybody else in the hallway was moving. Just standing there stuck in place as if a horror show was happening in front of their eyes.

It wasn't long and Abe and I squared off. Phil was down and who knows where Marty went. Abe was calling me a pussy, a queer, a fag – all the while beating his chest like a gorilla. But that day, squaring off didn't scare me. Nothing could have scared me. Even though my whole body was trembling so bad, from out my mouth came such a surprise – a deep voice from way down in my toes speaking out, loud and clear.

"Abe Martin," I said. "Always trying to get my pants off me. What's that about?"

Our bodies weren't apart for long. Abe wasn't going to let his ambush get out of control. He jumped and we were body to body. Over the years, one on one, Abe and I had been evenly matched, so our bodies knew what to expect. But this time it was different. And it was startling. The way we went at each other. Both of us wanted to kill.

What came next was one of those long moments. Heaving breath, yelling, cussing – fists and elbows, body slammed against body. One of my punches was straight out of John Wayne and right into Abe Martin's nose. Immediately there was blood. Then a blow to my right ear that after I've never heard out of quite right.

Just Abe and me. It was just us two swinging, lunging, falling down, and rolling. One point, Abe and I were on our knees, Abe behind. Abe had my head in an arm lock and I couldn't breathe and I fucking hate it when I can't breathe. My whole life somebody'd had that choke hold on me one way or another. It was rage, deep rage, and Big Ben that doubled over and threw Abe's body clean over my head. His back hit the hard cement floor. Sounded like everything was breaking. But he stood back up.

That's the way we were, two killers, barely standing, trying to get breath. Abe's shirt was torn. My belt was hanging loose. My fists were bleeding. Abe's nose was bleeding. My right ear gone haywire.

Slow and weird, the rest of the world started coming into focus. Just about then Mr. Sloat, the mechanical drawing teacher,

showed up. He was a Mormon bishop and never liked me much.
The moment, just as Mr. Sloat stepped in between, what I'd managed to say just then Mr. Sloat didn't take kindly at all.

"You're the one who's the queer," I said.

Abe Martin was a Mormon, too, so he didn't get sent to the
principal. The principal, Mr. Bagley, who was also a Mormon,
was filled with indignation and all sorts of authoritarian outrage.
He threatened to call my parents, not to let me be in the gradu-
ation ceremony, and a bunch of other stuff. But I could give a shit.
I'd finally stood up for myself. And I was higher than a kite.
And for a few brief moments in my life there was nobody in the
world who could hurt me.

THE THING THAT pisses me off most about Abe Martin, though,
didn't really piss me off until years later. It wasn't until after the
second time Big Ben knew that this was it and I had to stand and
fight that I realized something important.

I'd spent all my life in a kind of resignation. Shit was
always going to happen to me and I just had to learn how to withstand it. Bullies were going to come and go and I just had to
brace myself and somehow get through it. For instance, I never
once thought of getting even with Abe Martin. I mean he was
a real asshole. He didn't fight me fair. He ganged up on me with
his friends. With the intention of ridiculing me as I stood there
in the high school hallway with my dick hanging out.

I defended myself and I succeeded in my defense. And I'd
go on that way until the next time I needed to defend myself.
Fucking Catholicism, man.

TWENTY YEARS LATER, another bully. And once again he
wasn't alone. Two this time instead of three. In a basement in New
York City. Then, after I picked myself off the concrete floor, we
were out in the street.

Didn't know for sure what I was doing. Just knew I had to
do something.

But Big Ben knew. It was revenge.

I'D JUST QUIT my job at Café Un Deus Trois and was a full-time super. The building on Seventh Street, right next to the Ukrainian Catholic church, was a pain in the ass. The sewer always backed up. As soon as I walked in the foyer, which was every morning, if the basement was full of sewerage, I could smell it. Believe me.

It was a summer morning, because the mimosa tree in front of the church was blooming. The moment I unlocked the front door, I could tell it was bad. When I turned the basement light on and looked down, I couldn't believe it. Eight to ten inches of human shit and toilet paper lapping over the bottom step. It was a weekend, too, so my boss wasn't in the office. I immediately walked back to my apartment and put on my Key West shrimper boots. I almost didn't buy the shrimper boots because they were white, mid-calf, and looked kind of sissy. But as it turned out, those white, mid-calf, solid rubber boots saved my ass with all the shit I had to wade through.

Down in the basement, the only light was at the bottom of the stairs. I pulled my red bandana over my nose and mouth. Turned on my flashlight. My first step off the bottom stair was the scariest. I had to walk real slow to the sump pump. Just a beam of flashlight in a dark, dingy basement. Sloshing shit-water lapping up against the tops of my rubber boots. Fucking wade in the water, man.

Thank God that day the sump pump was working. It took a couple hours, but when the pump sucked all the water down, solid waste and TP still covered the cement floor. I didn't know what else to do, so I went for it. Pulled the red bandana back over my nose and mouth and started scraping. Human excrement down the sewer hole with the heavy duty metal push broom. Stepping careful because that shit was slick. Then I hooked up the hose and hosed down the whole basement. Sprayed out a whole can full of aerosol *Lavender Mist*.

But there was another problem that day. It was when I was

hosing away the shit away from the base of the boiler that I realized. The line on the side of the boiler. Sometime in the night, the shit-water level had reached over two feet high and the boiler had quit.

Back in my apartment, I left my boots in the hallway. Next to my phone was the list of emergency numbers to call. Repairs would be expensive on the weekend and my boss would be pissed but there was no way I could fix that boiler. I ran my finger down the list. *Frank's First Call Boiler and Repair.*

Two things about that company that fucked me up.

The first. It took a big dick just to call up *Frank's First Call Boiler and Repair.* You had to be prepared. If you fucked up the account number or the address the guy hung up. Then you had to be specific about what you needed. *Choose one: installation, replacement of parts, maintenance and cleaning, other.* You had to speak loud and clear and get to the point fast or the guy hung up. The first time I called them it took me all day to keep the guy on the phone.

And there I was again, my index finger on the telephone number. *Frank's First Call Boiler and Repair.* The Running Boy just wanted to run. Be prepared: I wrote down on a piece of paper the account number and the street address. Then how do you say in ten words or less your boiler was drowned in a shit flood? Fuck.

The guy on the phone was as tough as ever. John Gotti in New Jersey.

"What's your problem?"

I gave him the account number and the street address.

"What's your problem?"

"Other."

"What's your other problem?"

I said it fast, loud, and fuck you.

"Boiler emergency," I said.

There was a silence, just for a moment, and then the guy laughed.

"I remember you. You're the super getting the college education."

If you wait you lose. Before I had a chance to open up my mouth, the guy was talking at me again.

"Two hours," he said. "You be there on the stoop with the keys."

"If you're not on the stoop we don't stop."

In the shower, no matter how hard I scrubbed I couldn't get the basement turd smell off me. Poured a bunch of Polo after-shave into my hands and slapped it on my neck and face. Put on fresh clothes. Tied a new red handkerchief around my neck. Grabbed the flashlight and the keys. In the hallway. I slipped on my shrimper boots.

THE MOMENT THAT black van pulled up in front I knew. Which is the second reason why *Frank's First Call Boiler and Repair* fucked me up.

Marco.

Three months earlier, the last time I was alone with Marco, was in another basement. 211 East Fifth – the *first* time I'd called *Frank's First Call Boiler and Repair*. After getting hung up on all day, I'd finally I got a repairman sent over.

My boss gave me specific instructions to stay with the repairman the whole time. Just to watch him. *Make sure he doesn't goof off. Plus you might learn something.*

Marco arrived in a black van. Maria Callas playing a little too loud. Baldini. He was in his late twenties, tall and thin. Dark faux Aviator glasses. Under his ballcap, his hair was short and jet black. Orange coveralls, *Marco* sewed in red above his pocket.

He was sullen at first, you know like most straight guys, answered my questions with a grunt. I bought him a cup of coffee and he warmed up. Probably helped with his hangover. Turns out the oil pump had blown out and we had to undo the boiler assembly. I didn't know my ass from my elbow about boilers, but my boss had told me I had to stay, so I became Marco's assistant – handing him tools and running to his van for shit.

The first time I got a close look at Marco we were taking a break, standing outside in the sunlight in front of the basement door. A smashed nose that bent off to one side. One of those pencil-thin mustaches. Lips that seemed unreal, the way they were red. When he took his faux Aviators off, I mean I had to stare. His eyes were light brown, almost gray. Eyes like they could never look up into the sun or at God the Father or work for *Frank's First Call Boiler and Repair*. Those sensitive eyes, the thin mustache, and his red lips, man. Marco must have known about his eyes, how he had to keep them covered up, or maybe he was just weirded out by my stare, because he quick started down the basement steps. I waited a bit before I followed him down, and when I looked at him again, he was in the dark and wearing his safety glasses.

The cement walls of the boiler room were only a couple feet wider than the boiler itself. The motor and the oil burner assembly were on the floor of the boiler room right next to the pit the boiler was set in. The whole apparatus had to come off and then we had to bleed out the pipes. Or something like that. In any case, in no time at all, the whole magilla was torn apart. Just one light in the room. I had to plug in an extension cord for another light. Marco's hands were thick and calloused. Grease along the nails. On his left hand third finger a simple gold ring.

There were boiler parts everywhere and I had to be careful where I stepped. We talked some as we worked. Guy talk, as much as I can figure out what that is. I told him I was from Idaho and he mistook Idaho for Iowa then mixed them both up with Ohio. I didn't try and correct him. He was a Yankees fan and had a motorcycle. Some kind of fast Honda motorcycle. He didn't cuss like most guys. I went to ask him about his wife, and if he had any kids, but decided against it.

After a couple hours of handing him wrenches, after an afternoon of holding my monkeywrench on the bolt heads while he screwed the washers and nuts on tight, hours and hours of maneuvering my body around so I could get a better grip, both of us our arms up inside the dark hole of the boiler – there was no fucking way I couldn't not touch him – something changed. I have a theory about men working close in dark New York basements. Brings something out in you.

Sometime in the late afternoon, Marco stood up. He started making a big deal about how hot the basement was. A production number, him taking off his coveralls. Underneath he was wearing one of those Guinea T-shirts and a pair of jeans. White white skin. Lots of black hair on his chest. His jeans were some kind of designer washed-out jeans. When he bent over in those jeans. I mean he had to know he was showing hairy cleavage.

Propinquity. At this one point, I'm lying next to him on the cement floor, holding some damn oil pump burner thing steady, while Marco tightened a screw down. All the while his armpit's in my face. Sweat is what always tells the tale.

Marco smelled like my father.

And the most amazing thing. I didn't want to be in the next borough.

Later on, seven-thirty, eight o'clock, we were outside having a smoke. The boiler was back up and running, Marco was wearing his faux Aviators and his orange coveralls were back on. The tools were put away. The early evening was hot, and after a day in a dark basement, the bright burnt orange sky was good on my eyes and the air felt warm on my skin. I was sitting on the stoop. Marco was leaning against his black van. There was something different about Marco. The way he just kept standing there smoking. And his lips, Marco kept moving his red red lips, as if he was trying to say something. I wanted to say something too. I mean I felt like the boiler had lost and Marco and I were on the winning team. Didn't most guys feel this way after their hard work paid off for them? Wasn't that called *camaraderie*? Of course, I wanted to say something more. But Marco's lovely butt crack kept flashing in my brain. Made my breath stop. And how Marco smelled like my father. How fucked up I was that smell was sexy. So I didn't say anything. I had no voice, my heart was broke, same way as my dick was.

Marco pushed away from the van, walked through all the sunset bright orange, over to me on the stoop. I put my hand over my eyes. When his body was between me and the sun, I could see his hand stuck out. Marco shook my hand the way I always shake hands with men, too hard. All that overcompensation. Then he got in his van, started it up. I was halfway up the stoop when he called out.

"Hey, Ben!"

I had no idea Marco knew my name, so when I heard my name coming out from under that pencil thin mustache, from out of those red red lips, that place inside me that's always scared in that moment stopped being scared. How I stopped, looked at my arms, at my hands, looked around me at the world. Blessed fearless moment. When you're Catholic the way I am, you don't have to die to spend eternity in hell.

Marco had his window rolled down. On the window ledge, his black hairy forearm. He reached up under the visor and pulled out a pen and began writing on something. Maria Callas too loud. Just as he handed me out the business card, the way he turned his head, his faux Aviators shone the bright orange sky right into me.

When I got back to my apartment, I put the card under my reading lamp.

> Frank's First Call Boiler and Repair
> Marco Tucciarone

Scribbled on the back, his phone number and *weekends call after nine o'clock.*

About a week later, after a bottle of *Vin Santo*, I sat with my telephone in my lap, wrapping the curlicue cord in my fingers. Marco's business card under my reading light. *Weekends call after nine o'clock* written in strangely cursive handwriting.

THREE MONTHS LATER, on the stoop of 39 East Seventh, *Frank's First Call Boiler Repair*'s black van pulls up, double parks. At first I'm relieved because the too loud music isn't Maria Callas. It's hip-hop. The Italian guy that gets out on the passenger side looks like he's still in high school. His orange coveralls are too long for him and he has to stop and roll the pant legs up off his boots. He doesn't like that his coveralls don't fit. He's cussing the long legs of the coveralls, or cussing his short legs. I just know there's something he isn't happy about. He's bent over, his ass pointed my way. It's through his legs he sees me standing on the second stair of the stoop. He straightens up fast and turns around. The look on his face as he looks at me, his dark eyes, inside those eyes, it's hate.

"What the fuck you looking at?"

I have to remind my internal homophobia that I'm just standing on the stoop on the second step waiting for the boiler guys. And the boiler guys came and one of them stepped out, bent over, and started pointing his ass at me.

A gorilla this guy, the way he stares at my white boots, walks up to me, past me, up to the third step so he can look me in the eye. *Frankie Junior* sewn in red above his pocket. Puffed up in his chest, like Hank makes his chest, but I don't know Hank yet and this guy isn't pretty at all like Hank. He's mean, *Frank's First Call Boiler Repair* mean, and up this close his breath smells of beer and his skin is bad and there's something about his eyes. He isn't twenty years old yet, and his tiny brown eyes are dead.

"Frankie Junior!"

That voice. I know that voice. It's the voice who called out my name one evening three months ago in the glowing. Marco.

"Your dad's on the two-way. He wants to talk to you."

Frankie Junior's brown dead eyes go from my eyes down to Marco. It's in that moment I can see the hate in Frankie Junior's eyes doesn't have anything to do with me. He's got a chip on his shoulder, or a hangover, bad drugs, really bad gas, or he's just somehow fucked up and whoever he runs into has to pay for it.

Frankie Junior steps down, the too-long pant leg scraping the bottom step.

"Motherfucker!" he yells and kicks his too-long pant leg at the step.

"Orange cunt fucking pants!" he yells. "Can't fucking even walk!"

Marco stands tall on the sidewalk, his toolbox in his right hand. His thin mustache, those red red lips. Faux Aviator glasses. Even though I can't see his eyes, I can tell his dove gray eyes are not looking at me. They're not looking at Frankie Junior either. There's something resigned about Marco. Like this is my fucking job and this is my fucking life and this is my boss's fucking spoiled brat son and this guy on the second stair is the fucking guy who never called me back.

As I speak I try to put in my words a softness, some kind of apology.

"Hey Marco," I say, "How's it going?"

A quick breath in, Marco gets taller, his shoulders go up. His right arm lifts the toolbox, lets it back down. The fucking faux Aviators, man. He's not Marco Tucciarone. He's Boiler Man. And nothing's going to touch this guy.

Frankie Junior slams the van door.

"So where's this fucking boiler?"

I UNLOCK THE door to the basement, turn on the light. The shit smell is still strong. Frankie Junior's right behind me. By the third step he's cussing again.

"Somebody fucking die down here?"

On the cement floor, no sign of turds or toilet paper.

"Fuckin' A, somebody died," he says. "Shit themselves first, then sprayed it down with perfume water."

The single lightbulb is hanging right above us. Shadows of us puddle on the cement floor. Frankie Junior's standing right next to me. Marco steps out from behind him, bends down and opens the toolbox. When I look up, the dark shadows on Frankie

Junior's cheeks. His dead eyes are so dead they've become black holes.

It's time to tell them what's up with the boiler. My fucking mouth that doesn't know how to speak to big loud macho brute Italian guys, especially when the news ain't good is just about to speak, but the black holes in Frankie Junior's face, man. The black holes start sucking me in.

"Fuck man, I don't know who smells worse," Frankie Junior says, "this fucking basement or you. What'd you do take a bath in foo foo water?"

He's half a head shorter than me and his body is thick. Marco starts taking out tools and laying them on the cement. His faux Aviators reflect the lightbulb. You wait, you lose. That quick, Frankie Junior pulls a flashlight out of a side pocket, turns the flashlight on. Shines the light onto the boiler apparatus. The three of us all turn to look.

I hadn't sprayed it down. I was too freaked the boiler had stopped and I ran out of there and I didn't spray down the boiler apparatus. The black electric motor, the sparkplugs, the wires coming out of it, the oil filter, the copper tubing, the pump, the blower system – all of it. Covered in toilet paper and turds.

Frankie Junior goes ballistic. *Motherfucker* and *motherfucker*. Stomps up the stairs. Marco picks up a wrench, puts it back in the toolbox. It's when Marco realizes he's alone with me, he does that quick breath in again and his shoulders go up. That quick he follows Frankie Junior up the stairs. I stay in the basement, think maybe somebody should stay with the tools. The dark wet basement looks like a dungeon where people get tortured. The metal push broom I've left is leaning against the stairs.

In the foyer, Marco's standing in the vestibule. I walk up behind him slow, make enough noise so he knows I'm approaching. I stand next to him, not close, and lean up against the door-jamb. I'm surprised I'm taller than him.

Outside it's bright and hot. In the black van, out the passenger side door, Frankie Junior's stocky orange legs stick out into the sun. The upper half of him in shadow. He's yelling to John Gotti, Frank Senior, on the two-way.

Inside, next to Marco, I think of what I want to say, then say it: "I thought I'd got it all cleaned up."

Marco from the side looks like Michelangelo's *David* with a thin mustache and his nose busted off. He doesn't look around at me. Just pushes his ballcap up off his forehead. When he speaks, it's almost a whisper.

"Man," he says, "you should have said something."

Frankie Junior starts jumping up and down and banging the two-way against the van. He throws the phone onto the sidewalk and kicks it.

He's screaming: "Fuck! Fuck! Fuck!"

"Marco!" he yells. "Get the fucking toolbox. We're getting the fuck out of here!"

Marco's an orange flash down into the basement. I don't want him to get away, so I'm right behind him on the stairs. I'm saying, *you guys can't just leave. You're professionals. There's people in this building without hot water.* The whole time I'm talking, I'm trying to get Marco to look at me, but he's too busy checking around for tools.

Marco closes up his toolbox, latches the latch.

I'm standing between him and the stairs.

"I'm sorry, Marco," I say. "Really, I'm sorry. I called the number you gave me but the automated voice was weird so I hung up."

"Who *is* this fag?"

Marco says this. Because Frankie Junior is standing behind me.

Propinquity. I could say I didn't see it coming. But I did. Frankie Junior grabs my arms and pins them to my back. He's strong, body builder strong. Marco's fist hits me square in the face. Then a blow to my neck, and I'm down.

Things go away for a while. All I know is my face is on the cement floor and that floor had been covered in shit and I somehow try to pull my lips away from the wet shit cement. Frankie

Junior's talking. *Faggot boots. What's a red handkerchief supposed to mean. He takes it up the ass?* Then another blow. Something right between the eyes and the light goes off.

Inside forever it is only dark. Cast out. There is no breath. In my sternum, in the middle of my chest, a lightbulb you can see the filament flickering. It's when I hear the basement door close I wake up. Some deep fear of getting locked in. Panic in my breath and I grab my pocket and my hands are around the keys. I rip off my jacket, rip off my shirt. The metal push broom is the first solid thing my hand finds. I'm not sure of all that happens next. The dark stairway is only heaving panicked breath and then the door. The door crashes open because I don't put my hand around the door knob and turn, Big Ben slams my body against the wood door and wood splinters and there's light and I'm not in the darkness and I can breathe.

The black van is just pulling away. I'm running, Quasimodo breathing. Loud hip-hop from the van. Marco's on the passenger side. The window's open, the black hairs of his forearm. His faux Aviators.

The metal broom crashes down onto the windshield. The windshield cracks and caves in. The van swerves, hits a car on the other side. Marco yells at Frankie Junior, *Don't stop. Keep driving.* I swing the broom again, let it go. The van's side mirror goes limp, dangling down like something dead. The engine stalls. Frankie's cussing and the van won't start and he goes for his door. Marco grabs his shoulder. *No. Keep driving. Keep driving*, Marco yells. Steam's rolling out the hood. The van starts, the back tires spinning in reverse. I'm right at the passenger window. Marco doesn't try to close the window, he just looks over at me. I yell some kind of ancient fucked up grunt and jump, swing hard, hit him in the face harder than he hit me. Marco's head jerks back with the blow, his faux Aviators bent to shit. A jab of pain in my hand moves up my arm. Burnt rubber smoke. The van jumps and starts, trying to take off. I'm running right alongside. The Running Boy fucking loves to run. In his white rubber sissy boots he loves to run. Marco's still looking at me, right at me, blood streaming out his nose. Those dove gray sensitive eyes. He doesn't try to move away, doesn't bring his arm up. I leap again and yell, hit him in the face again. More blood. Blood smeared all over his face. The van is pulling away and I'm running and still he looks at me. Eyes like they could never look up into the sun or at God the Father or work for *Frank's First Call Boiler and Repair.*

Then all of a sudden everything's bright and loud and full and I'm in the middle of Bowery. Horns are honking and people are screaming. A yellow cab on my left is coming right at me. I jump back so fast it's like I'm flying.

What I remember next is I'm in my apartment looking in my bathroom mirror. My eye is a deep purple and almost swollen shut. Dried blood on my face from the gash just at my hairline. In the bright white light, there's blood on everything. Blood in my hair, blood on my white T-shirt, my Levi's, my white rubber boots, on the floor, on the sink, on the mirror, blood. The hot water's running into the sink. The sound of the water against the porcelain. My bloody red hand. The hot water onto a bloody white bar rag. And it's the damndest thing. I can't figure out where that bar rag came from.

4.

The West Side Y

OF ALL MY STORIES, HANK LOVED THE *FRANK'S FIRST Call Boiler and Repair* best. The white shrimper boots just too much. That big burst from down deep in him coming up fast shaking him around made Hank spit out his ham and cheese, he was laughing so hard. We were in a burger joint on Columbus Circle sitting at our table in the window. Every Wednesday night, after we both taught at the West Side Y, Hank and I went there. It was just a diner. Nothing special. Close to the Y. The food was cheap, plenty of French fries, and an endless cup of coffee.

It was *our place*, like the window table was *our table*.

And that was *our* joke. Since Hank and I'd been spending so much time together, people started to talk. One day Hank actually got a phone call. From Hal Taylor, another one of Jeske's students, who'd said: *certain people were getting the wrong idea*.

Hal Taylor ate, drank, and slept Jeske. I could just imagine Hal's face when he'd said that. His tongue poking poking out his cheek like he was sucking dick.

"No surprise there," Hank said.

And that's all Hank ever said about it. I tried to get more out of him, about what he really thought about people, his peers – friends dissing on him. But you know Hank. The Enigma of Hank.

Then one Wednesday night at the Y. I'd just closed the classroom door. There were twelve adult students, New Yorkers after a long day at work, sitting in their desks in a shiny beige room under the bright fluorescence. They were all looking up at me, standing behind the lectern as if I was the writing expert. This moment I remember well because this moment happened every Wednesday night at that time. Right after I took role. Just before I began to speak. The moment I knew that this was the class that would finally discover what a load of bullshit I really was.

Hank knew about this moment of mine because after we got our jobs at the Y that's all I could talk about. That moment in front of class when my heart froze, when my voice went haywire, the flickering filament in the lightbulb in my chest, when my breathing stopped, just before I started to speak.

That particular Wednesday, it was in that moment, after roll call, as I was just about to open my mouth, at that exact moment of terror, the door opened. He couldn't have timed it better.

Everybody in the class looked over at Hank. Just his head poked in, and his right forearm, white shirtsleeve rolled up. His long fingers against the wood of the door.

"I came here to out your teacher," Hank said. "He's a fraud."

The room got quiet. The whole building. All of New York City got quiet. The world hanging out there a round ball nothing holding it up. Only my breath and my pounding heart. Hank just stayed there at the door, smiling and looking in. I pulled the lectern into my belly. For a moment I thought *I* had said it. *Fraud.*

"And don't you think," Hank said, "he's really sexy?"

Hank's deep-set eyes, eyes you'd expect to be blue but weren't, were dark, almost black, right then looked adoringly into my eyes across the crowded room. Those sweet smiling lips.

"Gruney dear?" Hank said. "Let's meet at our regular spot for dinner, say 9:30?"

Really, Hank Christian. That fucker. Nobody made me laugh like him.

AND VICE VERSA. Like the night in our restaurant I told him about the shrimper boots and Frank's First Call Boiler and Repair.

A big spray of ham and cheese across the table. I had to duck.

"Fucking Grunewald!" Hank said.

Hank was calling out for club soda and picking lettuce off his white shirt.

"Christ," he said, "you're lucky they didn't come back and cut your nuts off."

Hank had knocked over his Coca-Cola too and we were sopping up spilt Coke off the pink Formica tabletop with paper napkins out of the tin dispenser.

The waiter, Silvio, *our waiter*, tall, one front tooth missing, brought over a glass of club soda and a bar rag.

"Thanks, Silvio," Hank said. "We'll tend to this. Sorry about the mess."

Hank grabbed the bar rag and started sopping up spilt Coke.

"I'll get that," I said. "You club soda your shirt."

Hank looked down at his shirt.

"Fuck," he said. "My good white teaching shirt."

"Salt helps too," Silvio said.

"I'll get another bar rag," Silvio said.

"It's always been a mystery," I said, "what it is to be male and what that means."

"So you attack two guys from New Jersey with a fucking *broom*?" Hank said.

"You find out what it is," I said, "by what it ain't."

The bar rag was soaked with Coke. I traded with Silvio, who was back with another rag. Fresh off the clean bar rag pile.

Somewhere in that moment everything stopped. In the middle of the big mess on the pink Formica tabletop, Hank's white shirt, the club soda, the clean bar rag, the salt, Silvio – all of it. Stopped.

That silence just before. Silvio stepped away. I looked over at Hank. Hank was looking at the bar rag in my hand soaked with Coke.

"Fuck!" Hank said.

His face was scrunched up the way sudden pain makes your face. Over the years, I'd see Hank's face do that a bunch.

The first time was that night when we'd stood in front of Auden's house and read the poem. This was the second time. We'd known each other six months tops.

"I'm crying again," Hank said, "and I don't ever cry. Fuck."

"Hank," I said, "what's going on?"

He was trying to get his mouth to work right. Then more time to breathe.

Silvio handed me the clean bar rag. Traded me for the soaked rag. Took himself back into the kitchen.

"It's the bar rag," Hank said. "You in the mirror and the blood on the bar rag and you trying to make sense of things."

Hank's body sunk down, folded in, more dense so he could have a part in the pain that was coming out of him too.

THAT GODDAMN BURGER joint. Can't remember the name of it. Torn down when that new Bloomberg building went up on Columbus. All those Wednesday nights, after class, Hank and I sat in there. Cheeseburgers and all that hope. Writers. We were going to speak a truth so real it wasn't spoken yet. We'd carve language so deep into our living hearts the reader would rip at the pages, would throw the book across the room, would fuck the book, would open their veins and run out into the street, cursing God Almighty or whoever it was responsible for this unfair unjust beloved torment.

THE BAR RAG. I laid the clean bar rag down onto the pink Formica tabletop next to Hank's hand, kept my hand on my end of it. Hank's long fingers drummed the Formica. Then suddenly Hank grabbed the other end. He started pulling on the rag. I grabbed onto my end of the rag and pulled too. I don't know why but there we were. The way we were pulling on the bar rag pulled our heads down close.

"Let me tell you about my sister," Hank said.

If I kept pulling on the bar rag, maybe I'd get more out of Hank than the Enigma.

"I'll tell you a story, "Hank said. "It'll give you an example of what kind of man I am," Hank said. "You'll see."

Hank had his end of the rag, I had mine.

"My sis was just sixteen," Hank said, "when she ran off to Ohio with this twenty-two-year-old cat named Darcy. On the phone, my mother was so fucking ballistic I couldn't make any sense out of what she was saying. When I finally got her calmed down, I told her I'd take care of it.

"I took care of it all right," Hank said.

Hank's black eyes were closer than they'd ever been. Right then I promised myself *never* to fuck with Hank Christian. To never be the reason those black eyes got so scary. Promises, man. So much for promises.

"My dad left before my sis ever knew him," Hank said. "I was her only father."

"And my stepdad – shit!" Hank said.

Hank grabbed the bar rag so hard he nearly pulled me over the table.

"My journalism years paid off," Hank said. "It took me no time at all to track this Darcy guy down. He was living in the burbs outside Cleveland. I packed up my car in the middle of the night and drove straight through. I was at their front door before the sun was up."

"Darcy opened the door in his shorts," Hank said. "Tall skinny guy. Didn't know what hit him. Peg came running out of the bedroom screaming at me to stop hitting him, but I didn't stop. All the while Peg was begging me, *Please Hank, I love him, Hank. Please leave us alone. Stop hitting him Hank, I love him. I love him.*"

"I took Peg *by the hair* – didn't let her get her stuff – Christ, all she had on was her jeans and a T-shirt – she was *barefoot*, and I dragged her to my van and threw her in and took her back to my mom's in Massachusetts."

"Two years later," Hank said, "when she was eighteen, Peg married the guy. He works in a record store and has his own DJ show on a local station. They have a son, my nephew, Johnny, a beautiful young man I'll never meet. Peg hasn't spoken to me since. And she never will. She won't even be in the same house with me."

Hank's knuckles pushed against mine. The bar rag only an excuse. Hank couldn't make his mouth move right. His chin started to go and it was no use.

"Gruney," Hank said, "the thing that's hardest to say was all the blood. The blood on Peg's jeans and on my shirt. On my hands. Hell, there was blood all over that van."

Big sobs, old broken things that scraped hard against Hank's heart as they came up out of him.

"I believed all that macho dominant-male kick-ass bullshit and look where it's got me," Hank said. "My sister. I've lost her. The only family I had besides my mother."

"My dirty little secret," Hank said, " –hell, it hasn't even been a secret. You have to think about it for it to be a secret."

Hank's dark eyes were two deep black holes in the world.

"Gruney," Hank said, "you're the first person I've ever told."

WHAT HANK SAID next, it took my ears a while to hear what he was saying. Strange when that part in you is touched how quickly you can fall apart. It's as if the words that are being said go to the deepest place, the place in you that's become the way you've become so you can keep on going. The helmet you put on when you were a kid that grew into your head and now someone is saying you have a helmet on your head.

"That first time I heard you read at Ursula Crohn's," Hank said, "it was as if the skies opened, or my soul opened, whatever, shit just opened. Your broken voice saying it is I who am broken, and it is human to be broken, and we are all broken, and it changed my life. I've never heard anything so beautiful."

"It was you who taught me, Gruney," Hank said, "to be authentic."

"It's you who taught me to be a real man."

5.
The women

THEN THERE WAS THE NIGHT HANK AND OLGA AND I GOT thrown out of Seville.

That's where we were going to meet that night, at Seville – a Spanish restaurant on Perry in the West Village. Hank said Olga said it was the best *Mariscada de Salsa Verde* in town. I didn't even know what *Mariscada de Salsa Verde* was, other than it was green. But I didn't care. It could've been fried green goat brains and I'd have gone. In the year I'd known Hank, besides Mythrixis, of all the girlfriends Hank had only mentioned now and then, Olga Rivas was different. She was from Nicaragua. Into Santeria. Her long thick curly black hair. Her eyes, her eyes, Hank couldn't stop talking about her eyes. Her English. The way she adorned herself with jewelry. And that night, I was finally going to meet her.

It was summer again and hot like only Manhattan can get. Humid hot with nothing green around to suck it up. Heat waves bouncing off concrete. I started out from East Fifth Street an hour early. Those days, my vacations were walking. My favorite route was to cut across Cooper Union Square to Broadway, then window shop Eighth Street with its cheap chic, shoes, and *salons de belleza eres*. To Fifth Avenue. My favorite corner. There was always a guy drawing with chalk on the wide sidewalks, wonderful drawings that looked like da Vinci or van Gogh. I always watched where I stepped so I'd never step on his drawing. And something else I loved to look at. One Fifth Avenue. That building was what my eyes always went to.

More often than not, that corner was my destination. There was a Hebrew National on Eighth, my favorite dinner out. Two hot dogs with sauerkraut and a Coke. I'd take my dinner to across from One Fifth, sit on the curb, eat my hot dogs, drink the Coke, stare up at the building. The Spanish terra cotta tiles, the mullion windows. The little round windows at ground level that looked like windows on big ships.

There I was, Ben Grunewald, so close I could reach out and touch it.

It. What George Plimpton had, what it takes to be Truman Capote. The penthouse apartment with the arched tall corner windows. The crystal chandelier you could see in there at night. Sometimes the curtains, like clouds those curtains. Vacations on Lake Como. *The Paris Review. The New York Review of Books.* Miles Davis. Sailboats. Those blue plates people hang on their kitchen walls. Pressed starched linen. Chablis Grand Cru. Truffles. Café de Flor. Museo de Chocote. Havana, Cuba. People to love you like Hemingway.

The myth of van Gogh coursing through my veins. One painting. He'd only sold one painting. So happy with my Kosher wieners and my Coke. Sitting there my ass on the curb, my feet in the gutter, next to me the guy chalking out *Starry Night.*

I'm looking up, always looking up.

I knew it was far away. That world. But no fucking idea how far.

If I had it to do over again, I wouldn't. I'd find someplace sunny. Always have tanned feet. Drink clear clean water from a thick green glass bottle. Find a big Catalpa tree to love. Eat dirt.

AT SEVILLE, THERE'S a line, and even though Olga has made reservations we have to wait. We're standing in the shadows the leaves make. A Mimosa tree I think. Soft lacy shade. Hank does the introductions. I don't look too closely at Olga at first.

Something makes me not look right at her. When she takes my hand I can feel the bones in her hand. How she holds my hand a moment too long. The lacy shade on her arms and face. Her famous long black curly hair, her beautiful brown skin. Black eyes that make Hank's look brown. Small boned, like her body has been reduced down twenty percent. Makes me feel oversized, clumsy. Her light see-through blouse is red. No bra. Pockets on the blouse so you can't really see her nipples. Gold bracelets on her wrists, lots of gold bracelets, a gold ring on each hand. How gold sounds rubbing against itself. Bright yellow shorts. Gold sandals with fake jewels on them. Toenails like her fingernails, so clear and shiny they didn't seem real. The way she says *Mariscada de salsa verde*.

The maître d'hôtel, a tall guy with slick black hair and a Don Ameche mustache, offers us a free cocktail. Olga orders a margarita – *maargaareeta* – margarita for me too. Then Hank orders a margarita. I look over at Hank real close when he says *margarita*. I'd never seen Hank drink hard liquor.

My eyes can't stay on Hank for long, though. They move with Hank's eyes to where he's staring. The way he looks at her. His eyes beholding her. As if she is something newly formed, precious, and as we stand, his breath is breathing life into her. And if he stops looking, if he skips a breath, if he looks away, Olga Rivas, this dark angel of a woman he has conjured up will disappear.

I don't like her at all.

Don't trust her. Women or men – doesn't matter. When they're beautiful the way Olga is beautiful, they know they can get away with anything.

There's a simple test you can try on beautiful people. You know how they look as if they know they're always being looked at? Well, try catching them off guard. And if you can't ever catch them without that looked-at look on their faces, if you can't ever catch them picking their nose, slumped over when they sit, belching, sneezing, yawning too wide, God forbid a fart – then you know you're in trouble. Stay away from these people like the plague because they're really not human – not until their beauty fades. And when it does, their beauty a blossom that has burst, when they realize they're no longer always being looked at, stand away because there's going to be a meltdown.

Believe me, I am watching Olga. She is ten, twelve years tops away from being human.

THERE IS A moment at the table. We are in one of the booths in the back, sitting in a half circle of red leather. Darkness and points of soft light hanging in the air around us. In the center of the round table, a votive candle in a red glass. Above us on the wall, a kitsch painting of a peasant woman with large breasts balancing a jar of wine on her shoulder. Olga in the middle, under the painting, facing out, Hank and I on the ends. We're some-where between our second and the third margaritas, high enough that the regular world has shifted just enough to let the shine come through. The all-important shine. Light – it feels like light – creeps into your body and things get clear and you know shit, important shit, and you speak easily because you're shining with what you know.

That's what I'm doing, shining, speaking easily. Who knows what I'm saying. Something important. Something about me. Going on and on and on. Pretty soon I get this feeling and I stop. I come back into my body back from out there wherever it is I was. Hank's staring at me. Olga's staring at me.

Olga reaches over and takes my hand. Her hand, a way that only a woman can touch. A touch that says she knows she'll never know you but still she's curious. From the other side, her touch, female. Tender even. The way an oncologist touches a cancerous tumor, or maybe in the zoo the way you see on TV a baby tiger playing with a monkey. The candlelight on the smooth brown skin of her arms, her gold bracelets. The sound of gold against gold.

"My buddy Gruney's really something," Hank says, "isn't he?"

Olga's right hand grasps my hand solid. Across the table, Olga's left hand is solid in Hank's too.

"I'd love to read your cards sometime," Olga says. "I don't know how to describe. You're like a feral."

"*Feral?*" Olga says. "Is that English?"

"Latinate," Hank says.

"Is okay?" Olga says.

"Says it perfect," Hank says.

"A feral child," Olga says, "who nobody ever listened to."

IT'S A GOOD thing I've had two *maargaareetas*. It's a good thing a third was coming. All that attention would have made the normal ordinary Ben Grunewald go tilt. Made my toes curl up in my shoes, made my balls pull up, poked up my shoulders. *Showing off again! Making a spectacle of yourself!*

Hank takes hold of my right hand. His hand, only a way a man can touch. A touch that says he knows that men haven't really got a clue. It's only an attitude. But fuck it, we can play and not get caught the way women can. The red votive light on his thick wrist, his smooth forearm.

That moment is one of the big moments of my life. When everything comes together. I feel a way I've only dreamed of. Too high really to ever remember it well. Only a trace, a thin drunk thread of memory going back over the years to find that guy, me, who was sitting there at that table, who let himself be seen. The three of us, on the red leather, darkness and points of soft light hanging in the air around us, the votive candle in the center of the white round table, the red glow of glass, between our second and the third *maargaareetas*, Hank's hand in Olga's, Olga's hand in mine, my hand in Hank's.

I'm about to make a joke, say something, anything, that will make the precious moment stop. I know I can do it. Move my shoulders, tilt my chin, laugh a little laugh. And I'm just starting, just past the shoulders, and in the middle of the chin tilt, when:

"Don't deprecate," Olga says.

"Deprecate?" I say.

"Latinate," Hank says.

"Yourself," Olga says.

"You must be careful," Olga says, "of what you say in front of yourself."

SOMETHING INSIDE ME, something ancient and infant, that hasn't looked out of me in a long time, looks out and over across the table at Olga. She is so perfectly doing that beautiful people looked-at look. Part of me wants to punch her, wants this all to stop, a big baby torpor, where is the fucking waiter with the tray of *maargaareetas*.

Then that looked-at look, I let it come out of me. Let my own beauty gaze back straight into hers.

Olga. Maybe it's because it's the first time I've seen Hank make his nod to hard liquor. Maybe it's because Hank's told me about Olga's Santeria, maybe it's because she'd asked to read my cards, maybe she is a witch, her beauty, maybe it's her black eyes that make Hank's look brown, maybe it's the gold, all the gold on her. The sound of gold. Maybe it's the three of us in a dark place hand in hand in hand around a flame. What scares me most is the secret I couldn't speak in Jeske's class. Can she see my shame? I watch Olga's red lips, ready for the brutal truth, but then she speaks.

"You've been with many women also," Olga says.

Maybe Olga's been talking to *Hank*. Thing is though, I've only told Hank about Evie, my ex-wife.

Maybe it's simply women's intuition. Or maybe what happens isn't because of anything other than it is. Hank scoots in closer, his hand a big bear paw around mine. Olga leans in too. Her hand in mine is like she's hanging onto a cliff.

The fact is Olga can see. In that moment, in that place, I

have no doubt. She can see inside me. All of my whole long history. And as she's looking, it makes me look too.

Many women also.

That look of Olga's. There's the *okay, he's gay look*, but then there's the other look – *he sleeps with women too*. That look. Women and men both, when they find that out, there's usually a long long look like they're trying to figure out how somebody – a *guy* – if a woman walks on both sides of the street that's somehow not surprising – but a *guy*, a man sleeping with women and sleeping with men too – *that* look is: *how can he switch gears like that*. And more specifically: *how can his cock switch gears like that*.

It's simple. Survival. For me it's been survival. The generous vascular congestion filling my cock with life while I'm touching, holding another human being, for most men an act as natural as blood flowing in and out of their hearts, for me, has always been elusive. A mystery. And by that point in my life, nonexistent.

No, there were no accidents as a child, no blows to the groin, no slip of a blade to the penis. But there was a wound. Most definitely there was a wound.

MY MOTHER, MY sister.

The Paradoxes.

There's one day that sticks out in my mind. My sister, Margaret, and I are going to 4-H camp. I'm maybe seven, Sis is ten. I'm excited to leave home, to go to some new exotic place. My sister and I hug mom and we get into our blue and white '57 Buick. My sister in front next to dad. Me in the back seat.

As my father drives out the driveway, I turn and look out the back window. My mother is standing alone at the back door of our skinny white house. She's in her red housedress and she's holding the iron frying pan. She's just scraped the food scraps out for the dogs. My mother looks up. That far away I can see it. Inside her almond-shaped hazel eyes, the deep loneliness she usually keeps so well hidden.

From the beginning, I was the one responsible for her sadness. I mean it was my job to stop it. Nobody told me to save her, nobody made me. I just knew. It was simple. My mother's sadness was something that happened inside my own body. How my mother was, was how I was. I had no choice. A pain too much to bear. And even if I wanted it to stop, my mother was what made life, life. I only kept her happy so I could survive.

Looking out the back window of the Buick that day, when I see my mother's eyes, I start crying. Really crying. My father hates that I'm crying. He thinks I'm crying because I miss my mommy. He doesn't know that I'm crying for her. That she is alone. That now that I'm gone she'll be alone with *him*. The man who doesn't see her.

My father's big arm, his hairy hand comes through the slot between the front seats. Knocks me across the back seat.

"Stop crying!" my father yells. "You damn crybaby."

Later, on the bus on our way to 4-H Camp, when I'm alone with my sis, Margaret makes sure that she and I sit in the same seat next to each other. Me inside by the window, her on the aisle. She has my lunch. She holds my hand safely in hers.

When the bus takes off, she whispers only so I can hear: *you damn crybaby.*

Margaret says it as if she's victorious, like she's the Grand Chooser and the only one who knows the truth. She whispers: *you need to grow up and start acting like a man. So your father can be proud of you.*

My sister, the paradox, who's bigger than me, who's always in control, who's the only one around to play with. The one who protects me from *them*: my mother, my father.

My crazy depressed mother and her mood swings, her insane rages, her migraine headaches. Her obsession with hell and damnation and fire and praying the rosary, praying the rosary. *Pray for us. Have mercy on us. Lord I am not worthy. I who am the most miserable of all.*

We hide under the bed when mother goes crazy. Margaret

lies down in front of me, makes a sandwich of me between her and the wall. She tells me to close my eyes tight. She pulls my arm around her and holds on tight. And we sing real soft our favorite song. "Over the Rainbow."

More than anyone, though, who my sister protects me from is my father. My sister Margaret is the only one who knows my terrible secret. Except my mother, and only she knows some of the time. But really, it's my sister, and only my sister, Margaret, who holds the key.

If my father catches me playing dress up, the wide world will open up a huge crack and I will fall in alone. Banished from the world of men.

My sister, Margaret, is the only one standing between me and that hell.

Yet when my father isn't around, and mother isn't watching, it's Margaret who puts dresses on me, curls my hair, colors my lips cherry red, hangs earrings on my ears.

If Margaret tells Ben to jump, my father always said, *Ben will ask how high.*

And something else that day on the bus. My sister Margaret does the thing she knows will hurt me the worst. She leans over, whispers in my ear: *Benjamina*. The girl name she knows I hate.

And all the while, as my sister whispers her betrayals, calls me the girl name, she unfolds my sandwich for me, she opens up my juice, she holds on tight to my hand. In my sister's eyes, so much like my mother's eyes, the way she looks at me happens inside my body too.

I'm protecting him because he's mine.

But what can I do.

The paradox.

I'm the only one she has.

Years later, when I'm twelve, maybe thirteen, the paradox of mother, the paradox of sister has only deepened. It's a fact. I am powerless. I am their slave.

In the sixth grade, during religion class, for the first time I really look at a drawing in my Baltimore Catechism. It's of a naked man at the very bottom of hell. He's in the deepest, hottest place in hell, *the most miserable of all.*

He has no cock hanging down there between his legs.

That's all the proof I need.

If I sin, if my cock gets hard, if my sister finds out, it's only a matter of time before she'll tell my mother. When my crazy mother finds out, she'll cut off my cock at the base, throw it in an unmarked grave.

My mother, my sister.

Fascists in the night come to kill my Lorca.

If the dictatorship is a success, I'll never get to say I miss it.

My mother, my sister.

Women I have loved.

And Olga sees it.

MY WIFE, EVELYN. Seven years of trying to make my Catholic promise work.

Idaho State University, 1967. Evelyn Marie Firth, Evie, is eighteen years old, blonde and tall and standing between the wall mirror and the staircase of my fraternity house holding a plastic cup of foamy Coors. She's so unlike the other helmet-haired sorority girls at the kegger. She looks like Twiggy.

'67 in Idaho, the year the Sixties really hit. On the front porch, I'm surprised when she accepts the cigarette. A Gamma Phi smoking a cigarette. So easy sitting next to her on the steps. Hazel green eyes under all that makeup. Short, dark pleated skirt and white polka dot pantyhose. Mary Janes. Her long legs press together and poke up from the second step. May in Idaho, one of those first hot days when everybody's been outside in the sun trying to get a tan. On the steps, my tanned feet next to hers in penny loafers, no socks. Duct tape holding the sole onto the left shoe. We'd mown the lawn that day and the smell of the evening was cut grass, the Marlboros, and her. Something clean and French. It isn't long and we are shoulder to shoulder.

"What are you doing this summer?" she asks.

"Going to San Francisco," I say. "Want to see what the hippies are all about."

I think that was it. Why she fell for me. An older guy, almost twenty years old, going to where it was really cool. Haight-Ashbury. Most guys back then, in Idaho, for my brothers at the fraternity, hippies were the last fucking place they wanted to go.

That's the first time I feel it with Evie. After I say *San Francisco*: the silence. Her faraway silence. Like suddenly the person who'd been sitting next to me just up and disappeared. I remember turning my head to see if she was still there.

"You'll never come back," she says.

I knew I'd be back. San Francisco. I was scared stupid.

"You never know," I say.

I come back. With hair over my ears and a mustache. A peace symbol around my neck. There's a big hullabaloo fraternity meeting. My acid trips and marijuana parties are a bad influence. *Hippy fag* is stuck onto my door every morning. *Commie queer. Phi Sigma Delta Love It Or Leave It.* I move out, find my own house to rent.

I've never taken acid. Smoked dope twice.

Idaho.

The fraternity formal we go to, Winter Carnival, our last attempt at status quo, Evie so bold as to wear a shiny silver blue bellbottom pants suit, her hair dyed pink, cut in an extreme angle across her face, huge silver earrings. Painted eyes you can see across the room. Me and my mustache, hair going down and down, in a vintage double breasted suit and a porkpie hat. Everybody else at the ball, some version of 1958.

Fucking scandalous, Evie and I. There are no limits.

A year later, Evie, in overall jeans without a bra, putting a torn bit of blotter acid onto her tongue. "All I want," Evie says, "is to take acid and sit in a blue room and listen to the Moody Blues."

Why she loves me. I don't know. She says it's Jimmy Webb.

I'm a sensitive man like the songwriter Jimmy Webb. That whole first year, the way she holds my hand, as if every moment is a perfect moment, and the moment is passing too fast.

Awkward Catholic-boy sex. *Working on mysteries without any clue*. Despite the fact that Lorca has long been murdered, I have my youth. And my youth has a cock. It's a faraway squirm of petulant flesh. Poetry bound inside a medieval contraption.

One day I stand in the shower, my cock in my hand, and hold it, look at my cock. Really look. I can't run away any longer. Something is definitely wrong down there. It's the first time I can admit there is a wound. I go to a psychiatrist and tell him I think I'm homosexual. He is Mormon and tells me I can't be. Homosexuals have their sex organs in their mouths.

Idaho. Not only is it the Middle Ages. It's Idaho.

There is a day in the kitchen in my rented house – a railroad they call this kind of house – a string of one rooms connected to one another, four rooms long. Each room an exterior door. That kind of siding that looks like fake brick. Gray. Evie and I have painted the kitchen yellow. On the kitchen exterior door, Evie's bought white curtains. The kitchen table is pushed up against the door. It's a glass topped table and there's a huge bouquet of bursting orange gladiolas in a mason jar from across the street in the cemetery. The sun that morning through the curtains. It's a Sunday and Evie and I have made pancakes and eggs. Our friends John and Maggie are over. The sunlight, the steaming food on our plates, four friends around a table, Peter, Paul and Mary on the stereo, *Late Again*. Percolator coffee and Marlboros. We're laughing because the day before our landlord had come over and was so shocked and obviously in awe of this new kind of young people, men and women living together so open and so casually, that he forgot to turn off the water supply before he changed the faucet. Water blew out a geyser. Pandemonium.

Laughing there, a part of me opens up and is aware. I am in a yellow kitchen with Evie and my friends and there's good food and we're laughing. And especially: I am wearing a yellow

T-shirt and blue-lensed John Lennon glasses that Evie's bought me. For no reason, she's just bought me these gifts. Things I love that she knew I'd love and she bought them for me. Under the table, Evie's knee is pressed against mine. She's doing her impersonation of her French teacher, *Monsieur Faggot*. In that moment, Evelyn Firth looks like everything I'd ever been waiting for.

1969, I'm 4-F. Flat-footed.

Evie's parents, my parents step in. Evie and I can't find a reason not to marry so we agree. After all, it's just a piece of paper. Halloween, at the university's Catholic Church, Evie wears a red wedding dress. Outside the church, just before, my mother attacks my mass of curly hair. The wedding starts late because I won't sit still. Our honeymoon is going to the movies. *The Invasion of the Body Snatchers*.

The beige round plastic dial Evie daily turns: the pill. Youth, marijuana, a couple of beers can make the dead rise. Lorca, I find, is Persephone, and twice maybe three times a week, I can will it to be spring. Ah spring! Evie! This lovely woman, her cunt, our moments of delight. A year maybe of decent sex. Then Evie, a full-on feminist, gives me the real deal. The details. I learn to give good head like Edith. You know, Edith Head?

In our second year, lying on the bed, my hand in Evie's hand as she pulls our hands across her naked belly. "Do you feel that?" Evie says. "That electricity, the spark between us?"

Another year. The old stucco house we bought. The inheritance: her grandmother's furniture. Her grandmother's fur coat. The paring knife that grandmother used to cut her oranges in the morning. "Look!" Evie says, "how the acid has eaten away at the blade."

The night I drive out of the service station in our old purple '53 Desoto. I'm talking on and on about Don Juan, about Carlos Castaneda. About *A Separate Reality*, Summerhill, The Primal Scream, R.D. Laing. The years with my mother, my sister, my scary father, the dictatorship, my chamber of horrors, the wound,

I'm only beginning to comprehend. As yet, no idea that Lorca even existed, let alone his murder.

"They're all just books," Evie says. "I can't really see what you get so excited about."

I create my own reality. I attract what I radiate. Believe that it hath been given and it shall be given unto you. Christ, all the New Age crap. I eat it up, make it mine so I can believe I have a say in this: who I am. It's only a glimmer. How fucked up I am. The task ahead is clear: to heal. But heal what. And how.

Seven years married. The separate bedroom where I keep my clothes. Her clothes are on the bed piled up so high you can't see the bed. The blinds always closed. Evie with the night-light on during the day reading a book, any book really, the TV pulled in there, in the bedroom, in where I sleep with her in that bed covered with her clothes, the smell of the room a burnt-out TV tube. It's my fault. Her unhappiness. If I were a real man. So I make her into a queen. Try and serve her better. My cock is not enough. Even with Edith, it's not enough. I am not enough. Nothing works. The day I get mad and throw the iron skillet and the iron skillet breaks. Tell her to wake the fuck up. She gets a job. Waiting lunch tables at an exclusive men's business club. She hates me for it.

I make an appointment with a therapist for Evie and me. Evie refuses to go. I make her go. I take her by the arm, walk with her out of the house. Force her into the car. I almost drag her into the therapist's office. During the session, Evie doesn't say a word. I try and talk but can't. All I can do is cry.

That last day, when the divorce is final and the house is sold and we've signed the papers and we've split the money, in the parking lot, when I get in the pickup I'll drive across America in, just before I close the door, I panic, stick my head out the window. I scream: "Evelyn! Evelyn! Evelyn!"

Her voice. The hope in her voice. I can hear the hope.

"What?" she says. "What?"

"Take care!" I yell. "Take care of yourself!"

The way I cry that day is the way I cry across the United States. Even still, now after thirty years, I cry.

A couple old songs: Judy Collins's "Who Knows Where the Time Goes." Leonard Cohen's "Famous Blue Raincoat." The line in that song: *And thanks for the trouble you took from her eyes / I thought was there for good / So I didn't try.*

Evie. Evelyn Marie Firth.

A woman I have loved.

And Olga sees it.

BETTE. LOVELY LOVELY Bette. Evie's best friend, the woman I have an affair with. Bette Ann Podegushka. She'd hung around with Evie and me for years, Bette, what a pal. All those nights sitting stoned with her and Evie watching *Saturday Night Live.* All the men Bette went through, the women. Really, Bette Podegushka was a walking soap opera series. It was her Marilyn Monroe ass and blue eyes. Hair that was sometimes red, or dark brown, jet black. Cut so short she looked like she'd had brain surgery. Ironed, shingled, permed, or naturally curly. Another day, another Bette. Always her own creation. She was too skinny or overweight, a gum-snapping Levi Lesbian, a femme fatale, June Allyson, Donna Reed, the girl next door you could always talk to. How I envied her fashion, her incarnations, her bravery, her life. When I grew up I wanted to be a free woman like Bette Podegushka. So many late late Saturday nights, Evie usually always long ago asleep, sitting across from Bette at the kitchen table, drinking and drinking and smoking and smoking.

One night, an empty bottle of tequila on the table along with a big bunch of crazy-assed fresh flowers and herbs from my garden I've jammed into a gallon bucket, cigarettes and marijuana, all the ashtrays overflowing cigarette butts, Bette tells me just about everything. I tell her, too, everything. And by telling everything, I learn something new. Lorca. I tell her how they'd murdered Lorca.

Who knows how it happens. The moment when friendship

is something more. The first thing, of course: I tell Bette I am leaving Evie.

Then there is that afternoon. I haven't moved out yet. I'm still living in my married home. Evie is out being a waitress, and Bette has just dropped in for coffee. Nothing unusual. We're sitting at the kitchen table. Like so many times before. Percolator coffee. Bette is just entering her Marilyn Monroe period. It's as if Bette's famous voluptuous ass has overwhelmed her and she's bleached her hair blonde and somehow the rest of her is just miraculously turning into Marilyn.

Bette Podegushka as Marilyn Monroe, the woman I fall in love with.

There's only one cigarette left, a Marlboro from a hard box, and we're sharing it. One of those first clear sunny Idaho days of spring. Warm outside, still cold in the house.

Bette wants to look behind the washer and dryer. I think it's strange but I go ahead and pull the washer and the dryer away from the wall. Bette sits down in the corner, I sit down next to her, together in the corner of the laundry room looking in behind the washer and dryer. The cobwebs and the dust balls, the hoses and the tubes and the pennies and nickels and dimes, the electric wires. Bette misses New York City and behind the washer and dryer to her it looks like New York City. And she starts yelling, *Neelie O'Hara! Neelie O'Hara!* like Patty Duke in *Valley of the Dolls*. I'm laughing is why I kiss her.

But we don't fuck. Not until weeks later when Evie announces that if I move out I can't expect her to act like a married woman.

I move out. Have a whole day to myself. Take a ride on a city bus. Eat a chocolate ice cream cone. Sit on a park bench under a budding Catalpa tree. God the way my heart feels free. Ever since that day, I've been trying to get that feeling back. That park bench feeling. Bette comes over the next day. Just that she knows about Dead Lorca, the careful way she touches me, my cock gets full and hard. And she *loves* how well I know Edith.

We fuck so hard we fall off the bed. We laugh so hard that we've fallen off the bed. I've never felt so safe.

Still though, I wish I'd had more time. Alone. It would have been better for me and Bette if I'd have had more time alone.

ALL THIS ENDS, or begins, with Bette and me in New Hampshire – long story – in winter, real cold, real drafty in a second story apartment decorated only with Bette's brass-bound steamer trunks and a futon with a faux leopardskin bedspread and shiny red sheets. My first novel that no one will ever read finished and a frozen chicken in the freezer.

The night there's a disco contest in a town, Rutland maybe, twenty-five miles away. First prize fifty dollars. Between Bette and me, we only have the money for enough gas to get there. But not to get back. We decide fuck it. We go to Rutland and win the contest.

The job I get waiting tables at The Mercedes Inn in Middlebury, Vermont, because the owners have seen Bette and me win first prize in the disco contest, because I am a writer, because at thirty-two, my beautiful off-the-rack-42-long body is expertly fitted into a classic gray tweed two-button suit, starched, pressed collar, and vintage Thirties tie. Bette Podegushka is not the only one who can have new incarnations.

The owners of the Mercedes Inn, Robert and Paul and Bernadette, are gay, or mostly gay. Bernadette is still married, but Bette and I can tell. Inside her there's a *Lesbienne Vraiment* clawing her way out. And then the owners, when they actually all meet Bette – her beautiful big ass, her blonde curls, her red lips, the unbelievable way that Bette Podegushka channels Marilyn Monroe channeling Judy Holliday is just too irresistible. Jesus, the way Bette could make people laugh!

Bette and I love gay. Before we move to New England, Bette and I spend two weeks in New York with her best friends, Ronald and Martin, gay men, in a tiny Greenwich Village apartment. The discos we go to. The drugs we take. Flamingo and 12 West

and The Loft and the Paradise Garage and Studio 54. MDA and
PCP and Black Beauties and Tuilinols and Quaaludes and marijuana and cocaine, each our own bottles of Ethyl Chloride, all
ingested in Ronald's expertly orchestrated order to manumit us
through the perfect disco night. Me and two thousand half-naked
gay men and Bette at The White Party.

The writing is on the wall. It's so obvious now how things
are going. How I am going. But as it's happening I am oblivious.
The drugs, yes, but mostly I'm hanging on for dear life. To Bette
Podegushka. At Flamingo, at 54, men in the bleachers, only
steps away, in front of God and everybody, their legs spread,
opened their assholes wide for other men to jam their cocks in.
While Bette and I, on the dance floor, keep on dancing.

The Dead Lorca in me no match for that.

New England isn't as crazy. Robert and Paul, the owners of
the Mercedes Inn, know of a furnished house right next to
theirs on Oak Lake. Bette and I move in and start our summer by
the lake. A summer house, inside the wood studs and wood
walls. Wood everywhere. The floor, the ceilings, the walls. When
you walk how your step makes the whole house sound. We even
have a little boat. Our breakfasts are the best, real coffee, not
percolator coffee, and yogurt and bananas and granola outside
on the picnic table. Somehow we always end up fucking on the
picnic table.

The picnic table, in the morning where I sit and write my
daily aspirations in my little notebook.

*I am loved. I am safe. Life is abundant and manifests itself
everywhere.*

The tiny green leatherbound book with gold edging Bette
buys at a rummage sale, *The Book of Oracular Symbols*, and
sets face up on the bookcase next to the stairs. How we always
check that book to see how it is how we're doing.

Bette and I work weekend evenings at the Inn. Me, a waiter.
Bette cocktailing. At ten o'clock Friday and Saturday nights,
Paul moves the tables off of Dining Room C and the Victorian

painting comes down and behind it's a disco booth and the ceiling rolls down into the wall and a disco ball descends and the disco lights flash and Donna Summer is singing "Bad Girls." It's me and Bette's job to start the dancing. So many times, I'd just be finishing up serving dessert to my tables and Paul, the beautiful blonde one who used to be the model for Marlboro Man commercials, would be pulling at my shirt tails, unbuttoning my shirt buttons. I'd go from a waiter serving coffee to a bare-chested disco dancer, a hot man dancing with a beautiful blonde woman in nothing flat, just like in the movies. I can still smell Bette and me, our bodies, after a night of waiting tables just after that first dance.

Really, the applause. There's a whole town in Vermont that will only remember, me, Ben Grunewald, as this half-naked dancer, their very own Fred Astaire, dancing with their very own Ginger Rogers. My Bette, beautiful Bette. Betty Ann Podegushka. We carry the dreams of that town through every move me make.

That's the summer, too, that Bette takes on a new role that will change everything. Community Theater. Playing The Girl in *The Seven Year Itch*. I swear, Bette Podegushka could manifest anything. The trouble is the rehearsals. I mean Bette doesn't have any problems taking on the character of The Girl or Marilyn even. The problem is that she takes the pickup and leaves me alone in the house by the lake. Our house next to Robert and Paul's, next to Paul that is. The beautiful model. The first night Paul kissed me, nothing's ever felt so right. But Lorca is dead. And I'm not about to go there.

But Bette catches us going there, Paul and me and strawberry daiquiris and once again amazingly Dead Lorca transforms into Persephone. Me, Ben Grunewald, with a man's cock in my mouth–the Marlboro Man's. In me and Bette's bed, one night, a Thursday, when she comes home too early.

The next evening, opening night of *The Seven Year Itch*, Bette–it's been a long rough night and worse morning–that afternoon isn't that great either–on stage she's doing great. In the second act, though, Bette in the middle of a long piece of dialogue, suddenly forgets everything, just stands there center stage and forgets everything and stares at the audience. Minutes go by. The other actor does what he can to help Bette out. But it's like she's left the earth altogether. Finally, looking straight out at the audience, in a clear crisp voice, Bette Podegushka says, "My mother never loved any of her children."

That night, that last night in our house by the lake, sunset, the time when Bette and I usually sat on the rockers on the back porch and rocked and looked out at the sunset on the lake and called each other ma and pa, I'm alone and the show is over. Bette's gone to behind the washer and the dryer, packed her brass-bound steamer trunks, her shiny red sheets, her leopard-skin bedspread, and has left for New York City, left for good. *The Book of Oracular Symbols* on the wood bookshelf next to the wooden stairs, that evening, when I open it: *The Symbol: A Delicate Bottle of Perfume Lies Broken, Releasing its Fragrance.*

Bette. Betty Ann Podegushka.

A woman I have loved.

And Olga sees it.

SEVILLE. SALT-RIMMED, THE slice of fresh lime drips down onto the waiter's hand. The hand reaches the frosty *margareeta* in the up glass across the table, over the fire in the red votive candle, past our eyes as if an apparition. The cocktail glass lands on the white tablecloth in front of Olga. Then it's Hank's glass, then mine. Our drinks on the table, we all rub the white tablecloth as if we have just landed, too. Each of us touch our glasses at the stem, raise our glasses, and toast.

"And there's even more women in there," Olga says.

"*A todas las mujeres!*"

"And here I thought," Hank says, "you were just a cock-sucking sodomite."

"Women," Olga says. "It makes you so much more interesting."

"That's Gruney for you," Hank says, "always a surprise."

Seville. A night on the town. Our booth in the back, in our half-circle of plush red leather, darkness and points of light hanging in the air around us. I'm way too drunk to know what's happened. Too drunk to remember. My journey into the history of my women. How much Olga saw, how much was only me, if I spoke any of it, or all, out loud. I do remember how close I feel to Olga. The fear of her beauty has disappeared, and we are friends, a friend meeting a new friend, and we are drinking and we are laughing. Hank's sweet lips, Olga's full red lips, my lips, puckered onto the rim of our salted glasses, taking the first sip. Sweet and salt and tequila and citrus. The shine. The all-important shine. Our youth.

"You know," Olga says, "we are breaking the Marilyn Monroe Law."

Hank keeps sipping. I keep sipping. Both of us, our eyes on Olga.

"Actually with Marilyn," Olga says, "it was martinis, not margareetas."

"They're like breasts," Olga says. "One's not enough and three's too many."

Hank and I then, our eyes go to Olga's breasts, her nipples just barely through the pockets of her red see-through blouse, then up to up above Olga. Just above her on the wall, the kitsch painting of the peasant woman. The woman's hair is long and black, tied with a red bandana, big gold earrings, enormous breasts, balancing a jar of wine on her shoulder.

Three's too many, Hank and I start laughing. The scooped elastic collar of the peasant woman's blouse is pulled way down off her shoulders. *Lots* of cleavage. The only thing holding the blouse up, her nipples. Erect nipples. *Diamond nips,* Hank calls them. And at any second, those suckers are going to sproing right out of the blouse.

That starts it. And that's how Hank and Olga and I get thrown out of Seville. First, it's Hank opening up his shirt, pulling his shirt down over his shoulders to just above his nipples. Then it's me. Then Hank and I trying to get cleavage. Olga turns around, checks out the painting above her on the wall. Three's too many, Olga isn't about to be outdone. She undoes the buttons of her red blouse, pulls her blouse down over her shoulders, to just above her nipples. Lots of cleavage. She doesn't have to try.

When the bouncer arrives at the table, Hank's big burst from down deep coming out fast shakes Hank around like I've never seen. How Hank laughing like that makes my laughter go global. Olga too. We try to stop laughing. We really do. But three's too many.

Never do get to the *Mariscada de Salsa Verde*.

Verde
Que te quiero verde
Verde Viento
Verde Ramas.

LORCA

6.

Pennsylvania ghosts

THAT SUMMER MY FRIEND ESTHER WENT TO LAS VEGAS for a week and asked me to stay in her house. On the train: New York to Philly, change trains in Philly, the last stop on the train to Paoli, then a ten dollar cab drive: Esther's house. One of those huge turreted turn of the century three-story mausoleums. Solid wood. Eaves and gables and lead glass windows and a wide wrap-around porch like something out of Hawthorne.

I was to Esther as Hank was to me; that is, she remembers the first time she saw me. In Jeske's class one night. I was wearing my brown tweed vintage suit. I looked like someone from the Great Depression, she said. Not so much because of the suit but because of what I looked like in it: on my last legs, wearing my best clothes.

A woman of a certain age, Esther. Maybe fifty-five. Long, white curly hair she tied up in a knot. Blue eyes that looked as if they were always crying. In class, I sat in the seat up front right next to her – across the room from Maroni. When she read in class, how her voice trembled helped me to be brave. Esther. One of those friends who were the best part of me. I don't know how I'd have made it without her. Any weekend I wanted, I could come stay with her and Roy, her husband, in the cozy, sloped-ceiling garret with matching beds and a bay window that looked south over the cherry orchard.

A dream come true. In the country, out of the city, and

paid eighteen dollars an hour in 1988 to take care of her yard. That kind of friend.

I was getting to know this guy Danny at work and I asked him to join me for the weekend. But something important had come up. I asked Esther if it was okay that Hank and Olga joined me over the weekend.

"The *Maroni*?" she said.

"Maroni," I said.

"*Jeske's* Maroni?"

"And his girlfriend."

"What happened to Danny?" she said.

"Something important," I said.

"What's so important?" Esther said.

"The Club Baths," I said.

"There's a bedroom in the basement," Esther said. "It's real cool down there this time of year."

"The one with the big-ass brass bed?" I said.

"King-sized," she said. "Only kind of bed for the Maroni."

WHAT A WEEKEND. Hank and Olga arrive Friday noon. I drive Roy's old, green Dodge Dart to pick them up. On a June afternoon, Hank and Olga and me, the weekend ahead of us, seems like the whole world is ours, driving with the windows down, on the windy, one lane road, every now and then a wagon load of harvested hay, an Amish man in a straw hat at the reins of a team of horses. Big white barns with hexes on them, the smell of manure and Holsteins.

Olga's brought all kinds of goodies for the weekend. Bagels, croissants, paté, Brie, a couple of other stinky cheeses, four good bottles of wine, a bottle of Hennessy, fresh coffee beans, gourmet corn chips, and her homemade salsa. And my favorite. Kosher hot dogs.

I put away the groceries and Hank and Olga settle in. Takes them about an hour. Fucking, I guessed, but I'm way past being jealous. In fact, I remember looking out the kitchen window that day onto the big weeping willow in the yard and thinking I'd probably never be jealous of Hank – who he was, what he created, or whoever wanted to fuck him. Whoever it was who would love him.

Twelve years later, Ruth Dearden, *got to go pal*, no fucking idea.

I'm on my last cup of coffee. Way over-buzzed. Olga comes up the stairs, freshly showered, her hair still wet. Long, black, wet curls. She's wearing a white summer dress, no slip. A wide-brimmed straw hat in her hand. Her bracelets, her rings, her choker. All her gold. The sound of gold against gold. The dress when she sits, a sound like paper. Olga lays her hat on the table.

A big sigh. "Oh my God," Olga says. "A walk in the country."

"There's a lake not far from here," I say. "When Hank comes down I'll give you the directions."

"I am walking alone," Olga says.

I set the coffee cup down exactly in the ring the cup had made on the placemat. Look up slow at Olga. She's smiling.

"Is it not possible," she says, "that a woman go for a walk by herself these days?"

Hank bangs up the stairs just then in his flip-flops and cutoff khakis and a wifebeater. The skin on that guy, all that olive. Wet hair dripping down his back. Wet drops on his white T-shirt. Maybe that is the moment, I think it is, just as Hank grabs a chocolate croissant out of the pink cardboard box, sticks it in his mouth, then opens the refrigerator. Showered and shaved and freshly fucked, the moment of Hank's life when his beauty has reached perfection.

"Be careful not to go too far," Hank says. "What's for lunch?"

"It's Amish country," Olga says. "These are pastoral people. They are gentle."

"Kosher dogs?" I say.

"Great!" Hank says.

"You should stay close, though," I say. "You never know."

"And you better take off some of that gold," Hank says.

AT ONE-THIRTY, SUN-SCREENED and bonneted, Olga is out the door. She looks like something out of a Matisse painting.

"She looks like something out of a Matisse painting," I say.

"She's worked hard on that look," Hank says. "Spent a fortune."

"At least she left her gold home," I say.

In Hank's hand, Olga's gold bracelets, her three gold rings, her gold choker with the little cross.

"Let's take it to town," Hank says, "trade it in for a trip to Paris."

HANK AND ME, a couple of kids trying to act grown-up. We make kosher dogs and sauerkraut with Grey Poupon mustard. A big pitcher of pink lemonade. We pour the lemonade into tall glasses over crushed ice, go out onto the porch, sit in the wicker rockers, put our bare feet up into the sun on the railing, brush away summer flies, rock the rocker arms against the porch wood, wolf down our dogs, sip lemonade, crunch ice cubes with our teeth, and talk about what we never can stop talking about. Writing and being alive. Both our first books are coming out the following March. Fierce beauty, hidden treasure, ancient secrets, old legends, adolescent boys and sex, in whispers, how we speak of them.

Our books. Hank will spend the weekend composing the dedication of his book to his father. I have rewrites on the last ten pages. Finally, finally, grown-up men, real published authors. The American Book Award, the Pulitzer, One Fifth Avenue, just around the corner.

About four o'clock. Hank's in the basement on the king-sized brass bed taking a nap. The steaks are marinating and I'm cutting up scallions for the potato salad. I look out the window. In Olga's arms is a big bunch of big red flowers, big yellow sunflowers, and lacy purple ones. Something about how she's walking. The brim of her straw bonnet bent back. Definitely not

on a casual stroll through the countryside. By the time she gets
in the kitchen, she's really crying.

"I've never been so insulted!"

Olga throws the flowers down on the table, then her bonnet.

"Oh what a horrible man!"

Hank is up the stairs in no time. He's still asleep, just in
his khaki shorts, that patch of hair in the middle of his chest.
He's working hard trying to make himself be present.

"What the fuck?" Hank says "What man? What happened?
Are you all right?"

Olga is throwing herself around. Beating on the wall,
screaming and yelling. Cussing a blue streak in Spanish. *Chingada
tu puta madre. Cabrón. Caga duro.* Her white dress not so white,
heavy with sun and sweat.

It takes Hank and me a while but finally we get her settled
down enough to sit at the table. I pour her a glass of pink
lemonade.

"What man?" Hank says. "Olga, what man?"

It takes Olga two pink lemonades to speak.

"Some awful man," she says.

"Where is he?" Hank says.

"Did he hurt you?" I say.

"What did he do?"

"What awful man?"

"Over there," she says. "In that house."

Olga points out the kitchen window. Beyond the weeping
willow, one of those oversized particleboard Home Depot-
windowed McMansion horrors. Only an evil man could live in a
house like that.

"Fucker," I say.

"I was just walking through the field picking wildflowers,"
Olga says, "and he appeared in his doorway and started making
demands of me."

"Demands?" Hank says.

"What demands?" I say.

"*Just what the fuck did I think I was doing?*" Olga says.

"What did you say?" Hank says.

"I told him," Olga says, "that I was simply on an afternoon stroll, picking wildflowers. Then he started screaming at me and calling me names."

"Names?" Hank says. "What'd he say? What kind of names?"

"*You dumb bitch*," Olga says.

"Where is this guy?" Hank says.

"*This is private property,* he screamed at me, *you dumb bitch*," Olga says. "*Don't you see the* no trespassing *sign? These flowers aren't* wild *flowers. These flowers are the subject of my doctorate at* MIT," Olga says. "And then he threatened to call the police."

Olga's really crying again. Along about then is when we hear the siren.

HANK'S WALKING BACK and forth between the refrigerator and the door. He's beside himself with being pissed. At the whole deal, pissed. The screaming neighbor, Olga, the cop outside. Pissed at himself, too, I guess. Never really seen Hank like that. The way he's talking to Olga surprises me. Hank's always one for the underdog, a guy who's got your back. But he's telling Olga she should've known better, didn't she see the no trespassing sign, what the fuck what she thinking – and it's only making her cry more.

"Hank," I say, "take it easy on her, will you?"

The way Hank's black eyes look at me. Fuck. His eyes go cold and faraway, and all of a sudden he's a big slab of marble staring me down and my stomach is full of ashes.

When he speaks, Hank's lips move but his teeth stay clenched together.

"Stay out of this, Gruney," Hank says.

IT MAY NOT seem like much, but this is a big moment between Hank and me.

The moment, however, is one that I take part in, but Hank doesn't.

It was more the way Hank said it than what he said. *Stay out of this* stirred up all Little Ben's shit. My big baby torpor was immediate and overwhelming. Little Ben was outside the grown-up male world again and there were rules going on and I didn't understand the rules. The code of honor. This is my woman and you don't get between me and my woman. All the while in me Big Ben is yelling: *Code of honor my fucking ass. Who the fuck are you to speak to me as if I were a child?*

What's also always inherent in moments like these is the total impossibility to talk about it while it's happening. After all, there was a cop walking up the driveway.

Plus, men just don't do that. They don't stop in the middle of everything and say *you just really hurt my feelings*. Isn't that a perfect definition of a guy who's a pussy? Isn't that what boot camp is all about? What could be more male than a boot camp and a drill sergeant calling the soldier in training a *little bitch*? What does the soldier do – stop and tell the sergeant that his feelings have been hurt?

I'm such a homo I just don't get it. Big Ben either had to bitch-slap Little Ben and tell him to cowboy up and take it like a man or stop and listen to Little Ben and see what it is that he needs.

In either case, I've got a big mess on my hands.

For Hank, the moment goes by without even noticing it. He's just an Italian guy who's letting off steam and feels crowded and needs his space.

THE COP IS a kid, barely twenty-one. A big round baby face, round glasses. I'm the one who goes out and talks to him. Esther's my friend and I'm the one responsible for the house. The sun is hot and he's sweating way too much for a cop to sweat. He's threatening to write out a warrant for Olga's arrest. Trespassing and the theft of valuable property.

Cops scare me. Even twenty-one-year-old chubby boy cops. Plus Little Ben is still smarting from what Hank said. I'm feeling shaky and it takes me a while. To talk. When the Fascists killed Lorca, they slit his throat. Cut his balls and his cock off first, then cut out his voice box.

Speaking and fucking. How they're the same. Penetrating the void, then putting something of you in there.

The words. I finally find the words and get my mouth to talk, and if that can happen, if I can actually get to the point of speaking words, then more often than not I can be very charming.

Propinquity. The cop stays two arm's lengths away. I tell the cop the situation. That Olga is a foreign exchange student, and that this is her first time in the countryside of America, and she has mistakenly thought the flowers are God's flowers like in her country and are growing there for free.

Hank walks out the door then, into the sun. The picture of cool. His chest up, his shoulders down, Hank's big guy walk down the driveway. Hank reaches out his hand, the cop reaches out his, and they shake hands, that firm manly handshake I've tried so often but usually overdo.

"Hank Christian, officer," Hank says.

Hank, all that guy stuff down in spades, in no time at all he and the cop have made the connection. I can feel it. That man-to-man thing. But how they do it, I'll never know.

"Would you like to come in and meet Olga?" Hank says. "And have a cool drink with us?"

The cop is loaded down with all kinds of gear. Sounds like a pack mule when he walks. Inside, Olga greets us in the kitchen, those black eyes of hers that make Hank's look brown, the cornflower blue sleeveless smock thing she's changed into, her nipples under the cornflower blue smock thing, her beautiful braided long black hair, the matching cornflower blue scarf in her hair, the gold hoop earrings, the gold bracelets on her long, thin brown arms, Olga's beautiful smile.

In her very best English-as-a-second-language accent that

makes her sound like someone Spanish speaking English-English not American, Olga says:

"Good afternoon, officer. Would you like a glass of lemonade?"

THANK GOD OLGA'S got her passport with her. And her visa.

A warning. That's all we end up with. A written warning on a piece of large pink paper that I'm obliged to give to Esther.

When the cop finishes his lemonade, he gets up, walks to the door. He has to be packing twenty pounds. Just as he grabs for the doorknob, before he opens the door and walks out, he stops. Puts his hat on, cocks it to the side. Turns his baby face around to Hank and Olga and me. In his best grown-up tough guy voice, he says:

"If I were you," the cop says, "I'd go over to your neighbor's house and apologize to him."

THAT NIGHT, AFTER our first bottle of wine, the sun making a spectacle of itself going down, is when Hank and Olga finally start to relax. Their visit to the enraged neighbor has cleared things up. I never doubted it. Just being close to Hank, to Olga, their physical beauty unnerves the gods. Plus their offerings of a bottle of wine, and Olga-made gazpacho and a blackberry torte. Turns out the neighbor and Hank had the same baseball team they liked. Philadelphia's, I think. The Phillies, maybe. Or is that football?

Something's still caught in my throat, though, between my throat and my heart, that place that hurts where I smoke. But it ain't smoke. It's Hank. *You stay out of this.*

We're on the screened-in porch, the dark night around us getting deeper. White linen, the good silverware. Tall candles, short fat candles, votive candles, candles and candles. Their light, the way it always moves. So full and golden. Big, heavy white dinner plates. Each of us, a water glass and a wine glass, crystal that hums a wet finger along the rim. On the table, Olga's big bouquet of red, yellow, and purple stolen flowers she's arranged into a large, blue glass vase. Hank gives me a wink then starts in:

Olga Rivas, he says, *so pastoral, so Keats and Shelley, in her white dress like in a Matisse painting picking lovely wild flowers and effluvious herbs in a garden meadow.* Not in a mean-spirited way. But the way like only Hank can do. Olga cusses, *hijo tu puta madre*, throws a baguette at Hank, then an Anjou pear. But it isn't long and Olga is laughing. She's sitting on Hank's lap and Hank and Olga are laughing.

I don't laugh. That big baby torpor in me. I try and tell myself that Hank's a guy and guys are just this way, and I'm not a guy, never been one, never will be, and it's just too fucking much to comprehend. Just let it go.

But Hank is my friend. My friend that I love.

It ain't long and way too loud, Big Ben just comes shooting out my mouth:

"Fuck, Hank," I say. "You and I got to fucking talk."

Olga and Hank stop. They look over to me like who's he? Olga's one eyebrow goes up. Spanish, the way she uses her eyes. Latina Attitude. She doesn't like it I got the attention. And Hank. The look on his face. At first he acts like he doesn't know what I'm talking about. But Hank's eyes, the way they get fuck-you blacker, Hank knows.

Olga gets off Hank's lap, steps away. She keeps her hand on his shoulder as she speaks.

"I'll go open another bottle of wine," Olga says.

"*Mi amor?*" she says, "you want the California cabernet or the Bordeaux?"

HANK'S BODY IS on alert, but still he slouches down in his chair. One leg is up and his bare foot sets on the seat. I can't quite see his face behind Olga's big bouquet of red, yellow, and purple stolen flowers. The way he holds his head, Hank's face is in the shadows of the candlelight. I slide my chair over so we can see eye-to-eye. At the sternum, right in the middle of my chest, a lightbulb that you can see the filament flickering. All the Running Boy wants is for me to get my ass out of there. It's a showdown, all right, we both know it, and I wish it weren't, but how else do you do shit like this.

"That's how guys do it, ain't it?" I say.

Hank stays hunched over, his head down, looking at his hands. Rolls his thumbs. Zeus is pissed and something big is going to blow. God the Father's going to kick ass. Supreme, the power of men. Terrifying, really. Something so terrifying about this moment and so familiar, but I don't know why.

GOT TO GO *pal*. The words that hurt. Years later, Zeus, God the Father, Hank must have sat that way in his house in Florida holding onto the pages of that last letter I wrote him. God the Father ready to kick ass, the sadness, trying to see through it. I should have made the joke about the hair. Made him laugh. But I didn't.

THERE ARE PETALS, yellow ones from the sunflower, fallen onto the white, starched tablecloth. The petals rub off yellow onto my fingers. I take a deep breath.

"That's why male love is back-to-back," I say. "It's about maintaining your position. If you love another guy you show support."

"Gruney?" Hank says, "what the hell you talking about?"

"*Stay out of this, Gruney,*" I say. "You hurt my feelings."

Hank's leg comes down off the chair and is a big thud on the floor. His face big and bright with candlelight. His empty wine glass right there. His fingerprints on his wine glass.

"Come on, man," Hank says. "I was angry. Don't take it personal."

"It's weird, Hank," I say, "how far away you can go and how fast. Then when you do speak, there's threat behind it."

"That's your shit, Gruney," Hank says.

"But really it's all bluff," I say.

"And if it isn't?"

"You throw a thunderbolt," I say.

Hank's face goes back into the shadows. Yellow is all over the place. On my fingers, on the tablecloth. Yellow fingerprints on my wine glass. I always make a mess of things.

"Hank, you were stressed, I get it," I say. "It just freaked me out you were talking to Olga that way. Does that make me a traitor?"

"I was angry," Hank says.

"Angry's okay," I say, "but is that the only appropriate emotion? Can't men be afraid and confused too?"

Out there in the dark, in the kitchen, Olga is opening drawers. Between Hank and me, the table and all the candles. The fires reflecting on the glasses, the shiny silverware. On the edge of flickering light and dark, Hank's face disappears, reappears. The way he holds his body so still. The Enigma of Hank. The Warrior Ghost.

The old house is big and dark. It holds our silence. Only Olga in the kitchen. The pop of a bottle cork. Hank goes to speak but he has to stop first to clear his throat.

"I thought that's what I was doing," Hank says.

"What?"

"Showing you how confused and scared I was," Hank says.

"Hank," I say, "when a man talks to me like that all I can hear is my father."

"Fuck, Gruney," Hank says, "you're doing it again."

"I'm not saying you're an asshole," I say, "or that I'm superior. I do shit like that all the time. You're my friend, man, and this is what friends do."

"Like that night at Ursula Crohn's," Hank says.

"Friends don't let friends get away with shit like that," I say. "I know I'm way too sensitive, but I don't want any shit to come between us, so I got to tell you when shit comes up."

When Hank speaks again, Hank ain't locked up faraway and he's the Hank I know again.

"Fuck, Gruney, you're totally right on, man," Hank says.

Hank's big arm with his big hand on the end of it falls out of the shadows, down to the table, rattles the china. He pushes his open palm out to me.

"Gruney Babe," Hank says, "I'm sorry."

FRIENDS. FUCK. FRIENDS again. Eating and drinking with friends. I'm feeling especially high because things for a while there looked so bleak. Hank apologizes to Olga and Olga says she should have known better and we all get pretty high off each other. I barbecue the steaks and Olga makes the salad dressing and Hank opens more wine. In that big, beautiful, dark old house.

After three hours of us eating and drinking, the table is a mess of meat scraps, corn cobs, wilted tomatoes, and greens. Our wine glasses, our fingerprints on them. Olga's red cherry lipstick. The three bottles of wine finished off, mostly by Olga and me, then there's the snifter of brandy. We'll all work a whole month paying this dinner off.

Olga wants a cigarette. I do too. So what does she do but pull a tin of Nat Shermans out of her purse. I've quit and started smoking so many times in my life. This is one of those nights I start.

The mean neighbor appeased, inside the screened porch, no mosquitoes, under a roof, a warm summer night, the three of us in that big house, no lights on, just the many candles on our table. Filled with good food, fine wine, our big snifters of Hennessy, Olga and me smoking. Still ahead, our desserts and espressos. Still ahead, our novels coming out in March. The night deep dark inside the house too. Only the candlelight. Around the table, each of us a painting by Goya. Out of the darkness, a slow contour of light, and as if miraculous, out floats a face, an arm, a hand.

Friday night. Ahead of us still Saturday, still Saturday night, still Sunday morning. The train ride back to the city still far enough away.

"Let's dance!" Olga says.

Hank lets out a little moan. Straight guys don't dance. I

take a candle into the next room, the living room, to Esther's
stereo hi-fi – a huge piece of oak furniture that is a record player.
My God, the albums in there. Ella Fitzgerald, Duke Ellington,
Billie Holiday, Count Basie, Rosemary Clooney, Nat King Cole,
Johnny Mercer, and Frank Sinatra before he was a Republican.
It takes me a while, but I figure out how the stereo hi-fi works.
Pile a bunch of records on and crank up the volume.

The song is "Lullaby of Old Broadway." I dance the candle
across the dark room back onto the porch. The table is an altar
with all the candles. When I get to the table, I set down my
candle, do a twirl. Hank's rolling his eyes. I take Olga's hand and
her cherry red lips are smiling big and we start dancing. Olga's
still wearing the cornflower blue sleeveless smock thing. It goes
all the way to her ankles. She twirls, the skirt lifting up, flowing.
We dance our bodies close at first, a two-step or foxtrot or
whatever it is, nice rhythm, fast, and lots of spinning. The sound
of gold against gold. Then we break out into a jitterbug. Olga
lets out a big laugh, throws her head back, her gold-hooped
earrings, flashes of gold light. Her cornflower blue scarf comes
undone, falls down around her shoulders. Olga tosses it away,
doesn't miss a beat.

Something you got to know about me and dancing. Maybe
it's all gay men, I think it is, at least most of us. Nothing can
make me happier. Except writing. Dancing is why I think straight
guys like sports so much. They get to move. They get to move
remarkably. People watch you and you get to show off how you
can move.

Bette Podegushka and me dancing at the Mercedes Inn
were the best dancing days. Nothing's come close. Except for
nights like this one. Olga and me and Hank. Hank's dancing with
us too, even though he's sitting. He just doesn't know it. Put on
an LP, a big band and Ella Fitzgerald on a stereo hi-fi, and that's
all it takes. In all of my life, of all the places I'll go around
the world, Paris, Nairobi, Mombasa, Marrakech, London, Rome,
Madrid, Barcelona, always the best times, the most exotic, the

most romantic, tender, the most intimate, is after a great dinner
in a home of a friend, bottles of wine, maybe a splif, turn on the
stereo and dance around the table with your friends.

"I'm Beginning to See the Light." My body feels good
moving. Dead Lorca, dancing is the only way to shake it off. The
heavens above and the earth below connect. My body is what
connects them. In the connection, transformation. What it is to
be alive.

Then the record's over and Olga and I are trying to get
breath. Hank's giving us a standing ovation. Olga walks over, grabs
his arm, "Fascinating Rhythm"'s on now and Olga tries to pull
Hank out to dance but Hank doesn't budge. I'm dying to pee.

The bathroom with just the candle light is too weird.
Strange shadows and big porcelain ghosts. I blow out the candle,
and in the dark, sit to pee because I know if I stand I'll miss
the pot. We got to leave Esther's house the way we found it. The
smell of melting beeswax. Quiet, so quiet in the room except for
my piss in the bowl.

Something like a ghost passes through me. Or maybe it's
gas. A trembling in my chest that feels sick. When I lean my head
on my hand, my forehead is sweating. I stand up slow and do
what I always do when my body starts acting up – pretend it isn't
happening. At the sink, it's cold water on my face, handfuls of it.

In the kitchen, I relight the candle, keep pretending
through the kitchen, through the living room. I think maybe if I
turn on the lights, the awful feeling will go away. But if I turn on
the lights that means I'm sick and I'm not sick.

The cigarette. It must have been the cigarette that fucked
me up.

The LP touches down and it's Billie Holiday, "April In Paris."
I'm in the doorway when I stop. On the porch, the table that is
an altar. Hank's bare-chested and glowing like a Catholic saint.
Olga's gold, little fires all over on her body, everything about her
is pointed at Hank.

Some songs can stop you in your tracks. Especially that

song. I go to take another step but can't. Too much red wine, I figure, the Hennessy, or maybe I stood up too fast. In one hand, the candle and the flame. My other hand waves through the darkness, looking for something solid. My shoulder lands against the doorjamb. In my ears, a pulse of heartbeat. Dizzy. I tell myself that if I fall I should fall so Hank and Olga don't see. A long moment when my body isn't mine at all. In fact, my body goes away altogether. I'm like the flames. No substance, only spirit. Long deep breaths. My eyes, whose eyes are they, look down at my chest. My hand, some strange guy's fingers. For a moment I actually think my heart is breaking.

Billie Holiday isn't singing, she's talking to me. Her voice, the way each word is in her mouth. How she licks it, rolls it around, makes the word hers. It's as if she's so present loving how that sound is in her mouth she doesn't ever want to let it go. *This is how it is, let me tell you, how Paris is in April, all this hope. Fucking hope, man.* But the way Billie loves each moment, every word, makes her hold on just a little too long. Why she lives is in this moment. Giving voice, so precious, she doesn't want to let it go. But any moment now she's going to fuck up the rhythm. But she always lets go just in time and she never fucks up.

In my chest, the sick feeling leaves as quick as it came. My heart is pounding strong, I'm back in my body, breathing deep, and so happy to be back home. I'm in my moment the way Billie is, holding onto it for dear life. All those years I spent trying to get out of my body, when all the while I was trying to get in. I slide down the door jam and my butt hits the floor. In my hand, I'm holding up fire on a candlestick. In front of me, just beyond, out there in the world on the screened-in porch, into the candlelight, Hank swirls up Goya.

I can't believe my eyes. In that part of the house between the screened-in porch and the living room is a stage. The candles are the dramatic lighting. Hank is on the stage. Just in his long khaki shorts. Olga's scarf a turban tied around his head. He is dancing.

Hank's not showing off. Well maybe a little. He's a man alone dancing a room, his eyes closed. He's dreaming with Billie in Paris in April. That thing in his shoulders and his chest that always seems to hold him up, isn't holding him up. How smooth his body is in the light. His feet are solid on the shiny, slick oak, his second toes longer than his big toes, thin ankles, his surprisingly hairless calves.

Olga's at the table, her curly black hair hanging down to her shoulders. Her hands are over her mouth, her gold bracelets down around her elbows, eyes bright and wide as if she is witnessing one of the wonders of the world.

She is. Hank Christian is dancing.

Slow, more like a man swimming than a man dancing, how a body moves against the water. That way straight guys won't move their hips, Hank is moving. *My ass is beautiful,* the way his hips are moving. The candlelight on the muscles of his back, his chest, his arms, that full, bright face framed in cornflower. His closed eyes, his nipples, his hairy underarms, the hair in the middle of his chest, light, dark, light dark, light and dark. Hank's gone. He's with Billie in her moment that she lives in that she expresses that she craves. Hank's body, how he licks the music, rolls it around, makes it his.

What have you done to my heart?

The silence after the song, LP scratches. Crickets. Warm, the night is warm. I'm still sweating. My eyes can't bear to look into Hank's, so I quick look away. The candlelight on the oak floor, the shadows around the table, the candlelight against the screen. Delicate. We are so delicate.

WHEN I WAKE up, I'm in my bed in my room upstairs. I don't know what the fuck. I'm just in my shorts and on the bed there's a pool of sweat between my shoulderblades. Night sweats. I'll come to know night sweats well. Something is flashing. It's outside, the flashing. Really all I know about the flashing is that it's not in me.

The pain in my chest is gone. I feel fine, a little drunk maybe. Then flash, there's a big, bright light, silver that for an instant makes every object super real and alien at the same time. The shadow from that light slanted, a weird, cold darkness. Moments later, a crunch of thunder.

Out the bay window, the huge dome of Pennsylvania sky is a road map of heaven. Long cracks of heat and light point bright fingers into the deep, dark earth. Silent flashes, repetitions of flashes. Every so often, thunder you can feel in your bones. The earth is a baseball getting hit out of the park.

Another big, bright light, a night sky crack, and the earth is the color of the moon.

On the nightstand, I try the lamp, no electricity. That's when I hear it. A blast of Beethoven or something like him. Music real loud that all at once is all around me. Then just as fast the music winds down, a 45 record going to 33⅓. Then boom the loud music again.

I go to the bathroom off the bedroom I stay in, turn on the lightswitch. No light. Strange how electricity and running water we just expect. I can see myself in the mirror. Mostly my white shorts. I put my fingers on the white tile around the sink. Position my feet firm on the floor. I take a deep breath. This shit's been going on way too long.

When I check in, my heart is fine, my breath is coming in and out. When I move my fingers, my fingers move. My toes wiggle. My shoulders, my arms, my legs. Still got my old pope. My mouth tastes like old cigarette. And my head is sore right in the middle above my eyes where it always gets sore when I drink and smoke.

Reality. Still, something's fucked up, even if it's not me.

It's the world. The *world* is fucked up. Maybe it's the end of the world. Outside, the heavens are flashing hallelujah and there's weird Beethoven music blasting out then slowing down, blasting out, slowing down. The only thing I can figure is that Hank and Olga are downstairs fucking with the stereo hi-fi. The two of them doing some interpretive dance to the light show outside. I don't even think *there's no* electricity *so how can there be a stereo hi-fi.*

Outside, through the bay window, it's far more interesting than the mirror. If it's the end of the world, I may as well witness it. Who knows how long I stand there. Make myself look close. If these are my last moments I'm a lucky guy. My eyes, these two round things inside my head that see, are delighted at the magic light show the gods are putting on. Then there's a new sound. A tapping that gets louder.

"Ben? Ben, are you in there? Are you awake?"

I open my bedroom door and it's Hank and Olga huddling around the flame of a candle. Olga's hair is down and she's just in her white slip. Hank's white shorts are like mine. Stretched out in the crotch and legs.

"Is that you guys down there," I said, "making that weird music?"

"No!" Hank and Olga say at the same time. "We thought it was you!"

LOOK AT US, three children with a taper, so close together you'd think it's one person walking through the dark house. It's funny, so we're laughing, but it's not too funny. That music ain't funny. Shoulder to shoulder to shoulder down the stairs. Bare feet against oak floors. Olga's spicy perfume, what's left of Hank's Polo after-shave. Sweat. At the bottom of the stairs, the foyer in the dark is every kid's nightmare of a haunted house. Right then, there's a big silver flash of light and when the thunder hits, it shakes the chandelier. Olga screams, then I scream, then Hank farts. One of Hank's famous farts. Then we're laughing so hard we fucking can't navigate.

Delicate. We are so delicate. Look at us. Inching to the living room carrying a tiny fire. To the big weird Beethoven sound, loud and then slow and then loud and then slow, coming from the living room.

THE BEETHOVEN MUSIC is coming from the Beethoven record that is the record on top of the pile I loaded up the stereo hi-fi with. Except I don't remember putting a Beethoven record on there. And Hank didn't put it on either, or Olga. But it's there, the needle in the middle of the record, Beethoven's *Fifth*. Hank reaches down and pulls the phonograph needle off the record. Outside, the storm keeps going. Blasts of light and thunder. But at least the music has stopped.

The only rational explanation Hank and I can come up with is that the electricity in the air somehow was fucking with the stereo hi-fi.

Olga has another opinion.

"Music is the structure of the invisible," she says.

When we go back to bed, we go together, all of us into the same room, my room upstairs. When we get to the room, the bathroom light is on. Ten minutes later, the lightning storm has passed.

In the bathroom, I brush my teeth while Hank takes a leak. He's got a set of kidneys on him. I shut off the light. When I walk into the bedroom, Hank's body, Olga's body are dark silhouettes pressed against the bay window.

"Look! Ben!" Olga says, "More mystery."

I press my palm against the glass. Once more, this weird lovely night shows its magic. Below us, on the ground, another light storm. Covering the lawn, beneath the cherry trees, and into the meadow. Fireflies. Millions of fireflies light up the earth. As far as we can see.

THERE'S ONE MORE thing about that night. Before the lightning storm, while I was passed out up in my bedroom, Hank and Olga fucked on Esther's Chesterfield couch, and Hank's splooge left a stain on the leather that wasn't ever going to come out. Esther wasn't too happy about the stain, but Esther is Esther and all she said was, "Well, at least it was the Maroni's."

LAST SEPTEMBER, ESTHER turned eighty. Roy is failing. She's sold her house and moved to Idaho. Sold that couch, too, at an open auction, along with most of the furniture. I'd give anything now to own that couch. To touch the stain Hank Christian left on a piece of red leather.

So many times, I've looked back on that night, the three of us in Pennsylvania in Esther's big old turreted, gabled house something out of Hawthorne. Lovely Olga like in a Matisse painting, in her white dress, a young beautiful maid picking flowers in a garden. That cop, when he saw Olga, didn't know what hit him. How I spoke up about my feelings and my friend Hank heard me. The candles that made the table an altar. Hank's dance, what it is to be alive, how he moved his hips like straight guys don't. Haji Baba the cornflower turban on his head. Billie Holiday, "April in Paris," her voice, all that is broken and doesn't fit giving voice to hope.

So many times, I've wondered at the lightning that night. Really, I've never experienced a storm like that since. So many times, usually a little stoned, I've told the story of the Beethoven record. It never fails, the way people laugh at that one. Then I have to tell the one about the fireflies.

Why I believe this, I don't know for sure. So many times I've thought it, was afraid to say it. Said it quiet but never out loud. Truth is, most of the time I've spent trying to forget it. But now, so many years later, I know in my heart it has to be true.

Olga said it. *Music is the structure of the invisible.*

The ghost that passed through me that night, passed through Olga too, and Hank. All of us. The magic of that night: how the invisible touched us. After that night, none of us were ever the same again.

The first time death brushed up against us and left its print.

Death, so theatrical when it first appears itself to youth.

For years it was a pool of sweat on the bed, between my shoulders at night.

Hell, these days death's a pair of old shoes sitting by the door.

Olga, her double mastectomy.

Me, the hangover the next morning that lasted a week, my seroconversion to AIDS.

Hank, the tumors that started on his cock, that went to behind his eye, then settled in his liver.

Delicate. We are so delicate. So easily we die.

7.

The Spike

THE SEXIEST THING MY EYES EVER SAW HAPPENED LATE
October in a Manhattan bar. The Spike is a leather bar, heavy
duty, and it was usually winter when I went there, during the holidays, always late at night, and I was always fucked up. Or it was
hot, that New York heat. In August, what air conditioning and
aftershave do to a man's sweat. Winter or summer, each time it
was the same. After the bouncer, I sucked my gut in, led with my
shoulder, and made my slow way through the jam of men to the
bar. It was a tough journey for my propinquity, but I was stoned,
and sometimes I'd imagine I was a stowaway on steerage in a
huge ocean liner, or third class traveling in a freight car in a Third
World country. Usually the bar was three people deep. That meant
more shouldering. When I finally made it to the counter of the
bar, when I finally got my beer, I turned around, kept my back to
the bar, didn't move from the bar for anybody, and watched.

This time at the Spike, though, is different. It's an afternoon,
and I'm meeting a friend from my old days at Boise State, Sam
Tyler. Sam's in town on some kind of sabbatical. Poetry. Sam
knows his way around New York, and especially his way around
the Spike. Sometimes when he came to New York, Sam didn't go
anywhere but the Spike. On the West Side Highway, somewhere
in the twenties. Infamous, this bar. In the window, its only adver-
tisement, a red neon spike just on the small side of a raised
forearm and fist.

Mid-afternoon, there isn't a bouncer. A couple of guys at

the bar, but the place is empty. Surprising, the way the bar looks. Like hell might look during the day. A big room, twenty-foot ceilings, dark gray-blue walls, long, sloping, oak floorboards, low waves through the room, salt on the floorboards. Sunlight through the chips in the windows spray-painted black. A line of whitewashed pillars rubbed to bare wood between a man's shoulder and his ass. The oval bar in the middle of the room, what at night the universe of cruising men circle, like a roller rink, or in the Forties the way a dance floor looked with couples going round and around. Like any ordinary closed-in bar where people seriously drink and smoke, the smell, except for the poppers, the lube, and the sex. Napalm. It's what I imagine napalm to smell like.

Sam's a big guy, big cock too, or so I'd heard. I don't know from where. Those kinds of things in the gay world just get around – if you're large or if you're small. It's just information, something your ears hear. First name: Sam. Surname: Tyler. Cock size: ten inches tumescent.

Thick black hair and a black graying beard. Tall, real tall, a big-chested guy. Big, deep voice and intelligent brown eyes. For me, Sam's brown eyes, *intelligent*, what makes him sexy. Not that we ever had sex. That night we tried but couldn't get past my Dead Lorca. Plus the size thing. The cock-obsessed gay world, size is something very important about you. And if what is important is wrong, when you're lying next to ten inches of hard cock, it's difficult not to launch into an obsessive Woody Allen.

Portnoy ain't got nothing to complain about.

Actually, Sam has no trouble with my cock, even with the fact it doesn't get hard. *Some of us are just shy,* he says.

Guys with big cocks always say things like that. Because they can. They're like the rich: they're different from us.

Hugging Sam that afternoon at the Spike was like hugging a big bear. We order beers, sit on two high stools by the cigarette machine close to the front door, watch the bar, go through all the small talk you have to go through at first.

Outside, on the other side of the red neon spike, I can see a white delivery van pull up across the avenue. It does a smart piece of Doris Day parking. A stocky guy, wearing a dark brown khaki uniform and boots, no cap, long brown curly hair, steps out of the van – one of those tall square things with no windows. The guy looks a lot like Hank. He's wearing a jacket with a company's logo on it. The guy looks up the avenue and down, takes his jacket off, throws it in his van and locks it. Nothing I can see is written on the van. Sam says something to me just then, I don't know what, in fact, the whole following conversation with Sam is lost on me. Moments later, the guy from the van walks into the Spike, makes a beeline to the bar and orders a beer. *Tom* on his shirt pocket. He slumps his body over onto the bar, stares into his beer. Thick legs and a big, strong ass. Every once in a while he looks up, takes a quick look around. The Spike is definitely new territory.

Not long after, another guy walks in. This guy's a big guy. Big as Sam. Crew cut. Carries himself like he's important. Takes his time and checks it all out as he walks. Clint Eastwood, make my day. Levi's and a brown leather belt. A blue work shirt with the sleeves rolled up. His cowboy boots, long strides, creaks in the oak floor. The smash in his short hair where he's worn a hard hat. Sam checks him out, too. Isn't long, neither of us are talking. All we can do is watch.

The big guy walks up to the bar right next to Tom but doesn't touch him. Tom stands up fast. The big guy's a head taller. The two of them look each other in the eyes. The kind of look where everything else goes away. Tom's doing his best not to fall over. The big guy has it all down. But you can tell. He's stepped into some deep shit. They're straight men, or men in the world living as straight. The big guy more than likely has done this before, but it's for sure this is Tom's first time. And something else that's clear. Both of them have been waiting a long time for this moment.

Each of them takes a step forward, and since there's only one step between them, when they meet it's a collision. Tom has his chin raised, his head back, and the big guy leans down. The way their lips meet. You can hear the kiss all the way across the room.

Count Vronsky and Anna Karenina at the train station. Tom's big hands press against his lover's head, the big guy's big arms around Tom's waist, Tom's tiptoes at times barely touching the floorboards. Faces and lips smash together, each one trying to crawl inside, they kiss and kiss as long as they can until they come up for air.

Romance such a strange emotion in a leather bar.

The big guy goes for his beer. They look around for a moment, but not for long. New York City, the city where nobody stares, and everybody is staring. Trying not to look like it. The big guy whispers something into Tom's ear. Tom looks down, sees the name on his shirt, unbuttons his shirt, takes it off, stuffs his shirt into his back pocket. Tom, down to his white T-shirt. We're all wondering what else he might take off.

Another kiss. Body to body, hungry lips eating it all up. My God, these guys are going to fuck. The kiss, the kiss, the kiss, the kiss, forever and ever the kiss. They pull away again, breath trying to come in and go out, their chests bellows of air, Tom's lips sliding up the big guy's face, Tom pulling himself all the way up to the big guy's ear.

They go on that way at least an hour. Sam is there and we're talking, but I am someplace else. Kiss and kiss and kiss then come up for air, those two. Lost lovers in the only place that will have them. Nowhere else to go. There's the back room where they can fuck, but I don't think they know that. Or if they do, their fucking is just for them.

When they leave they leave together, nobody seems to notice. Maybe Sam notices because of how much I've noticed. My heart feels so happy for them. One way or another they're going to solve their problem. Outside, across the avenue, on the other side of the red neon, Tom opens the back door of his white van. The big guy looks around then gets in first. Then Tom gets in. The way that van starts bouncing it's all I can do to stay sitting in my chair.

"THE WAY THAT van started bouncing," I say, "it was all I could do to sit in my chair."

It's Wednesday night, after teaching at the Y. Sometime around Thanksgiving. Hank and I are at *our table*, at *our restaurant*, eating cheeseburgers, fries, drinking Cokes. Hank has a mouthful of cheeseburger. When he stops chewing, Hank looks up at me, those black eyes of his straight into mine.

"Would you take me with you sometime?" Hank says.

"Where?" I say.

"The Spike."

It's my turn to spit cheeseburger across the table. I mean, I don't spit cheeseburger, but if I had a mouthful, I would've.

"Why would you want to go there?"

Hank is bringing his shoulders down, starting to pump up his chest.

"Because *you* go there," he says. "And everything you've said about it, sounds like a pretty interesting place."

"Hank," I say, "it's a heavy-duty leather bar – a *gay* leather bar."

"I'm quoting," Hank says. "*Napalm.* You said the bar smells like napalm. *Social conventions distilled down to a single purpose to fuck or get fucked.*

"But that's not the real reason you go there." Hank says, "I like why you go there and I'd like to go with you."

"Why do I go there?" I say.

"You're curious about human nature, especially men," Hank says. "When you go to the Spike, it's like getting in a satellite to orbit Pluto."

"I'd like to see Pluto too," Hank says. "And I'd be in good hands because I trust you."

44">

4">4

44"> segment 44

444">4

4444

CHRISTMAS HOLIDAYS. THAT night before Hank comes over, I feel I'm some kind of lascivious despot corrupting an innocent child. Hank Christian, an innocent child. Fuck, we're all so homophobic.

When I open my apartment door, I can't believe my eyes. Hank's dressed in clean jeans, a black belt, white tennis shoes, and a button-down, long-sleeved blue Oxford shirt tucked in his pants. A shiny green winter parka. His hair washed and shiny. Standing there in the hallway of my building, he looks like he was going out on a date. A heterosexual date.

"What?" Hank says.

"Nothing," I say.

"Don't I look enough like a gay?" Hank says.

"Come in and sit down," I say. "I'll get us a beer."

Hank unzips his parka, lifts his right arm up, smells his pit. Then his left arm.

"See! No pits. And it's hot in the subway," Hank says. "Mennen Stick. Always works good."

I step back, let Hank walk in, then close and lock the door. That place right there, one of the only two places in the apartment big enough for two to stand, for a moment we stand. Mint breath. Mennen stick. A quick touch of hands. Not the way guys usually touch, but this is Hank. His eyes, always takes me a while to look right into Hank's eyes.

That night, after my deep breath, when I look, Hank is scrubbed and shiny as a new silver dollar. Light coming out of him as if light was what he's made of.

I've cleared away the papers on my writing desk, pulled up my other chair, so we can sit. Hank takes off his shiny green winter parka. I get us two Buds out of the fridge, find the opener in the drawer, sit down next to Hank.

"You don't go to Pluto looking like Jupiter," I say.

Hank laughs up his chest, takes the beer.

"I ain't got no leather hats and chaps and shit," Hank says.

"Only got four shirts and two pair of Levi's, and I'm wearing one of each."

Maybe I'm jealous of all that light is why I feel I need to cover it up.

"You don't understand," I say.

"You want to *be* the drama," I say, "or *watch* the drama?"

"Gruney," Hank says, "for Christ's sake, I'm in *jeans and a blue shirt.*"

"You want to disappear, right?" I say. "Well, believe me, right now you look like."

"A straight guy," Hank says.

"Yeah," I say. "So let me give you some homosexual leather bar fashion tips."

"But the way you've talked about it," Hank says, "these guys don't care about fashion."

"I'm just saying there's a uniform," I say, "with not a lot of variables."

"Plus," I say, "you're beautiful."

"Come on, Gruney," Hank says.

"And we need to put a lid on it," I say, "Believe me, you walking into the Spike looking like a beautiful straight guy, every man in there is going to want a piece of you."

AT THE BACK end of my apartment, really only two steps from my writing desk, under my loft bed, just at the door to my bathroom, I have a little space only I ever go into. The only other place in my apartment where two can stand, but nobody ever makes it that far. On the wall by the bathroom door is a full length mirror, to the left there a bookcase and my stereo. On the other side, under the steps up to the loft bed, my closet and my chest of drawers. A space shaped like a horseshoe just long enough to lie down in, wide enough to turn around. How many nights I've danced in front of that mirror, the fluorescent light from the bathroom slanting down in, to Luther Vandross, Teddy Pendergrass, Barry White, Randy Crawford, The Reverend Al Green.

That night that Hank steps into my place where only I ever
go, when he stands in front of the mirror, what I've planned
on doing is getting Hank out of that blue ironed Oxford shirt and
into something less frat boy, more street.

But when Hank walks into that private space of mine,
there's something in my chest like I can't breathe. Propinquity.
Hank's just right there and he's taking off his blue shirt and it's
for sure I'm going to fall over. I take his blue shirt and hang it up
on a hanger. Then it's his sparkling white T-shirt you can see his
nipples through that's got to come off. So the T-shirt comes off.
And there I am standing in the tiny space holding onto Hank's
white T-shirt that smells like Mennen stick and Hank's subway
ride down from the Upper West Side. In order to get to my chest
of drawers I got to move and there's no way I can move and not
touch Hank's naked arm, or his naked back, or his naked chest,
or all of the above. So I do what I always do when I don't know
what to do. Drop what I'm doing and grab whatever is nearest.
Hank's white T-shirt is on the floor and what I have in my hands
is a Marvin Gaye album and I put it on the turntable. By then
I've maybe touched Hank's naked chest and back a hundred
times. I stand there trying to find breath, watching the turntable
arm lift up, watching the turntable arm move over onto the
record, watching the turntable arm hit the record. That crackle.

That quick, it's magic the way things happened with Hank.
"Got to Give It Up" starts playing. I'm rummaging through my
chest of drawers looking for God knows what. "Got to Give It Up"
is the best dance song ever. Sure enough, Hank starts dancing
with himself in the mirror. The same way I dance when I am alone.
In that same spot.

"So how'm I supposed to look?" Hank says.

Hank looks exactly the way he's supposed to look and that's
the problem.

"Incognito," I say.

"Latinate!" Hank says.

Hank goes to the fridge and gets more beers. He wants to

hear "Got to Give It Up" again. So I pick up the turntable arm –
that loud record crush through the speakers – set the turntable
arm back down, and it's "Got to Give It Up" again. Hank hands
me a beer, we touch glasses, do a toast, and before we know it,
we're fully involved. Hank and I are dancing and carrying on and
shit, *Vogue*-posing in the mirror way before Madonna knew
about it. Things go from bad to worse and instead of going to my
extra-large dark T-shirt drawer, I go to my disco trunk. In no
time at all Hank and I are deep into disco drag. I forget all about
dressing down and we're dressing up. In that tiny space, *No
more standing outside the wall / I done got myself together, baby, and
I'm having a ball.* Trying on outfits for the leather bar the way
two high school girls try on dresses for the prom. Really, I wonder
if I've ever laughed so hard.

At one point, Hank is wearing the black platform shoes with
green glitter on them I wore at Ursula Crohn's, a pair of white
silk boxer shorts with an embroidered snake coming out the fly,
a black fishnet wifebeater, and a blue sequined skullcap.

Me, I'm in a black leotard, a leopardskin T-shirt, and a
bowler hat.

Showing up like that at the Spike. Shit. We'd never get past
the bouncer.

WHEN HANK AND I finally get out of the apartment it's past midnight. Hank's wearing two or three old T-shirts of mine, black
and extra-large that hang down over his ass. Big sleeves that go
down past his elbows. A pair of my work boots – a size too big,
and my old green expandable baseball cap that comes down to
Hanks' eyes and covers up his shiny black curls. An old thermal
sweatshirt with a hood.

I wear the same thing, only different.

There we are, Hank and me, covered up, dressed down,
anonymous males, going to the place that is the extreme of male,
a homosexual leather bar, the Spike, and the around around

macho pose the top the bottom do-si-do big hard cock staredown sex dance of the underworld. What life is like on Pluto.

THERE'S A WAY you can be high. Back in those days it was two shots of tequila, a hit of San Simeon, and beers to nurse 'til you drop. At the Spike that night I'm high that way. Hank isn't far behind. Our backs lean against the bar, Hank's elbow against my elbow, our ballcaps pulled down. Hank and I are sipping Buds, Hank and I are watching. Behind us, the bar back with its bottles, glowing green, glowing blue, clear, amber, glowing Wild Turkey dark brown. From underneath the bar, Judy lights from down low so the bartenders can see. Hank and I, our backs are to the bar. In front of us, three men deep. Beyond, the bar is dark. Smoky dark. A foggy night, an ocean of men, dark waves. They have a sound, the waves, here and there bursts of pirate laughter, then no laughter. And underneath, always underneath, the deep voices of men, their low sex chant, the sound just before the hurricane hits. Disco music so loud Hank and I can't talk. We try at first but we have to yell.

"Chthonian!" I yell.

Hank cups his ear. "What?" he yells.

"Chthonic!" I yell again.

"What?"

"Latinate!" I yell.

"Sounds Greek to me!" Hank yells.

Hank, the way laughter moves up through him. The men standing around us at the bar all turn, inspect our intrusion, lots of attitude. So we quit laughing, quit talking, just lean against the bar. Every now and then we smile, but mostly we're overwhelmed, just taking in the whole huge Pluto Greek chthonic thing.

Hank's clearly out of his element, but as far as I can tell, he's doing fine. Looks like every other guy there, except for those who want to stand out. We've both taken off our thermal hoodies and tied them around our waists. There's a Bud in his fist, his ballcap is pulled down, he has that fuck-you, tough guy face.

Looks like a real regular. Plus, his arm is against mine, and if anything goes wrong, I'll know right off.

An hour goes by, maybe two, more beers, more smoke, more men crowd in. When Hank and I first got to our spot at the bar, besides Hank's elbow, my body could stand free without touching another body. I could see the bouncer at the door. There's too much smoke to see much now. On the other side of Hank, there's an especially tall guy facing the bar, but other than him, all I can see is Hank and the men in front of me. Beyond them, not three deep but five, the foggy night, Pluto, the swell of ocean, dark waves, the sound of the waves. Disco beat, you can feel it in the floorboards through your shoes, in your elbows from the bar. At times, when the men recognize a song, "We Are Family," "Love Is In The Air," "Bad Girls" – ten years we've been listening to these same fucking songs – the pirates whoop, they holler, shake their asses. Sometimes my feet can leave the floor.

Two more guys squeeze in, order beers, then stay. They're wearing only chaps, their bare asses hanging out. The one guy in front of Hank, his ass is smooth and hairless. The guy in front of me, a trail of dark brown hair up and out his ass crack. Only inches away. Hank raises an eyebrow, puckers his lips, points with his lips down at their asses, gives them a thumbs up. My buddy Hank.

The circling crowd is a long slow snake eating its tail. As the night goes on, the bar is jammed. Bodies press right up against us. The heat of bodies. No room to move. Those bare asses right there. Propinquity. You'd think I'd be freaked out, but that night with Hank, because I'm worried about *Hank* freaking out, I realize something. Why I go there. Drunk enough, high enough, I am jostled, pushed, poked, and shoved. Just a normal guy. Another guy in the crowd. There's no way I can't be touched.

Hank is keeping his hands high, but so far I get no sign from him he wants to go. Then there's an elbow poking me in the side. It takes me a while to realize it's Hank's. He's got something to say. The way we do it, the way we find to talk, Hank starts it off.

He turns his ballcap backwards, dives his head down, puts his lips right up to my ear. He enunciates every syllable and keeps it short. Disco Speak.

"So how do you get a cock up your ass?"

Surprise. Surprised because the way Hank is looking at me he really wants to know. But it's a question I can't answer in Disco Speak. So I turn my ballcap around, dive my head down, put my lips at Hank's ear, say the next best thing.

"Carefully," I say. "Or not."

Hank's not satisfied. His head dives down, moves in to my neck, puts his lips in close.

"Seriously."

Disco Speak in the middle of chaos. I turn to the bar, try to get a bartender to look at me. I have to wave my arms and yell. The place is so loud I can't hear that I'm yelling. Really I don't need another beer. But I need the time. Something to do while I decide how to answer Hank. What words to use. Just when is ass-fucking too much information. Plus I've never talked about getting fucked. To anyone. When shame is that close to you, when it's a part of you like breathing, you don't even know it's shame.

The three bartenders are pouring beer, popping bottle caps, pouring shots. They are gladiators in their bright arena, the crowd yelling for blood. On the mirror above the bar: *no sissy drinks – Coke, Sprite, tonic, club soda mixes only.*

The bartender who finally looks at me, looks at me because of the five dollar tip I've left him last time. He has the kind of face that needs to shave twice a day. Sweat dripping off him. Big silver loops in his nipples I'm afraid he'll catch on something. His eyes when they look into mine are surprisingly innocent.

"Two Buds! A shot of tequila!"

I give him a ten and a five, wave my hand so he knows to keep the change.

Hank downs his beer and I hand him another. I down the

tequila. My head is an airplane and Hank's shoulder is the runway. The way we're diving and bobbing, I'm thinking of cranes making love or maybe giraffes.

"Ever sodomized a woman?" I say.

The Judy lights from behind us light Hank's face up from the bottom. Like when you were kids and you put a flashlight under your chin. Just as Hank's about to dive in with some Disco Speak, in the crowd there's a thrust, men are pushed and then push back. For a moment I'm third class on a bus in India. Thank God for the tequila shot. In no time at all, the two chap guys got Hank and me pinned to the bar. My chap guy's got his ass pushed right into my crotch. Hank's guy's got him too. Hank's arms are in the air and his head is pushed back. Hank's face, for a moment, I think he's going to split. Then, as I'm watching him, Hank looks over at me. I catch him checking me out to see if I'm getting off with this guy's ass in my crotch.

That's when we turn, the both of us into the bar. Our backs to the chthonian hurricane, the marketplace, the waves. The extra tall guy next to Hank doesn't move. We dig ourselves in there like a World War and it's the trenches. Somewhere a high-pitched wail. Then suddenly, magic again. Hank Magic. And it's just Hank and me heads down, the wet hardwood counter of the bar, our hands on the bar around the long neck Buds, the ice scoop and the glass-clink of the bartenders somewhere around the tops of our heads. We're shoulder to shoulder to each other, and ass to ass with our chap buddies.

"So," Hank says, "sodomy."

"You like it?" I say.

"Hell yeah," Hank says. "You have to be rock hard to get in."

Hank lifts his bottle, takes a drink. I can feel the muscles in his arm move, we're that close.

"Secret's in the preparation," I say.

"K-Y," Hank says.

"And your mouth," I say.

Hank's beer bottle goes down hard. His arm, those muscles that were so close, now there's space between us.

"Seriously?" Hank says. "You put your mouth down there?"

"In there," I say. "My tongue."

I'm afraid a little for what Hank's face does next. A look my father gave me when he caught me in a dress.

"You eat *ass?!*" Hank says.

A grossed-out frat boy now, Hank's face. Shame is Deadly Nightshade blooming in my heart. But I'm determined. I move my body slow, back in again, just barely, my shoulder against his shoulder.

"He's got to be clean," I say. "Fleet clean. Sometimes, before I go down on his ass, I spit in whiskey or tequila or whatever I got."

Hank stands up from leaning in on the bar. It takes me a while, but I stand up too. Tall as I can get. Which is taller than Hank by a half a head, but the tall guy on the other side of Hank is still a head taller. We take up less space standing. Nature fears a void and the bodies move in. Hank's black eyes look inside my eyes, in deep.

"You little ass-eater!" Hank says.

Hank tips his bottle up, pours the beer down his throat.

Then: "Yeh, I've et it too," he says. "With a woman down there it all becomes just one big *place,* you know, asshole, cunt, clit. I just love eating pussy and sometimes I get so carried away, it ain't just pussy I'm eating, it's ass too, it's everything. It's the whole fucking world.

"It's all good," Hank says.

"I'm a good friend of Edith's too," I say. "Or used to be."

"Edith?" Hank says.

"It's a joke," I say. "Edith gives good."

"Huh?" Hank says.

"Head." I say, "You know Edith Head."

Hank obviously wasn't married to a feminist in the

seventies. We go back into our huddle, crouch down, elbows on the bar. Men all around us push.

"Olga said you were good at it," Hank says. "Eating pussy."

"And that's a little confounding," Hank says, "that Olga can know something like that."

"Psychic," I say.

"She's a witch," Hank says, "and you better not be eating her pussy."

Hank and me with the same woman. The way we laugh then has so much force, we push the bare-assed chap guys away. In fact, the whole fucking crowd has to step back. I'm stupid laughing so hard I start to cough. After a while, I don't even know what I'm laughing at. I'm just trying to find breath.

The good old days. When we didn't know. If you laugh like that the gods will hear.

Ruth Dearden.

Got to go pal.

For what no man doth believe / the gods can bring about.

Hank and I lean down, dive back in. Hank's burp is long and extra loud. The burp bounces against the bar, comes up smelling beer piss.

"Still though," Hank says. "Going from women to men. And then back again. I don't know how you do it."

"I touch them, but they don't touch me," I say. "No one touches me, so it doesn't matter what sex they are."

Just as I speak these words, pirate laughter, a big burst, way too loud. Hank doesn't hear a word I say.

"This one time for a prostate check," Hank says, "the doc had me hold onto a metal shelf. When he stuck his finger in, I pulled the fucking thing off the wall."

Still I try one more time: "It's like required reading," I say. "You read Virginia Woolf because everyone says you should. So you read her. But she doesn't touch you."

"What?" Hank yells.

I wave my hand, *forget it.* Hank dives his head down in again.

"How you get it up there," Hank says. "I can't imagine."

Back to Disco Speak. This time I'm so close to Hank's ear, my lips touch his fat ear lobe.

"Your girlfriend got it up there."

"What?" Hank says.

"That's different," Hank says.

"What's different?"

"She's a girl," Hank says.

"Assholes got no gender," I say.

"No," Hank says. "Assholes are *female*. That's why guys say *I got your back*."

My hand is high, my gesture broad and Judy lit, a sweep across the room.

"Not all guys," I say.

Hank's face looks drunk and in the drunk way I've only seen Hank look a couple other times. Something pissed off, maybe even mean. His black eyes look around the room.

"You can see this anywhere," Hank yells. "Men hitting on men is no different from men hitting on women. You don't have to go to the Spike to see men act like assholes."

What I say next surprises me. Not that I say it, but how. Directly into Hank's ear. It's a challenge.

"We can see a lot more if you'd like," I say, "in the back room. Men fucking."

Hank's black eyes come straight across at me.

"Okay, Napalm," Hank says. "I'm following you."

SOMETHING HAPPENS THEN. Just as Hank and I start to move away from the bar toward the back room. We're just entering the slow circling Ouroboros, just about to be swept away into the crowd, when, for some reason, Hank and I stop and both of us look down on the floor. What makes the tall guy so tall is that he's standing on a plastic milk case, *Dellwood* along the side. Hank and I both, our eyes, travel up this guy's body. Just when our eyes are at the skull tattoo on his pink arm, the tall guy raises his beer to his mouth. Where his arm and the skull tattoo used to be, framed between his chest and belly and his arm in the air, Hank and I see it. On the bar, his fly open, his ballsack spread way out and thumb-tacked to the wooden counter. Stretched out ball flesh, a many-pointed hairy star, pink thumbtacks, and a nub of circumcised cock sticking up out of it.

Hank. The shock of seeing that guy having a quiet beer while tiny beads of blood well up around pink thumb tacks is a blow to him as if he's been kidney-punched. He puts his hand on the bar, steadies himself.

"You all right?" I yell.

Hank's a battering ram through the crowd, an offensive lineman plowing through, headed for the door. That quick, the crowd fills in where Hank has pushed. I can't see him anywhere. Getting my body through that crowd isn't as easy for me. I push and push. It takes forever. Outside, when I finally catch up to him, Hank's bent over in the gutter, big vomits splash out of his mouth into the curb.

"Hank," I say before I touch his back. "It's me."

IT'S JUST AS hot outside, only different. For about a minute. Then the wind whips off the Hudson and I'm froze solid. My thermal sweatshirt goes on quick. My ears still pound with disco. In the cold night air, my body's happy to move free again. The West Side Highway, speeding bright white headlights of cars and trucks and cabs, yellow numbers on their roofs, red lights, orange lights, their blink and blink. Above at the intersection, the traffic light down and up, green, amber, red. The night is a blur, a loud long roar and blur. A big truck blasts past and the hot air and exhaust blows against us, hot ghosts onto ice. Hank's up, putting on his thermal, and walking. We take a cross street east. In the city we love, we're walking again. When things have gone bad, when things have gone good, when things have dumped shit on your head, when you're in the stars, when you're fucked up, when it's too hot, when your ass is freezing, when you've just heaved your guts out into the curb, walk, just walk. Keep on walking. Our breath pushed out just ahead of us.

"Good thing you didn't bang into that guy," I say. "He'd be dangling."

Hank doesn't laugh, doesn't look at me. He just keeps walking, shivering, his hands fists in his Levi's pockets. Even in the dark, I can tell. The way his face is pale. We keep on walking. Side by side, not one in front of the other, not Hank stepping back in the narrow spots so I can walk first. Just walking. It's quiet enough we can hear our footsteps break the ice. At the next avenue we stop for the Don't Walk. In the neon, Hank's face looks green.

"The wind coming down these long bright avenues at night," I say, "fucking freeze your nuts off, man."

Just then a blast of wind so cold it blows right through us to the bones.

"I didn't throw up because of the sex," Hank says. "I got a weird thing for needles."

Passes out easily, Hank, throws up if anything gets too far out of kosher. Makes my heart cry out. Hank and his cancer. All those days and nights, all those years in and out of hospitals, the biopsies, the chemo, the radiation, bed pans, the throw up, the IVs, the incisions, the needles, the shits. Hank in Florida, me in Oregon. All those years, I was never there. Couldn't brush back his hair. Didn't hold his hand. In spirit, yes. But my body, well, my body was having some problems of its own.

The first deli we come to, Hank stands under the heat lamp in the doorway outside. I go in.

"Pepsi," Hanks says, "and some peanuts maybe."

Hank rips open the bag of peanuts, chucks the whole bag of them into his mouth. His bare hands in the cold night. Chews like he's way too hungry, then downs the Pepsi, two big gulps. We're way too young, too healthy, to know about blood sugar. Above us on the left, the top of the Empire State Building is Christmas red and green.

"I'm glad we went there," Hank says. "It's always cool to

see the world with different eyes. But that wasn't what I was look-ing for."

Hank takes the Pepsi bottle by the neck between his second and third fingers. A quick thrust of his arm and the bottle flies into a vacant lot, breaks against the cement. The broken glass, little pieces of light, fall onto a flat of old linoleum floor with other bits of broken glass and ice.

It spooks me, the Pepsi bottle. How quick it happens, and violent. My body jumps. At the sternum. In the middle of my chest, a lightbulb that you can see the filament flickering. Fear. The beaten boy in the world of men, running. Their strange sudden inexplicable violence.

We don't stop, keep walking as if the Pepsi bottle never happened. It takes me a while but then I get it that I'm a child who's walking with his fucked up father, and I need to say something.

"So what was it," I say. "Exactly. That you were looking for?"

ALL THE WAY across town, to the Flatiron Building, to Union Square, to NYU, past Tower Records, Eighth Street, to Astor Place and the big metal square you can push against to make it move, Cooper Union, down to East Fifth Street, not a word. We walk, our heads down, our hoods pulled tight, our hands in our sweat-shirt pockets, frozen snot in our mustaches, right past my apartment and keep walking, not a word. To Second Avenue, to Sixth Street, five in the morning, the Indian restaurants, masala, curry, lamb vindaloo. Past the Pyramid. The skinheads. Not a word.

At Auden's house at #77 St. Mark's Place, we're staring up at the poem Wystan Hugh Auden wrote that's under the second-story window. We've been standing there for I don't know how long. Daylight's making shadows where it used to be only dark. Wind like to knock us off our feet. I'm so fucking cold I'm numb. That poem. How very perfect that poem is. True the way truth can make you wince, make you cry, make you proud. The guy standing next to me is the old Hank again. He undoes the string around his hood. Takes off his cap. He's got hat hair. It's the poem that has made Hank, Hank. His shoulders are going down, his chest going up. For a moment, I think he's crying.

"So," Hank says, "sodomy. You haven't said. Do you like it?"

"I mean," Hank says. "Do you like getting fucked?"

AUDEN IS SMILING. I'm sure of it. Probably laughing out loud. All of Homosexual Heaven in an uproar. My queer forefathers and mothers, a hierarchy of pederasts, sodomites, dykes, fags, queers, sissies, bisexuals, fairies, trannies, old maids, butches, poofs: Homer, André Gide, George Sand, Christopher Isherwood, Tchaikovsky, Wagner, Coleridge, Gertrude Stein and Alice, Cole Porter, Leonardo da Vinci, Sappho, Stephen Spender, Robespierre, Sir Isaac Newton, Oscar Wilde, Molière, Bayard Rustin, Walt Whitman, St. Augustine, Michelangelo, Socrates, Francis Bacon, James Baldwin, William Burroughs, Allen Ginsberg, Paul Bowles, Yukio Mishima, Jean Genet, E.M. Forster, Proust, Henry James, Aristotle, Cavafy, Christopher Marlowe, Billy Strayhorn, Tennessee Williams, William Shakespeare, Herman Melville, Rumi, the *simpatico*, the martyred Garcia Lorca – we've all had to answer the question: homosexual? It's always a fucked struggle, fought in isolation, even for Auden, even for Tchaikovsky. Just look at Oscar Wilde. *Homosexual*, self with the self, the battle, can be so internal that we can live our lives never being able to look beyond ourselves to see there are others like us.

New York City 1987. To know what is right in the dark night of your heart and pursue it with clarity during the day. I'm lucky enough to be born into a time and a society that I can say this chthonic, deep down thing out loud. I am a proud gay man. Although *proud* is a work in progress. Hell, I can't even get it up.

At Auden's door, Sunday morning early at 77 St. Mark's Place a proud gay man at the Gates of Homosexual Heaven, I'm standing half dead from exposure to ice and cold before the poem that breaks my heart. Breaks it open. My friend, My "April in Paris" Friend, *what have you done to my heart* Hank, is standing next to me. His hair's a mess, greasy, his breath is bad, and he looks like he feels. A long shower and ten hours of sleep will do him good. He's just asked the second question after the first question – *homosexual?* – that follows sooner or later: *do you take it up the ass? And do you like it?* This is right after maybe only an hour before he's said: *Assholes are feminine. That's why guys say I got your back.*

The lightbulb in the middle of my chest, the flickering filament. Run. Just get the fuck out of there. But mostly always I run, then fall, stumble, trip, crack, break, then try to get up again, try to put it back together. That morning, though, looking up at that plaque, I'm staring at my history and all the lives that have gone before.

The deep down part of me, Big Ben, that part of me that's never really ever let me go, no matter how fucked it is I've got to bring into the light of day my dark and dreary soul. Always the breath, first, before I speak – the breath I can actually see that night – the inhale, the exhale, the constant proof that life's a miracle. I call on Homosexual Heaven for help. Their answer is a garbage truck that pulls up, stops. The hiss of brakes and the roar clunk of the huge truck eating garbage. It takes me a while for my teeth to stop chattering.

"I liberated my asshole," I say. "That's why I moved to New York City. I used just go out with guys and tell them that's all I wanted. No kissing, no hugging, no foreplay. Just lube and get it in there. Hurt like hell. Every time. I punched a guy once. Damn that pain is like nothing else. Pain that can fucking overwhelm you."

Manhattan garbage trucks are the loudest in the world. Metal cans banging. The huge hydraulic shovel arm that smashes all the shit in. How the cold makes it all the louder. Hank steps away from me, not in fear or revulsion, I think, but just with the impact. My words, how they come out of my mouth, I always overdo it when I know it's going to be difficult.

What happens next, all the while I'm talking, I stand

myself close to Hank. The way we were huddled at the bar even though now it's outside and daylight. After his first step back, Hank doesn't try to move away, although I sense he wants to. In a way, though, it's like a train wreck the way I'm talking and Hank doesn't want to miss the gore. For me, the whole world becomes only Hank's black eyes – that and a quality of light. The early sun and the cold sky blue and pink and orange. Light that doesn't shine, that glows.

"It happened one night," I say. "The restaurant where I worked was having a staff party. We started out at the Monster on empty stomachs and drank a bunch of cocktails. Then we all piled in cabs and drove across town to this Cuban restaurant that had our table waiting for us. We're all totally drunk and starving when we sit down. In front of us is the normal place setting for a nice restaurant, a napkin, fork, table knife, wine glass, water glass, you know the set-up – well, along with the table setting, at the top of each of our plates was a little blue paper plate with a big oatmeal raisin cookie on it. What none of us knew, and not even the people at the restaurant knew, this guy named Stephen Something, a friend of the owner's, had put a very special ingredient into those oatmeal cookies. Hashish. Fuck. Of course, we all wolfed down that oatmeal cookie as if it was a speck of dust. I was the first one to get up from the table. They hadn't even served the first course yet. Later on, I found out that nobody made it all the way through that dinner. Everyone got so stoned they left the planet. So I'm walking home, and really I've forgotten how to walk. I'm that high. So I just put it all on autopilot. When I wake up, I'm lying naked in my apartment with my big ceiling fan on high. That fan was spinning. My undershorts were on one of the blades of the fan and all I could do was lie there and watch my panties go around and around. Then I realize the radio is on and somehow the radio can control my thoughts. Some part of me knows that none of this is normal, so I figure I've got to get to the phone. Then I realize I don't have a phone and I have to walk across the street, go into a bright laundromat and

call the only person I know to call. His name was Dick, if you can
believe it. Dick had taken way too much acid, was a total splotchy
alcoholic, and all he ever wanted to do was *merge*. I never did
fully understand what *merge* was, but believe me, I'd tried. So I
call up Dick, who's asleep because it's something like four in
the morning and he's got an attitude, but I tell him please he's got
to help me, I'm real fucked up."

Over Hank's shoulder, the garbage truck driver comes
round to the back to pull a lever. He is big and dirty and black in
heavy duty orange Carhartts. Hank and I are standing too close.
The driver sees us, wants some attention too. He throws a metal
can in our direction. Hank doesn't notice. His black eyes are too
busy tracking my story. He's ticking off every detail as if each
one is his own.

This next part, before I speak it, the ghost of air I suck into
my mouth. The miracle of it. When you get close to the vein
that's pulsing truth, when you open that vein, you can scrub your
soul clean with the blood.

"So we go over to Dick's apartment because mine is freaking me out, and it was that night, totally stoned out of my fucking
mind, that Dick works his cock inside me."

Hank's eyes go a little off as if all he can hear is garbage
truck.

"Suddenly," I say, "my ass sucks in his cock as if his cock is
life and I'm a dying man. Fucked me like I'd never been fucked.
A fist jammed through my burning ass, reaching up to my heart,
holding on tight, cradling me like a baby. Everything is exploding.
Merge. There's no other word for the way I come. I go away, far
away, then come back, then realize I'm something, someone, who
can go far away and then come back again, so I go far away
again. To the very top of a tall tall tree. I'm stuck with a root from
deep in the earth up my ass, its branches wrapped around my
heart. I'm dripping sap, swaying in the wind."

Hank doesn't blink. The way his black eyes look, I know
something's changed. The garbage truck is loud, loud. All of

Manhattan, a hissing, whirring, banging, crashing, colliding, crunching, freezing, fucking garbage truck.

"To tell the truth, Hank," I say, "Just talking about it I could come again."

PART TWO | *Idaho*

8.

The most miserable of all

OVER FOUR MONTHS GO BY AND I DON'T SEE HANK. AFTER all that going on about getting fucked in the ass, I figured if there was anything left to say it was Hank's turn to say it. I didn't call him.

And damn. During those four months so much happened. Winter to spring, a whole season passed. Hank's book got published and my book got published. Pub dates, my reading at Dixon Place, reviews, that's a lot to happen. You need a friend more than ever during times like that.

Sometime in there, Ursula Crohn called and proposed a combination book party for Hank and me, but I never heard anything more. Probably just too gay. Hank and Ben: The Book Party.

After our night at the Spike, at Auden's door, the sun coming up big, yellow, and freezing cold, when the garbage truck drove off, how silent it was on St. Marks Place. Big old snowflakes falling. Hank walked uptown and I walked down. Both of us knew something had changed. Neither one of us was for sure what. A sick feeling in my chest that went up and across my shoulders. Atlas. I was carrying the world. I'd got in too close to my friend Hank. The kind of big mistake you make when you love and because you love you get in too close. The kind of sick you get only after a mistake like that.

You put your head down and just keep going. While I swept sidewalks, shoveled snow, unplugged toilets, fixed door locks, replaced broken window panes, servicing the boilers. My insides hurt. Couldn't get away from it. In my apartment, walking the streets, sitting on the frozen stoop, coffee in a Café 103, at my typewriter, I was lonely the way you can only be in this city. Surrounded by a million other lonely motherfuckers. You're just another one of them. You've put your time in, worked hard for it, you've claimed your right. That's the way it is for New Yorkers. You wear loneliness on your sleeve. Anywhere else you'd just be alone.

One evening sometime in February, I take the R uptown and press the button for Hank's apartment. No answer. I leave a note on his mailbox to give me a call.

A couple weeks later, I call Hal Taylor. He's especially interested why I'm asking about Hank. *What's the matter, you two break up?* No surprise there.

At St. Mark's Bookshop, there are two copies of Hank's book. The cover is Jupiter golds and reds. $15.95. On the back cover that photo of Hank. He's in profile, not looking at the camera. The background is gray and his hair and his body are black. His body is hunched forward a bit, like it's cold behind him. Like he's Atlas too. The light is all on Hank's face, his eye in shadow, and he's got that look, sad, faraway, but the way he holds his mouth you know.

Over the next four months, sitting at my desk in my little circle of light, I read Hank's book four maybe five times. Strange, I'd listened to Hank read the stories, read them myself, critiqued them, proofread. But those nights alone with Hank's sentences, I felt such an intimacy. The actual pages, the feel of them, an old map to a lost treasure.

A LATE AFTERNOON the end of May. Summer hot already though. At the Strand Book Store, Hank Christian and I run into each other. It's a big town, New York. On days like this it ain't so big.

The Strand, in the basement, jammed to the ceiling with books, aisles and aisles of notched steel posts that hold up platforms of books on wide plywood shelves. Way back in the corner, dark back there. Bare lightbulbs, the kind you can see inside their bright wires. Lightbulbs like that hanging down every six feet or so just above your head. As you walk on the cement floor your shadow runs into you, then into inside you, then long out behind you. Shelves of books going way up high on each side, over and over your shadow on the cement as you walk.

On the other side of the bookshelf, I see his shoes, those ultra-white tennis shoes. Levi's straight-leg coming down onto the white laces. Suddenly I have a sense of the whole big of him, all at once, as if he were a ghost. A blast of aftershave and his body. New red potatoes in a shovelful of earth. Just like that he passes into me then back out again. At the same time, in the aisle on the other side of the bookshelf, I know all this is also happening to Hank.

Below us, on the wide plywood bottom shelf, there's a huge pile of my book, blue and aqua and moss green. Next to my pile, a huge pile of Hank's book, orange and red and sunny yellow.

Remainders. Seventy-five cents a copy. Hundreds of them.

We walk along the bookshelf, Hank on his side, me on mine, our shadows on the cement floor doing that. At the end, at the intersection of a wider aisle, under the lightbulb, our shadows merge into a two-headed hunchback, festering, low, and lonely.

Hank Christian, you'd figure his eyes would be blue, but they aren't, are dark, almost black. The efficient line of Roman nose. Above the square jaw a bit of cleft. Hank's sweet lips are a smile, but really there's no smile in his smile.

"Hey Gruney," Hank says. "What's up?"

As if the last four months haven't even happened. Hank the Ghost gone back into himself. One day he'll pull back in so far he'll disappear. Fucking straight guys, man. Basic training. Always keep that female ass covered.

My breath, how I'm out of it. My pounding heart. Christ, I've never been able to hide a thing. But Little Ben is doing his

best. To stand and not run. And it shows. As soon as Hank sees
Little Ben, Hank's smile becomes a real smile.

"I've missed you," I say.

"My pile's bigger than yours," Hank says.

"What?"

"The remainders," Hank says. "My pile is bigger."

"Seventy-five cents," I say. "Fuck."

"Been looking all over town for a copy," Hank says. "Couldn't
find a one. That's because they're all here."

"Ursula Crohn call you?" I say.

"Yeah."

"So," I say, "did you have a book party?"

"No," Hank says. "You?"

"No."

"Well, the upside is," Hank says, "my twenty dollar bill is
going to buy more than one book."

"I thought I'd at least see it on a shelf in St. Mark's," I say.

"Or here at the Strand," Hank says. "Upstairs, I mean."

"I even looked up at Columbia."

"Nothing?"

"Nothing."

"Congratulations on the *Times* review," Hank says.

On the cement floor our shadow stretches. A two-headed
hunchback who's been long asleep. Stretches so far it almost
splits in two. Then there it is, here it is, one of those moments in
your life that lasts so long you don't know how you survive it.

"Jeske said France bought your book," Hank says. "And it's
going paperback.

"Gallimard," Hank says. "Fucking great."

Little Ben inside me scrambles for some words to say that
can be true.

"It's a cult hit," I say.

"Fuck that cult shit," Hank says. "When you're good and
when you're different it scares people."

This long moment. Hank hasn't had one review. I know it

and he knows I know it. If I say one word the wrong way, we'll be a globbed up bottle of A-1 Steak Sauce stuck in the back of the refrigerator forever.

"Thanks," I say. "That means a lot to me."

"That first night at Ursula Crohn's," Hank says, "I heard it."

"Hank," I say, "I'm sorry about that night at the Spike."

"What did you do?"

Hank's black eyes are way too much. On the cement floor, the two-headed hunchback is two different shadows.

"I'm not sure," I say. "But that's always been my trouble. I don't know when to stop, I guess."

One shadow each at the bottom of our feet. Still the moment. The lightbulb right above our heads. Bright lightbulb light with the insides that you can see. Books in a basement, the smell. The smell from my armpits. Hank's Mennen stick. Red potatoes and earth. Fuck.

"Getting any writing done?" Hank says.

"Nah," I say. "How's Olga?"

Laughter inside Hank, how it jumps up in his chest.

"She threw me out," Hank says. "Literally, she threw my clothes and shit out the window. My computer and printer were sitting on the front steps."

"What the fuck?" I say. "What happened?"

Hank, the way he holds his cards so close to his chest, I didn't figure at all on what he says next.

"She found some fuck poems I was writing to this girl at work," Hank says, "and she went all Latina Bitch on me."

"What did you do?" I say. "Where are you living? Is she okay?"

"Olga's fine," Hank says. "She has a tradition of righteous indignation to fall back on. I'm living in Brooklyn. Third stop on the L Train. With Mike Yamada. You remember him from Jeske's class?"

"He's just got a story in *Esquire*," I say.

"That's him," Hank says. "You doing any book tour?"

"Idaho," I say.

"Idaho?" Hank says.

"Got a gig in Pocatello," I say. "Maybe even Boise if we want."

"We?" Hanks says, "Who's we?"

Hank's black eyes, something in there. Adventure.

"My brother Ephraim," I say." Remember him?"

"The Indian?"

"Native American," I say.

"Yeah," Hank says.

"He's giving you and me a book party," I say, "in his sweat lodge. He's invited both of us."

"He don't even know me."

"He loved your book," I say. "He knows you well enough."

"He read my book?"

"Will they let you off at work?"

"Can we sell any books?" Hank says.

"We've got two hundred books right here," I say.

"I can only afford twenty of them," Hank says.

"You'll sell twenty books then."

My friend, Hank Christian, is here again. In the basement of the Strand, under the clear lightbulb with the inside filaments, holding his body that way. His chest pushed up and out, his shoulders down, flexing his biceps.

"Can you lend me some money?" Hank says.

"The bank gave me a credit card," I say. "Can you believe that? Five hundred dollar max."

Hank's smile. The way his eyes look at me, Atlas shrugs and I'm pulled away from planet Pluto where I've been stuck. Back into the free breathing air of mother earth in a basement in New York City.

"Fuckin' A, man," Hank says. "I've been searching for an excuse to get out of this fucking town."

TWO WEEKS LATER, Hank and I are in the friendly skies. He's got the window seat and I've got the aisle. An empty seat between us. We've each got a backpack and we've each checked one suitcase. In the backpacks are our clothes. In the checked suitcase Hank has twenty-two books, in mine is twenty-four. If we sell them all at ten dollars apiece we'll pay for the trip.

1988, Hank Christian and Ben Grunewald. We're there in our bodies while it's happening, of course. We feel the magic, the freedom, the adventure. But we have no idea. How events can fuck you up, make your soul, finally bring you to your knees. That's the kind of journey we are on. We can sense it. But all we know what to do is drink beer on the plane. I smoke a cigarette while we go over our pages. Hank asks for more ice cubes and flirts with the stewardess. Hell, I'm Big Ben. Even I flirt with the stewardess. Even she can tell we're going for something big.

Idaho.

It ain't New York.

In New York we ended up in a pile in the basement. But in Idaho we're going to read and people are going to sit in an audience and listen to our sentences. The following day, Friday, there will be a book signing at the university bookstore. Then Friday night, a reading at the Blind Lemon, a beatnik bar in the Sixties that's still there on Center Street. The bartender, Wilbur Tucker, still reads from *Howl*, from *On the Road*. He's larger than life, Wilbur, and looks like Papa Hemingway. In the middle of the bar scene, eight o'clock sharp, Wilbur rings the fire bell those four times the whole bar shuts up. And he reads: *I saw the best minds of my generation destroyed by madness.* He reads: *because the only people for me are the mad ones, the ones who are mad to love, mad to talk, mad to be saved, desirous of everything at the same time, the ones that never yawn or say a commonplace thing, but burn, burn, burn ...*

Idaho.

Wilbur Tucker is going to ring the fire bell again. But this time he's ringing it for Hank Christian and Ben Grunewald. He'll be ringing that bell for me.

In Idaho too is my brother Ephraim's sweat lodge. For Hank that's nothing short of *The Last of the Mohicans*. And something we haven't planned on at all. Old friends of mine in Boise, Reuben and Sal and Gary, have invited us to travel up into the mountains, to a ghost town called Atlanta, where we'll be reading in the original Old Town Hall.

Idaho.

A beatnik bar. A sweat lodge. A ghost town. Go west, young man.

Idaho. Anything you can possibly dream of.

Now, twenty years later, those two young men, what was in store for us, I'm just beginning to comprehend.

AS SOON AS I'm out of the plane, just as my foot lands on the first step of the stairway down to the tarmac, my lungs breathe in the sagebrush and high mountain air. The Idaho night, the wind against my bare arms, as soon as the wind is in my ears, my body remembers something I've forgot. That other thing about Idaho. Idaho is home. Home is family. All those years I've been trying to get away.

My big sis, Margaret, has been in Bernie's Lounge drinking margaritas all night with her boyfriend, Kevin. There they are, she and Kevin, standing in the newly built bright Pocatello airport with red helium balloons floating off them.

"Hurry up!" Margaret yells. "Bars close in an hour!"

By the time Hank and I get our bags, even though drinks are more expensive, our best bet is just to stay there in the airport lounge. We're all in a padded corner booth, Margaret and Kevin and Hank and me. Margaret and I sit as close as we can get and still be brother and sister. Red balloons bobbing all around us. We've all ordered margaritas, except for Hank, who orders Coors, but I have something to say about Coors.

"Harvey Milk," I say.

"Budweiser, then," Hank says.

Margaret looks good. Those big dark brown eyes. *Bette Davis eyes*. Down deep inside them the sadness she always hopes I can see. It's her birthday tomorrow. Forty-five years old. She's just got a perm and her hair is a little too chestnut brown but close enough to her real color. Looks like she's just walked off the golf course. Mary Tyler Moore in *Ordinary People*. She's smoking a Virginia Slim. Ever since I was in the seventh grade, and Margaret was a sophomore, she and I have been smoking. I'd just recently quit with the AIDS scare and all, but I'd just had a cigarette on the airplane, and it's my book tour and I've already slipped, so fuck it, when I see Margaret light up, I bum one off her and light up too.

Idaho.

This is what we do in Idaho. Smoke. Our father smokes, our mother smoked. Movies we watch, Rock Hudson is smoking, Doris Day is smoking, Brando, Natalie Wood, James Dean, Warren Beatty, Montgomery Clift. Smoke. In high school, only Mormons don't smoke and Mormon ain't cool. Light up a cigarette and you're a man. Light up and you're a gorgeous woman.

A carton of Virginia Slims is what I've bought for Margaret's birthday. She smokes over a pack a day. Switched from Marlboro to a healthier cigarette.

When she was a girl, Mom told Margaret she wasn't pretty so she had to be clean. After that, Sis kind of disappeared. That's what Margaret is doing when I look over at her that night in the airport lounge. She's holding out her Virginia Slim so Kevin can light it. She inhales deep, in her throat too, as if she is swallowing the smoke. Her hair is perfectly coiffed, her fingernails manicured, her Weight-Watchers body slim, her blouse, lightly starched white and sleeveless, her khaki shorts pressed, her legs tanned, her white white Keds. She exhales. Somewhere underneath all the smoke is my sister.

Dad always said, when I was a kid, if Margaret told me to jump, I'd ask how high. Margaret's three years older and for my first seven years she was all I had. Out there twelve miles north of town, on a square one hundred and sixty acre farm, all there was, was Mom and Dad and Margaret and me, the Catholic Church, and all the chores we had to do. The pigs, the chickens, the hundred head of cattle, spring planting, fall harvest, and all the fucking work that's in between. Sis had girlfriends at school, Betty and Fergi, but never could spend time with them when it wasn't school because we lived so far away and because of our chores. And boys. Boys were cruel to Sis because she was ugly and fat, she thought, and not popular and didn't have any boobs. No one to talk to. I was the only one who listened. I was her best buddy, her confidant, her stand-in girlfriend, and at Catholic youth dances, when the boys didn't ask her to dance, I asked her. It was my best pleasure asking my sis to dance. I couldn't stand it if she felt lonely. Pretty much all the time Margaret felt lonely. With my mother it was the same way. She was lonely, too. My mother, my sister. Those females and their faraway look. But Mom had Dad and all Sis had was her little brother. Me. The one she'd say jump to and I'd say how high.

There's a video my cousin converted from eight millimeter. Most of the video is dead relatives, but there's this one segment that I can't stop watching. It's of me and Margaret sitting on the cement steps of a front porch. Sis is maybe eight and I am five. She's wearing that plaid coat with her red scarf and I'm in my bomber hat and the jacket with a belt that were two metal links across the waist. Sis has her arm around me. Me, Little Ben, sitting in close to my sis, her arm around me, and we are holding hands. The way we sit, the way we touch, everything about our bodies is saying we are safe, this is my little brother, this is my big sister. I'm protecting him because he's mine. I'm the only one she has.

When the camera pulls back, I am surrounded by women. My mother and all her sisters. Great beauties, all of them. The noise they make, magpies or crows, they all talk at once. My five-year-old eyes don't know what to do, who to look at first. Tall, glamorous, my aunts with the Veronica Lake swirl, with snoods, with penciled-on eyebrows and shoulder pads. Katharine Hepburn, Hedy Lamarr, Ava Gardner, Gene Tierney, Rosalind Russell. It's 1953 and these are the women who worked the nation

through the war. And the war has given them something back.
In their Catholic hearts, film noir is just meeting the Virgin Mary.

THE AIRPORT LOUNGE, in the booth, Margaret and I, hip to
hip, are still two kids sitting on the cement steps. We're not holding hands, but the way we talk makes Hank look up and watch.
Hank's across the table from Kevin. They're talking straight guy
talk. The smile, the distance, the autonomy, the polite regard,
the kind of talk that's always about things or events, sports on
the radio that sounds so exotic when I hear it. But whenever I try,
I sound the way I always sound when I try – like I'm trying too
hard. Kevin's in his orange I S U Bengal cap. He's got an alligator
on his shirt. Ten years ago, living in Chubbuck, Margaret's man
wore a cowboy hat and beat her with a pitchfork. *You've come a
long way, baby*.

All those red balloons bouncing up around us. The cocktail
waitress has got the big Eighties hair and earrings that are holo-
grams all the way down to her shoulders. A hint of cleavage. Lots
of space between her teeth on top. She looks familiar. I think
maybe a girl I went to high school with. She wasn't popular. Future
Homemakers of America. Becky maybe. She doesn't remember
me either. She smells of *Halston*.

"Last call," she says.

"Three more margaritas," Kevin says, "and a Bud."

Hank raises his hand, tries to pass on the beer.

"Oh come on," Margaret says. "How often you get a book
published?"

Then to the waitress: "We're celebrating," Margaret says.
"My brother, Ben, and his friend Hank Christian here are famous
authors. They're reading tomorrow night at the Blind Lemon.
You should come."

What Margaret says next she says like she's still just a kid.
"And it's my birthday!"

We all take Margaret's cue. We toast our glasses, we all yell:
"Happy Birthday!"

OUTSIDE THE AIRPORT lounge, it's the wind. The Idaho wind
that's always there. The sky is black and stars are bright as flash-
lights. The yellow moon, three-quarters full, the man in the moon
has no left cheek. Beyond the runway lights, miles and miles
stretch out into darkness in all directions. High desert plain, coy-
otes, sagebrush. Just due south, giant sprinkler robots roll huge
wheels over the ground, their high arcs of water sprayed onto
the earth of the Michaud Flats. Just beyond, it's Magic Valley. Its
square, irrigated fields are third crop alfalfa, are stubbled wheat
fields, J.R. Simplot potato vines waist high, and acres of barley
dark amber almost rust.

Inside the airport lounge, so many margaritas, so many
dreams. Tomorrow friends from high school and university will
come to the ISU bookstore for Hank and me to sign their books.
And the reading at the Blind Lemon, Wilbur Tucker will ring the
fire bell, his voice saying Hank's name, my name out loud for
all my home town to hear. *Ladies and Gents, Pocatello's own Ben
Grunewald.*

Hank, my buddy Hank, him and his book, right alongside
me.

So many dreams. May as well have been dreaming of
parades and marching bands. The mayor giving me the key to the
city. But more than anything. Although I didn't know it then.
Not like I do now. More than anything was the moment in the
spotlight at the Blind Lemon, standing in the spotlight in front
of all those people, and the best dream was that my big sister was
in the audience, Margaret, sitting there so happy and proud
that I, her little brother Benny, was standing up there in that
spotlight.

A dream bigger than that, better, I couldn't imagine.

THE NEXT MORNING Margaret's at her stove frying eggs. She's
smoking a cigarette. The reason I notice the cigarette is because
after smoking cigarettes at night, a cigarette in the morning
always made me sick. I'm filling the percolator with coffee. I'm

feeling sick. Hank's in his white T-shirt and his jeans, sitting at Margaret's round oak table in the kitchen of her double-wide, buttering whole wheat toast. None of us got to sleep before three, six o'clock New York time. Hank slept on the couch. Me on an air mattress on the floor. Sleep, if you can call it that.

Outside, the sun is bright coming in through the lace curtains. The fresh coffee smells good. I've never seen Hank look so hungover.

"How do you like your eggs, Hank?" Margaret says.

"However I can get them."

Margaret puts out her cigarette in a big, green glass ashtray, washes her hands in the sink, puts lotion on them, then sets a big oval orange plate of fried eggs, ham, and hash browns onto the table. Both Hank and I go for the food. We didn't really get any supper. Margaret sits down at the table, slides her chair in. She makes the sign of the cross, folds her hands. I know I probably should too. But I don't. Instead, Big Ben gets up, pours coffee all around. When Hank sees Margaret, he bows his head, too.

Idaho. This is what we do in Idaho. We pray. To Jesus Christ to have mercy on us. To the Virgin Mary to save us. To all the saints to intercede for us. We pray for the poor souls in purgatory. We pray for the missions in Africa. We pray for the defeat of communism. We pray so that it will rain. We pray it won't rain. We pray for more snow pack on the mountains. We pray it won't freeze. We pray for our immortal souls. We pray we won't go to hell.

"Happy Birthday, Sis," I say.

"Yeah," Hank says. "Happy Birthday."

Margaret slides an egg, a slice of ham onto her plate, grabs a piece of toast.

"I didn't tell you," Margaret says. "Kevin's rented a stretch limo. A white Cadillac. Tonight, we're going to hit all our favorite bars in Pocatello."

A hitch in my breath. Something behind Little Ben's eyes fries a little. Hank looks up, too. Margaret sees my look and, fast as she can, she says:

"It's a white stretch Cadillac," she says, "with a driver. It's one of Kevin's birthday presents."

Hank's black eyes are checking me out. Christ I'm always an open book.

"You still going to make it to the reading?" I say.

Margaret goes for her pack of Virginia Slims, pokes out a cigarette, lights it, inhales deep.

"What time is it again?" Margaret says. "Eight, right?"

"Eight sharp," I say. "Wilbur Tucker's hitting the fire bell eight o'clock sharp."

"Oh sure," Margaret says. Exhales. "Anyway we should make it by eight."

IN MARGARET'S TINY bathroom, Hank showers first. Hank shaves while I shower, or tries to. He can't keep the steam off the mirror. Halfway through my shower, the hot water goes. I let out a yell and jump out of the shower. Hank's got a towel wrapped around him, white shaving cream half on his face. His black eyes look over at me, at my body, and his eyes look down. No big deal. Every guy is curious. I go to cover my cock and balls but I don't. Little Ben acts like I think a straight guy would. That it's perfectly normal to be standing naked in a tiny room so close we're almost touching.

MARGARET WORKS AT the university and she's set the book-signing gig up. She didn't have much time. Big Ben had made the whole Idaho Book Tour thing up on the spot in the Strand Book Store. In the two weeks, she's managed to get the book signing and the reading at the Blind Lemon advertised in the *Idaho State Journal*, plus she got the ISU bookstore to agree to let Hank and me bring our own books to the book signing and not take a cut.

That morning, we load our books into the tiny trunk of Margaret's blue Mazda sports car. Margaret drives us to the university, Hank and I jammed in both on one seat. Hank's on my lap, or let's say his body is part on my left leg and part over the gearshift. Hank's either got to bring his left leg close into him so Margaret can shift, or he has to open his left leg way out so she can reach between his legs to shift. That's when it starts, the laughter. Then halfway to the university, Sis drops her cigarette. Somewhere down between our tangle of hips and legs and arms, there's a cigarette burning. By then we're laughing so hard Margaret has to stop the car. Good thing there's no traffic on the country road. The cigarette has rolled down by my left foot, I can see it, but can't get to it. Sis reaches down through our legs and I look and I can see the manicured, polished nails of her hand feeling around down by my foot.

"Little more to the right," I say.

Sis's hand goes onto Hank's white tennis shoe. It ain't long and Hank says:

"The other right."

Laugh. That's what we do in Idaho. So hard I have to roll down the window.

Finally somehow Margaret gets her Virginia Slim back, and gets it back between her lips and we're off again. Hank's big arm at the back of my head. My head pushed down into his armpit. Mennen. Red potatoes, raw, and earth. Never smelled Hank up that close. Sweat is what tells the tale true.

In the parking lot, Hank has to reach down to grab the door latch because my whole left side is dead and my right side is too smashed against the door. When the door opens, Hank and I fall out, two of the three stooges.

Idaho. The Book Tour.

Hank and I each get our suitcase of books out of the trunk. Margaret's just pulling away when I grab the car at the open passenger window. Margaret stops the Mazda. She looks at me like she's always looked at me. A mixture of tenderness and something else. Her little brother.

"Remember," I say, "eight o'clock."

"Okay," Margaret says.

"Kevin knows that the reading's at eight, right?"

"See you then," Margaret says.

"Blind Lemon," I say. "Wilbur Tucker rings the fire bell at eight sharp."

HANK AND ME, both our suitcases are luggage. You know, those Samsonite-looking things. Hard rectangular boxes with latches that snap. A lock in the middle that tiny keys unlock. Hank's is covered in a faux dark brown leather, and mine is powder blue. I can't even remember where I got this fucking powder blue piece of shit luggage, but there it is, heavy, really heavy, in my right hand.

That moment. Little Ben standing in the ISU parking lot next to Hank, in the wind, in the hot noonday Idaho sun, holding onto the handle of my stupid powder blue suitcase filled with my twenty-four books, watching Margaret drive off in her blue sports car. I should have known better. But what there was to know wasn't knowable yet.

That first time, my first book, I thought there was no longer any reason for the world not to pay me attention. I'd shown that I could do it, make something of myself, make art, important art, and the *New York Times* had said so. The truth is, I thought the publication of my book had bought me passage. From then on my destiny would be different. Finally, I could get on the sailboat. At One Fifth Avenue, I'd take the elevator up to the penthouse with the arched tall corner windows. Switch on the crystal chandelier you could see in there at night. The blue plate on the kitchen wall. Pressed starched linen. Chablis Grand Cru. Truffles. Café de Flor. Havana, Cuba. People to love you like Hemingway.

Love. The hole in me I didn't even know was a hole it was so big would be filled and I could stop the way I lived in the moments of my life, empty. Love, not a speck of it.

Havana, Cuba. Now there's where I should've gone. Instead I go straight to Pocatello, Idaho.

If you can make it there, you can make it anywhere.

In a world of shit. And Little Ben didn't have a clue.

You never go back to your hometown if what you're looking for is love.

"IT NEVER FAILS," Hanks says. "As soon as I walk onto a college campus, I always got to take a shit."

In the student union, everything is like it was. Clean, shiny expanses of windows, granite floors, mopped and waxed. The sun shining in. Back in my day, Friday at noon, things would be hopping. On this Friday, though, from where I'm standing, there's only two tables of people in the cafeteria. No receptionist at the front desk. On the events calendar, a happy face with magnetized letters that say: *Have a fun weekend!* Outside on the quad, I count seven people.

In the main floor lavatory, the toilet stall where Hank's taking a dump is the place where I scored my first ounce of marijuana.

Twenty-four hard-bound books are heavy. I set my fucking powder blue suitcase down. The air condish seems to be running overtime. Still, beads of sweat roll down from my armpits.

IN THE BASEMENT, just as you walk into the ISU bookstore, on the right of the door is a wooden table covered with orange and black ISU Bengals stickers. Behind the table, two orange plastic chairs. Overhead bright fluorescence. On the table, a sign, swirly red letters, outlined in gold: *1:00pm – 3:00pm author signing.* There's a woman at the cash register who smiles when we walk in. She looks up from her book but doesn't greet us. The black and white clock above her head is straight out of grade school. Hank sets his suitcase down, unloads his suitcase. I unload mine. Gold, diamonds, rare pearls, truth, the way we touch our books, lay them onto the table, one book on top of another, spine to spine. Hank with his yellow orange books, me with my blue green. In two piles, in three piles, finally four short piles each with one book propped against a pile so passersby can see the cover.

By one o'clock we're set up. Hank's piles of twenty-two books in front of him. My piles of twenty-four in front of me.

Hank and I move the orange chairs around, sit our asses down onto the hard plastic. Hank's wearing his good white shirt. I'm wearing my blue Oxford shirt. Good Catholic boys. On time. Prepared.

In the glass partition, bright wavy reflections of Hank and me. Hank's forehead is way too shiny. He's sweating Budweiser big time. I don't look at my reflection. In lighting like this, you don't look at your reflection. The display table next to us is piled high with Bengal Tigers, stuffed with potpourri. Lavender, eucalyptus, patchouli. Hank cuts one of his famous farts and it isn't long and we have to move a bunch of those Bengal Tigers over onto our table.

1:45. HANK SAYS, "How many years ago you say you graduated from here?"

At first I say, "seven," and then add again, then say, "seventeen."

Seventeen years.

Across the double doors from us, at the cash register, the woman is middle-aged with light brown hair in a flip. Under the overhead bright fluorescence her hair looks gray. Her dress is a blue printed shirtwaist that goes below her knees. It looks gray too. Twice now, she's come over and asked Hank and me if we would like a refreshment. Each time, Hank and I say no, and each time, after she leaves, Hank says, "*A refreshment*? What is *a refreshment*?"

"She's Mormon," I say.

"That explains it?" Hank says. "*A refreshment*? How do you know she's Mormon?"

"The frock," I say. "The hair. You just know."

2:15. THE UNRELENTING fluorescence from above reflects onto the glass counter. A faux German beer mug with *ISU Bengals* printed on the side sits next to the cash register. I put my hand on the glass counter, lean onto it. The way the Mormon Lady smiles at me would freak any New Yorker.

"Excuse me," I say. "The campus seems so empty. Where is everybody?"

That smile of hers stays put.

"It's the weekend," she says. "Most students have gone home."

"Wow," I say. "It's so different from when I went to school here."

That smile doesn't change one centimeter. I expect the Mormon Lady to ask me when that was, or how long ago was that, or that must have been decades ago, but she doesn't say anything. Her glasses are tortoise shell, big and round.

"This book signing was advertised in the *Idaho State Journal*, wasn't it?"

"Yes," she says. "In *Buzz of the Burg*, just last Wednesday."

"Has anyone called or ordered any books?"

She takes off her big round tortoise shell glasses, folds them, lays them next to the faux German beer mug. Her eyes are blue, but under the light look gray.

"No," she says. "No one has called."

The place on the glass where my hand has rested leaves a smudge. I walk across to our table, sit back down in the orange plastic chair. At the counter, The Mormon Lady's got out the Windex and a rag.

Hank says: "Maybe these people's children, who are just now graduating from high school, will come in and buy some books."

Hank laughs his chest up when he says that, but for a reason I don't understand yet, his words hit hard, almost knock the breath out of me. I can tell how I look by how Hank looks at me. Little Ben is all over on my face. Of course I'm trying to cover up, and of course I can't.

"Gruney! Baby!" Hank says. "What's going on?"

"Nothing," I say.

Hank scoots his orange plastic chair up against mine.

"Your sis will show up tonight," he says. "Don't worry."

Hank's knee touches my knee. That's all it takes.

"It isn't just that," I say. "I don't know. I just thought."

I'm biting my lip. Little Ben's fucking chin is going to start turning into rubber bands any second.

"It's been almost an hour and a half," I say. "No one is here. I thought at least Bob and Jim and Brent, maybe Fred, from high school would show. They all read the newspaper. What the fuck? And then there's my fraternity brothers and Diane and Mitch and Lloyd and Suzanne. They all work here at the university for Chrissakes."

"You heard the lady," Hank says. "It's Friday and everyone's gone home."

Over at the cash register, the Mormon Lady is pretending she can't hear us.

Hank says: "Did you make plans to meet with any of these people?"

Hank's question is like a foreign language. Plans? Big Ben doesn't make plans. I was reviewed in the *New York Times*. People should just know.

"Not really," I say.

"Did you send out any invitations?" Hank asks.

"No," I say.

"Why?"

"They're all Mormons," I say.

"Then why the fuck do you expect them to show up?"

Things start crashing in about then. The dream in me, ancient and so strong I hadn't even considered that it wasn't real. Like the dream I was dead and everybody who'd hurt me was standing around my open coffin crying their eyes out. My dream of coming home had played so many times in my head, I couldn't imagine any version where I wasn't the exalted hero.

In that moment, under the bright fluorescence in the hard orange plastic chair, I tried my best to answer Hank, one part of my mind trying to contact another part, but I didn't come up with anything. Couldn't say what I didn't know yet.

Havana. I'd have been much better off in Havana, Cuba.

What Hank says next, he says no different from how Hank usually says things. Direct. No nonsense. And way too loud.

"Do they know you're gay?"

The Mormon Lady looks up. The black and white clock above her head, the red second hand, stops. 2:37. Everything stops. All the traffic lights in Pocatello, the seven people left on campus. Stop. My heart. My breath. Even Hank stops.

A pain right between my eyes. Dizzy. Fire on my heart like the sacred heart of Jesus. My stomach doing flips. Last night's margaritas, today's bad gas. Then something really weird. Something my body remembers but thought it had forgot. But it's more like a somebody.

It's Little Ben, the tormented Catholic nightmare version of him, me. That picture in the *Baltimore Catechism* of Heaven, Limbo, Purgatory, and Hell. At the top, the clouds and the sun and the bearded white God in a heavenly gown, the trumpets, the rays of light, the angels. Then down and down and down, the descent into suffering, Limbo, Venial Sin, Mortal. How my eyes went down, straight to the nastiest, the most miserable of all, at the bottom of hell. Every time. That naked guy down there, with his front to you and he's got no cock, just a straight line down there, his crotch like a woman, flames all around him up to his ass. Suffering without hope.

Little Ben down there all alone in hell. Just him and his original sin.

Everybody up in heaven pointing down at him and laughing.

THAT MORNING ON her bed, on the white chenille bedspread I don't remember, September or October 1948, lying in the patch of sun. The Johnson & Johnson Baby Powder. She is my mother, without her I will die. I look close into her eyes to see how I'm going to be. She sprinkles the white powder on my cock and balls,

around my bum. It feels cool and dry and something else. I kick
my legs, let go a big smile for my very first time.

The audacity to get hard in front of the Virgin. Our mother,
Mary. My mother, Marie.

My sin.

The first time Virgin Mary Marie was alone in a room with
a hard dick she could control.

All those Vatican statues with their cocks lopped off. Somewhere down in the catacombs, drawers and drawers of Dead
Lorca severed penises.

Cock-hating, fucking Catholics.

How can a cockless man in hell, full of hate, flames up to
his ass, no fucking way out of this mess, do anything but blame
himself the way his mother blamed him? Then the humiliation,
the degradation, the sharp needle adrenaline rush, the sick pain
he begins to jones for: to lose, to lose, to lose and never win,
to always be wrong, off, to be cast out, never to be good enough,
big enough, hard enough.

Mother Church, Papal Bull. Hell is your Virgin mother got
inside you. Once that shit gets in, it grows and grows and
doesn't stop growing. The world outside a loop, outside what is
inside, one example after another after another. How you're not
good enough. How everybody else has got it better.

THE BLACK AND white clock above the Mormon lady's head
says 2:38. Hank's face is up close. *Gay* is a blinking red neon word
between his black eyes and mine.

"No," my mouth is saying. "Well, probably. Yes, I'd imagine."

One big fucking tear comes rolling down my cheek.
As soon as I feel it on my chin, I try to laugh but it doesn't work.
Hank's big hand, his long fingers, give my knee a squeeze.

"Hometowns, man," Hank says. "They always fuck you up."

THE BATHROOM IS the bathroom next to the pool hall. Twenty
years ago, I'd go into that bathroom just to read the one line of

graffiti that maintenance didn't catch for months. Near where the stanchion is bolted to the wall: *suck cock Tues here at 4.*

Tuesdays at four, those months, I always knew where I was. Never in that bathroom.

The day of the book signing, I am in that bathroom. Projectile vomiting eggs and ham and hash browns and tequila. Loud, strange, animal sounds coming from deep inside. It's forever I'm on my knees holding on to the big white toilet.

In the mirror, when I can stand, the me who tries to talk to me is trying to talk to me. But I'm nowhere around. All there is to see is the Most Miserable, the naked guy without a dick at the bottom of hell. His finger goes to near where the stanchion is bolted to the wall.

At the sternum, right in the middle of my chest, a light bulb that you can see the filament flickering.

Idaho.

This is what we do in Idaho.

The Most Miserable of all is everywhere.

And all we know how to do is run.

2:55. WHEN I make it back into the bookstore, Betty and Fergi, Margaret's friends from grade school, are standing at the table. They're hot and out of breath, not yet used to the air condish. Hank stares up at them. I stare. The Mormon Lady stares.

"I hope we're not interrupting anything," Fergi says.

"We thought we'd be too late," Betty says.

"Are there any books left?"

Betty and Fergi each buy one of Hank's books, one of mine. When I go to make my first author signature in Betty's book, I write *thaks* instead of *thanks*. Crooked shaky penmanship. Fuck.

Fergi's tall and still has her ratted black hair from the sixties. Betty's not a bottle-blonde anymore and a mom three times. In her, I can just barely see the girl from my childhood. They talk at the same time and too fast and ask a lot of questions. Life in New York. How it feels to publish a novel. What they want to ask, they don't. Are you really a homosexual? And: Is Hank your boyfriend? The Great Omniscient Hank watches me, watches them, watches all. I ask about their marriages, their children.

When Betty and Fergi leave, both of them give me a hug. I try to make my body not stiff. Close my mouth tight, my breath. They hold Hank's hand a little too long. He looks them back in the eye. Let's them see they're being seen.

OUT ON THE quad, in the bright hot windy day, the wind feels good on my face. In my lungs.

Idaho.

In a moment I understand why I've always liked the wind. The way it blows on your ears you cannot feel alone.

Hank's got his brown faux leather suitcase. I've got my powder blue. Two books less each and twenty dollars richer, Hank and I have each sold our first book and Hank's hungry.

"I heard you in the bathroom talking to Ralph," Hank says. "You feeling all right?"

"Tequila and fried eggs," I say.

My mouth moves but I wonder who it is that's speaking.

"She's not a Mormon, you know," Hank says.

"Who?"

"The Mormon Lady back at the bookstore," Hank says. "She's not a Mormon. Her name's Frieda Cooper and she's studying to be a librarian."

Hank's shadow, my shadow are a little ahead of us east on the perfect grass.

"She says our books won't sell because we say *motherfucker* too much," Hank says. "You say it once and I say it five times."

Laugh, bless Hank's heart, Hank has made me laugh. I reach over and smack Hank's shoulder.

"That makes you five times a better writer than me," I say.

"But would she carry our books in her bookstore?"

"She says she would," Hank says, "until somebody raised a fuss."

"Then what?"

"She'd take them off the shelf 'til the mishigas was over," Hank says, "then she'd put them back."

"*Mishigas?*" I say.

"She said *mishigas*," Hank says.

"They all think you're gay, you know," I say.

"I am," Hank says. "Whenever I'm in Idaho I'm gay."

"Does that mean I can fuck your ass?" I say.

Hank's black eyes come around at me. Sooner or later one of us had to say it. The Spike, the last time we were at Auden's door, those four months we didn't talk, that pain, it's there in the Idaho sun on the ISU quad between us.

What Hank says next and what Hank does next happen together. What he does is grab hold of my shoulder in a way that men don't grab hold of each other's shoulder. What he says is:

"Houston," Hank says, "I think we have a problem."

Hank's arm stays cupped around my shoulder, his chest pushed into my arm. We're laughing easy, Hank and I, and that's good.

Then: "We're cool, aren't we?" Hank says.

"Of course we're cool," I say.

FIVE O'CLOCK. IN the bar at Buddy's Pizza. A big part of my college career took place in this smoky room. It's no bigger than half of Margaret's double-wide. Crosby, Stills and Nash are singing *something's happening here*. On the table, the waitress has just set down an extra large sausage extra cheese pizza and two of Buddy's salads with the famous salad dressing. I'm drinking a Red Eye, some call it a Montana Mary, which is tomato juice and beer, which Hank can't imagine. I tell him it's good for hangovers, but Hank still goes for his draft Bud.

"Hank," I say, "I'm sorry about not selling more books."

The pizza's too hot and Hank's waving the napkin at his mouth. He chews and chews, has to wait to swallow his pizza.

"Gruney," Hank says, "just being out of New York is enough."

He takes a big sip of beer, burps.

"Plus all this sun and fresh air," he says. "And the wind is incredible. If we didn't sell another book, I'd still be having a great time."

Hank jabs a forkful of Buddy's famous salad into his mouth, wipes his chin. I wish I was hungry too.

"This salad dressing is incredible," Hank says. "How do they make it?"

"It's Buddy's big secret," I say. "What are you reading tonight?"

"The story of the little girls calling in the cows," Hank says. "You?"

"The intro pages," I say. "About the sky and the red pieces of cloth on the fence."

"I've been looking at that Idaho sky," Hank says.

My slice of sausage extra cheese stretches cheese from the pan to my plate all the way across the table. Across the table from us, just then a bald guy starts talking about a big white stretch Cadillac limousine.

"They plan to hit every bar in town tonight," he says. "When Margaret and Kevin left here they took half the bar with them."

7:30. HANK AND I haul our suitcases down Pocatello's dark side. Center Street: the old Block's Men Store, the Shanghai Café. The Hotel Whitman. And all the bars: Satan's Cellar, The Office, The Back Door. As we walk, all around our bodies, on our forearms, our necks, on our faces, the wind, the unending Idaho sky with its long sunset that's peach and gold and rosy pink.

I expect to see a big white stretch Cadillac limo, but there's no limo.

Above the bar at the Blind Lemon is a painting that starts at one end and ends at the other. It's a painting of a painting of a reclining nude woman whose head is a skull. The painter has painted himself into the painting and he's looking at the woman sideways as if he doesn't really trust his invention. The painter looks like a young Wilbur Tucker, but in all the years I knew Wilbur, he always said it wasn't him, was his buddy he roomed with in college, who'd bit it in the Korean War.

When we walk into the Blind Lemon, I expect to see a bar full of old ghosts. High school bullies. Old girlfriends. Or worse, the Most Miserable. But the bar is just the bar, the Blind Lemon, loud and busy and smoky on a Friday night and above the bar that huge painting of the pendulous breasts and the skull. The podium is there, too, just like it's supposed to be, with the built in microphone. It's set up between the big dirty window facing Center Street and the curve of oak bar. The fire bell, big and shiny brass, setting right there at the end of the bar.

No Sis.

There's two empty stools at the bar, Hank and I pull them up, set down our suitcases. The bartender is not Wilbur Tucker. He's a young man. Something about him makes me think: gay. He's someone I've never seen before. Before I speak, I do that thing in my throat I always do in public to make myself be heard.

"We're here for the reading," I say.

"Starts at eight," the bartender says.

He's mixing margaritas. He's got one of those pencil mustaches and his hair is a buzzcut. That new look gay men are starting to get into.

"This is Hank Christian," I say. "And I'm Ben Grunewald."

The bartender looks at Hank, looks at me, puts a wedge of lime onto the salty rims of two frosty rocks glasses. He's smiling too big. He doesn't know what to say.

"We're the readers tonight," Hank says.

"Oh yeah!"

"Where's Wilbur Tucker?" I say.

"He's running a little late," the bartender says. "I've got you all set up."

"Eight sharp," I say. "Wilbur rings the bell at eight sharp. Who's going to ring the bell if he isn't here?"

"I will," the bartender says. "Or one of the cocktail waitresses."

"But he'll be here right?" I say. "Wilbur?"

The bartender's back is to us. He's reaching for the top shelf. If he's heard me, he doesn't let on. When he's turned around again, he's pouring Hennessy into snifters.

"So what do you boys want to drink tonight?" he asks. "Two drinks are on the house, after that they're half price."

"What about a big white stretch Cadillac limo," I say.

"That's new," he says. "What's in it?"

"No," I say, "I mean have you seen one tonight?"

7:45. NO BIG white stretch Cadillac limo. No Wilbur Tucker. No Sis. The bar is a group of drunken children in football jerseys. Hank goes to the rest room first. It's been a long day after a long night. He comes back with his thick wavy hair wet, his face scrubbed pink. I'm looking forward to a touch-up too. In the bathroom, though, there's only that same tiny mirror with soap splashes on it, the sharp smell of beer piss, a bar of cracked gray soap, and some paper napkins. The cold water on my face feels good but it only rubs the grease around. The soap helps. When my hair gets wet it just lays down flat on my head. I try rubbing my hands through my hair, but know there's no way to win at the game I'm playing.

7:55. NO WILBUR Tucker. No big stretch white Cadillac limo. No Sis. I'm on my second Red Eye when it happens. I've been too preoccupied with everything else and it hits me hard: I've never really read aloud to a group of people I didn't know. In the middle of my chest, the lightbulb, flickering. I double over. Running Boy, it's a panic attack and I can't breathe.

To speak aloud the things that are in my heart. The audacity of it.

I'm off my stool and on my way back to the john. But there's a commotion at the door. A man in a wheelchair is being wheeled in. A tank of oxygen hooked onto his chair. The man is old, real old, about to die old. That quick, I forget all about the bathroom and walk toward the guy. When I get to his feet sticking out, I go down on one knee. Take his hand in my hand. His good hand. The one with the cigarette in it. The other hand is crooked on his lap. Under the silver comb-over, inside those blue eyes, there he is. Wilbur Tucker. From deep inside and far away he looks at me. One side of the oxygen mask tilts up a smile. The slightest squeeze around my hand. He tries to speak but has to cough. Finally:

"I read your book, Grunewald," he says. "It's a good book."

8:00 SHARP. WILBUR Tucker in his chair stays close to the door but far enough he don't block access. He's clear across the room, he can't stand, let alone stand up, let alone get to the bar. No way that hand of Wilbur Tucker's could ever ring the fire bell.

Hank and I have flipped and I go first. The bartender takes hold of the clapper, pulls it hard, four times against the brass fire bell. The bell is so loud and so loud for so long it makes you cover your ears.

The silence after the loud bell.

When the bartender says my name he says *Gruneburg*.

I make my way to the podium, I don't hear the applause, but Hank says later, *man did you hear that applause*. My finger is sticking in the page of my book where I'll start. The podium, the big oak heft of it. To my right is the dirty window and outside it's Center Street. No big white stretch Cadillac Limo. To my left, the big brass fireman's bell. On the podium slanting up, my blue and green book, my first novel, reviewed in the *New York Times*, bought in France by Gallimard, about Idaho, the dreaded place where my heart sings, my home, its endless skies, the wind, the racist motherfuckers who live there. The spotlight is so bright in my eyes. The mic, out of the bright like some big black phallus, just in front of my mouth. But the mic's tilted too high. When I touch the mic to pull it down, the feedback sound. My lips start trembling and shit. My ass feels like shit spray. In the audience there's no Margaret, no big sis. No one to be the ears that can hear me. I make myself think of Wilbur, what it took to get himself here. My deep breath. When I hear my voice over the microphone, it's tiny, it's shaky, it's timid.

Cockless Most Miserable Little Ben at the bottom of hell.

The Catholic boy with a big apology.

All of heaven laughing.

AFTER THE READING, on Center Street, it's a wild Friday night. Loud music from basement bars. Cop cars flashing red, white, and blue. Hank and I walk with our suitcases, we don't know really where to. Just glad to be out in the air. On the street, no big white stretch Cadillac limos.

10:30. In the lobby of the Whitman Hotel it's finally quiet. The reception desk is white marble. Charles Russell reproductions on the wall. Cowboys and cows and Indians and sunsets. A couple straight-back wooden chairs. A cigarette machine. The night clerk is tall, his bones poke through his short sleeve purple shirt. He is smoking. Behind him is a clock that's a black cat whose eyes and tail move the seconds in opposite directions. I ask the clerk if we can sit someplace and have some water. Lots of water. The clerk points his long skeleton arm to our left, picks up the phone, dials a number, talks into the phone. The cigarette doesn't leave his mouth. Hank and I follow to where the clerk has pointed, through a coved archway into a big room, a lobby, that feels like no one ever goes in there. Tables and chairs, we try to find a place where it feels like we can sit. We settle on the table in the corner by the window. Hank and I set our suitcases down, sit our asses down. It's old, the hotel, kind of creepy. Fake wood paneling on the walls that go up to coved ceilings. Rock and roll somewhere from a back room.

I've never seen Hank so high. For a long moment we just stare at each other and don't say a word. Then we high slap our hands and start laughing. We are rolling around, trying hard to hold on to the excitement. How are bodies feel heard and seen the way writers are supposed to feel heard and seen. Two little boys, we're making weird sounds and jumping up and down.

Hank and I, our readings at the Blind Lemon, we were a hit.

For me, it took a couple sentences to get my voice calmed down. By the end of the first page, though, I'd hit my stride. The audience, I could feel them. My words and my voice speaking the words were holding the audience up. As if they were people in deep water, found my little rowboat, crawled on to safety, and were floating.

Then Hank. I got to watch Hank go to where I'd just been. His voice on his words wasn't no rowboat. We were all of us in the bar floating on his ocean liner big as the building. *Mother-fucker motherfucker motherfucker.* Gave us all permission. At one point, my eyes were closed and I was listening hard, the sudden awareness that my lips were moving to his words. Lip-synching. I quick opened my eyes to see if anyone had caught me. Thank God all the eyes were on Hank.

And something else, standing outside looking in like that, at Hank, my friend, behind the podium, his lips at the mic, I saw him in a way I'd never seen him before. I mean I know I've always admired Hank. But that night, he was one of King Arthur's knights or a cousin of Chief Joseph's. A warrior. Bold, big, full of light. Maybe, just maybe, someday I could see myself a warrior too.

Afterwards, there was a swarm of people and Hank and I got out our suitcases and sold a shitload of books. Could have sold more but we only took cash. Standing there in the middle of it all, people crowding around us, felt good, felt the way we were supposed to be feeling. People wanted their books signed. They wanted to talk about writing, to talk about New York City. People wanted to talk about the meaning of life. All the while, I'm scribbling away, fucking up my Catholic School penmanship. Still, I kept looking for my sis.

Two beers into it, talking to a guy from Idaho Falls and a

girl from Leadore, I remembered Wilbur Tucker. My eyes went straight to the door where his wheelchair had been.

Outside on the sidewalk in front of the Blind Lemon, on Center Street, as far as I could see, only street lamps and twenty year olds. No wheelchair, no oxygen tank, no Wilbur Tucker.

I was going to leave a note for Wilbur with the bartender, but Hank and I got so caught up that night, it wasn't until way later on the air mattress on Margaret's living room floor that I remembered.

Wilbur Tucker. I never got to thank him. To this day, twenty years later, I still remember I forgot. Now, more than ever I know how important a thank you from a student can be.

Sometimes that's all you got.

HANK GETS UP, does a little jig around the table. The way he moves is like the night at Judith's he danced to "April in Paris." In the lobby of the Hotel Whitman, Hank shaking his ass. After a while the double doors behind the curtain of orange hanging beads open and there's a blast of rock and roll. *Welcome to the Hotel California*. The waitress with her small round tray walks through the orange hanging beads. Big red hair, lots of cleavage. The skirt of her blue-striped polyester uni is short. Textured pantyhose. Spike heels. They click with every step she steps to our table in the corner by the window. She sets two glasses of water on our table and a yellow plastic pitcher.

"If you boys want cocktails," she says, "you've got to drink them in the bar."

I watch Hank watch her. When she goes back through the orange hanging beads, she doesn't close the doors.

It's no longer quiet in the lobby. I'm thinking of the old man in "A Clean, Well-Lighted Place." At least that's how I remember it. That's what it is for me, now that I'm an old man, memory: a short story by Hemingway about an old man in a café. Way too many *copitas*.

But the loud rock and roll doesn't bother me. I check Hank

to see and it doesn't bother him either. The world has just spun us around a loop we've never spun on before. Live rock and roll can't hurt us. Even when it's local and bad. We look at each other as if we stop looking at each other the night will go away. It never ceased to startle me how Hank and I could look at each other. Mad to love, mad to talk, mad to be saved. All that's important, all of it, we're full to bursting, we're talking talking talking.

MIDNIGHT. ACTUALLY THE black cat on the clerk's wall says 12:10. I finally take a breath. The lobby where we're sitting is twenty feet tall. On the walls, bad seams in the four-by-eight fake wood paneling. From the middle of the room, a huge swag light from the Fifties that hangs down – something too bright with gold projectiles that looks like the Jetsons. Two black marble columns. Black wrought iron tables, glass tops. White plastic outdoor chairs. Floors made of those tiny white square tiles. At the check-in counter, an orange and red throw rug. The deco sconce on the wall behind Hank's head pushes light up the shiny brown plastic wood.

"This place is weird and fucking ugly," I say.

"Historic landmark meets trailer park," Hank says.

About then, a woman steps through the orange beads. Mary Tyler Moore just off the golf course. Bette Davis eyes. My big sister, Margaret.

Some moments come along in your life, there's so much going on in them, you don't know what to feel first. Actually I always know what to feel first. I mean my body does. The problem comes after the moment passes and I don't know how to say it right, all the things I felt and in what order.

Here's some of it: just like always, my heart jumps up the way it always jumps. How high is going to depend on her. Then I'm sure of something. She doesn't show it, but I know. The way she makes her face have no expression. Her chin, the higher that chin gets, the more I can tell.

Shit-faced. My sister Margaret is totally shit-faced. I mean she's staggering.

The orange beads behind Margaret sway and clack against each other. Margaret stops, looks over at Hank and me. For a moment, that empty face, her chin a little higher, she pretends to, but really, she doesn't recognize who we are. Then it's like we're somebody she knows she thinks she must know, so she smiles, gives us a goofy laugh.

"Somewhere around here's a cigarette machine," she says. "You guys know where the cigarette machine is?"

Hank's black eyes are on me. He's watching me like a writer watches for humanity. That's when I remember. I mean how could I forget. But it really isn't a memory at all, I mean it's not in my head, the way everything, my body, gets heavy, slows down, sinks. There's a crash too. Hit by a fucking truck.

Margaret didn't make it to our reading.

I'm amazed at how I am a child. How much it hurts me that she didn't make it. The hurt is in my chest, the fire bell going off in my chest. So loud I have to cover my ears. My teeth at the back of my mouth grind down.

But this fire is a fire I can't feel for too long. It is too hot. Plus what's underneath. Something way too derelict, too dark, and I won't have any part of it.

HANK GIVES THE night clerk five bucks to watch our suitcases and at the cigarette machine I help Margaret with her change and pulling the right knob for her Virginia Slims. She's standing too close. Her hand and her perfect fingernails, her forearm against me. Hell, it ain't long and her whole body is leaning against me. I'm her little brother Benny she won't let go of. Before Margaret's got her cigarette lit, she's apologized over and over maybe five times.

"There was so much going on," she says. "And so many people. God, I didn't know I knew so many people. And we were having so much fun, and we were all drinking and some of us were pretty f'ing drunk and I didn't want to go crashing into your reading with twenty drunken people."

It makes sense what Margaret says. Immediately I'm sorry for the sulking, all the ways my heart's been sore.

"Hey, *no problemo*," I'm saying, "*no problemo. Nada y pues nada.*"

That's about it for my Spanish, besides *salon de belleza eres, mariscada de salsa verde*, a few cuss words, and a short poem by Lorca about the color green. Still, a part of me wonders why the fuck the sudden switch to a Romance language.

ON THE OTHER side of the hanging orange beaded curtain, it's the Round Up Room Friday night forty-five minutes before closing time. Everything glows toxic orange and it's jammed with people and smoke and noise. Up on the bandstand, the local band, in matching white western shirts and white cowboy hats, is singing "Desperado." Margaret's got both me and Hank by the arm, her in between. She's leading us through the bar. Really though, Hank and I are holding her up. Everyone we come to, Margaret makes a fuss, she pulls her mouth up close to their ears, she yells in their ears, and then everyone looks at Hank and me, sticks out their hand and laughs extra loud. Hank and I, all we can do is smile, shake hands. There's no way to hear a fucking thing. Except every once in a while, *stretch Cadillac* and *Happy Birthday*.

At the line of parquet where the dance floor starts, just then the band starts up with "China Grove." Jitterbugging and two-stepping, way too many bodies are way too drunk flying around in a cramped space. Making it across that dance floor is more like making it over an extreme sport obstacle course. Then, in the middle of all the bodies, in all the noise and smoke, Hank on one side of Sis, me on the other, there's a moment and a memory: Hank and me at the Spike.

Kevin's in the booth next to the bandstand with a bunch of other people. They all shout when they see us and clap, then scoot over to let us in. Hank smashes in against Margaret,

Margaret smashes against me, Kevin smashed in on my other side. Three other people at the table, two men and a woman we're introduced to. They all look right off the golf course, but there's no way I can get their names. Kevin is saying something to me but I can't hear. I move my ear in real close.

"Your sister had a great time tonight," he says.

I lean back and look at Kevin. He's a sturdy guy, thick in the neck and his wrists and chest and arms. A blue and green Hawaiian shirt, a couple buttons open down the front. Blonde. That blonde thick hair out of his shirt and on his arms. What I see is how much Kevin loves my sister. What a pleasure it's been for him to give her this magical night. That quick it's pretty clear to me that I need to give the shit up. My sister is in love with this man and he's in love with her and he's gone through a lot to get the limo and set the whole night up and all. And those plans were made long before Big Ben decided in the Strand Book Store back in New York City that he and Hank were coming to Idaho. Really, to hold on to the fact that my sis didn't make it to the reading all of a sudden seems selfish and silly.

And something else. Some part of me sees a bigger picture. Sees me and Kevin as two guys in competition for my sister's attention. At that very moment, in fact, I'm the guy sitting between him and his loved one. What I feel next is a shitload of drut. I immediately want to get up and get away from in between them. But there's no way. I can barely move. So I take a deep breath, breathe in all that smoky orange alcohol air, and just let it the fuck go.

When the cocktail waitress gets to us, Margaret orders margaritas. Hank tries to say no. I try to say no. But everyone is so trashed and it's so loud, it's no use.

THE SINGER AT the microphone pushes back his sweaty white cowboy hat and announces to the crowd last call. There's high whistling and boos and one long cowboy yahoo. Then something strange, something you'd never figure. The band goes into a song my ears can't believe they're hearing. I look over to Hank and his black eyes are already looking right at me. That bass line, you can't mistake it. Lou Reed and "Walk On the Wild Side." Then from out of nowhere it's the Mormon Lady from the bookstore. Frieda, Hank said her name was Frieda and she wasn't a Mormon at all. She's standing at the end of our table and asking Hank for a dance. Hank's got that I'm-such-a-smooth-ass-lady-killer smile on his face. Margaret loves it that a woman has broken the rules and asked the man for the dance. She puts her Virginia Slim into the ashtray, laughs hard, big wide smile, rubbing her palms together. Something in her face changes. Her eyes. She is looking at Hank in a whole different way. I know that look. It's the way she looks at our father.

We all got to get up so Hank can get out. The dance floor is too crowded, so he can't get far away from our table. But he wants to. I know how stingy he is with his dance moves. Especially since everybody at the table will be watching his ass. There's not room to breathe, let alone move, but somehow Hank manages to get Frieda's butt toward the table and his own self behind her. They do a moderate straight guy two-step dance. Still, whatever Hank does, it always turns out sexy.

We're all sitting there, admiring the fuck out of Hank. There are two margaritas lined up in front of me. My elbows on the table, I'm smoking one of Kevin's Marlboros. The wood table is a mess of empty glasses, piled high ashtrays, cigarette butts. My big sis is on my left, Kevin on the right. Both of them know what this song's about and because it's what it's about they think it's about me. Margaret leans forward, Kevin leans forward, and they smile at each other across my chest. It's like I'm a puppy and the song is "How Much is that Doggie in the Window?" Still, though, it's cool.

That's when it happens, somewhere around in there, the moment. Margaret lights another Virginia Slim, inhales, swallows the smoke, blows the smoke out, leans into me, puts her lips right up against my ear.

"I'm surprised you're not out there shaking your ass," she says. "You love so much how people watch you when you shake your ass."

Every word that Sis's lips speak, clear as a fucking bell. My chest jumps up to catch a breath and it comes out a little laugh. I'm surprised really and trying to figure out how to take this shit in.

What Margaret's just said is right on. Nothing's better than to be lost in a song and I'm dancing and maybe somewhere out there people are watching. But nobody knows that about me. Except her. Margaret's the only person.

The pain between my eyes again. Dizzy. Maybe the Return of the Cockless, Most Miserable of All. How well my big sis knows Little Ben, how predictable he is. I am amazed at how I am a child.

Shaking your ass.

There's something mean in the way she's said it. And not just mean. Downright cruel. How her chin went up. Her empty face. In that tiny instant how her lip curled up. For a moment, I didn't even recognize her.

Her little brother, who's not at all like their father, would like nothing more than to be like their father, but has been banished from the world of men. My big sister Margaret knows this all too well. How when we were kids, that's how she got to me. I can't tell you how many times. And what this little brother does best is something their father would never fucking ever ever do. No real man, really, would ever do that with his hips. Just look at Hank.

Shake your ass.

From over Frieda's shoulder, Hank looks down at me, gives me a wink. That guy can always make me smile. I down the margarita closest to me, set the empty glass aside, drag the next full one over the slippery wood and set it in the ring in front of me. I smash out the Marlboro. The ashtray is nasty ashes and smashed-out cigarette butts. Right next to my elbow, Margaret's tanned elbow. Her perfect fingernails. She's pulling hard on her Virginia Slim. Her eyes are still looking right into mine.

My sister Margaret's auburn eyes. Inside in there, there it is.

Idaho.

This is what we do in Idaho.

We get drunk.

We go to truth-telling tequila land, the place in us where our dark mother dwells, and in the middle of a crowded loud bar, we set our target, we find the moment, we strike the blow.

I know I can hurt you and because I can, I will.

9.

Sweat lodge

THAT NEXT MORNING IN MY SISTER'S DOUBLE-WIDE, I
wake up early, get my stuff together. I don't try to be quiet. Make
all the noise I have to make. Every step shakes the whole house.
But Margaret doesn't wake up. My guess is that morning nothing's
going to wake her up. I call a cab and by seven o'clock Hank and
I are in a blue Chevy Citation, *Pocatello Taxi* on the side, black
lettering curled over a red Bannock Rose, our backpacks, Hank's
brown faux leather suitcase, my powder blue one in the trunk,
headed for the rental car place. Hank, of course, thinks I'm fucking
nuts.

"Trust me on this one, Hank," I say. "I got to get out of here."

HUNGOVER. A JUNE morning in Idaho and it's already hot and
way too bright. Hank and I, all the windows rolled down in our
rented red-orange Ford Pinto, drive the old two-lane Highway 30
to my brother Ephraim's house in Fort Hall. Fort Hall's just a
wide spot in the road on the Bannock Shoshone Indian reservation. A trading post on one side of the highway, and on the other,
across the railroad tracks, low government buildings set in among
the cottonwoods.

When I was a kid, my family traveled from Tyhee to Blackfoot every Sunday. Grandma and Grandpa and most all our
relatives lived in Blackfoot. When we passed through Fort Hall,
my mother made sure all the doors were locked. More often
than not, too, we were praying the rosary. Any chance my mother

got, she prayed the rosary. Hell was such a terrible place. About
the time Fort Hall rolled by outside the Buick's locked doors
and rolled up windows, we were generally somewhere near the
fifth and final mystery, whether it was glorious, joyful, or sorrowful – usually sorrowful, and all there was, was only ten more Hail
Marys to get through and the damn thing would be over.

Turn left off the highway and a quarter of a mile on the dirt
road is Ephraim's house. That morning, we could see the smoke
from the fire as soon as we turned off the highway.

Ephraim lives in a beige HUD house with his granny and
his mom and any other relatives who need a place to stay. He's
always got the place looking good. New roof. New siding, and the
addition to the back of the house for the new laundry room.
The lawn mowed. A row of apple trees and a row of cherry. Rasp-
berries and blackberries. Big weeping willow in the front yard.
Birds all over the place.

Quite some drama when we drive into the yard. Clouds of
dust and barking dogs chase the car, other dogs chase cats and
the cats are running. I park between a dead pink Nash Rambler
and a green Oldsmobile 88 on cinderblocks. Behind the Olds
is the chicken coop. Behind the chicken coop, a ways out, in the
middle of a bare field, is the fire pit and the fire. Ephraim's
standing out there. Looks like a scarecrow with his big hat and
floppy pants. When he sees us pull in, he waves, starts walking
toward us.

When Hank and I open our doors, on Hank's side there's a
yellow lab with three legs wanting him for lunch. On my side,
two dogs, Border Collie and Austrian Shepherd mix. Between
them they have two eyes. No way I'm going to move another inch.

One holler from Ephraim sends the dogs off under the
Chinese Elm.

Ephraim's a big man. Got twenty pounds on me. Solid. He's
wearing his straw hat he bought in Bermuda and an extra lovely
blue and green flowered shirt and what looks like pajama bottoms. He's smoking his ever-present More Menthol. As he gets

closer, I notice he's wearing his Birkenstocks and socks, too, even though it's hot, because he has to be careful with his feet.

"Brother dear!" he calls out. "Welcome to the rez."

Ephraim's nickname on the rez is Owlfeather. I'm just a little taller, not much, so we fit together well. Our arms go around each other. We turn our faces in and kiss. Ephraim's wearing his light-sensitive glasses, so I can't really see his eyes.

"You look tired," he says. "You okay?"

"Margaritaville," I say. "I need to sweat."

Hank standing there looks like he doesn't know what to do. I think maybe he thinks he's supposed to kiss Ephraim, too.

"This is Hank," I say.

Ephraim holds his hand out and Hank steps up and Ephraim takes Hank's hand, lays his other hand on top.

"Nice to meet you," Ephraim says. "I liked your book."

Never seen Hank blush before, but there he is in the high noon sun, Hank Christian as red as a beet.

Inside the house, the blinds are drawn and a fan's going in every room. The TV's on. Ephraim's mom, Rose, is on the sofa, a big Navaho rug with shades of gray and red spread over the sofa. She and Ephraim look so much alike. She's a nurse at the Fort Hall clinic and she's in her pink nurse's uniform on her lunch hour. On her plate is a bologna sandwich, one slice of bologna between two slices of white bread. She's drinking a Tab.

"Benny Grunewald!" she says. "We never get to see you anymore."

"This is Hank," I say.

"Make yourself a sandwich!" she says. "You guys must be hungry."

In between the doorway to the bedrooms and the front door, Ephraim's grandmother's in her old rocking chair. Her hair in pin curls. On the dining room table next to her, a glass of water with her teeth in it. She's fanning herself with a paper fan, red Chinese letters and the name of a Chinese restaurant. On her shoulder's her pet monkey, Charlie Brown. He's eating a banana.

"Hi, Granny," I say, "This is Hank."

"You boys going to sweat today?" Granny says. "Boy it's sure going to be hot."

In the middle of my chest, the lightbulb. Big Ben's always gung-ho for a sweat lodge. Then when it comes time, Little Ben's the one who's got to step into a hot dark hole in the afternoon. Ephraim knows how scared I can get, and when I look over at him, he takes a puff on his cigarette. His eyes look at my fear like it was just another part of the day.

THE REASON YOU go into a sweat lodge is so you can go back to the womb. The dark, the heat, the water hissing on the rocks, the smoke; it all comes together to put you back in a place where you're naked and it's cramped and hard to breathe, so you can come out the other end with the feeling of a new beginning.

That afternoon, under the dome of cross-hatched willows covered by hides and canvas and heavy blankets, Hank and I sit, our skimpy white towels wrapped around our middles, knee to naked knee. When all the hot rocks are handed in and put in place into the fire pit, Ephraim reaches up and pulls the flap down. So sudden the pitch black. The pitch black, and then from out of the black, the sparkling pile of smoky red rocks only inches from my bare feet. An arm's length from my face.

The problem is I'm not in a womb. I'm in a pressure cooker.

At first I think the pressure cooker is my hangover, so I'm bearing down, the heat crackling down my back. I inhale deep and when I exhale, try and blow the shit out. But then it's my claustrophobia kicking in and panic starts and when panic starts, that's what it is, panic. The flickering lightbulb in the middle of my chest is a blaring fire alarm and I can't run and I'm totally fucked.

Between a rock and a hard place. We've been invited by Ephraim to participate in a Shoshone ritual and I'm trying hard to pray and be holy and respectful. I'm inside his sweat lodge, a place specifically designed to force you to confront the ghosts inside you. And believe me, the afternoon after the morning I left my big sister's house, I have some old ghosts to confront.

Plus, I've brought Hank. Hank's never gone into a sweat lodge before and he's looking to me for what to expect. Just what I need. To be a fucking role model. And believe me, it's no consolation that Hank, his white towel now wrapped around his head, has his whole naked writhing body smashed up against mine. Both of us, our mouths eating dirt and grass, trying to get to the last bit of oxygen.

Lying there, the heat crashing down, in the dark, can't breathe, the terror. Just as I look, a big rock clunks down into the fire. A burst of heat against my face and shoulder and everything stops. Deep in my chest, my heart, an old rag doused with gas, is the fire. This time, it isn't a word *claustrophobia*, or some blind fear. This time it's an Idaho Shit Storm, and the guy without a dick at the bottom of hell is back. Little Ben The Most Miserable of All.

Terror like that, when you feel it, time can go on forever.

1972. MY FIRST job was working as a counselor for Social Services at Idaho State University. Don't ask me why, but my boss made me advisor of the Indian Club.

Those first days on my job mostly I wanted to hide. So I gave myself the job of alphabetizing the books in the Indian Club's library. A big room in one of the oldest buildings on campus. The safest place I could find. Tall ceilings, big windows you could sit in, hardwood floors that creaked. Morning sunlight coming in. My morning cup of coffee. That's where I ran into a copy of *Bury My Heart at Wounded Knee*.

That particular morning, I was standing on a stepladder, putting books onto a high shelf alphabetically, my job, but the copy of *Bury My Heart at Wounded Knee* in my hands had taken me over. I was halfway through it, couldn't stop, and I was out of breath. There was nothing else in the world but me hunched over that book. The heartbreak of it.

A memory: on the yellow school bus number 24, when I was ten or eleven, I'd wanted to sit in a seat but the Indian woman in the seat behind was saving it for her friends. She was a big woman who always wore a long blue wool coat. Her hair in a page-boy. Big red lips. Both her hands were spread out wide across the top of the seat. She was in high school. No way in hell that woman was going to let me sit down.

"You big fat slob!"

That's what I called her, what my mother called them, Indians. Big Fat Slobs.

The woman didn't say anything back. Just gave me the evil-eye staredown.

Years later, there I am in the Indian Club Library, standing on a stepladder, lost in an old staredown, *big fat slob* on my lips, the heavy orange book *Bury My Heart at Wounded Knee* cuffed between my wrists and elbows – America's racism, my racism, the shock of recognition, going through my head, making my heart sore.

It took me a while to realize that a young Native American man, a big hefty guy, had walked into the room.

"Where'd you buy them pants?" the young man, Ephraim, had said.

Them pants. The famous green corduroy pants. Seventies' cut, high waist, sans-a-belt, bell bottoms. Tight at the top, loose at the bottom. No pockets on the ass.

Now when people ask me how I got so into Native American spirituality, I just tell them *green corduroy pants.*

Eight months later, it's Indian Days at Idaho State and Ephraim has his tipi set up on the quad. I am wearing my green corduroy pants. When I duck down and pass through the flap of canvas, when I stand up again, I'm in a whole different world. First time in my life in a tipi. Buckskin, beaded backrests, buffalo hides, stacks of Pendleton blankets. A fire in the fire pit. So much to look at I quit looking. The feeling I have is I am home with someone in their beautiful house.

It all goes by in a blur. Ephraim shows me how to always walk to the left, where to sit. I sit and he picks up his long pipe with gold threading on it. Ephraim takes a whittled piece of stick, puts it in the fire, lights the end of the stick, then brings the fire to his pipe and lights it. Smoke pours out of the pipe, out of his mouth and nose as he offers the pipe to the four directions. The whole time he's whispering prayers in Shoshone. When his prayers are finished, Ephraim hands the pipe to me. The pipe to me is like any tool when it's in my hands. It doesn't work. A lot like my dick. But I am trying with the pipe and I smoke the pipe and move it around in the four directions in some kind of way like Ephraim did and I guess I'm praying, too. After I hand him back the pipe, we share a cup of tea. A special herbal tea.

Then: "Are you ready for this?" he says.

Ephraim's eyes have a slant that makes you think of Cleopatra and the Egyptians. Dark brown, a touch of copper. Long black hair down to his shoulders. A curl in that hair, the French in him. That day his hair is braided and he's dressed in his finery. Beaded moccasins, leggings, porcupine breastplate, turquoise necklace, turquoise bracelet, silver hanging on him everywhere. More French in the shape of his smooth nose. How his lips fold out longer than you think they should. The way how they point up in the center like a Kewpie doll's.

"We're going to make a promise now," he says. "In blood."

Ephraim and I, we could talk about just about anything. Art history, Walt Whitman, Vietnam, Carl Jung. Fort Hall and the reservation where he was raised. Tyhee, where I was raised. Him an Indian kid on the reservation on one side of the boundary. Me a tybo, a white boy growing up on the other. Not more than ten miles apart our whole lives. We talked about our fathers, our mothers, and most especially, the history of the West and the story of his people. Racism. I really loved it the way he put up with all my dumb white-guy questions. But what we were really talking about, we couldn't talk about. Neither one of us had the words. And if we did, our lips just couldn't form them.

Over the years, Ephraim and I've had some good laughs over them green corduroy pants. How they looked, what they meant. The way we were innocent like we'll never be again.

Blood brothers. No way we could do that these days. Body fluids are different now.

THE PROMISE. IT took us a while and a bunch of cigarettes to decide what we wanted to promise each other. I had some trouble with the word love but I figured I was just a white guy and needed to get over it.

What we came up with was this: *no matter what happens, I will keep you with love in my heart. I'll help you out whenever I can. I will be kind. I'll respect you and the choices you make. If I don't agree with you, I may tell you I disagree, but I won't stop loving you. This sharing of blood marks this promise and makes it real. I'll keep this promise until I die.*

Propinquity. It takes everything I have. I let this big Indian chief guy take hold of my right hand. He lays my hand wrist up onto his knee. He picks up the bowie knife, pulls the knife out of its sheath, lays the shiny silver blade across my wrist.

That's when things start to change. He starts to giggle.

"I've never done anything like this before," he says.

It was his gay nerves, that was his problem. But of course we weren't gay yet.

Plus his bowie knife was dull. Maybe it's the herbal tea spirit, but it ain't long and Ephraim and I, a couple of misplaced Idaho boys, we get to laughing so hard, we can't hold still long enough to get the knife anywhere near a wrist. Laughing around inside the tipi that day's when I first fall in love with him, my blood brother, Ephraim. Never knew I could laugh like that 'til then.

Must have taken us hours, but finally, my wrist looking like a hand saw had been to it, raggedy pieces of skin sticking up and shit. One clear line of blood bubbling up, and Ephraim's wrist, how I finally couldn't stand it and leaned into the knife hard, maybe a little too hard, the yelp out of me when I saw the pain in Ephraim's eyes, finally. Finally we each had a proper line of red blood and we pressed our wrists together, blood flowing into blood, and we promised.

To hold each other in our hearts.

To help each other when we can.

To be kind.

To agree to disagree.

With blood.

With love.

INSIDE THE SWEAT lodge, forever it's only dark, only hot, smoky, and there is no air. Inside the pressure cooker there is no breath. No sound. Nothing moves. Not my belly or my hand or my legs. My mouth is full of sand. I wonder if my eyes are open, then I've forgotten how to open them, or what open eyes are like. Finally a glow, something shiny, deep, and alive.

From where my head is on the ground, the fire pit is a huge mountain of lava glowing red. The whole world is red and is on fire.

Something then that creeps over me, or out of me. It's a sensation from down low, although how my body is, inside or out, up or down, I don't know. It's when it comes up over my back, crosses my shoulders, that it's in my head.

Fear is no longer a word that can say it. Not panic, not claustrophobia.

I am the Most Miserable of All, the cockless man at the bottom of hell. I've always been in hell. Was born in hell. Raised in hell. I've always been alone down here in hell. Where there is no hope and the Catholic Fuckers in heaven are laughing. I'm crying, and I've always been crying. It's the only way I know how to gather myself up into a self, to be.

So much hope in a hard-on.

So far from grace.

Terror like this can go on forever.

Out of the dark a hand grabs a hold of mine. Ephraim's

across the fire pit, so it has to be Hank's. As if that hand can see in the dark it slaps flat palm to palm into mine. Holds my hand in a death grip. I squeeze back.

Fuck is this ever going to end.

There's a loud sound and a bright light and the bright light is the sun and the flap is open and there is breath. The way that moment is dramatic. The fresh air and the sun rushing in. I take a big deep breath of that air, then look over close at Ephraim. At first he's just part of the bright, then his eyes. They're scared a way I've never seen them. And his lips, how he doesn't know what to do with them. Sweat coming off him in buckets, chest going up and down. And Hank. There it is, Hank's hand still sucked onto mine. He's leapt up onto his knees. His face pushing out into the open air.

"Something is really going on," Ephraim says. "It ain't ever got this hot before!"

I'm slow slow to breathe again, and when I do, I feel the scorch. Another breath and the mountain of lava is gone and I'm not that guy in the bottom of hell. I'm me, Ben Grunewald, the luckiest guy. Another breath and I'm still me and the world starts to move again. Relief or love, fresh air in my lungs, whatever it is that feels so good. Outside there's a killdeer bird. Gusts of Idaho wind through the open flap.

Breathe and listen to what you can hear. The water on the rocks. The steam. It makes me smile that I can hear the steam. The rocks in the fire pit so red they're pink or purple, or some new color altogether.

The Most Miserable at the Bottom of Hell is gone.

Breathe and the world's right there for you to see. The terror's gone that covers it up. In front of my eyes, dirt real and flesh and my eyes can't get enough.

My brother Ephraim. His dark eyes with the lick of copper in them, the Asian lids exotic Cleopatra. The two hundred pounds of him. The sweat on his skin. His sunburnt muddy arms. His red neck. My *Indin* brother's a redneck.

Hank's hand in mine is still a vise grip. He looks over at me a look. Mud on his face, in his hair. For a tiny moment, all in the world there is worth seeing is burnt into those black eyes. He squeezes my hand even more, then lets go. Lays his head down on his muddy towel. He wraps his body into a ball, his back to me, his eyes looking up at the sky and the sun. All flesh and muscle, the long black curls of his hair, the way in marble Michelangelo did hair. Skin white as marble. The slant of sun across his shoulder, mud on his shoulder, mud on his back, his ass. Drips of sweat making pools on the earth. The slow way air comes in and out of his chest.

We keep the flap open the rest of the afternoon. Something unheard of, really. That a sweat lodge can be that hot. Breath and then breath and then breath, one long sweaty afternoon inside a cave looking out, watching the sun go down. Ephraim and Hank and me. The wind, the killdeer bird, breath and breath and breath. Cramped and naked coming out the other end.

LATER, FRESH AND new, cleansed by fire, we're showered and dressed. I'm sitting in a blown-out blue-green lawn chair next to a sagebrush as big as the Ford Pinto. There's a tall cool drink of water in my fist. I'm wondering where fear goes when it leaves. My eyes look for it, the way terror lays on things, hides behind, but I don't look for long. I know where terror goes, somewhere inside your breath, so I take a long drink of cool water, swallow. When I take a deep breath, I'm safe and the sun is in my eyes so I have to squint and I don't even remember terror anymore, and really what's the big deal about some Catholic nightmare version of me.

Hank pulls up a stump next to me. He's sitting lower than me and I have to look down. Hank leans forward on his haunches, breathes in deep the sagebrush and the sunset. Once more there he goes again, he slaps his hand into mine, holds my hand tight. I set my glass of water down.

His face in the low gold sun. I think maybe he wants me to

206 | TOM SPANBAUER

look at his face in the sun, so I do. His hair combed back off his forehead, his cheeks burnt red from sweat lodge heat. Under that, his skin a color I've never seen in Manhattan. Moments go by and I'm all of a sudden not sure what's going on and maybe there's something I should do. That's when I get it. Hank's trying to get his mouth to work right. I look away then, because it's too much, what I can see, but Hank pulls my hand in close.

"That's someplace I've never been to," Hank says. "Thought I'd been everywhere."

Hank makes a point of looking his eyes full on into mine. It never ceased to startle me the way Hank and I could look at each other. That golden sun making his face glow. Too long he looks, but I don't look away. He's still trying to talk.

Finally: "I don't know how to thank you."

"Thank Ephraim," I say.

"I will," Hank says, "but still, you brought me here."

"You'll never be able to repay me," I say.

That jumps Hank's chest up. He's laughing now or so I think. That's when he does something, then I don't know what the fuck to do. He takes my hand and places my hand on his shirt, above his heart. Laughing or crying, really it's hard to tell. Whatever it is, Hank can't talk.

After a while I figure I'll talk.

"What was it?" I ask. "That was so new?"

Hank just keeps holding my hand on his heart. Under his T-shirt, his marble skin, his chest hair, his nipple. I'm trying to keep thinking about his heart.

"Right now," Hank says, "I don't know how to say. But I'm working on it."

ON THE PICNIC table under the Chinese Elm, the feast Ephraim's mother and grandmother have made. Fry bread. Roast beef stew with potatoes and onions and tomatoes. Corn on the cob. Coleslaw. A big pitcher of purple Kool-Aid. White paper napkins and silverware on a red checkered tablecloth. The shadows going long. The dogs at our feet. Grandma's put her teeth in and her crazy little pet monkey Charlie Brown's on her shoulder eating fry bread. Ephraim's mom. How his face is hers. Two copies of my book, two of Hank's, on the table, signed, to Rose, and to Granny. We're brushing away the summer flies. Mosquitoes at sunset.

GOT TO GO *pal.*

Over the past thirty-six years, I've said *got to go pal* to Ephraim a couple of times. And he's said it to me. We've been through some tough times, him and me. My divorce, our sexuality, coming out, blood brothers, and for a while there we thought, maybe even another kind of brother as well. And then there was the new gay designer disease that everybody was freaking out on.

But we're together. We've always had our promise. The ritual of that promise. And we've always come back. And we always will.

Hank and I never made a promise like that. By the time it got to us, 1988, cutting our wrists and sharing blood, all hope was gone and it wasn't safe.

Maybe even if we couldn't have shared the blood, we could've still shared the words. Maybe that evening after the sweat lodge, just before supper, when Hank pulled the stump up next to my lawn chair. In those moments, in that gold piece of sunlight, the world smelling of sagebrush and fry bread, terror nowhere around, Hank holding my hand onto his heart, I could have risked it and spoke in my clear voice the words that were true in my heart.

Hey, Hank, while we're here let's promise each other the way Ephraim and I have promised.

We could've that day. We were that close. We could have done it easy. Looked in each other's eyes and promised love. If only I'd spoken the words.

Or maybe if I'd have made the joke about the hair.

Maybe that would have been enough.

10.
Sister

THE LAST LEG OF OUR JOURNEY. BOISE IS TWO HUNDRED
and seventy miles away. Five days to go and Hank and I will be
back to Manhattan.

Our night at Ephraim's was another late one. The three of
us on his long couch, percolator coffee and talking talking, listening to Ephraim's albums that are stacked on the hi-fi. Beethoven,
Schumann, Tchaikovsky, Merle Haggard. Ephraim lighting one
More Menthol off another. The smell of the cigarettes.

Hank and I have been in Idaho three days and it's our first
night without booze. And so quiet. Outside the screen door,
crickets and frogs. The way the three of us sit there in the low light,
my left knee against Ephraim's, my right knee against Hank's.
Like I am finally home. A couple of times I start to talk about the
Most Miserable, who's been following me around. It's the perfect
time and place to talk, but when I step up to say something,
there's nothing. Most Miserable disappears when I try to put
words on him. Which just adds to the problem. Finally, I just give
in. The naked guy with no dick at the bottom of hell just won't
let himself be talked about. Not yet. Maybe this is the same
place as Hank's. Where he'd never been before that he couldn't
talk about.

It's about two o'clock when Hank, his head against the back
of the couch, his eyes closed and his mouth open, just starts
snoring away.

All Ephraim's got is a single bed, so my bed is four big

cushions on the floor. Either that or it's sleep with his mother, or granny.

"Too bad," Ephraim says, "there's not more room on the couch."

"He is a beauty," I say. "Ain't he?"

"You're like me," Ephraim says. "We always fall for the same kind of guy."

"What kind of guy is that?" I say.

"Straight."

THIS DAY ON our way to Boise is Monday or Tuesday, I think. The next day, Wednesday, Reuben and Sal and Gary will drive us up in their Jeep to Atlanta, Idaho. The ghost town in the Trinity Mountains and our reading in the Old Town Hall.

Hank is driving. For some reason, and I have no idea why, we're driving down the main street, North Arthur, in Pocatello. The Interstate to Boise bypasses Pocatello altogether, but there we are, driving through downtown Pocatello, past all those old buildings. Idaho First National Bank, Fargo's, Molinelli's Jewelers, Bitton-Tuohy, the Oasis Bar, the Chief Theater.

The windows are rolled down and even the wind is hot. Our backpacks are in the back seat. Hank's faux leather brown suitcase, my powder blue one are in the trunk. Hank's in his Hawaiian shorts and his wifebeater, flip-flops. Me, I'm sunning my Manhattan white feet on the dashboard, in my cutoffs and Fruit of the Loom T. The best thing about driving is the open windows and the wind and the music on the FM stations. Golden Oldies. Music from the Sixties and Seventies. Back in Manhattan, there's no time for golden oldies.

Both Hank and I see her at the same time.

Margaret walking out of JC Penney. Always when I see my big sis, something inside me does that little jump. Hank lets out a New York whistle that stops cabs. It's so loud everyone on the whole block looks around.

It all happens so fast I can't do anything to stop it. My hand

211 I Loved You More

goes over to cover Hank's mouth but stops halfway because there's no use. The whistle is blowing and there's nothing can stop it. I want to smack Hank and tell him to shut it, but how's he to know what's going on with me and my sis.

And something else: already I can tell. Big Ben has made his decision. And Little Ben is trembling. At my sternum, in the middle of my chest, the lightbulb that you can see the filament flashing. Time to run.

After all the years, Margaret and me, finally the moment is here.

Hank pulls into the gravel parking lot across from the old Dairy Queen right next to Sis's blue Mazda sports car. The crackling of the tires against the gravel. Hank pushes the silver-handled gearshift knob into park. Turns off the key. Always the bright Idaho sun and the gusts of Idaho wind. No place where there's shade. No place to hide. Hank's looking at me like he knows more than I think he knows. That look on his face like his message on his answering machine. *You know what you got to do.* Just like that, Hank slaps his hand into mine, holds it there.

What I got to do. Even though I don't know exactly what that is. I open my door, step out into the sun. Close the door behind me. Lean against the Pinto. Sis is close enough to touch when she stops. She's wearing a blue and white sun dress. Over her Bette Davis eyes, large, octagonal, clear-framed sunglasses. Her purse is something like fishnet, a yellow woven bag over her shoulder. Yellow sandals. A gold *M* around her neck on a gold chain.

When she speaks, her voice is almost a whisper, an excited whisper, the way she's always spoken to me when she knows that something's wrong.

"What are you doing here?" she says. "You left so early. I didn't know where you went."

I put my hand on my forehead, my fingers together, shade on my eyes.

"Ephraim's," I say.

"I figured," she says. "But I don't have his number."

"Sober yet?" I say.

"Oh, I know," she says. "That was quite some birthday. Are you leaving today?"

"Boise," I say. "We're going to Atlanta with Reuben, Sal, and Gary."

"Are you going to stop in Jerome and see dad?" she asks.

I take my hand away from above my eyes. My eyes squint. Put my hand down to my side. Really, I don't know what to do with my hand.

Idaho.

This is what we do in Idaho. We smoke, we pray, we get drunk, we walk the *via dolorosa*, carry the old wooden cross back to father.

"No," I say.

"He's getting old, Ben," she says. "Since mom's died he's a different man."

"I'm not stopping in Jerome," I say.

"You're just angry," she says. "Ben, I told you. I'm sorry we missed your reading."

It's all there in my chest. All that I want to say and don't know how. I'm a kid again and my big sis has just told me she's spent my allowance I lent her and she's not going to pay it back. A big baby torpor in me, a tantrum the size of hell. Yet I don't dare speak my mind. I can't take the risk. From day one, she's the person in the whole world who can love me back.

Big Ben has other plans, though.

"Margaret."

As soon as I say her name, Little Ben is sobbing. Right there in the Idaho sun on North Arthur in Pocatello next to the Dairy Queen. The sound that comes out of me is the sound of the Most Miserable of All. How loud it is. As if that sound isn't even coming from me. I'm surprised by the power, the way it just comes blasting out of my chest. The suffering I can hear in me as if I am an audience. Then too I wonder about Hank behind me in the car, what he'll think. Yet I'm so relieved. But then there's the high whine, the tears, the chest sob, all the weird pauses for breath, the snot, the way my chin is moving like I have nothing to do with it. My shaking hands. My shaking body. I'm barely standing up.

All this because my sister missed my reading. I'm ashamed for being so petty. The longer I stand there, though, the more I just let myself feel, the clearer things get. All my life I believed my love for my mother and my sister was their only hope. I was their only hope. Without me all they had was my father. With my father they were lost, lonely, ridiculed, enslaved, full of fear. Then I was born, their beautiful boy. The bringer of a new testament of hope and joy and beauty.

And in return they loved me for it. That is, when they didn't hate me. After all, I was their boy, not a man, the kind of man a woman wants, my father. God the father. Even I wanted him.

My sister would say jump and I'd say how high.

"Margaret."

I look up into my sister's big, octagonal, clear-plastic sunglasses. Behind the dark glasses, those eyes. She's freaked that I'm losing it on North Arthur. She's saying *Benny Benny Benny* and she's tried to touch me a couple of times and she tries again but I won't let her touch me. She thinks I'm just her crazy little gay artist brother and one of his dramas. I hate how her voice has that big sister sound.

"Margaret."

"Margaret," I say, "I love you too much. Too much for a grown man to love his sister. So much more than you'll ever love me. I'm going to go away for a while, far away."

"You're always so sensitive," she says. "It was just a joke about your ass."

"Sis," I say, "I can't be like this and live anymore."

"Oh, Benny," she says, "I love you too. I'm your bestest buddy and you're biggest fan."

Margaret ducks her head down after she's said that. Her hand is going through her purse. For the Virginia Slims I can see down there at the bottom. That's when her glasses slip off her face. The big, clear-plastic octagonals bounce on something then land somewhere down on the gravel. At the same time, Margaret and I bend down and both her hand and my hand are on the glasses. Before I know it, Margaret's got her arms around me. She pulls me in close. I don't try and stop her. On our knees on the gravel between two parked cars, I hold her close, too, press tight the yellow fishnet purse between us. Sis, the person who was how I learned to love. How I learned tenderness. How she always held me when I cried.

I am crying. Trying to stop, trying to breathe, but really just crying and crying. Finally, one last big deep loud sob goes through me. Cramps my toes, makes my knees weak, pushes up out of me like vomit. Pain like that. How we carry it around and don't even know it.

My chin on her shoulder, my eyes can't see for tears. Snot pouring out I try and keep off her sundress.

"I won't ever love you like this again," I say. "You got to understand. And I'm not stopping in Jerome."

The palm of Margaret's hand pats my back.

"I understand," she says. "I understand."

BUT MARGARET DIDN'T understand. Not that day.

Years later, and we're not young and we're sick and we're getting old, and our mother is dead and our father is dead, Margaret will call me on the telephone.

"What happened between us?" she'll ask. "We used to be so close."

My end of the phone line will be silent. And Margaret will cry. The way I cried that day. So no, that day, in the rust-red Pinto with Hank, pulling out of the gravel parking lot onto North Arthur, Margaret, no way she understood.

For years and years, she and I had been life for one another. We'd saved each other from abuse, from death even. The love, the resentment. How profoundly it had shaped my world.

Now that was over.

In the Idaho sun, on the corner in front of the Dairy Queen, when I look out the back window, my big sister in her matching shoes and purse, her big, clear-plastic octagonal dark glasses, waving. The same old pain in my chest. How lonely Margaret looked. Just like my mother. My mother, my sister. But I knew this new thing about myself, and because I knew, I'd taken a step. The first step.

And I could never go back.

ON I-84, SUN beating down, wind. The Idaho desert. The green exit sign says, *Jerome*. Hank's black eyes look over at me.

"Are you sure about this, Gruney?" Hank says. "He's your father."

Bugs all over the windshield. Madonna's on the radio singing, *Open Your Heart*.

"Keep on going, Hank," I say.

Out my window, to the east, where my father is, sunlight on something shiny. A flash of light in the bright afternoon.

11.
No hay palabras

ATLANTA, IDAHO. SOMETHING MAGIC ABOUT IT. MAYBE it's the Sawtooths, the lithium in the water, maybe it's because up there you're more than a mile high.

Or maybe the magic is something else.

At the turn of the century, tens of thousands of people from all over the world crowded themselves into that valley. Their one single effort, to dig for gold. The history of the town, just the story of the gold itself – six million tons of gold ore mined out of Atlanta – could give you fever.

Twenty-nine people live in Atlanta now. Half of that in winter. More dead people in that valley than there are alive.

Or it's the wind. Maybe the magic is how the wind blows down along the river and into town.

Maybe it's because besides chopping wood, preparing food to eat, eating the food, boiling the water on the cook stove, and cleaning up after – breakfast, lunch, and dinner – all there is to do is walk, or sit in hot pools, or sit on the bank of the North Fork of the Boise River. The water's too cold to swim. Fly fish for trout if you're into it. Or sleep.

Then, too, maybe after all, the magic *is* the gold. One of gold's properties is its high electrical conductivity. Maybe Greylock, the mountain peak looming high above Atlanta, is still so full of gold that it's conducted us to the only place in the world where I could be with four friends, together at the same time, at a time when most of my friends were either dead or dying. In a ghost town for chrissakes, not much to distract us.

Or maybe what made Atlanta magic wasn't Atlanta at all. Maybe the magic was just the time. Destiny, fate, fucking fortune, whatever it is. The way the earth was spinning it spun the five of us together, our good health and our youth, still immortal, in a way we'll never be spun together again.

Or maybe what made Atlanta magic was the mushrooms.

LATE MORNING IN Boise, Idaho. Reuben and Sal and Gary, Hank and me, all of us climb in Sal's Jeep Wagoneer. We're all big guys and we're traveling with food and provisions for five men for three days and three nights. There's no electricity in Atlanta, at least in Gary's house. No refrigeration. So the Wagoneer is jammed.

The first hour out of Boise, we're still on the plains. When we get to Lucky Peak Dam the road starts to climb. In Idaho City, we stop for hamburgers, coffee, French fries, and pie. Not long after Idaho City, we turn off the tarmac.

Then it's three and a half hours of dirt road, the Wagoneer going straight up, going straight down mountains. Around every hairpin corner, we slow down, honk the horn. Around every hairpin corner, visions of a huge logging truck barreling down on us. Always on the one side of us, a rock wall. On the other, dropoffs like to clench your sphincter closed forever.

Three and a half hours of hanging on for dear life to a one-lane road. During the times when we aren't just about to drive off a cliff, though, we're talking, dishing, and talking talking. My old friends Reuben and Sal and Gary – it's been ten years since we've all been together in Idaho. I've told them Hank is just a friend, but when they meet Hank they fall in love, too. Who wouldn't. They've all read his book and they want to know everything about him.

At one point, I look over, take a good long look at Hank. The last time I'd really looked at him seems like ages ago, just two days before, at Ephraim's in Fort Hall in that piece of bright sun after the sweat lodge. He'd just taken my hand and put it over his heart. *That's someplace I've never been to.* Ever since Hank said that, there hasn't been much else I've been thinking about. What that place for Hank was.

But this day Hank's in a car full of chattering homosexuals. First Indians, now queers. Far as I can tell, Hank's doing fine. In fact, more than fine. Who wouldn't be, traveling with these characters?

We cross the bridge over the North Fork of the Boise River and start up the last mile of straight low grade to the town of Atlanta. The sun is just going behind the mountain. On the right, from out of the pines, the first building, a two-story gray ghost, old wood from a century ago. Its wavy windows, sun in its cataract eyes look right into my soul. That glint of light I'm not sure happens inside me or out.

THE ATLANTA TOWN Hall is the old Atlanta Club, a flat-roofed rectangular concrete building that's modern for Atlanta. Built in the Twenties. We all pile out of the Wagoneer and stretch. Hank lets out a high-pitched fart.

"Mountain lions," Hank says.

Reuben hears the fart, looks at me, and says:

"He gambled and he lost."

Then Gary says: "She was a poor dog. But a good one."

Always proud of his farts, Hank. Me, I'm as far away as I can get from him. Then in a moment, something else has my attention. The way the mountain air lays on my skin. I have to stop. Cold on my ears and in my nostrils. My breath in deep, when I breathe out I can see my breath. Magic.

The Atlanta Club has a shed roof overhang above the front door. A half dozen or so people, bundled up on two old church pews, are sitting in the fading light. One pew on each side of the front door pushed up against the building. Above the pews, two windows you can't see through.

In the back of the Wagoneer, Hank finds his faux leather suitcase, I find my powder blue one. By the looks of things we don't expect to sell any books, so Hank grabs one book and I grab a book and we walk inside. It's one big high-ceilinged concrete room. The warm hits us first. And the smell of wood fire. To the left is an old wooden bar back, looks like oak, that goes on forever, stained dark and rubbed to raw wood where, over the last century, men and women have bellied up to it. Dark dark all around in the corners and on the floor and above you on the ceiling dark. The brightest light is a kerosene lamp set on a low table, oak too, setting in a circle of high-backed wooden chairs ordered together like old Mormons in front of the potbellied stove.

In the back corner there's another kerosene lamp. For going out to the outhouse. And something else. Music. There's a guy back there by the lantern and he's cranking an old Victrola. Billie Holiday singing "April in Paris." I do a quick look at Hank, but Hank doesn't remember his "April in Paris" dance that night in Pennsylvania. He's busy shaking hands with a woman with bright red hair in a blue parka who's introducing herself as Misty Rivers.

Magic. The big casement windows that line the west wall shine out of the dark as if church windows, four frames of bright red-orange fire.

We all sit in the Mormon chairs around the low table. I sit next to Hank. We both know to sit our asses near the stove. On the table, cheeses spread out on thick white plates, baguettes, bottles of red wine, a huge plate of cookies, stemware, a coffee press, old coffee mugs, hot water, tea bags. Cream and sugar in those kind of blue dishes.

By the time everyone has their coffee or their wine, the bright shine of the windows is gone. Everything is black. Pitch. Just us human beings there crowded around the kerosene lamp and the stove. There's maybe twelve of us. One chair is empty. The kerosene flame from the table below us comes up light into our faces. The guy who was playing the Victrola sits down in the empty chair. His hair is gray but he looks young, something wild, rugged about him. Gray chest hair coming out his shirt collar. He's not wearing shoes. He looks over to Hank and me. Like everybody else is looking, he looks too.

I've never heard a place be so silent. The way time is not a measurement but something you are perfectly still in.

Hank puts a chocolate chip cookie in his mouth, then two more. He presses his knee into mine. That knee press means I should go ahead and do something. Since usually I go first, I open my book. I have to push the pages down into the light. My voice in the big dark room, echoes of it, all the spirits listening. Maybe even one Most Miserable in particular. At first my words tremble, finally I hit my stride.

Those twenty minutes I read that night in the Atlanta Club, while I am reading, more than ever before or since, in all the world the feeling I love the most. When I'm finished reading, nobody claps, nobody steps up, takes charge, pours more wine all around. The way the faces all look at me it's as if I'm still reading. Or maybe some other guy is reading now only I can't hear him.

The black dark, the silence, the light of the kerosene flame. The flicker on the faces of the people in the circle. Twelve, I count them, twelve of us sitting, including Reuben and Sal and Gary, Hank and me, Misty Rivers and the Victrola Guy.

I've never felt so listened to.

Those of us around the table, it's as if we are dark houses in the dark, windows shuttered to the night, a light on inside. Each of us with our front door wide open.

Or this is a séance and Hank and I are the channelers.

The dead speak as Hank begins to read. My favorite story of his. The same story he read at the Blind Lemon in Pocatello. About the little girl who calls in the cows. I cover my mouth with my hand because I don't trust my mouth not to lip-synch. Why I love Hank's story so much is why I love it even more that night, because more than anything the story is about light, fading light, and the little girl narrator, her lists of cows' names and family members, how her voice becomes a litany of blessings on them all.

With my mouth covered like that, I look my eyes around the circle. I make a blessing, too. On this strange gathering of people, or spirits, who sit in high-backed Mormon chairs around a low oak table and a kerosene lamp 6,000 feet high in the middle of the Sawtooths. Seven people I don't know. Five, including me, I do.

Reuben, not like the sandwich, but roo-BEN, is directly across the low table from us. He looks French in his black beret. A big mug of Earl Grey tea in his hands. He's just had his teeth capped and the kerosene lamplight shines off his white teeth. Sal is sitting next to Reuben, as close to the cookie dish as he can get. He's particularly fond of the double chocolate fudge. Sal's wearing his trademark big white long-sleeved shirt. Not his red baseball cap though. He just wears his hats in the sun.

I met Reuben Flores and Sal Nash on a September afternoon in 1973. The very next day was my first day as a high school English teacher and my hair was down to my shoulders.

I could've gone to any barbershop in Boise. Three bucks and I'd have been acceptable. But I'd given up hope on so many things. The Sixties were over and the Seventies looked like married and a job. And now I was even going to give up on letting my freak flag fly. But I just couldn't let some redneck give me an American haircut. I figured if I was going to sell out, then at least I could take the risk.

Truth was I wanted more than it looked like I was going to get.

Beauty by Gustav, I opened the cut-glass, big, heavy door. Man, the smell in that big beautiful old house. Smelled dangerous. The problem was you needed an appointment.

But then Reuben Flores walked out. Really, this guy's a cross between John Leguizamo and Diana Ross. What a smile. If I could wait just ten minutes, he'd be right with me.

What I remember about that haircut was that Reuben

offered me a cocktail, and the offer surprised me, and I tried not to act surprised, and then I was sitting in his barber chair drinking a rye and ginger, and we were talking talking. Not guy talk. We were talking about life and breath, his guru named Bhabhiji, and I felt so at ease. I wasn't searching for words.

Reuben has a story about that day as well. The tall lanky man with long ash-blonde hair standing in the foyer of the beauty parlor and how surprised he was when I got in his barber chair that I asked him if he was homosexual.

I don't remember that. What I do remember is that Reuben pointed out the window. Outside in the garden was a young man wearing a red baseball cap. His lover, Sal Nash. The strong back muscles under his white shirt. His hands dug deep into a flowerbed. The way Reuben spoke of him, Sal Nash was no corporeal human being. Sal Nash was a heavenly angel. I didn't doubt it for a moment.

And something else. Something Reuben said just as he pulled the drape from my shoulders and I was about to get out of the chair.

"You know, Ben, what it all boils down to is love."

That's when Sal walked in from outside. Actually, at first I couldn't tell it was Sal. All I could see was a huge bundle of red flowers.

"Ben, this is Sal,'" Reuben said.

The red flowers parted and under the bill of the red ballcap were two blue eyes. Maybe not blue. Maybe crystal or silver and just the red flowers made them blue. Like to look right through you, those blue eyes. His thick dark-red hair and full beard. Fucking Alan Bates right there in Boise, Idaho.

"Hi Ben," Sal said. "Would you like a dahlia?"

Reuben, Sal, the beautiful big house, my new haircut, the smell of the salon, red dahlias, love.

Maybe the Seventies weren't going to be so bad after all.

And. Homosexual. Maybe one day, I just might start walking on the other side of the street.

224 | TOM SPANBAUER

HANK'S READING THE part about Grandma Julia Mae. Nobody in our circle has made a move. As if we're in a trance. Gary Whitcomb, Atlanta's honorary mayor, keeps his knee a steady press against mine. He's done a lot of work setting this reading up. He owns the Atlanta Club and everything in it. Even the Mormon chairs are his. Gary's a big guy, solid. Sandy red hair, what he has of it. So he mostly shaves his head. Usually a beard, sandy red, too and trimmed short. Tall, rugged-looking. You'd think he was a real Idaho Spud, but when he opens his mouth, that voice. High-pitched and so gay. That's what attracted me to him in the first place, I mean besides his big shoulders, and a quiet way that made him seem sad. Then that laugh would come out of him. Mostly I liked him because he was a painter who always had paint on his Levi's and on his boots.

It was a mosquito. I couldn't sleep because there was a mosquito in the room. It was just after I'd left my wife, Evie, and I was staying in the extra bedroom with Bette Podegushka and her roommates, Will and Leo. Everybody was out dancing. I'd turned on the bright overhead light and I was standing naked on my bed jumping up and down trying to kill the fucker with my pillow.

That's when Gary Whitcombe walks into the room.

I quick sat down and pulled the sheets up around me. Gary let out that laugh. I had to laugh, too. Turns out I'd left the front door unlocked. Gary had a six-pack he was going to share with Will, so we started in on beers. After a while, Gary turned off the light and we sat there in the dark. I smoked cigarettes and we talked. About everything. Evie and Bette and sex and Idaho and art. That's the first time I heard about a place called Atlanta, Idaho. Gary talked about his house up there and the hot springs. The old gold mines. Greylock mountain. I remember how comfortable I started to feel. In the middle of all the changes, all that fear, that night I felt comfortable. It wasn't long and Gary and I were lying on the bed and I was curled up into Gary's armpit.

I remember something else, too. Gary didn't get hard either.

When I asked Gary if that upset him, he said, "No, I never get hard the first time."

That a man could know that about himself and be okay with it and then say it out loud. I liked that.

YEARS AND YEARS these guys, my pals. Reuben Flores, Sal Nash, Gary Whitcombe. Like Ephraim, they're men who've known me through it all. Beauty by Gustav, a married man, a high school teacher, buying a home on Boise's North End. Then 1978 comes along and everything changes. My affair with Bette, maybe a bisexual, for sure a disco sister. Then a few years later, I'm a full-blown homosexual. Currently a resident of the Lower East Side of Manhattan, a graduate of Columbia University, and now a published author. 1988. And we're together again in Atlanta, Idaho, in a big dark concrete room, huddled around a kerosene lamp and a potbellied stove, no electricity, way high up a mile closer to the moon and the stars, sitting around a low table listening to Hank Christian's little girl call in the family's cows.

A family.

ONLY THE FLICKER of the kerosene lamp when Hank is finished. Inside the stove, a chunk of wood settles deeper into the fire. So quiet. The faces stare at us, stare more. Their front doors wide open.

Hank grabs a handful of chocolate chip cookies, hands me one. It's only then I realize I'd forgotten about dinner. After a while, Sal starts clapping and then everybody else claps too. Misty Rivers unzips her blue parka, lights a cigarette, takes a deep inhale. On the exhale she says:

"Both of you read us some more. Please."

"Yeah," the Victrola Guy says, "I haven't been read to since my grandpa died."

Around the table, all of a sudden, everybody's moving, talking back and forth. People grab their coffee cups, pour more wine, move their chairs, uncross their legs, stretch their backs, light cigarettes.

Don't stop. Keep reading. No, don't stop reading.

Hank's black eyes, a spark inside, bright as the kerosene lamp. I'm surprised, too. Magic. The silence, what we took for bored locals, has turned out to be something else.

Hank reads his story about live nude girls. I read the part of the novel about the Blackfoot State Fair. Then Hank's story of his high school sweetheart. Then me, the part about my father's saddle room. We don't get out of there 'til midnight.

Everybody carries the dishes from the low table to the sink behind the bar. There's two chocolate chip cookies left. I take one and Hank takes one. Gary opens the door to the stove and checks the fire, turns the dampers down. As everybody is leaving, Misty Rivers unzips a pocket of her blue parka, pulls out a checkbook. She lays the checkbook onto the table, opens it, bends down, and begins writing. The kerosene lamp shows the silver roots under her dyed-red hair. One check for Hank's book, one for mine.

When she hands Hank his check, she looks him straight in the eyes and shakes his hand.

"You've made a wonderful evening for us in Atlanta," she says. "Thank you."

And to me:

"And you're from Idaho," she says. "We're real proud of you."

Her hands are small and strong, the skin is slick.

OUTSIDE, GARY LOCKS the Atlanta Club's front doors. Sal's got the Wagoneer going.

"Let's walk," Gary says.

It's chilly after sitting by the stove, but the night air feels like pure oxygen. We walk together, Reuben, Gary, Hank, and me. At first, it's so dark we can't see our feet. No moon in the night sky. The night sky so full of stars so close you know the earth you're walking on is part of the cosmos. I take a step and where I step the bottom isn't there, and my foot goes down and down and finally hits the ground. For all I know that step could have been

a cliff. Ahead of us, Sal driving slow in the Wagoneer. The headlights make a place of light onto the dirt road. The brake lights
more stars. Red stars.

"You guys are part of Atlanta history now," Reuben says.

"How's that?" Hank says.

"Misty Rivers just bought your books for the Elmore County
Public Library."

GARY'S HOUSE, THE *Main Spread*, is darkness inside of darkness. On the back porch, Gary takes a flashlight hanging from a
nail and turns the flashlight on. Everything is blacker on the edges
of the light. I can see an old table. A washtub on the table. A
brick chimney, and an old screen door painted white. Gary pulls
open the screen door, pushes open the back door. Hank steps
back and lets me walk in first.

Each step I take into the house is a decade back into history.
And with the flashlight beam bouncing around onto things, the
house feels like an old silent movie. Through the kitchen, it's more
like the museum of a kitchen than a kitchen. But there's no red
velvet rope and you're not a tourist and you're just walking deeper into the past. Over the polished creaking floorboards, past
the iron and chrome *Majestic* cook stove. Past an oak table with
four wooden high-backed chairs. A tall wooden bookcase full
of books. The big white dishes in the cupboards, the glasses in
the hutch, rattle with every step.

I know I'm haunted, but by the time I'm in the hallway I am
a firm believer in spirits. Fucking spirits are all around me,
crowding in. They seem more curious than anything. They touch
me the way you want to touch things sometimes because they
are exotic. On the right of the hallway is Gary's bedroom. A bed,
neatly made, covered in an old quilt. The light through the window, the way it makes the lace curtains glow, proves that we've
entered another reality. Ahead of us down the long narrow hallway is an old full-length mirror. The flashlight beaming into it
shows us that we're the ones who are the spirits. I look away as

fast as I can. Hank bumps into me from behind and my throat makes a high gargle sound. Hank's hand grabs my shoulder, doesn't let go.

We walk through a door to the left and through a bedroom. On one side of us a midget stove, stove pipe straight as an arrow through the roof. A double bed in the corner covered in quilts, two big white pillows.

"Reuben and Sal will sleep in here," Gary says. "You guys are in here."

Gary opens heavy wine-red curtains and points the flashlight down three steep wooden steps, then steps down into the room.

"Watch your step," he says, and points the light to our feet.

Hank's still got his grip on my shoulder. I step down the steps, then Hank.

The room is a larger than the first bedroom and across the room it has a door, painted white, that Gary opens. It leads outside.

"If you got to pee in the night, stick close to the house," Gary says. "There's been a bear around town causing some trouble. Some wolves, too, but they're as scared of you as you are of them."

Gary's high-pitched voice talking about bears and wolves makes me think he's joking. But then when he closes the door, the way he pushes the door in with his shoulder, so the latch snaps tight, I know this ain't no joke. Hank standing in the dark next to me, knows it too. His hand on my shoulder is a tight squeeze.

The flashlight goes to the double bed. A white chenille bedspread with white pillows at the head and a folded quilt at the foot of the bed.

"This is a great old bed," Gary says, "from the 1860s. Quite some stories about that bed. Some say it used to be Peg-Leg Ida's, but there's no real documentation."

"Peg-Leg Ida?" I say.

"She was a whore up here got her leg froze off," he says.

Gary's got the flashlight up close to the ironwork at the base of the bed.

"You see how the iron work links two circles in the middle?" Gary says.

"It's what they call a wedding ring bed."

Hank's hand is off my shoulder soon as he hears *wedding ring bed*. Gary sets the kerosene lamp on the desk.

"Sleep tight," Gary's high voice. "Don't let the bed bugs bite!"

Gary's up the three steep steps. He closes the heavy wine-red velvet curtains behind him. Hank and I, taking off our clothes, make strange huge shadows onto the walls.

"Can I sleep on the outside?" Hank says.

"Sure," I say.

I'm stripped down to my undershorts. The bed bounces and creaks and the sheets are cold against my legs and arms. I pull the covers up to my chin. Just as Hank blows out the kerosene lamp, I see the painting on the wall. It's that painting of George Washington, his shoulders and his head, looks like he's floating on a cloud. The room is so fucking dark. Hank stands in the dark for a moment. I guess that's what he's doing. It's not long and his warm body settles in next to me. No doubt about it, we're both freaked out being in the same bed. And we haven't really talked since the sweat lodge. If it was up to Hank we'd probably lie there and not say a thing. But we have to say something. Something.

"Best reading so far," I say.

"Unbelievable," Hank says.

"Misty Rivers," I say.

"Elmore County Library," Hank says.

"The Victrola guy," I say.

Hank is a big deep low snore. I'm worried about that snore at first. That I'll have to touch him, get him to lie on his side or something.

A GRINDING SOUND wakes me up. I lie there with my eyes closed trying to figure out what that sound is. But I can't place it.

Hell, I don't even know where I am. It's cold and there's a smell, not a bad smell, just very particular and odd.

Then I open my eyes. The ceiling of the room is high and made of rough-cut barn wood. So are the walls. There's a window to my left at the foot of the bed. White curtains, the kind my mother used to wash and dry out on a stretcher. Just beyond my feet, through the double rings of the wrought iron bed, an oval mirror hung on the wall. Below the mirror, a table with a white doily. A yellow water pitcher on the doily and a smooth yellow bowl. Two big wine-red curtains hanging across the doorway. To my right, over the lump of quilts next to me, George Washington on a cloud is staring me down.

In the top corners on each side of the room at the ceiling, triangular cracks of sunlight coming through chinks in the wall. Around the room, an armoire, a steamer trunk, a wooden desk. Old books and papers on the desk.

The particular smell is the smell of the whole room. Old wood, old wrought iron, old books, and the sheets and the old quilt on top of me. That's when the quilted lump in the bed next to me moves.

Holy Christ, it's Hank Christian.

Those black eyes under a mop of messed up hair.

During the night, while me and Hank were sleeping in the wedding ring bed, no bears and no wolves had eaten us.

"Mornin' sweetheart," Hank says. "What's that grinding sound?"

Inside me, all around me, on my skin. Something mysterious. Magic.

At first I think it's the spirits in the house, then I think it's that I fucking woke up in the same bed with Hank Christian. But it's something else. Some old part of me. Maybe the Most Miserable is back. I close my eyes. Take a deep breath. That old spirit ain't nowhere around.

Turns out that sound is Gary in the kitchen grinding coffee beans in his hand grinder. Then there's a smell. This mysterious

thing has a smell. A smell I haven't smelled in years. Fresh coffee
and bacon frying. Magic.

THE *MAJESTIC* STOVE is going and it's hot in the kitchen.
Reuben and three big black iron frying pans on the stove. One
with scrambled eggs and tomatoes and cheese, one with bacon,
one with hash brown potatoes. Reuben's got a white apron tied
around him and doesn't hear us at first because of all the frying.
The tall wooden bookcase is full of cookbooks. On the oak table
with the fancy kerosene lamp is a green bowl of red salsa. On the
transistor radio, mariachi music. I walk up to Reuben, give him a
kiss on top of his perfect haircut.

"Mornin' boys," Reuben says. "Did you sleep all right in
that lumpy old bed?"

"Fine," I say.

"Yeah, fine," Hank says.

"Gary's got the coffee ready outside," Reuben says. "Just
grab a cup and sit yourself down. Breakfast'll be ready in ten
minutes."

SUNLIGHT, MORNING SUNLIGHT, coming down not too hot
yet, onto the backyard. The backyard is a stretch of green lawn
to Gary's barn and the outhouse. On the lawn is a wooden bench
that was painted turquoise once. Tubs of water on the bench.
One for washing dishes, one for rinsing, the next for rinsing too.
Scattered across the yard are old porcelain pans filled with water.
Half dozen or so.

Gary and Sal are sitting with their legs over the side of the
porch. Sal's in his long-sleeved white shirt and red ballcap
and Gary's still in his PJs with a sunbonnet on. Into a big white
mug, Sal pours me coffee so black and thick it looks like what
Arabs drink.

"Italian Roast," Sal says.

Hank gets his cup, too. I sit down on the porch between
Gary and Sal, sun on my Levi's and shoes. My face in the shade.

Hank squats down on the lawn, takes two sips off his coffee, gets up and walks the twenty steps to the outhouse. The door sticks but he gets it open. Ain't long and we hear a loud shit blast then a thud.

"Bye Bye, Mr. Chocolate Chip Cookies," Hank says.

Magic. On the back porch, June morning sun, Idaho. Mile high in a ghost town. Porcelain pans of water reflecting sun. Wired on Italian Roast. Bye Bye, Mr. Chocolate Chip cookies. We're laughing our asses off.

That's how the day begins.

AFTER BREAKFAST WE all pile in Gary's World War II Jeep. That kind of Jeep that doesn't have a top, just four big wheels, a front hood, fenders, front and back seats, a steering wheel, and a gearshift. I'm riding smashed between Reuben and Sal in the back seat. Hank's in front. Because of the sun, I'm wearing one of Sal's ballcaps, *John Deere* across the front. Hank's got on a wide-brimmed straw cowboy hat. The air smells of wood fires.

"Where we going?" I ask.

"Alturas Bar," Gary says.

I think it's a little early for cocktails. But it's probably past noon. Maybe a Bloody Mary. But when we get there, Alturas Bar is something else altogether. It's an immense formation of rock. Not one big rock but millions of rocks. White rocks stacked twenty or so feet high, even higher. The valley is narrow there and the white rocks go from the base of one side of the valley all the way to the other side up to the bank of the river. Round boulders mostly, the size of, say, a bathtub or smaller. But they are all sizes and shapes. Some rocks as big as half a house. Some as big as your hand. All of them white.

Gary tells us all about the place. The story goes something like this: back in the olden days, the gold ore was dug out of the ground and then sent down the mountain in wooden chutes that carried the gold ore to the gold mill and then all those cast iron contraptions extracted the gold out of the ore. The rubble and rock that was left over when the gold mill finished with it was sent down more wooden chutes and ended up at the river.

The river is where the Chinese worked.

The Chinese, at the bottom of the rung, down at the river, scoured over every single rock that descended down the mountain for any trace left of gold. Millions and millions of rocks and each rock was stacked by hand by Chinese workers over a hundred years ago.

One big sculpture, Alturas Bar. Like the Vietnam Memorial, although there's no name carved into every rock.

Hank and I start walking. Walking and jumping from rock to rock. Like we're on the surface of the moon, all that expanse of white. It's amazing how solid the formations are. And what at first looks like a flat white rock surface turns out to be its own complicated geography of valleys and craters and hills.

There's a point where I'm standing on a rock shaped like the palm of a huge hand. All around me, under me, not millions – there's a billion rocks stacked just so. White white and above, the sky is so blue it's a blue I've never seen yet. And two hawks, red-tails gliding slow as a dream in all that blue. Hank's way across the surface of the Alturas Bar moon, on the other side of a crater, over on a spire of stacked rock. A tiny man standing on something immense. For a moment I think he's a spirit, some gold digger in a cowboy hat from another time. Just below him is the river at a place where the river bends. The river is low, mostly white water flowing shallow over rocks, but close in the bend, right below Hank's feet, an elbow of water, a deep blue green pool.

I spread my feet across the rock that's shaped like the palm of a hand. It wobbles back and forth. The sun bouncing down on the white rock gets so bright I have to cover my eyes. I wave at Hank and when Hank waves back he points to the hawks. I take off my John Deere hat and wave it back and forth so he can know I've seen the hawks.

Hank motions that we should head back to the Jeep.

I'm about to turn and go when one of the hawks screeches out. It makes me stop, put my hand over my eyes. The wind is coming down the valley along the river. A big gust hits me and blows my hair around. Idaho. The wind around my ears that always makes me feel I'm not alone.

Across the crater, Hank steps off back toward the Jeep. Just then, one rock, about the size of my head, tumbles down. It rolls down the rock hill, rolls down the century, the century and a half, rolls and rolls and bounces down against other rocks set there by hand just so by a Chinese man, a boy, a girl, a Chinese woman, and hits the edge above the river and falls into the air down down and into the deep, dark, blue-green pool. A little splash in the afternoon.

BACK AT THE Main Spread, on the back porch again. We're all sitting in the shade on the north side of Gary's back porch. Around two o'clock, after bologna sandwiches and potato chips and beer, someone mentions mushrooms, psilocybin, I forget who. Probably Sal. But then it for sure could have been Reuben. Then, maybe it was Gary.

Myself, I've been around the world, and around the block, a bunch of times, but I've never taken an hallucinogen. I figure I haven't really got much of a hold on this reality, let alone take off in some other one. Hank's not up for it either. He's got all kinds of excuses. But it ain't more than an hour later and I've got three of them nasty things in my mouth and I'm trying like hell not to vomit. And Hank. Hank is in fact vomiting in the bushes.

And I'm thinking, *Holy Fuck*. What the fuck did we think we were doing.

Of course, my biggest fear is that hallucinogenic mushrooms would open up the gates of hell. And in hell, I'd meet the Most Miserable of All, suffering down there at the bottom, dickless and without hope. Hallucinating.

We all start out sitting around under Gary's old apple tree. Reuben is lying with his head in Sal's lap. Gary is leaned up

against the tree rolling a joint. All of us close enough to touch.
Just in the shade on a sunny day as if nothing is different.
The wind blowing in the tree. The way the shade moves across
our bodies. Everybody acting like you're supposed to act
when you're tripping. Talking low and laughing. Grooving on a
lazy afternoon. Hank has quit throwing up. I'm glad of that, I felt
responsible. Now he's just lying there totally relaxed in a way
I've never seen him, on the grass, his black eyes wide-eyed,
staring up through the leaves of the tree.

I don't know how it starts but for some reason everybody
starts acting like themselves. I mean Reuben is Reuben and Sal
is Sal and Gary is Gary, Hank is Hank. That's somehow amazing
to me that we each of us know how to act like we are who we are.
And every time one of us does something or says something,
none of the other of us who didn't do it or say it could've done it
or said it. Fucking remarkable. For example, how Sal is touching
Reuben's head, only Sal can move his fingers like that. No matter
how hard any of the rest of us try, we'd never move our fingers
like that. *Just* like that. Or even *have* fingers like that. Or Gary
when he laughs. I almost shit myself when he laughs because it
is so *Gary*. In my lifetime I could never make a sound like that.
And Hank, the way his body lies on the grass. His arms, his legs,
his hat hair. Totally individualistic. No possible way any of us
could lie that particular way under that tree.

It's like there's the cosmos, see, and it's all one big whirling
entity that perpetuates itself and each of us are a part of that
cosmos, but only a particular part. As if a cookie cutter has cut
out each of us into a certain form and we are stuck in this form.
For example, this being called Reuben Flores. While he's a part
of everything, he's also only what the cookie cutter has cut out for
him. And he can't do or be anything that he isn't.

But then something else starts creeping in. After a while,
it starts to feel like we are imitating ourselves. The way, for
example, Gary lights the joint is exactly how Gary would light a
joint, and he knows it, so he does the perfect imitation of

himself doing it. Gary Whitcombe lights the joint exactly how Gary Whitcombe would light a joint. Trippy. Then everybody isn't just doing what they do because of who they are, but they're doing it because they *think* they know who they are. They are doing what they are doing because they know that's how they would do it and so they do it that way.

Then I get the incredible insight that in fact we can go beyond the form of ourselves because the form isn't a given, it's a taken as given. The cookie-cutter cutout isn't an objective reality. It's only an *idea*, what forms us is only an idea, and all we're doing is perpetuating this idea. Ergo, if who we are is simply a manifestation of an *idea* we have of ourselves, then we could change the idea and break the cookie-cutter form and fuck all.

So all this was going on in my head. It's when I started talking that I run into trouble. And I haven't been talking long at all. I'd just pointed out that the way Hank was taking a pee was the way only Hank could take a pee, and that in fact, Hank in taking a pee, is doing the perfect imitation of himself taking a pee, because after all, all we are is an idea that we perpetuate about ourselves.

It isn't long after that's when Gary taps me on the shoulder and says, "Ben, we're going for a walk."

And I say, "Okay."

And Gary says, "And you're staying here."

And they take off, all of them, even Hank. And leave me alone sitting under the apple tree.

Some friends. As soon as they walk out of the front gate and they're out of sight, immediately the worst thing that could possibly happen, happens. I get that fear. I am really high on a hallucinogen and all alone in a ghost town in the middle of the Sawtooths and anything in the fucking world could happen to me. A bear or a wolf. But it isn't even something real I'm afraid of. Fear is fear is fear and what I am afraid of is being afraid. My whole life, everything I've ever done, everything I do, even the way I walk down the street, I walk that way, so this fucked up giant fear that is always sleeping somewhere inside me don't wake up. Walking on eggs, being quiet in the house, mother with her migraines that could hit her like lightning or sudden murder and you had to be really quiet or father in the saddle room with his belt and my bare ass, or dreams when you have a fever and your hand was as big as the world and you could grab the world, fucked up stuff that makes no sense that's happening to you. Hallucinations. Or the bullies on the bus, or the bullies at school. I couldn't even form a fist, let alone stand and fight. Or those two weeks after *Psycho* I couldn't sleep and I couldn't tell anyone I couldn't sleep because it was just a fucking *movie*.

DNA fear.

Original Sin.

I was a sinner, I was detestable and ugly and weak and deformed, one of those untouchables, not a man, and God the Father fucking hated me when I was born, because I was born, because I was conceived in sin. And he's hated me ever since and there's no place to get away from him, only way's to walk around him, to not wake him up, the Giant, the Catholic, the almighty God.

Ben The Most Miserable of All Grunewald. Dickless, powerless, alone at the bottom of hell. Without salvation, without hope. The cry that never ceases.

And on a bright sunny day here he is, the Most Miserable of All, the Fear Giant, sitting with me under the apple tree.

Sitting inside me. Death, man. Red fringe and all. Fucking death.

I'm curled up into a ball. Sweat pouring off me. My belly full of lead, full of dread. The only way to breathe, big gasps.

WHEN I FINALLY open my eyes, I can only see my hand. And just at the moment when I open my eyes, my thumb moves from against the knuckle of my hand to the tip of my index finger. I start moving my thumb back and forth like that, the way a child would, distracting himself while he sits in the hard chair under the crucifix in the outer office of Mother Superior. Perhaps if I can pay attention to this thumb long enough, the Giant will go back to sleep.

And an amazing thing begins to happen.

When I put my thumb against the knuckle of my index finger the fear goes away. Completely. That first time I move my thumb, it happens so quickly, so I move my thumb back to the tip of my index finger where it was, and there he is again, the blaring fucker Fear Giant.

So I quick move my thumb back to the knuckle and hold it there.

No fear. The Giant is gone and the sunny day and the apple tree are back.

The wind in the tree and the shade of the leaves moving over me. I sit up. I can breathe, my stomach isn't shit spray. I've stopped sweating.

I sit there like that for a good long time, my thumb up against the knuckle. I don't dare move my thumb. Not until Reuben and Sal and Gary and Hank get back. Then I get to thinking about earlier, when I had the insight that all we're doing is imitating ourselves because it's simply the only way we've learned how to do it. Form is only the idea of form, and since we are only ideas of ourselves we could change and fuck all.

I move my thumb back to the top of my index finger.

Fear like hell.

I move my thumb back to the knuckle.

A beautiful Idaho day under an apple tree.

I move my thumb to the top of my index.

Horror, terror, the dark angel, the worst.

I move my thumb back to the knuckle.

Under the apple tree. Peace and tranquility.

Fuck.

The Fear Giant is only an idea of mine. Dickless Most Miserable alone at the bottom of hell without hope, another idea.

We create our own reality. And since we create it, we can change it.

Under Gary's apple tree, tripping on mushrooms, that I was an idea of myself, a story that I continued to repeat, that insight, finally got me to lift my thumb off my knuckle and let it go free, holding back, holding off nothing. I was alone and fucked up and out of control hallucinating in the middle of nowhere and I was doing fine. More than fine.

About that time is when I start looking, I mean really looking, at Gary's porcelain pans of water sitting on his back lawn. The sunlight on them. How the water and the porcelain and the sun all come together to make one thing.

A vessel of light. Hard smooth white with a chip now and then down to black. Made you want to stick your hands in, or your face, wash the water onto the back of your neck. Then just sit there on the grass, the cold water running down your back, letting the sun off the water flicker onto your closed eyes.

That's what I'm doing, letting that light flicker against my eyes, then pouring porcelain pans of water over my head, when I hear people laughing.

"What we want to know," Reuben says, "Is Ben Grunewald back?"

"I think it was Nietzsche," Sal says.

Then Hank's next to me. My big brother, my little brother, my father, my son. Such a consolation to see him. His hand on my shoulder, those wonderful black eyes of his so full of being so ecstatically stoned.

"Hey buddy," Hank says. "Thanks again. Yet another place I've never been to. Life is beautiful, no?"

"This fucking water in these porcelain pans," I say, "is fucking great."

"You think *that* water's great?" Gary says.

"Let's go to the hot springs!" Sal sings out.

"I'm ready!" Reuben says.

"Hot springs?" Hank says.

I stand up. Under my feet and all around me the lawn is soggy, wet, and green. My Manhattan-white feet are a deep rose-brown. The hairs on my legs are wet, too, blonde in the sun, and the skin of my legs is rose-brown too. My cutoffs are wet, and my T-shirt. Hank's hand moves down my arm and holds my hand at the wrist. Between the top of Hank's shoulder and the straw of his cowboy hat, past his ear, two or three steps beyond, is the corner post of the back porch that holds up the purple tin of the shed roof. Above the shed roof, the brick chimney stacks up to a crown. Above us all around up there the sky is royal blue.

The sun isn't high anymore, it's going west. Still it's so bright. I put my hand above my eyes.

Everything is touched by a slow warm wind. The hops growing against the side of the house, the lilac bush by the back door, the grasses of the lawn, the apple tree, quake just enough to play the light. Something about the way the air smells. Mile-high, mountain-air fresh. But something in the fresh. Pine sap and dirt, river rocks. Granite, if granite has a smell. Wood smoke. Rust. And another smell. As if fresh oregano or borage has been pinched into your nose – the outhouse with lace curtains in its windows. All around me, around me and Hank holding onto my arm at the wrist, porcelain pans of water, vessels of light, reflecting sun.

The rock. In Alturas Bar the rock as big as my head bounces down and down and down the centuries. Into the air it falls. The deep pool of blue-green water. A tiny splash in the afternoon.

Hank's hand drops away. I pull back the wet hair from my face. Under my T-shirt, slow water drips down my back.

"*Lithium* hot springs, man," I say. "Let's get going!"

FROM THE SIDE of a hill, hot water rushes out of rust-brown gravel and splashes down mossy rocks. Sunlight on the water, thousands of tiny bright flashes. Boils of steam rise knee-high into the late afternoon, sunlight on the steam, thousands of tiny rainbows. The sound I'm not sure at first is really outside my ears or is a sudden high-altitude pop. Thousands of tiny pops. In between the gurgles and the ripples there are whispers. At the bottom of the hill, the waterfall funnels over the edge and drops the length of a man into a pool.

The shored-up pool is clear, but blue-green clear the way water looks. The pool is the size of the Wagoneer but not as deep. From where my rose-brown feet are standing, on a solid smooth wet blue-gray rock, all around me it's miraculous. The river and the sun are behind me and the trees along the river, poplars, cottonwoods, ancient pines, are pushing their shadows at my back. Upriver and down, the solid world is melting, gone totally liquid, and floating down the valley.

I don't stop to think. My T-shirt is off and my cutoffs, my shorts on top of my towel on a dry rock. Naked like that in the day, a lick of wind finds my ass, my balls, that quick. A quick whip up my back around my shoulders into my hair and around my ears.

Hot water up to my ankles, my knees, I'm cupping my balls as I sit down into the water. A flinty smell and a taste on my tongue, lithium. At the bottom of the pool, my ass against smooth slick pebbles. Clear hot water up to my chin.

The lithium, the hot water, the psilocybin.

All around me in the blue-green waters I can feel it bubbling up. Old dark river, centuries slow and underground, infernal heat, compression. Underwater, I keep my eyes open. Out and through the tiny blue-green rocks, smooth pebbles, the river surges against me. Above me, the waterfall crashes down, water into water. I stay below until I can't. A deep breath pulls me up, out. I come up behind the waterfall, the rusty gravel hillside against my back. The hot water spills out into the air in front of me, a liquid wall of wavy glass.

Tumbled down from above, rolling over rocks, thick black moss, filling up into pools, then down again, down, free, the waters chattering I am free I am free. Hot water on my head, coursing past my ears, the sunlight through the water, I am free too.

Finally, what I've been waiting for forever.

As if I were never the pope's, my father's son, my mother's child, or my sister's little brother. A sterling moment so clear the glimpse I have. And something unlooses inside me, my thumb moves from one place to another, an old rock tumbles down, and I am different, new.

I'm stoned, I know and this new free place may only be in me for moments.

I bring my hands up through the waterfall, my hands as if water is flowing out in fins from my hands, and look close. I breathe deep, look hard at my hands, making my body remember. I'm praying but I don't know who to, to whatever is miraculous, to whatever it is that pulled back the veil so I could dwell in a place I never knew existed.

"WATCH OUT FOR the chiggers!" Gary says. "They stay close to the ground around your ankles."

"What're chiggers?" Hank asks.

"No-see-ums," Gary says.

"Itch like hell," Reuben says. "The secret's to never start scratching."

Outside the waterfall, it's naked men. Reuben pulls down his Ralph Lauren white boxers, picks them up between his toes and catches them with his hand. The sun in the pool near his feet reflects a shine across his face. He's thin and wiry, a line of black hair across his chest. Then down, the hair spreads out black at his crotch. His cock is hiding, it bounces heavy when he walks. If a man is his cock, or the cock is the man, then Reuben is, Reuben's cock is a fox or a coyote, something that wiles you, beguiles you, a dazzle and in one quick trick you're lunch so fast you don't even know it.

Sal. Never trust a man that beautiful. At least I can't. That's my fault not his. Look at him squatted down naked at the edge of the pool. Always in the shade, or under a hat. Skin like marble statues. One of those southern white flowers that bloom in the

night. He's got that Sal look on his face. The one that says I know
I'm beautiful but isn't beauty ridiculous. If a man is his cock
or a cock is the man, then Sal is, Sal's cock is Vivien Leigh. A little
crazy, too much acid and way too much chocolate. Scarlett O'Hara
swinging down there in all that red velvet.

Gary's watching for chiggers, so he doesn't stay long out of
the pool. He's just in his overalls, so when he takes them off
he's standing there in the altogether. Two big steps and he's a hot
splash in the pool. A big body a bit like mine only thicker in his
shoulders and arms. Freckles. He's another white guy should stay
out of the sun, but he's always in the sun, peeling. If a man is his
cock and the cock is the man then Gary is, Gary's cock is Gary
Cooper in *Friendly Persuasion*. Only with freckles, a high voice
and a gay attitude.

Hank. Well you know all about Hank. Today though, the
way he walks on the rocks, his tender feet pearly white, there
seems something crustacean about him. A hard outer shell that's
hard because inside is so soft. The way the muscle of him is in
his trunk and arms. His butt and gams a footballer's, too, but his
calves and his ankles and his feet. Fragile, not made out of mud
and rock like the rest of him. Glass. Easily shattered. Atlas standing on Achilles' heels.

The only straight guy here and he suddenly knows it and
his face is doing that *Ecce Homo* thing, that him-presenting-
himself thing but not like back at the main spread when everyone
was pretending to be themselves. It's just that Hank is nervous.
Makes me love him more.

Full on in the sun Apollo. Greek gods just falling out of the
sky. His olive skin soaking up the sun. A very full and languid
Mussolini hanging down. If a man is his cock and a cock is the
man, then Hank's not a man, he's a legend.

That's what we were for each other, Hank and me, and that's
where we failed.

Legends.

No human can dwell in such exaltation forever.

And somebody else.

Me, Ben, only a head and wet hair bobbing in the sun above the pool's crystal waters. If a man is his cock and the cock is the man then I am, my cock is Dorothy and the Tin Man and the Scarecrow and the Cowardly Lion. I am the man who followed the yellow brick road and got himself out of hell. At least for a while.

In that place most miserable, somehow there is hope.

ATLANTA FUCKING IDAHO. Something magic. Half-dressed and wiped down, we're heading back to the Main Spread. On a winding dirt road in a World War II Jeep, on each side of us pines and spruce and Doug-fir and trees and trees and trees. The late summer air just at dusk against my face, my chest, my arms. The sun in the west full in our faces. Warm, hot almost. The mushroom rushes have passed and what's left is an ever-expanding moment. My body is a gestalt of my body. Not just a head with arms and legs that do things and a cock that just hides out down there. I'm one big warm fleshy thing with blood beating and sperm and breath. My towel is around my neck. It's still wet and smells of lithium. My hands hold the towel at each end. I'm in the back in the middle, jammed between Reuben and Hank. Sometimes when I look down I can't tell whose legs are whose. Reuben's shoulder, Hank's, against my shoulders. Skin stuck to skin with sweat. I look over at Reuben, then at Hank. Their smiles are my smile, content, aware, full of wonder.

A strange sensation in that space between the crack my arms make with my chest and just above my nipples, underneath in there, where I might have wings, the spirit in me starts to rise up and out, and when I lift my arms, that spirit soars up high to the heavens. For a moment there's a heaven above. It's so clear there's a heaven above, because what's coming out from under my arms is connected to it.

Gary shifts down and turns the Jeep. Suddenly, we dip into the shadow of Greylock and below us is a mountain meadow.

Cool, smooth green, the river, rusty, rocky earth. A mule deer does a slow lope into the trees. We all make the same sound, the gasp of air in our throats. Above us, the sunset clouds are dramatic. Gold and pink. Just above Greylock, the beginnings of a dark gray sky.

"Looks like we're in for a storm," Gary says.

IN THE KITCHEN at the Main Spread, our five bodies, the high-backed Mormon chairs, the oak table, the stove, the cupboards, the tall wooden bookcase full of cookbooks, there isn't room to move. The transistor radio is playing Patsy Cline.

Reuben's in his white apron in front of the blazing Majestic. Pots and pans boil and sizzle. Gary and Hank and Sal sit around the table. The fancy kerosene lamp on the table is lit. There's another kerosene lamp on top of the pie safe, one on the bookcase, and another on the warmer above the stove. The light on the room makes it feel like Christmas.

Outside it's started to rain, light at first and then the rain pours down. Gary checks the kitchen ceiling for leaks.

My chair, number five, is by the kitchen window. The lace curtain smells like dust. Steam on the window, rain drops running down. The four legs of my chair wobble on the dark wood planks of the floor. My rose-brown bare feet. The back door is open and the planks shine with what's left of the light of the day. The rain against the tin roof, the roar and noise above us, we are covered with it. The rain on the lawn in the backyard. High splashes of rain on the porcelain pans of water.

Reuben's cooking tamales and Spanish rice and red beans. On the table, next to the fancy kerosene lamp, is the green bowl of dark red salsa, a plate of cheese and a basket of tortilla chips. Cold Dos Equis. I don't think I've ever been so hungry, so thirsty. All of us, we're starving farm hands the way we eat. Aware of our hunger, the delicious satisfaction of eating. We can't help but make fun.

When dinner is finally served, my big white plate full of

tamales, cheese, red beans, salsa, and rice disappears in a heartbeat. Then a second. On the table, the green bowl of salsa is
empty first, then the bowl of rice, then the bowl of beans. Hank
goes for the last tamale. One more round of beers.

Outside the windows it is night. No stars. No moon. Only
light rain. Inside it's a steamy room, cozy, warm, Christmas
light on a room full of dirty dishes, pots and pans. On the back
porch, I put on my socks and shoes, then fill the big kettle with
water from the hose. Simple actions like these, my body moving
through them, are full of enjoyment and wonder. When I set the
kettle on the wrought iron of the Majestic stove, there's a high
snap and sizzle.

Reuben pulls out a pack of Nat Shermans. I can't resist.

I inhale on the cigarette so deep I inhale every aspect of the
night, the place, that moment: the kerosene light, the heat from
the stove, the draft from the back door, the drizzle of rain on the
tin roof, the smell of the rain and the smell of tamales and
boiled beans, the smack of hot sauce on my tongue, the tang of
beer. *Close the door, light the light* on the transistor. Sal with his
Levi ass and white shirt-back to us, scraping plates into the compost bucket, singing along, *you don't have to worry anymore*.
Gary, kerosene lamplight on his shaved head, just in his OshKosh
overalls, the straps against the freckles of his shoulders. He's
taking a long pull on his beer. Reuben's finally sitting down, his
legs crossed, his zip-up black Prada boots, one arm hooked at
the elbow on the back of the high chair, exhaling from his Sher-
man. Hank, his hair pulled back from his face, Hank's beautiful
face in the kerosene light, his black eyes still the psilocybin
twinkle – all of it, everything.

"All we need now," Hank says, "Is a chocolate cake."

Sal stops scraping plates, washes his hands in the pot of
hot water on the stove, wipes his hands. He steps across Gary and
me, walks down the hallway that Hank's got his back to. Nobody
thinks much about Sal leaving. Minutes later, though, Sal walks
in with a pink box and stands behind Hank. Reuben picks up

Hank's plate. Out of the pink box, Sal pulls out the biggest chocolate cake I've ever seen. Sets it down in front of Hank. The look
on Hank's face, my God, it is Christmas and Hank's a four-year-old.

"Bye bye, Mr. Chocolate Cake," Reuben says.

And the day ends. The way it began. Laughing.

AFTER THE ASSEMBLY line of washing and drying is finished
and every knife and fork and spoon is put away into drawers.
After every plate and cup and glass is back into the cupboard. The
counters, the table wiped down. When the fire in the Majestic is
only coals, after Gary turns the damper down. When there is only
the one flame of the fancy kerosene lamp on the table, and the
room is back to shadows, to spirits. We all embrace and thank
each other for the day.

It was a great day, a day like no other, and I look into Gary's
eyes, Reuben's, and Sal's, hold onto their hands as I tell them
goodnight. They listen as I touch them and praise the day, the
marvels of it, the deep understanding, the importance of their
friendship. But the more I talk the more they laugh. How I'm
still way stoned.

I *am* still stoned. When I open the wine-velvet curtains and
walk down the three steep steps into the bedroom, Hank is
standing in the middle of the room holding up a kerosene lamp,
just in his undershorts. Next to his feet, Gary's bucket is catching the drips of rain through the hole in the roof. The wedding
ring bed right there. The way George Washington looks at me,
the way Hank looks at me, I know I am, I know Hank is, still way
stoned.

Hank moves the kerosene lamp so we can see inside the
bucket. The drips from the roof are constant and fast, almost a
steady stream. There's maybe two inches of water in the bucket.
Hank and I stand and stare at the water in the bucket, stare up
at the roof for a long time and listen to the sound of the drips.
It's something so odd we just have to witness it.

A big gust of wind. In the corners on each side of the room

at the ceiling, the triangular chinks in the wall, the wood is dark brown wet and dripping down water. Hank and I feel it about the same time. It's fucking cold.

I open up the steamer trunk, pull out extra blankets, lay them on the bed. In no time at all, I've got my clothes off, keep my shorts and socks on, and I'm under the covers. Hank blows out the flame in the kerosene lamp. The springs bounce and creak when he gets in bed. For the longest time we lie there with the covers pulled up, shivering. It is so dark. I'm still high all right, the way my head floats on the pillow. I want to talk and talk and catch up with Hank. So much to say, but I keep quiet. I think probably I've said enough that day. When I start to warm up, I just can't help it. I keep my voice low when I speak.

"Is that door closed tight?" I ask.

"Yeah I checked it," Hank's voice is a whisper.

"Bears," I say.

"Wolves," Hank says.

Hank says, "Gruney, holy fuck!"

"I know! I know!" I say, "Holy fuck!"

"What is this place?" Hank says.

"Fucking psilocybin mushrooms!" I say.

"A ghost town," Hank says.

"Have you ever been in a place so pitch dark?" I say.

"What a journey!" Hank says. "Where the fuck are we?"

"Alturas Bar," I say. "The hot springs."

"The chocolate cake," Hanks says.

"The rain dripping in the fucking bucket," I say.

"Fuckin A," I say.

"Fuck!" Hanks says.

"The wedding ring bed," I say.

Hank lets go one of his farts. It's so loud. Through the heavy wine-velvet curtains, on the other side of the solid wood wall we hear Reuben say:

"He gambled and he lost."

Way across the house, Gary says: "She was a poor dog, but a good one."

Christ the way we laugh. I plug my nose and laugh and laugh and laugh until I am asleep.

WHEN I OPEN my eyes, the drip from the rough cut boards of the roof is an icicle about a foot long. The triangular chinks in the wall in the corners at the ceiling are knuckles of ice. Now and then, little drifts of snow are spirits across the room. In the oval mirror, I can see that outside it is snowing. Hank's curly head is on my chest, my chin on his head. His body right next to mine, not an inch of space between. Our arms and legs, I'm still getting them confused. As far as I can figure, his legs straddle my right leg and my left leg is over his leg. Only an inch out away from our bodies, the bedsheets are freezing. It takes me a while to figure it out that the hard thing against my thigh is too high for a knee and his other hand is on my ribs. And a very strange miraculous feeling. My cock is hard too. The full hopeful feeling of that. But it's the one part of me, besides the top of my head and back, that's not touching Hank.

One big deep breath jumps into my lungs when I realize where I am, where Hank is, how close we are. After a while and some real concentration, my breath goes back to something like normal. The light through the mirror from the window is snow bright and barely morning. I don't try and move away, or act startled, or worry about Hank when he wakes up. That he'll think I planned this, or that it's my fault we're lying this way.

My God, so this is what it feels like to be touched. I must still be high, I think. So content. Natural comfort. Perfectly in the place I've always wanted to be.

Hank moves his hand a little across my chest before he speaks. His voice is as if in a dream and so low I can barely hear him.

"In the basement of the Strand Book Store," Hank says. "My God, how long ago was that?"

"All those months we didn't talk," I say. "What happened to you that night at the Spike?"

Only our breath, the wind and the snow outside. I let my hand move on the skin of Hank's shoulder.

"We could've frozen to death last night," Hank says.

"It's still last night," I say. "I'm still so high. Are you still high?"

"I'd better be," Hank says. "I've never been this close to a guy's nipple before."

"Three months we didn't talk," I say.

"I'm not sure if I remember why," Hank says.

"Sure you do."

Hank's ribs fill with air and stay full. When the air comes out his mouth, I expect bad breath, but Hank just smells like Hank.

"It was getting fucked in the ass," Hank says. "You said you liked it and it freaked me out. I'd been thinking about *Kiss of the Spider Woman* and how Raul Julia is a friend to William Hurt and so he fucks him and maybe that's what you and I should do, only I couldn't imagine it."

A gust of wind hits the house, everything shakes and rattles. A piece of tin on the roof makes a racket. Suddenly inside me the lightbulb in my chest. The flickering filament and I want out of there. Hank's way too close and there is no breath. But I'm high and I've traveled far and learned too much. My thumb the day before, how it made the fear come and go away.

So long ago, the day I'd cut my finger and my uncle Bob chased the Running Boy all over the farm.

Lying there in bed with Hank that morning, it was a great big revelation that there had never been a place that was safe for me. And yet there I was. With a hard-on and finally safe. In the wedding ring bed in an old house in a snowstorm in the Sawtooths, embracing Hank. Whatever had got me to that place, I had to trust. Besides, really there was no place to go. Outside the bed I'd freeze to death.

"How do you do that? I say. "Just go away like that?"

"It's something you learn," Hank says.

"What's to learn?"

"Never show fear."

"What's the trick?" I ask.

"You shut it all down," Hank says. "Screw it down hard. Make it so nothing can touch you."

"How do you do that?" I ask.

"You just do it," Hank says.

Through the triangular chinks at the ceiling, a swirl of snow high up across the room from one wall to the other. I look down and see there's a dusting of snow on the quilt. I go to kick the snow off but don't. I'm afraid to move. Afraid the embrace, the magic, will end.

"Was this what the whole Idaho Book Tour was about?" Hank says. "Getting me into bed?"

"You got in this bed all by yourself," I say.

"But say it," Hank says. "You've been wanting this all along haven't you – me," Hank says, "sex with me."

"And now all my dreams have come true!" I say.

"We're not having sex," Hank says.

"We are to me."

"Then this is enough?"

"I've had a fucking apparition after me since Pocatello," I say.

Hank's hand moves across my heart and holds on to that side of my ribs. The Running Boy again, but I move my thumb and it's all so ridiculous, it's only an idea, something I've learned, to live my life in fear.

"Fuck, you cried so hard in the car," Hank says. "You and your sister. That's some heavy shit."

"There was this drawing in the *Baltimore Catechism*," I say, "of hell and there's this guy in hell, at the very bottom. He's naked and he doesn't have a dick and his face is terrifying."

"When we were in the sweat lodge," Hank says, "I saw my father."

"He tried to kill me," Hank says. "My pops held me under the water and I really fucking believe he was trying to kill me."

"That sweat lodge was so fucking hot. I was in hell too," I say. "Remember you reached out and grabbed my hand?"

"Ever since my father," Hank says, "that's how I've treated men. That bullshit about male love being back to back is bullshit. The only way I really know how to treat a man is to kill him before he kills me."

"Was that the place you meant that you'd never been before?"

"Yeah," Hank says. "Before the sweat lodge, before yesterday and getting stoned on shrooms."

"Before you," Hank says, "front to front with a man was death."

"God, that night at Ursula Crohn's," Hank says. "Your voice. I'd never heard anything so vulnerable and so clear."

"So maybe it's been you along," I say, "trying to get *me* in bed."

"Wish that was the case," Hank says, "but it ain't."

"But you're hard," I say. "I can feel your cock against my thigh."

"I'm hard every morning," Hank says. "Besides, you're cute."

"*Every* morning?" I say. "You ever not get hard when you wanted to be?"

"Been times," Hank says. "I'm no different from any other guy."

"*That's* no different?" I say. "Erectile dysfunction is not different?"

"Come on, man," Hank says, "I'm a man, not a machine."

"I can't let people touch me," I say. "I've always had a terrible fear."

"But *I'm* touching you," Hank says.

"My mother and my sister did that," I say. "If I got hard for sure my sis would find out. She always found out everything. Then she'd tell mom. She always told mom. So I could never let her find out. It was my secret and only I could know. Nobody else could know. Nobody. If they found out, they'd cut it off. Take Lorca out in the night and slit his throat."

"Lorca?"

"Dead Lorca," I say, *"Portnoy's Complaint.* That's what I call it."

"But you're hard now," Hank says.

"Don't I know it," I say.

"I promise I won't tell your sister," Hank says.

Hank, fuck. No matter where we are, Hank can always make me laugh. Even here in the wedding ring bed talking about my hard-on I'm laughing. In fact, the two of us get to laughing so hard, we're covering our mouths, trying not to snort. Two boys in bed, shits and giggles, trying to be quiet, mom and dad just outside the door.

Hank's voice is a fake whisper.

"Let me see it!"

I close my eyes and shake my head. This can't fucking be happening.

"Come on," Hank says. "Show it to me. It's important that you show it to me."

"I can't move," I say. "I'll freeze to death."

"Just lift the covers," Hank says.

"Will you show me yours too?" I say.

Hank and I turn into one big arms and legs two-headed laughing man. The way laughter hurts in our stomachs. How our laughter makes us move from our warm spot in bed. The freezing fucking sheets. Our little screams. Long moments, our mouths wide open when neither of us makes a sound. Then finally deep inhales of breath. Laughing. Fucking laughter, man.

I reach my hand down, how easy it is to pull up the covers. Hank and I look down inside the cover tunnel. Down there it's my shorts and my cock poking up in them. I'm so surprised I'm still hard and I start to think about being hard then stop thinking about it. My hand pulls back the elastic and boing. Just Hank looking at it makes it bigger.

"What'sa madda you?" Hank says. "That's a right fine Johnson you got poking up."

"It's not very big," I say.

"From the bottom of the palm of your hand to the tip of your middle finger," Hank says, "You're for sure moving onto seven inches," Hank says.

"Here, look!"

Then down in through the under the cover tunnel, Hank's hand moves his shorts off his cock and up and out bounces full-of-blood Mussolini. Our cocks are leaning into one another, almost touching. It's like they're saying *hello, how are you, been looking forward to meeting you for a long time now.*

"It's so much bigger," I say.

"Eight inches," Hank says. "Believe me, I've measured."

Hank unhooks his legs from mine and lies down flat. I pull down my shorts. Hank pulls down his. We hold up the covers. Hip to hip like that, lying parallel, our cocks stick up. If a man is a cock and the cock is the man, then Hank is Hercules and I'm the fair Adonis. Both of us tent poles.

"Bigger around," I say.

"But look at your head," Hank says. "Way bigger than mine. And the way you've been cut. That's an Italian cut, man. Great for the backstroke."

"No doubt about it," Hank says. "That's a gun a man could be proud of. All these years you've just had it on safety."

Hank's black eyes, I look up into them. He is still high and because he's high the way he keeps his eyes sometimes shuttered, they're not shuttered, they're wide open, generous, full of innocence. Then it's as if that love in him jumps over, an electrical arch, a big blue buzz into my eyes straight to my root and I'm seeing myself as he sees me. My cock gets even harder.

What Hank says next, I don't see it coming.

"Ben?" Hank says, "can I ask you something?"

That moment. Fuck. Right there. That moment.

"Are you freaked out about AIDS?"

Slugged in the heart. That's how I jump. My whole body slammed by a blow of grief. In the wedding ring bed, George Washington on his cloud staring us down, two pilgrims.

Sex. We are all shy. We're all worried. Sex. We're not quite sure what's going to happen next. But it's the most catastrophic, enthralling thing that could possibly happen. Every deep unspoken part of us is coming up and out, becoming aware, and longs to merge. The risk of being hurt. We are so fucking delicate. The cookie cutter is so delicate. We bring our mayhem, our despair, our hopes. Who we believe we are, who we aren't. What we know as true, what we don't know. All our infernal lying. How much all this is like death.

Hank holds me and I weep. Sometimes I can't get my breath.

On the other side of the wine-red velvet curtains, Reuben is up, and Sal, the fire is lit, and Gary's grinding coffee beans. Somehow there's sun in the room. Something like sun in the mirror. But it could be that Hank and I are just that bright. My face in the crook of Hank's neck, trying to hide, snot and tears, fuck. Then in a moment. The tears go and the racking of my chest, the heaving, and my body stops. In Alturas Bar, the rock falls over the edge, a splash into the deep blue-green. It's only then I realize. The sobs, the snorts, the gasps for breath, haven't stopped at all.

Hank is weeping, too.

Book Two
Ben & Ruth

12.

The real world

MANHATTAN, OCTOBER 1988. A LATE SUNDAY MORNING, hungover from Saturday night beers on the stoop. Outside, it's hot, bright, gray, and humid. Garbage all over the sidewalks. Inside, Little Ben is sitting in front of the Darth Vader fan. Way too much coffee. Sweat dripping in my eyes, down my neck, under my arms. The Sunday *Times* is all there is.

Fucking Sundays, man. Sisyphus Sundays – in the morning it's the hangover from Saturday night and the afternoon's spent tripping on all you have to do Monday morning.

The deep longing for someplace green and wild and soft. I don't go to Central Park because Central Park ain't Atlanta Hot Springs. Designer Nature only makes my desire for wilderness worse. Manhattan will never be the same after the Atlanta magic. Nothing will be the same, because I'm not the same. Before I didn't know what I was missing. All those years the fear my body remembered, now my body also remembers the sunlight on the water in the porcelain pans, the falling rock at Alturas Bar, the mushrooms, my thumb and what it taught me, Hank's Hercules, my fair Adonis – all these things are now a place in me, too. A place where I'm hard and healthy and there's hope. A place I won't forget.

But I'll forget. You can count on it.

We are so fragile.

What's coming up – destiny, fate, fucking fortune – whatever it is that's in store for me, no fucking way I could've had any idea.

All I know is it's a Sisyphus Sunday and I'm hungover and I miss Hank and Atlanta. Maybe there's a movie somewhere. A movie about someplace green and wild and soft.

My apartment is clean, I've washed the dishes, I've taken a long shower. Side one of George Michael's *Faith*. Side two to shave. In the bathroom fluorescence in the mirror, my Idaho tan is gone. I tie the white towel around my waist and sit down in front of the computer. But I start to cough and the cough goes on so long I have to stand up and lean against the kitchen sink.

It's so French and so cool to smoke. The pack of Gauloises in the ashtray I grab with my fist and crush and throw into the garbage can under the sink. The white towel falls from around my waist. I look down at my body. That's the moment Big Ben decides it's time. To cowboy up and go get tested.

ON THE DAY of the test, I take the number six train up to 86th and Lex. The train is hot and Little Ben is hungover again. You can get HIV tests for free at clinics all over town, but Big Ben won't have it. I call up my editor and ask her for the name of a good doctor. With a proper doctor, Big Ben decides, I'll have a better chance.

The doctor's office is a well-appointed brownstone. Maple trees turning yellow and red-orange. Dappled shade on the set of broad granite steps that curve up from the street to the first floor door. The day of the test I don't meet the doctor. I sit for only moments in the waiting room on a large taupe-colored couch. All the room done in earth tones. On the spotless glass of the Noguchi coffee table, along with the regular magazines, my choices of reading material are the *New York Review of Books*, The *Economist*, and *Granta*. A Persian carpet the same design as the carpet in Ursula Crohn's apartment. For a moment, I stand in the place on the carpet where the stool was on Ursula Crohn's. Memory is a drunk old man in a Hemingway story. My green glittered toe and my smelly feet.

Hank's been busy with graduate schools. Looks like he's

got a gig at the University of Florida. The past month, since we've been back from the Idaho Book Tour, Hank's been more in Florida than Manhattan. I want to tell Hank about the HIV test, but every time I talk to him on the phone, he's so jacked about studying with Barry Hannah I don't want to bring him down.

In the bright cubicle, a nurse with a name tag *Y-Vette*, sticks the needle in my arm. My blood so red, the skin of her hands so black. Everything else in the room is white.

A MONTH LATER, I'm on the number six train again. During that month I've tried to quit smoking but smoke twice as much. I've quit drinking, though, for the whole month, except for the Saturday night before the Monday of the appointment to get my test results. A real binge that ends up Little Ben at the Spike. Hank's got into Florida. His letters, his phone calls are all Barry Hannah this and Barry Hannah that. Fucking Barry Hannah, man. Big Ben gets all my hair cut off, a Fifties fucking buzzcut. Mornings I sweep the street, pick up dog shit, hose off the sidewalks. It's November and New Yorkers are back in town, so there's toilets to unplug, windows to putty, locks to fix.

Silvio, the waiter at Hank's and my restaurant on Columbus is dead. Randy Goldblatt, David, Gary, and Lester from Columbia are dead. Sam Tyler, my friend from Boise State is dead. Rock Hudson is dead. At St. Vincent's, I visit Dick, the guy who fucked me the night of the hash brownie. Pneumocystis. As I walk through the hospital hallway, room after room after room, young men who look like old men with oxygen masks and IVs, tubes coming out of every orifice. Urine, ammonia, floor wax, recycled air. Computer screens that blip green lines or yellow. When the lines are red you're dead.

When I go to walk into Dick's room something happens to my body. The man who lies on the bed ain't Dick at all, he's a skeleton. How the lips stretch back into a wide smile when the body is that wasted. It's not fear, it's the hand of God that stops

me from going in. Because my body cannot move, because I am
a pillar of salt.

Outside St. Vincent's, sitting on the curb, a young man holds
his head and weeps. I stand for a long time on the sidewalk, only
a couple feet away from him. I'm trying to breathe but the air
is only bus exhaust. Really, I want to console the guy, maybe offer
him a cigarette. The way he weeps, though, I can't stop weeping.

The lightbulb in the middle of my chest, the filament
flickering. I look down at my thumb, move my thumb to the no
fear place. But there's no fucking way.

THE DAY OF my appointment, the night before Little Ben
doesn't sleep. I call up Hank but get his answering machine. *You
know what to do.* I don't know what to do, so I hang up. I polish my
black wing tips, put on my vintage blue linen suit, a white shirt,
and a clip-on bow tie. I can feel my heartbeat in the tight collar,
so I take off the tie, undo the top button. The lightbulb and the
flickering filament has moved from the middle of my chest to low
in my gut. My heart is an echo chamber in my ears. How my
arms shake, in my hands, my fingers, the flickering, how it gets
stuck in the knuckles.

It's cold but the sun is extra bright. I never wear sunglasses,
but that day I buy a pair of Ralph Lauren knock-offs from a guy
on the street. The number six isn't crowded and I can sit. It's good
I can sit. The subway car is one of the old cars where the seats
are lined up on both sides against the walls. Across from me, my
reflection in the glass. My short hair. I'm my father wearing
sunglasses.

What I'm about to tell you next may sound contrived or
overdramatic. But you'd better believe me. Because what happens next I swear is true.

From my left I hear it, the door between the subway cars
opens. The roar of the train on the track gets louder and then the
door closes. Coins shaken inside a tin can. That left turn from
looking at my father in the reflection is such a simple movement

of the head. No longer than a second. What I see, when I take my sunglasses off to make sure of what and who I'm seeing, I take as an omen. It's a woman with a white cane. Around her neck is a sign: *Blind and have* AIDS.

The woman on the TV special. It's her. In the middle of an epidemic an upbeat moment on the local WCBS Channel Two News. Six months ago, I'd watched the special tucked away safe in my loft bed on my black and white TV with the coat hanger that's an aerial. The woman was pretty and young, short bouncy hair. She worked as a secretary and had just been tested positive. The woman kept going on and on about her faith in God and her high hopes and what an important thing it was to maintain a good attitude. Something so young and fresh about her, so Debbie Reynolds the way she talked, her sense of purpose. Her expression of great faith gave me faith. Stopped that hard piece of terror that had been growing in me since the day I first heard the devil speak its name: GRIDS. *Gay Related Immune Deficiency Syndrome*.

And there she is, the bouncy young hopeful woman, scabs on the skin of her eyes, her light brown dishwater hair greasy, on the six train uptown with a tin can and a white cane and sign around her neck.

THE DOCTOR IS a woman and I'm sitting in her high-ceilinged, oak-paneled office. She's my age, maybe younger, with long dark brown braided hair. The braids folded up around her head. Lots of eyebrows about her. The way she moves her eyebrows. Silver half-glasses that set on the end of her nose. Dark red lipstick. Her dress is something tailored and comfortable and blue and she sits in an ergonomic leather chair behind her large oak desk. The window to the street behind her is a bright rectangle. Tiny strands of her long hair stick up in the light. I can't actually see her face. She's a silhouette with eyebrows. What I can see, what I can't stop looking at, are her hands. Smooth and tanned, fingernails short and neatly manicured, they are folded on top

of her blotter under the light from one of those desk lamps with
a green glass shade and a brass pullstring. Her wedding ring
is gold with green stone. The way the green stone sparkles, I can't
stop looking because I've never seen a real emerald before.

"This is what they tell me to tell you," she says.

The only movement I can see that she makes are her
thumbs. She rolls her thumbs.

"You are HIV positive," she says. "Two hundred forty
T-cells. And because you are HIV positive, you are going to get
sick. And because you're going to get sick, you are going to die."

IT STARTS AT that moment. Big Ben gets on his Big Fucking
Bull Horn:

*Get out of this office and fast. This doctor woman is too power-
ful, she's behind too big a desk, her emerald is real, and this house
impresses you way too much. You could start believing this shit.*

Running Boy running down Lexington. Running and running. Each time a wing tip hits the sidewalk, the heat burns my
foot, shoots up my leg. A blur of black wingtips, a Road Runner
cartoon, underneath me. That's all I can hear too. No traffic,
no city noise, just my wing tips pounding cement. I'm running so
fast my sunglasses fall off, but I don't stop. At intersections
sometimes I float over the whole street, a long distance high
jumper. I swear at times I'm really flying. Big Ben is yelling *look
how strong you are. You've been running for blocks and still you
have breath, still you are strong. These fucking doctors don't even
know for sure if it's HIV that causes AIDS. It's all in your attitude. A
good attitude can beat any diagnosis. All you have to do is believe.
The secret is to believe.*

PENNSYLVANIA STATION IS the first place I recognize. At first
I don't believe my eyes but I'm in Pennsylvania Station. Wet.
As if it were raining, I am wet. My vintage blue linen suit sticks to
my arms, my back, the backs of my legs. Through my white shirt,
my belly hairs. I've run from 83rd Street to 34th Street and in

Penn Station I'm still running. It's Esther I want to get to. Get my
ass to Esther in Pennsylvania and in Esther's big old house.
Solid wood, I'll be safe. In the cozy, sloped-ceilinged garret with
the matching beds and a bay window that looks south over the
cherry orchard. Safe. I'm running and my hand is searching for
change in my pocket so I can call Esther and tell her I'm on the
next train. Somewhere in there I pass out. Mid-stride, mid-air, the
lights go out. The hard gray floor.

SILVIO SHIT HIMSELF to death. Silvio, that smile, his one
tooth gone, his smooth olive skin, sweet sweet Silvio died shitting
on the toilet. All the nurse could do was hold his hand. One last
shit-spray and his para-sympathetic nervous system went tilt.
Gary slit his wrists in the tub. Long cuts up the arm with a sheet
rock knife. Deep cuts, over an inch deep. The red how it pumped
out in pulses into the bathwater. Is that when he screamed? His
neighbor said she heard him scream. Randy died in a straitjacket. They had to tie his hands down. Dementia so fierce he tried
to tear his face off. Lester overdosed because the AZT was making
him so sick. Tom's heart just gave out. Dick finally just gave in. In
one exhale he was his skeleton.

And these are only six. Six men I know in a city of thousands and thousands of men sick and half-dead, infested with
scabs and pustules and tuberculosis and thrush and skin fungus
and flesh-eating viruses. The way it eats at your brain, when you
sit quiet you can actually hear the virus in your head.

Thousands. Thousands of men full of fear and dread and
alone with their fear. Each man's fear as contagious as the virus
itself. Fear and fear and fear feeds the collective fear and the
city is the horror the horror the fucking horror so thick it's the air
you breathe the same way years later the air you breathe from
the World Trade towers is thick.

IT'S STILL PENN Station. I'm still on the floor. No one has come
to help me, but New York instinct, I've already checked for my

wallet. No one has ripped me off. My elbow is sore, though. A puddle of sweat on the floor under my face. At first I think it's blood, but the eye that isn't pressed into the floor looks and it's only sweat not blood and I'm happy it ain't blood. AIDS blood. If it were blood, I'd get up again and run like I ran when I was a kid and Uncle Bob chased me all over the farm.

In a heap, my body. I don't even know where my legs are. Only what I see I can know. My hand is way out there in front of me two tiles away just lying there. For a moment I'm sure my hand is dead, but I know it ain't 'cause it just checked my ass pocket.

The lightbulb in the middle of my chest.

Over the years nothing has changed. Fear has ruled my life and now it will rule my death. No matter how long I run or where I run to.

Then my hand is in Atlanta under Gary's apple tree and I'm looking at my thumb. Remember? The amazing understanding I had about fear and my thumb. How was it exactly that my thumb moved? At what position was there fear? What position was there no fear?

Look at you sprawled out sweating like a pig in some other dandy's clothes, looking one eye across two gray tiles at your thumb. Your thumb, your thumb, your goddamn thumb. Too afraid to move your thumb because you can't remember where the no fear position is, and maybe your thumb is already in the fucking no-fear position. And it can get worse. You know damn well it can get worse.

Maybe what you found on mushrooms under an apple tree in a ghost town in Idaho won't come back to you now that you're down and out in New York City in a puddle of sweat.

Lie there, Little Man. Try and move your thumb. It is your only hope – not the consequence of what comes after you move it, but that you can summon up the will to move it at all.

The worst thing about hope isn't when you can't find it.

It's that you stop.

13.

Portlandia, 1995
Seven years later

MY THUMB IS AGAINST THE KNUCKLE OF MY INDEX FINGER, on the no-fear spot.

I've just got back from a week in Montana and it's a summer night in Portland. Hot for Portland, and the miracle above all, it's not raining. It always rains until July Fourth and July Fourth is four days away. The house is clean and decorated with white candles and white crepe paper streamers. I've cooked up a huge barbecue of ribs and chicken. It's a full moon and a blue moon. A Summer White Party.

My birthday. Forty-seven years old.

Six o'clock, an hour before everybody gets there, I'm just out of the shower, heading upstairs to put on my party duds. I'll be wearing a pair of white long johns. The double doors to the deck are open and in the distance, Mount Hood on the horizon is a piece of sharp white. Just down the stairs of the deck, under the clematis, sunlight there on the second step. There's only a minute or two before the sun goes behind the hill.

The patch of sunlight is just big enough for my face and shoulders. And my hand. The sun on the thumb and the index finger of my hand. On the knuckle, the no-fear spot. I take a deep breath. Move my thumb to the tip of my index, to the fear spot.

That evening, my forty-seventh birthday, in the patch of sun on the second step, there's no lightbulb in my chest, no flickering filament, no Fear Giant. Only the sun on my hand and water from my wet hair rolling down my back. I move my thumb back to the knuckle, then back again to the tip. Back and forth, back and forth.

SEVEN YEARS AGO, back in the puddle of sweat on the floor of Penn Station, I finally got my thumb to move. If you can make it there you can make it anywhere. Nothing changed. I mean the fear didn't just go poof. But I figured that since I moved my thumb I could move something else. Besides, how long really can you lie on the floor in a public train station.

Lots of people were staring. Most of them New Jersey or Long Island people. New Yorkers wouldn't stare that way. I sat for a while on the gray tiles, then Big Ben made my knees do it and I stood up. Had to stand for a while, too. Kept forgetting what I was doing or why I was doing it.

At the curb I got a taxi. Nothing like a quick taxi to fix things up. Give you a sense of power. I even had enough money to pay him. Tipped him good. A dark brown guy with huge black eyes and pock-marked skin from one of those unpronounceable -*stan* countries. Incense burning on the dashboard. I think he knew he was my guardian angel.

After I showered I sat down at my new computer. I started writing because I didn't know what else to do. It was a longshot, this novel, but I trusted my heart, I followed my bliss. I stayed centered with a positive attitude. I shot my arrow of intention into the air. The secret is to believe. It all sounds like bullshit, but what else you got?

Imagine it and it will come. One day the phone rings and through a bunch of mysterious events, on the line it's an old friend of Randy Goldblatt's. Randy, from Jeske's class. The guy on the phone, his name is Tony, and he wants to have coffee. Tony Escobar. Another long story and not an easy one to tell.

We meet for lunch at Café Orlin. Tony's odd and funny and looks like a heavyweight Billy Zane. Neither one of us knows what to say at first. Randy's dead and he died of dementia strapped into a straitjacket. What can you say.

Tony orders the *huevos rancheros*. Tony raves so much about the *huevos rancheros*, I order the *huevos rancheros* too. The table is small and the restaurant is crowded. Our knees touch under the table. Tony was right about the Mexican eggs. Delicious. We hit it off pretty quick and soon enough we get to talking about Randy. Tony tells me he and Randy were roommates as undergrads at UCLA. They got real close. Then Tony says something that surprises me.

"You're all Goldie talked about," Tony says, "that whole semester he was in Jeske's class."

"Goldie?" I say.

"Randy, Randy *Goldblatt*," Tony says.

"Poor Randy," I say. "That first day, Jeske made Randy say it. That he was fat. Made him fucking cry."

Three years older than me, Tony, a Sagittarius. His father's family from Spain and his mother's Black Irish. He's a recovering Catholic, too, and a professor of English at Reed College and he's just finishing up his sabbatical in Manhattan. Single, out, and gay, and he lives in Portland, Oregon. Smooth olive skin and a clipped beard but not too tidy. Blue eyes that jump out of all that black hair. Lips like Marco's lips, cherry red.

It ain't long and we're talking about our HIV positives. We're talking about sex. What we can do and what we can't. What is safe if you're both positive? Just talking about sex, we both get a little crazy.

I know. This guy Tony is too good to be true. God bless Randy Goldblatt. God bless Goldie. But the best thing about Tony is his dick. He doesn't get hard right off. His dick isn't as big as the rest of him is and he's shy about it.

Shy. That's it right there. I'm totally smitten.

Room 523, the Hotel Olcott. The days of my propinquity are over and we get naked and we talk, have a little wine. The bathtub is huge and green and Tony's got bubble bath. It ain't long at all and there's bathwater splashing. Then sex again on the bed. Tony's bed is actually two beds pushed together and we're lying in the middle of the beds and our fucking pushes the beds apart and I fall to the floor as I'm coming. Tony looks over the edge of the bed the way I was hollering to see if I'm still alive. Tony laughs like Hank, a whole-body laugh, lots of chest. A lot of things about Tony remind me of Hank. Dinner at Raoul's that Tony springs for. Later on that night, we find a park bench in Central Park. We sit on the park bench in the shadows. Out in the street, the yellow lamplight, the wind blowing the gold leaves, Tony reaches over and holds my hand. Propinquity.

After Tony reads my novel he's convinced it's love. I'm convinced too. He wants me to come live with him. I want to come live with him. We set the date for the end of June the following year.

Tony leaves for Portland in early December.

For Christmas, he sends me a Fairy Drag Queen ornament to put on the top of my tree. It's a Ken Doll dressed up as Christmas Angel Barbie, only Christmas Angel Barbie's got a black beard and hairy legs. Her lopsided halo you can plug in. Under his dress is a red jock strap. A wired connector on his asshole so he can sit, a proper star, on the very top tip of the tree. In his Christmas card, Tony tells me he bought the Fairy Drag Queen at a benefit for AIDS on Christopher Street.

By April Tony is dead.

Systemic non-Hodgkin's lymphoma.

AT PORTLAND'S PIONEER Cemetery, I stay away from the crowd of mourners. Look hard to see which woman is his mother. Which man his father. Lots of young people gathered. Students, I guess. A young man plays his guitar and sings. *"Ne Me Quitte Pas."* Fuck.

When everyone leaves and the dozer has filled the grave, I just sit there on the wet grass among all the flowers. It's a beautiful spring day. The tall trees. Everything so quiet. Green like I've never seen green.

Big Ben finds a house for rent not more than a block away.

Three hundred dollars a month for a whole house and backyard. On the FOR RENT sign it says: *See Horace next door,* and then an arrow. Next door in the front yard there is every kind of blooming flower there is. Horace is about sixty. He's bald and wears a red T-shirt. His pants held up by red suspenders. Those wild kind of eyebrows old men got and spectacles. *Spectacles,* I think as soon as I see Horace's gold-rimmed glasses. The way Horace's blood-shot eyes look at me he can tell I've been crying. In Horace's hand a copy of *Moby-Dick.*

"Good book," I say.

"Have you read the feminist version?" he says.

I don't know what to say. I clear my throat or some shit like that.

"Moby Pussy," he says.

Horace doesn't laugh when he says this, so I don't laugh either. Really, I'm afraid to start laughing. I take my wallet out, take two hundred cash out and give it to him and tell him I'll send him the rest when I get to Manhattan.

"Manhattan?" Horace says.

I start to apologize for the missing hundred then stop.

"Grew up on Orchard and Delancey," he says.

Then Horace goes in his house and closes the door. I can hear him in his front room rustling around. When he opens the door again he hands me two keys.

"Same key opens the front door and the back," he says. "You've got two there. Duplicates."

"Full rent is due by the fifth of every month," he says.

At Tony's grave with all the flowers I tell Tony about my new house and ask him if he's read the feminist version of *Moby-Dick.*

A WEEK LATER, back in New York, Little Ben thinks I can't possibly leave New York. Who am I if I'm not a New Yorker?

One morning I get up, throw on my work clothes, grab my broom and dustpan, open and close and lock my apartment door, walk out the front door of my building. Down on the street, some asshole has ripped open the garbage bags and there's shit all over creation. The night before I'd spent a couple hours bagging up that garbage. So I set myself to the task at hand. Get the mess cleaned up. All the while people are walking past. One guy in a black Armani overcoat hacks up a loogie and spits right at my feet. It's nothing personal. It's just that I'm invisible. But it's the backed up sewerage in the basement of 39 East Seventh that's the last straw. I leave my white Key West shrimper boots on the bottom basement stair.

If you can make it here you can make it anywhere.

THE DAY I leave Manhattan, Hank is up from Florida getting the last of his shit out of storage. We meet at #77 St. Mark's Place, at Auden's door. It's the afternoon of *Cinco de Mayo*. Already hot. After this day, I won't see Hank for eleven and a half years. Hank's in his gray hooded sweatshirt and Levi's. Still wearing the straw cowboy hat Gary gave him from Atlanta. His new white tennis shoes. His hair's cut short and his beard shows gray. The Eighties are about over. I'm wearing the green coat Gary gave me with Idaho Dairy Association on it. Levi's, my Red Wing boots. Sal's red baseball cap. I've brought an old bike along somebody'd left in one of my basements. Hank said he could use the transportation in Florida. It's one of those stripped down bikes with ten gears and knobby tires that's good for dodging through traffic. Hank's standing on one side of the bike, me on the other.

THOSE BLACK EYES that should be blue but they're not. Hank looks tired. But I do too.

I don't tell him about Tony. I try to but I can't. But I do tell him about the house I've rented in Portland. I make up some shit about going back to the Pacific Northwest. Hank's still going on about Barry Hannah.

When we embrace the bike is between us. We're front to front and Hank holds onto the bike, keeps the bike right there between us.

I wonder why that bike is there.

But then I got to figure. It's been eight months since Atlanta and the wedding ring bed. And Hank Christian, The Enigma of Hank, The Warrior Ghost, is back to holding his cards close to his chest.

Hank Christian, man. Fucking Hank Christian.

I'm trying not to cry, but I cry.

Fucking Auden's poem gets me every time.

THAT FIRST YEAR in Portland I spend more time in the cemetery than anywhere else. There's a huge old cedar tree I like to lean against. Smells great under that tree. Pioneer Cemetery. Mostly poor people buried there. Couldn't find a spot for myself right next to him, but I got one close by.

Tony Escobar, man. Fucking Tony Escobar.

AND THAT'S HOW I got here, Portland, Oregon, on the second step. The sun is warm on my face, my shoulders, my hands. Five years and three months since Tony died. Five years and two months I've lived in Portland.

It's my birthday and people are coming to my house for a birthday party and I have enough money to buy the food and the booze. I have two books published and I have a contract for a third and the third book is busting my balls but I love it. I'm writing about what only there is I can write about. AIDS and New York.

Something else that's important to know. Not a day has gone by in these last seven years that Little Ben hasn't woken up afraid. AIDS. That bright flickering filament in the middle of my chest. Every day at Bikram's College of India, with every drop of sweat I think of AIDS. I quit smoking, quit drinking. Every day when I want a smoke I think of AIDS. Every day I want a smart cocktail I think of AIDS. My organic breakfast, the organic vegetables for lunch and dinner, the naturally grown meat I can't afford at the fancy grocery. Every night I put myself to sleep reading Louise Hey and other self-help books. Flip the *I Ching*. Do the tarot cards. Trying to keep the Fear Giant at bay. One spiritual book tells me my urine is my own secret personal medicine cabinet, so every morning I drink a cup of my urine. Every morning with my cup of piss I remember AIDS. It's not so bad, just tastes like piss. The secret is to believe. Not one moment since that day I lay on the floor in Penn Station, not for one fucking moment have I let myself forget what the doctor on East 83rd had said.

Positive = Sick = Death.

Then there was Montana. Just the week before, as a birthday present for me, Ephraim arranged it so that I could dance with a sacred medicine pipe. Me, the only white man that's danced with that pipe. When the old native man asked me why I wanted to dance with his pipe, I looked into his dark eyes. They were the eyes of a child, nothing in between. I've never felt so looked at. I told him about my friends who died and the virus called AIDS and the test that I had that showed I was infected. I told him I was dancing with his pipe so I wouldn't get AIDS.

We can do that, the old man had said.

ON THE SECOND step the sun is almost gone. I take another breath, a deep inhale.

It's that day, in the patch of sun, in Portlandia. All that Montana sacred pipe spirit flowing through me. That moment there on my forty-seventh birthday, I decide.

My thumb is on the no fear spot and I move my thumb away. It's time to let the fear go. My birthday gift to myself. Big Ben steps up and declares: I am healthy and I'm going to stay healthy and I'm not going to get AIDS.

As if it were up to me.

The patch of sunlight is gone. That breath is a difficult breath to let go of, but when I do, it's the first time in years. No fear. Clear and clean and smooth and as soon as I finish my proclamation of health, the phone rings. It's Hank Christian.

"Dear sweet man," Hank says. "Happy Birthday."

"How's Barry Hannah?" I say.

"We're armwrestling," Hank says. "Three to two my favor."

"Dr. Christian," I say, "if you ever graduate you should come teach with me. What a team we'd make. Just like the old days at the Y."

"Hey, I'm serious," Hank says. "I'd love teaching with you. Nobody else is doing what you're doing."

"There wouldn't be any tenure," I say. "But that doesn't mean there ain't no benefits."

Hank's big laugh coming up and out of him.

"You could say *motherfucker* all you wanted," I say.

"And no freshman comp," Hank says.

"I ain't much at armwrestling," I say.

We laugh some more after that. Then we talk as long as we can but neither one of us are good on the phone. So we make our usual promise that we'll visit one another. But I have my new book to work on. And Hank has to find a job. It will be five years before we talk to each other again.

IT'S THAT NIGHT I have a gin and tonic, two. I smoke some reefer too. Weird. I'd completely forgotten what a funny fellow I can be. Of course, you can't smoke reefer and not have a cigarette. Before I know it, I'm completely stoned and I'm Big Ben and there are so many people in the house it's hard to move. Most of the people are from my class. It's when my favorite song comes on, "Got to Give It Up," that I look around for someone to dance with.

Ruth Dearden's been dancing all night, nonstop, as if the back patio was a place of magic. Sometimes alone, mostly with other women. Ruth is completely unselfconscious, and often the way she moves is quite dramatic. For a moment I think she's high, then I remember her husband.

Ruth always leaves right after class. Most students hang out, have some wine. Usually someone lights a joint. Later on,

Ruth will tell me it was because of that joint that she left early. She was afraid her husband would find out and he'd make her stop class because there were drugs.

At first, I dance alone next to her. The last time I'd danced to this song was with Hank that night before we went to the Spike. All around Ruth on the patio are puffs of chiffon that all night she's been tearing off her dress.

The moment when Ruth sees that I'm close, she smiles way too big. I take her hands and we begin to dance. Jitterbugging I guess is what you'd call it. My sister taught me the steps when I was in the fourth grade and I've been doing them ever since. Modified the steps with Bette Podegushka for the disco years.

"Oh my God!" Ruth says. "My teacher is dancing with me and he's in his long johns!"

Some women just know how to follow. Don't ask me how they do it. I can't do it. Ginger Rogers as good as Fred Astaire only Ginger did it backwards and in high heels.

Some women Ruth ain't. As soon as I touch her hands and begin dancing with her, the unselfconscious, dramatic dancer that was Ruth Dearden, all of a sudden loses her rhythm. It's like she isn't listening to the music at all. She actually begins to clown, throwing her arms and legs around. I'm surprised she makes fun of herself like this. Then in a moment I get it. Ruth Dearden has a propinquity problem. I quick let go of Ruth's hands and we dance together without touching.

On her chest, just above the chiffon bodice of her white dress, her skin flushes scarlet. Ruth knows her skin is doing that, so she puts her hand at her throat. She's looking for something to say, anything, so she says:

"Happy Birthday!"

"You look like you're having a good time," I say.

"My husband isn't here," she says.

"Your dress is falling apart."

"I'm ripping it apart. It's my wedding dress," Ruth says. "I've always hated it."

"A little girl's dress," she says. "Or a doll's. So puffy and so First Communion. I don't know what I was thinking."

What I say next. You got to be high to say shit like I say next.

"If you keep at it," I say, "you'll be like Shingli-shoozi."

Ruth Dearden isn't as tall as me. She's barefoot and I got two inches on her. She's not fat or plump. She's just big. By the time she meets Hank she'll have lost twenty-five pounds. Her skin is that strawberry blonde that freckles. The flush still on her chest. Maybe a heat rash. Her hair is thick and red that hangs to her shoulders. Curly hair that won't frizz. I want to touch it. Because of the color and how it looks silky and because I'm high.

"What did you say?" she says.

I have to stop because I'm laughing. That happened a lot with Ruth. There was a way so many times when we were together I'd start laughing and not know how to stop and the moment would expand and expand. I'd just suddenly find myself in a place I couldn't explain that was never ending. And I'd be laughing.

"Shingli-shoozi," I say. "It's a Betty Grable movie. Betty's singing and dancing on a stage in front of a red curtain and there's a pocket in the curtain and she steps inside the pocket and changes into a skimpier outfit."

"It's a game my sister and I played," I say.

The way Ruth is looking at me. Her big plastic glasses a little crooked. Her bangs hanging down into her eyes. That asymmetrical jaw of hers and her mouth open. The flush is on her cheeks as well.

"I made up the word," I say. "Or my sister did. When I was five. I was so fascinated by Betty Grable's pocket in the curtain and her quick wardrobe change I called it Shingli-shoozi."

"Shingli-shoozi!" Ruth says.

"My father hated it," I say.

"Betty Grable?"

"No," I say. "That I made up the word."

"Was it you who made it up," Ruth asks, "or your sister?"

"Men can't do that, you know," I say. "Women are lucky that way. You can step behind a curtain, change your outfit and your makeup, and voilà, you step out a whole new woman."

"Jeez," Ruth says. "Wish I knew how to do that."

That was the first time Ruth hit me. Knocked me the fuck down. I mean she didn't mean to. It's just at that moment, Ruth decided to do one of her dramatic dance moves and she twirled with her arms out and when her arm came around, her fist hit me square in the face and knocked me down.

I put my hand to my nose, blood on my hand.

"Ben!" Ruth says. "I'm so sorry!"

She leans down, and with a tuft of chiffon she's ripped from her dress, she goes to put the chiffon to my bloody nose.

"HIV!" I almost yell it.

LATER ON THAT night, when the full moon is hanging above the chatter and the music of the party, I pass out the words to a song. It's an old song from the Thirties and what's a better thing to do on a Cancer's birthday than sing to the moon.

I turn the lights out and each person lights a candle and we gather close together in the backyard and we're all in white and we all look up. The full moon up there in the dark night sky, a bright silver ball. The night is clear and warm, and the moon feels close, how we can see that it's a ball hanging up there, the craters on its surface. The way it shines is the way we all shine when we know we're beheld.

> *Blue moon*
> *You saw me standing alone.*

VOICES RISING TOGETHER in song. It can get me every time. All of a sudden, my body feels the bodies close around me. My birthday, my friends, my students, this new world in Portland, Oregon, the shine up there shining just for me. The breath I take is another new breath, a breath without the constant fear.

I heard somebody whisper please adore me
And when I looked the moon had turned to gold.

It's on the refrain that I look around at the group of us. Mortals singing at the moon. We're all children, really. No wonder people sing to feel united. Each one of us, alone in our body, gives voice to a sound that goes up and out into the world. Our voice is joined by other voices, and by some miracle, what joins our voices out there dives down into our throats back into our hearts.

Then I hear it. One voice I can hear above the rest. It's not a strong singing voice. There's something fragile about it, yet clear, determined.

Ruth Dearden, a candle under her chin, her big plastic glasses. All the chiffon tufts of her dress torn off. Her head is tilted up. The way she's looking at the moon, somehow you just know.

All her dreams are going to come true.

14.
Father

THE CAR I RENT IN BOISE IS A GRAY CHEVROLET ASTRO. I stop off at their houses, but Reuben and Sal and Gary are still in Atlanta. On I-84 it's the Mountain Home desert. All the windows are open and my elbow's out the window. August in Idaho. It's mid-day and my shirt's off. No shoes, my baggy cutoffs, my bare legs, bare feet. Wind blowing through the Astro and the radio cranked up high, I'm alone singing loud to the golden oldies the one hundred and fifty-four miles to Jerome.

God, I miss Hank.

Tony would've loved Idaho.

MY FATHER'S HOUSE is set a ways off from the highway. The country mailbox Grunewald with the red metal flag, set on a rail-road tie stuck in the ground in the gravel right where the drive-way intersects with the highway. My mother used to back her Buick out of the garage, pull it up back to behind the house, just to where the Buick's nose was even with the board fence, then hit the gas. She'd hit sixty before she got to the mailbox and still have time to stop. The distance less than one city block from starting line to finish.

The house is a tile-roof red-brick house with a picture win-dow. My father built the house for my mother when they sold the farm. This new house is almost identical to the house I was raised in. The same three-bedroom ranchburger. Same kitchen, same vaulted-ceiling living room with used-brick walls and exposed beams, the same front porch with a loveseat for two that is a swing. Identical to the old house, almost. It's what is not identical that makes me crazy.

My mother's not in it. She's dead.

I pull the Astro to into the driveway and park next to my father's red Chevy pickup. The sun is late afternoon hot and bouncing bright off the cement driveway and the white vinyl garage doors.

The car engine shut off, the engine still ticking. This is always the point, Christmas or summer or whenever the visit, just as we're about to get out of the car, just before we enter into the portal of the family house, is when my sister Margaret always said it: *Cowboy up, Ben.*

Immediately, that day getting out of the Astro, I have a quick moment of shame and I want to cover my naked chest and arms, my naked legs, my bare feet. According to father, a man is always in his boots, in his Levi's. Only long-sleeved shirts that you can roll to the elbow. And a hat. A man always wears his hat.

Fuck him and his hat. I'm bare-headed, barefoot, half-naked, and he's almost dead. I am too. Still got three and a half years. But I don't know it. Don't want to know it.

My feet are hot on the cement. I do a back stretch and when I lean forward I fart. Think of Hank. Think of my father. Both of them big on farting.

On the sidewalk, just below the mudroom door, is the old chain-linked metal mat you scrape your boots off on that's been in front of the mud room door since I've had a memory. The metal presses little squares into the bottoms of my feet. The mud-room door is unlocked. Up the four steps, the kitchen door is unlocked too.

The silent way that door opens. Not like the creak of the door of the first house. I call out hello, but the house is silent the way only the second house can be silent. More than silent. The way nothing arrives at the ear. This second house, just empty, because it's trying to be the other house, and it will never be the other house, plus she died in this house.

Only the grandfather clock in the living room. That tic tic tic. At a quarter past, the chime, so German, and at the half-hour, and at quarter 'til, and then on the hour the big to-do with the chimes and the cuckoo. Like to drive you fucking nuts.

But it's not just that my mother isn't here.

The first house he built her had a promise. Something about that first house – how it expanded out past the green lawn she kept so perfect, past the log pole fence I built her, past the Four o'Clocks and the Austrian Copper rose, to the Tyhee Road, and from there through the fertile valley into town and from there on out it was the world.

This second house was a ruse. A stage set of the first house built on a hill in the desert with a wind break of half-dead pines and scrub Russian olives. Something to keep her going, to stop her spine from bending completely forward at the waist. To stop the psoriasis and her hair from falling out. Something to get her to start baking apple pies again, au gratin potatoes again, chocolate cakes, carrot pudding, start playing her piano again – anything to bring her back. But the day she walked into that new house – at the very place my bare feet are standing that day – when the door closed behind her, she knew she'd never leave it. At that moment, one step in, so much like the old house but not the old house at all, this new house was a prison and she fell and broke her ankle.

The linoleum is cool under my feet. The same pattern as the old linoleum. The countertops the same Formica green. The white cupboards. The same early American drawer pulls. The wallpaper with rows of yellow roses. But this kitchen is the mausoleum of the old kitchen. Not even a ghost of live food. Feels like you're standing in a large hallway that happens to have a refrigerator and a stove and a sink in it. Everything so clean, so antiseptic the way she'd have kept it. My father takes care that everything stays exactly the way she'd have kept it – the kitchen table with the grapes and apples and pears oilcloth tablecloth, the salt and pepper shakers that look like milk cans in the center of the table, the lamp you can pull down so the bright light isn't in your eyes, the green wall telephone, the fancy pen with the feather on it on the built-in table under the green wall phone. On the wall next to the phone, the faux-weathered wood sign that says: *Vee get too soon alt and too late schmardt.*

That day when I walk into the bathroom, there they are, the set of forest green bath towels and hand towels and washrags one Christmas I bought my mother at Bloomingdales monogrammed *J&M*. The set of towels she only hangs out for company. That is, for me. The bath towels hang perfectly lined on the rack above the bathtub. The hand towels hanging perfectly lined next to the sink. The forest green washrags with the monogrammed *J&M* folded over each towel. The forest green toilet seat cover, the green rug on the floor around the toilet.

For a moment, I wonder if he's hung the towels out there for me. But *he's* had a stroke. *He* is almost dead. Maybe already dead. How could he possibly think to hang the Forest Green Monogrammed Bloomingdale Towels out. Maybe since she'd died, my mother was the company he'd put the towels out for.

Probably it was my sister. Above the toilet is a blue and white ceramic mother duck with three blue and white little ducks swimming behind. They're all swimming with their beaks lined up with their mother's in a straight line – then there's the odd duck, the black duck with his bill tipped down. Always been an odd duck.

In their Dusty Rose bedroom on the same carpet but different, mother's worn blue fuzzy slippers next to her side of the bed, side by side exactly, her rosary with the beads that glow in the dark on the bedpost. Her folded jeans on the chair. The blue cotton blouse. On the wall, the paintings of The Immaculate Heart of Mary, the Sacred Heart of Jesus, the woven palm fronds from Palm Sunday stuck into each frame. The round mirror of my mother's vanity. The infant I was from my crib who stared into that mirror. Inside that mirror, the bedroom reflected, somehow in there is the most terrifying of all.

The last time I'd seen my mother was when I'd visited in 1988. I was studying at Columbia and working at Café Un Deux Trois. One evening, after supper and apple pie and ice cream, my mother and I sat on the brown davenport and drank coffee and smoked cigarettes. She'd fluffed up her hair and wore her Orange Exotica lipstick. My father sat at the kitchen table, his back to us, the lamp pulled down, that bright light onto his big hairy hand, onto the purple grapes and the red apples and the yellow pears on the oilcloth tablecloth, onto the pages of the *Treasure Valley News*, my father a looming torpor of silence, stirring his tea with three teaspoons of sugar with his teaspoon – while I was with her in the living room, her hero. Full of romantic stories of famous people and faraway places. Frank Sinatra ordering a Manhattan, Ingrid Bergman's daughter spilling ketchup on her blouse. When I tell my mother that Tony Bennett's toupée looks like a rug on his head, she laughs 'til her gums show.

The next morning is the morning I have to leave. In the kitchen, I've just shook hands with my father and am hugging my sister, when over her shoulder I see my mother. She's in the hallway motioning with her finger for me to come with her.

In the bathroom, mother locks the door behind us. Surrounded by the Forest Green Monogrammed Bloomingdale *J&M* towels, the black ceramic odd black duck, my mother puts her hand around my arm, her slick palm, and squeezes. Her almond-shaped hazel eyes.

"Ben," she says, "you have to take me with you. Take me out of here. This man I live with doesn't look at me or talk to me or take me out. He never thanks me. All I do is cook and clean. That's all that's left. There's nothing bright or special. Nothing new. I'm going to die here in this damn house someday while I'm mashing his spuds and I don't want to die that way, so you got to take me with you."

This is the mother whose insane rages, as a child, my sister

Margaret protected me from. This is the mother of the weekly enema. Warm salty water, the rubber hose. Even my insides weren't mine. This is the mother, and I her male child. My cock, the first cock she was ever in charge of, her rigorous Catholic-in-celibacy training, my God, my cock never had a chance. This is the mother. The woman who was my story, who I was for, however she wanted to see me, how I finally left her behind. That indelible story she told me, who I am, that I'm still trying to retell.

This mother, my mother.

And so I sit on the toilet, not on the closed forest green covered toilet lid, but on the toilet hole, as if I were going to shit, only with my pants on, holding the huge Catholic Virgin Tyrant Mother Mary, my little crooked mother in my arms. The way she weeps. My mother's snot and tears rolling down my neck. How I'd spent my life trying to keep those tears away.

"Take me out of here," she cries. "You've got to take me out of here."

Three years later, the night before her funeral, Margaret and my father and I are sitting at the kitchen table. That dead silence of the second house. The fucking clock. The purple grapes, the red apples, the yellow pears of the oilcloth tablecloth. The salt and pepper shakers that look like milk cans. The lamp you can pull down, that bright light shining on *Certificate of Death*. Margaret lights another Virginia Slim. She is the ghost behind the cloud of smoke. My father has spread out his hand onto the oilcloth, over the purple grapes. His black hairy thick knuckles. He's stopped crying. But just long enough to speak.

"Tomorrow at the funeral Mass," my father says, "one of us has got to take the urn from the altar and lead the procession out to the internment spot."

When my father knew my mother was dying, he left her bed in the hospital and drove home. He didn't want to be with her at the moment of death because he was afraid that she'd shit herself.

Margaret takes another drag on her cigarette. No way she's going to carry that urn. My father can't carry the urn out because once she died he hasn't been able to stop crying. Years of beating and berating his son not to cry, for three days straight the man cannot stop crying. The three or four years he survives without her, that's really all he does. All he can do. My father cries.

The next morning, after the funeral Mass, the priest looks over at me. The Hierophant's Nod. It is my sign. Like an altar boy who knows his way around the hardwood steps, the scarlet carpeting, the incense and the ringing gold bells, I get up, walk to the altar. The urn is copper and oval-shaped. I'm surprised I don't think it's tacky. My hand reaches out and grabs the urn, brings it in close to my chest. Puts the oval copper urn in there secure so the klutz don't drop it.

I turn around and face the congregation. That's when I hear it.

"Take me out of here, Ben," my mother says. "You've got to take me out of here."

IN MY MOTHER'S second house, on the pad with the fancy feathered pen on the built-in table below the green wall phone is a note in Margaret's back-sloping loopy handwriting.

At St. Luke's, Room 585. Hurry up.

The next three days, Margaret and I take turns with our father. His left side is paralyzed. He is conscious but he doesn't speak. Doesn't make a sound. Doesn't move. He can't eat. He can breathe and keep his right eye open. Every once in a while he moves his right hand, his index finger. As if he's pointing at something.

That first day I walk into the room, his bed surrounded by monitor screens that blip, tubes everywhere, my father is just a head, a huge head with a huge nose under an oxygen mask, and huge ears. That huge scary body of his, now only long skinny bones under the sheet.

Margaret can't stop talking. Her little girl voice. She calls him daddy. A running commentary. *Lookit here, daddy, your long-lost son has just walked into the room. Isn't it great to see Benny again?* The only time she shuts up is when she goes to smoke. Thank God she smokes a lot.

On my second day, there's something about his right eye. Something come to life in there. He recognizes both of us. I don't know how we know this, but both Sis and I know. It's that one dark eye, how it follows us when we move.

Daddy, Daddy, Can you hear us?

That night, Margaret goes home to get some sleep. It's the first time I'm alone with him. I try but can't remember the last time my father and I were alone. How I stare at him. Long, long, and long. His eye stares back. Never blinks. It feels like a stare-down, but I'm not sure that's true. I think maybe that's just how his eye is now. But the gaze between us, whatever the medical condition, has the same feel it's always had. The way that eye looks at me. The challenge to look back.

I pull my chair up to the bed and don't ever stop looking back.

Late that night, I've fallen asleep, my head on the mattress. In my dream Hank is touching my head, or is it Tony? When I wake up it's my father's index finger that's touching me. I don't move. Just let my head lie there on the soft mattress, my father's finger a gentle scratch at the back of my head, in my hair. How his touch goes to every part of me. It's only at that moment, while my father is touching me, that I know fully what it's been like not to be touched by him.

A man shut out from the world of men. Full of confusion and misery. And something else. I know it with all my heart and soul. For a son your father is the one. One day, you're in diapers, in the afternoon, in the morning, just before you go to sleep, by a river bank, in your nursery with the blue sailboats, strapped in the carseat, out in the raw dark brown earth of the sugar beet field, when your father hands you back to your mother, there's a moment he beholds you. The way he touches you he believes you into his world. He gives you back to your mother but now you're his.

Most fathers don't know this touch or even when they give it. But still they give it. If your father doesn't give you his touch, doesn't claim you, it's because he himself is lost, or dead, or not there, or too drunk or stoned, or the mother is too strong, or the father somehow decides against you.

But really, all I know for sure late that night in St. Luke's Hospital, Room 585, my head on the soft mattress, about sons and fathers, is what is true for me. My father's touch gives me presence in my body in a way I've only always wished for.

When I turn my head around, my father's eye is right there, just beyond his finger that keeps moving up and down across my eye and nose. I pull my head back. In that moment I'm sure I've found the clue, discovered the secret. It's the deathbed scene and finally my father's given in.

I stand up, lean my arms against the bed and lower my head down. I don't know what I'm going to do. Rest my cheek against his cheek. Maybe kiss his forehead. Lay my head on his shoulder. Touch my forehead to his forehead. Whatever it is, I will show my forgiveness to him for all the broken years.

My head lowers down closer in. Out the corner of my eye, I see his finger's still moving. I have the thought that maybe this is a mistake and his finger is just moving like it's always been moving and in my sleep I rolled my head over and my head just happened to be there where his finger was and that's the only reason that he was touching me.

My chest low, almost touching his chest, close in to my father's face, we're eye to eye, only a breath apart, and his other eye opens. One eye, so much less than half of both his eyes. Together my father's black eyes are the full force.

It's only then I realize. He thinks I'm going to kiss him on the lips.

His homo son.

My father, who hasn't moved or spoken or shown any signs

of life besides breathing and his one damn open eye, now two eyes, and his fucking index finger, now gathers all his strength and stretches his neck away, turns his face up, his lips away from mine, and yells some kind of animal grunt.

I pull his face back around, pull his oxygen mask off. Hold him by his huge ears. Make him look at me.

Dark, almost black, bloodshot, in that moment, I am beheld all right. Those critical fucking eyes. Full of hate and fear. The fucked slant of dark sun that was my nourishment. So this is the gaze that made me. How I'd stretched my body spindled and crooked for light. In his gaze, as I was ruined, I was ruined in every corner of the world.

If I were a better man, hell if I were any kind of man at all, I'd thank him. Like Johnny Cash thanking his father for naming him Sue.

But nowhere in my body is there a thank you.

Man to man, front to front, face to face, eye to eye with him.

My father is my enemy.

And I fucking hate his fucking guts.

15.
Misery

MAY 13, 1996. OVER THE YEARS I THOUGHT I KNEW THE depths of it. But I had no idea. My whole body goes down. And I don't know what the fuck. An alarm inside. A special alarm. The one that only goes off when the body knows it's about to die.

May 13th no different from most mornings. I wake up at eight-thirty. Make coffee in my French press, make toast. The coffee is a good blend I bought at Nature's. The toast is whole wheat and organic and the butter is unsalted organic and the orange marmalade is homemade, no preservatives.

I'm sitting at the kitchen table, reading a *New Yorker*. It's just after I finish the first cup of coffee and one of the pieces of toast.

That moment. If you're diabetic or hypoglycemic and you have a sugar crash, it's something like that. Or a grand mal seizure even. Imagine the worst feeling ever and then imagine that worst feeling won't ever go away. Fight or flight that hits you so fast all your systems shut down.

And all I'm doing is sitting at my breakfast table.

I make it out my door, somehow walk the two blocks to the Pioneer Cemetery, lie down on my spot close to Tony Escobar. Figure I'm dying, so I might as well die right there so all they have to do is roll me over then dig the hole.

Lying on the earth is the only thing that helps. But it starts to rain and the rain is good but pretty soon I'm shivering. If I could run, I'd run. I throw up and think I'll feel better after I throw up, but I don't. My pituitary gland, or whatever gland it is, is still pumping out stress hormones. I say that to myself: *your pituitary gland is still pumping out stress hormones,* but saying that only makes me think of my father's only joke: *You know how to make a whore moan?* As if he'd know.

I need to eat. What I need is protein, but I'm trying to be a vegetarian, but what I need most is protein. Meat protein, not that wimp-ass protein you get from soy drinks or tofu. What I need is to quit eating wheat. I'm fucking allergic to wheat, but I have no clue about wheat. What I need to do is quit drinking coffee and eating sugar. I'm exhausted from battling this virus and from being afraid. What I need most is rest. What I need most is to get my ass to the hospital.

But I have no insurance. And I've never once been to the hospital. Only to visit my friends who have died in the hospital have I gone to the hospital. Just walking in the hospital doors, how I was going to pay for it, fuck.

There is no one to call. The only person I can talk to is Tony and he's dead and I can't walk that far anymore. I call Hank but always get his machine. I never leave a message. Ephraim is in Bermuda. My students, of course, any one of them would come to help me. But I can't ask help from them. I'm their *teacher*. And teachers don't call up and say *what the fuck is happening to me*.

I don't know how I get through that day. My body isn't even mine to move. Just lying there on my spot, if I move my head, the world swirls around and even bounces. Things up close are far away and vice-versa. I can't find my regular breath. It's raining hard and I'm lying in a puddle. When Big Ben finally decides to move, it seems like hours it takes to stand up. Then standing up is its own horror. Each step is one step and one step is all I can imagine making.

The next morning I can walk and I can breathe. I get on my scales and I weigh one hundred eighty-three. Usually my weight is around one ninety-six. The next couple days I order in pizzas,

Indian food, Mexican food. Watch bizarre daytime television. Eat all the shit I shouldn't be eating. But I can't eat anyway.

The day of class, I'm barely holding it together. In fact, I don't hold it together. I start talking about how weird I feel and pretty soon I'm crying. The teacher puts his head down on the table and cries.

Ruth Dearden leans across and puts her hand on my head. Her hand feels cool and I want her to keep her hand on my head, but I'm the teacher and I'm in front of class.

Things in the world are just things. Your house, your table, your notebook, your computer, your bed, your toothbrush. Your clothes, your shoes, your socks, your car. Food. They have a life of their own unconnected to you. It's as if you're already dead and the world does not recognize you. And something even more. Because the things in the world don't recognize you, because your world isn't *your* world anymore, is just *the* world, instead of the familiar connection, you feel the empty place where you used to be connected, and without that connection, the way you're floating, things appear to you as having an energy barrier around them. And the energy of that barrier is a whole new weird deep anxiety.

My astrologist tells me the tough time I'm going through will end in December.

So Big Ben figures I just have to wait it out. Seven months.

That's German Catholic for you.

I make it through the next seven months that way. I mean Little Ben does.

Two hundred and one days. Every day.

Four thousand eight hundred and twenty-four hours.

Two hundred eighty nine thousand four hundred and forty minutes.

Seventeen million three hundred sixty-six thousand and four hundred seconds.

Shitting and shitting and shitting. My asshole gets so sore I can no longer use toilet paper. I wash myself off in the shower.

My body can actually feel itself dying. Every night sleep is one long nightmare.

Stubborn, dutiful, get what you need to get done. Be strong. Don't complain.

That's denial for you. Big Ben had decided I wasn't getting AIDS so I wasn't getting AIDS. It was an imperative from High Command. All the psychics had said so, the Native American Medicine Man said so. The *I Ching* said something different every time I threw it. Forget the tarot cards. But that's all I do. Throw the *I Ching*, lay out my tarot cards. Count every breath, every heartbeat.

That's fear for you. The fucking epidemic of fear. There's no asking for help. I'm the Running Boy and no place is safe.

Once a week, *arbeit macht frei*, Big Ben sits in front of class and demands I be a teacher. Finally, at Halloween, Little Ben just can't anymore. I take *a couple weeks off to get some rest.*

ON THE MORNING of December 1st, I call Ruth Dearden. I don't remember much. Ruth helps me get out of bed. I can't walk alone. We get lost in her Honda Civic on the way to the hospital. Fucking Ruth Dearden, man. I'm half dead and we're lost in the West Hills and I'm laughing. At the hospital emergency room I weigh in at 162. The on-call doctor is a young man wearing green scrubs. He says I probably just have the flu. Ruth grabs my hand and squeezes my hand when the doctor says that. Her hair's a mess and she's wearing what looks like pajama tops and sweat pants. Clogs.

"We'll give you some antibiotics and then we'll let you go," the doctor says. "But first we need to take a look at the X-rays of your lungs."

I have to pee. I walk down the hallway. I guess I'm walking alone. In the hallway I go past an open door. Inside the room, there are doctors looking at a chest X-ray. The beautiful white lines, hundreds of them, fluorescent long white worms, flowing down beneath the rib cage.

I'm on a gurney. They're wheeling me off. I don't recognize the on-call doctor because his face is upside down.

"Mr. Grunewald," the doctor says, "we're taking you to ICU.

"You have AIDS."

THEY WHEEL YOU across a long skybridge and put you in a blue room all alone. *Quarantine,* the sign on the door. Doctors all around you. Insurance people trying to get information. I don't qualify for the Oregon Health Plan because I've made too much money the year before. Twenty thousand is too much money. Doctors, nurses, ask me my name, ask me to subtract seven from ninety-three. I've got tubes up my ass. I'm under an oxygen mask. There's an IV in my arm. I'm skin and bones. I'm sweating like a son of a bitch.

Later on the doctor will tell you, *we almost lost you.*

But I don't tell the doctor, tell anyone, about the night they almost lost me. Things were sketchy and the dream world was not far away.

The night orderly was a big guy, heavyset. Round glasses and a lot of talk. He asked me to subtract seven from eighty-six and keep subtracting for as long as I could. It wasn't the first time I'd been asked that since I'd been in the hospital. But it was three in the morning. I don't know how, or why, but I did it. Little Ben always does what he's told. While I'm subtracting, in the middle of the night, they almost lost me, the heavyset night orderly puts on rubber gloves, tells me he needs to check my prostate. I'm subtracting and subtracting. One finger is up my ass and I'm subtracting. Two fingers and I'm subtracting. Three fingers, they're way up there up in my asshole and the pain is so great I think I stop breathing.

16.

The promise

THE DAY I GET HOME FROM THE HOSPITAL, THE *WALL Street Journal* publishes an article about the new AIDS cocktail, which I'm taking, which is making me sick. But I don't know from sick.

Hospital rules, they have to wheel you out in a wheelchair, but at the curb you're on your own. At the curb, Ruth is waiting in her silver Honda Civic. I've practiced walking in the corridors of the hospital, but this is the first time I've been outside. Of course it's raining. When I stand up from the wheelchair, Ruth is right there. Her arm around my back is strong. I know as soon as she touches me if I start to fall she can hold me up. The umbrella, the rain, standing up, taking the step off the curb, getting my long body to fold up into that tiny car, I have no idea how we do it.

Inside the car, my knees are almost poking me in the chin. Ruth has to reach down between my legs to push the lever so my seat will go back. Her hair smells of Herbal Essence shampoo. Inside Ruth's car is like everything of Ruth's. Chaos. I'm an every-thing-in-its-place kind of guy. My mind is chaos, so my world is ordered.

Ruth's dashboard is an altar. Two Wonder Woman action figures. An old peace symbol. Feathers and dried flowers and rocks. *If you're not mad you're not paying attention.* A Barbie doll head hanging on a chain from the rearview mirror. In the gear-shift console below the radio and CD player, the little box for change, in the box Ruth's got dried Rosemary and Lavender. And change, mostly pennies. On the floor is a beat-up copy of *Zyzzyva*, *Antioch Review*, an *Elle* magazine, a bubble gum wrapper, and a tin of Altoids. CD cases and CDs all over creation. *A Woman Without a Man Is Like a Fish Without a Bicycle* taped across the glove compartment.

With my index I tap the *woman fish* sticker and look over at Ruth. I can tell underneath it all she's nervous, but she's determined to get my ass home in one piece. The flush on her neck and on her cheek. I tap the *woman fish* sticker again. Ruth's eyes, under her bangs, under the oversized plastic contraption covering her eyes, are blue. She gives me a big smile. It's a smile a kid would give you.

"The divorce came through," Ruth says. "You're looking at a free woman."

With that, Ruth punches in a CD. It's David Bowie and Queen singing "Under Pressure" way too loud. She pulls up on the emergency brake, lets it down, rides the clutch, shifts into first. We're on a hill and she pulls off without a hitch. Just a tiny screech of tires. Already I'm laughing.

RUTH HAS CLEANED my house from top to bottom. I've never seen my kitchen floor so clean. She's even dusted. Fresh flowers in every room. When I ask about the flowers, Ruth tells me they're from friends and students. But there are so many. Later on I get the real story. Ruth is stealing the flowers from the cemetery.

"The people are already dead," Ruth says. "And I don't ever take more than a half dozen from one grave."

Those first three months, if you can make it through them, they say you'll make it the rest of the way. The first three months don't look so good for me. I can't stop shitting. I have an appointment once a week that Ruth drives me to. About the fifth week, my new doctor, who isn't a doctor, is a nurse practitioner, Madelena Papas, decides to give me medication for a yeast infection of the stomach. It's not a week later and things are back to normal. Or as normal as they're going to get. But it does my spirit good not to always be on the toilet.

Ruth's always there. I mean she's not always there but she's there pretty much every day. Ruth got alimony for two years in her divorce settlement. Don't ask me how she got that. Thank God for the both of us. Her alimony gives Ruth two years to figure out what she wants to do.

The Oregon Health Plan decides I'm eligible because the last three months I had no income. So I get Medicaid and Medicare, and Social Security says I'm disabled and I get a disability check every month. I'm so whacked out I don't know any of this. Ruth does. Ruth gets it so my disability check is automatically deposited in my checking account. She pays my rent and my utility bills. I'd imagine there were months that Ruth paid some of those bills herself but she never copped to it.

My medications. You can't believe the number of pills I have to take a day. At certain times of the day. Some with food. Some after not eating food for three to four hours. Some in the middle of the night. Ruth organizes my pills into a weekly pill dispenser. These pills in the morning. These in the afternoon. These in the evenings. These in the night. There's a list for me thumbtacked on the wall which pill to take and what color the pill is and what shape the pill is and when to take it.

For someone who seems like walking chaos, Ruth Dearden sure as hell knows how to organize a world.

After seven weeks, I can get up in the mornings and scramble eggs. For lunch, a lunch meat or tuna sandwich on spelt bread. Sardines at four o'clock. Ruth makes dinner or delegates someone to make dinner. I eat as much of my food as I can.

In fact, it's Ruth who figures out that so much of my stress level is due to my diet. That I need protein, that I'm allergic to wheat, that I need to stay away from caffeine and sugar.

My bed is set up in my old lean-to office just off the living room. That way I don't have to walk up the stairs. Ruth has hauled my old TV in and set it up at the end of my bed. After dinner some nights, she sits on the bed with me and we watch a movie she's rented. Always something upbeat. *It's a Mad, Mad, Mad, Mad, World*, *Some Like It Hot*, *The King and I*. One night Ruth rents *The Heiress* and at the end when Montgomery Clift is knocking on Olivia de Havilland's door, Ruth and I, our hands are gripped into one fist, rooting for the Heiress.

Ruth's nickname for me is Queen Lowlighta because of all the small atmosphere lamps and lava lamps with soft glows I've got all around my room. The night she called me that, we were both a little surprised. After all, I was her teacher and she was my student and there she was calling me Queen.

Fucking Ruth Dearden, man.

One Saturday night in March, I've asked Ruth to rent *Last Tango in Paris*. Upbeat it's not. But I'm ready for some art. Big Ben shows up and says I need some art. Ruth's never seen the movie, so when the movie's over it's just Ruth and me in my little space in the lean-to that used to be my office that's now my Queen Lowlighta bedroom fixed the way Cancers can make little homes out of nothing. It's close to midnight. Outside, it's raining buckets. I'm lying in my bed under a blanket and Ruth is lying on top of the blanket next to me. Really, we're so under the spell of the movie, we aren't at all uncomfortable lying close the way we are. Besides I'm under the blanket and she's on top. That evening I've showered and shaved and I'm in fresh pajamas. So I don't smell the way I think I usually smell. Ruth's in jeans and her Peruvian sweater. Her shoes are off. Long slender white feet.

All of a sudden, Little Ben is trying hard to say something to Ruth about how much I appreciate her and all she's done and how close I feel to her and how thankful I am for her generosity of spirit. It's all coming out awkward and full of clichés. Horribly fucking wrong, really stupid, and so I kiss her. On the lips, soft. Like Saint Bernadette would kiss you. The way Hank and I used to kiss. A kiss full of love and appreciation and respect and *agape*. That kind of kiss.

Ruth doesn't kiss back. I mean her lips just stay flat and let my puckered lips touch hers. Something happens in the room. But it's not in the room, it's in Ruth. Ruth's up off the bed and has her socks on, and her shoes and she's out the door. As she leaves the room, she calls back:

"Thank you, Ben," she says. "Goodnight."

IT'S TWO WEEKS before I see Ruth again. There are dinners frozen that I can eat and groceries that show up on my doorstep, but no Ruth. I think I've lost my friend for good. How is it that when I get close to a woman I always fuck it up? It's a hard two weeks, being alone. I've become so dependent on her. Some part of me is happy, though. To be on my own. To be well enough to be on my own. Even though deep down what a joke it is to think that I can make it on my own. I'm barely walking and I haven't left the house.

That's when it first starts to settle in. The enormity of what has happened to me. I'm forty-eight years old and my youth is gone and my health is gone. That's all I asked for, that I wouldn't get AIDS. All the positive thinking and Indian dancing and psychics and *I Ching* and the secret is to believe. That whole thing up in Atlanta about human beings being stuck in a form and if we could just see that we are who we think we are we'll be able to change who we are. And then what was it? We're not a form but an idea of a form and so since we are ideas of ourselves then change the idea.

Yeah, well, change this, motherfucker. My T-cell count was seven and my viral load was over nine hundred thousand. *Believe that it hath been given and it shall be given unto you.* Yeah, well, I believed. Way down deep, I believed. Every particle of me believed. I couldn't have wanted something more, believed more. Believing more wasn't fucking possible. And there I am. Either it's fucked up to believe that it hath been given or else it's back to being *your* fault and you just didn't believe that it was given enough.

Fuck this Secret Shit. The secret is hold on to your balls

because what you're in is a pinball machine and when you rack up enough points you either win or go tilt.

For me it was tilt. You attract what you radiate. Which means I got AIDS because I was looking for it. I had no fucking say at all in the something that meant everything to me, my life.

Big Ben is so full of shit.

THAT'S WHEN I stop sleeping. I mean I barely sleep. Three or four hours a night. I didn't know what the deal was then. But I can tell you now. The spirits, the guardian angels, I thought were in charge of my fortune and well-being had never even existed. All there was, was me and I'd better keep an eye on me. And how can you keep an eye on things if you're not awake.

The lightbulb in the middle of my chest, the filament always flickering.

The Running Boy couldn't stop running.

It must be all the Catholic stuff. That if you pray hard enough the Virgin will hear you. I mean, my mother, if my mother didn't have her faith she couldn't have existed. With all the Catholic shit I tossed out, I'd held on to a very precious belief. A belief that is the most essentially Catholic. Jesus can save you. If you can't get to Jesus, talk to his mother. I'd just turned Jesus and his mother into Don Juan and Louise Hay.

At my next appointment, I take a cab to the hospital. It's really weird being out in the world alone. I'll say it again. It's really weird being out in the world alone. I tell Madelena, my Nurse Practitioner, that I'm having trouble sleeping. She refers me to a Dr. Mark Hardy, a psychiatrist.

DR. MARK HARDY'S office is in the basement. Dark, *film noir* dark. I'm standing in the reception area waiting to sign in. I notice the bright yellow tape on the gray carpet but I don't know what the tape is for. In a moment, a big bald security guard walks up to me, grabs me by the arm. He's yelling *always remain behind the yellow line.* He pulls me by the arm to the back wall.

Sit down along the wall with everyone else until you hear your name called.

I want to protest. I'm not just like all the rest. I'm Ben Grunewald. I've published two novels. I've been reviewed in the *New York Times*. But then I don't. I'm shaking so bad all I can do is sit down on a gray folding chair.

That moment, so much in that moment. The bully guard, that I don't stand up to him. Maybe I'd lose my insurance. Or the doctor won't see me. They'll put me at the end of the line. Fuck, when you're weak like that, when you need so much, how overwhelming it is. There's no fight left, and all you can do is cower.

But the guard was right. I did think I was better than those people sitting along the wall. Those people were crazies on public assistance. Homeless, drug addicts, drunks, dirty bag-people.

As I sat down. On one side of me was a heavyset woman with no teeth and long stringy hair. An orange parka and stains on her T-shirt. The young man on the other side was gothed-out, some kind of strong perfume, spiked hair dyed black. Full of piercings. Music so loud on his earphones I could hear the punk rock noise.

DR. MARK HARDY'S office has a window that is a window well. Spiderwebs and spiders and leaves and shit fill up the window well. The smell of walls that have just been painted. There are bright colorful posters on the wall. Bright colorful posters that pretty much say you're fucked.

Dr. Mark Hardy is young, just barely thirty, and beautiful, I mean radiant fucking beauty. This guy isn't just movie star beautiful, he's surfer dude beautiful. Long brown wavy hair as long as Roger Daltrey's. He reaches across his desk and shakes my hand. His hand is meaty and dry and his large square fingernails are shiny as if he polishes them.

He asks me to sit down. I sit. My elbows on the arms of my

chair poke my shoulders up. My neck is stiff. My lips are dry. I'm going on ten hours of sleep max in the last three days. Doctor Mark sits with his one leg crossed over the other. The shin of his right leg making a ninety degree with his left. He holds his hands like pictures of Jesus' hands, the tips of his index fingers at the base of his nose and his third fuck-you finger on top of his nose. Thumbs on his chin. Now and then he plays with the blotter on his desk. Lining it up with the edge. He asks me ridiculous questions – my mother, my father, my sister, my education – straight from the textbook. I answer him as if these questions are important. Finally, he says out loud, like it's suddenly just dawned on him:

"Paxil!" he says.

Just before I walk out the door of Dr. Hardy's office, I ask him:

"Have you ever been depressed?"

Dr. Mark Hardy is surprised. He gets huffy. Coughs a couple times. His face turns red the way Ruth's neck does.

"Once," Dr. Hardy says. "When I broke up with my girl-friend in high school."

Then he asks me, after all the textbook questions, he looks at me like I'm a guy, and not just another patient who's got AIDS. He flat out asks:

"Why are *you* depressed?"

"Failure of spirit," I say.

PAXIL FOR ME is like taking speed. My body is flushed and it feels like I can't keep up with my breath and I can't sit still, let alone lie down. I call up Dr. Mark Hardy, seems like dozens of times, but I either get the receptionist or his voicemail.

My message is always the same.

Are you sure this stuff isn't an upper? I'm a total speed freak on this shit. Please call me. I'm in a terrible predicament.

Dr. Mark Hardy does not call back. I have to wait two weeks

to see him again. In the middle of the first week I get a letter. It's from Ruth.

The envelope is off-white and the paper is soft with a nub. A postage stamp of James Dean. My address in Ruth's penmanship so perfect as if she'd gone to Catholic school. Just like Ursula Crohn's letter. The stamp, the stationery. The penmanship. The fancy paper. Who is it that can get their shit together to create a letter like this?

Ruth Dearden. I expect the worst.

Inside are three pages handwritten on the same paper as the envelope. The written lines don't slope or slant or go awry.

Dear Ben.

Ruth starts her letter with the first moment she sees me. Sitting in a class room at the Sitka Center at the beach in Otis, Oregon. I walk up to her wearing a red ballcap and a white T-shirt and Levi's, look her right in the eyes, take her hand and introduce myself. The way I look at her, the way I speak, something new comes alive in her. It's a way of looking at herself. And she falls in love. Just like that. A big funny man she knows she'll never have a chance with. Tall and handsome and a New Yorker. Such an exotic creature. Profane, irreverent, passionate in a way she's never known a man to be. It's how I smell in the hot classroom that gets to her more than anything. Gay, but the rumors say there'd been lots of women. So there is hope.

I'm so unlike her ex-husband, her fucking perfect older brother Phillip, so unlike any man she's ever met.

The night of the White Party dancing under the moon. When I ask her to dance, how clumsy she gets as if her body has never danced. The song we sing to the moon, a moment so profound she doesn't go home 'til dawn.

Over the years, around the writing table, how her love changes. The way I support her, give her room to speak and argue and state her opinion help her have the strength to leave her husband. Along with her therapist, Judith, I'm the one to thank for her new freedom.

Then about a year ago, she begins to see in me another man.
Fragile, afraid, wounded, aloof, impenetrable really. The day
in class I cry. She wants so much to give back all that I have given
her. She'd give her life if only I could only let her love me. Then
the kiss. It pisses her off, the kiss, because it means so much more
to her than it does to me. She's had two weeks to think it over,
though. And she's decided. She hopes someday I can love her
back. But whether I can love her or not, whether I can love her at
all isn't important. And then she promises. To love me forever
without conditions. Just being around me, taking care of me is
all she wants.

THAT NIGHT I'M lying on my bed vibrating, trying to watch a
Cary Grant movie. I think I hear a knock on my door but I'm not
sure. Since the Paxil my ears have been ringing. Then it's Ruth
standing in my bedroom doorway holding a vase of purple and
yellow flowers. My freaked out body is so startled it slams against
the wall, which startles Ruth, who drops the vase of flowers.
Broken glass, water. Purple and yellow flowers all over.

The fiasco. So many fiascos with Ruth. She tells me to stay
in bed, she'll clean it up. My feet are bare but I get up anyway,
careful where I walk. I'm leaning down, picking up glass off the
floor. That's the second time Ruth hits me. Knocks me the fuck
down. With the broom in the side of my head as she walks in the
bedroom. Blood again from a cut on my ass where I land. The
cut isn't bad, it just bleeds a lot. Then it's Ruth standing in a puddle of water, posies all over the place, me leaning across the
bed, fucked up about the blood and AIDS and Ruth. Made her
put on rubber gloves. Ruth trying to put one of those large
square Band-Aids on my hairy ass. The rubber gloves. Fuck.

Really, what else can you do but laugh? At least at that
point with Ruth and me. Years later, the third time she goes to
hit me it won't be funny at all.

ONLY TO GO to the doctor do I get out of my pajamas. That night, though, I put on my walking shoes, my khaki pants, a white T-shirt, and my black sweater. My wool overcoat. A red knit cap. My God these old clothes, how they don't know how to fit. Ruth thinks I'm trying to get away from her. She says, *No, I'll go. You don't have to go. I'll clean this mess up and then I'll go.* I don't tell her what I'm doing because I'm laughing. Ruth thinks I'm laughing at her, and I am, but not just *at* her. It's like that song in *The Sound of Music. How do you solve a problem like Maria?*

What Ruth doesn't know is what a relief she is. Even with all the mess and the broom upside the head and the pain in my ass, the way I'd been shaking with that Paxil shit, how my bedroom and my bed had started to look like a horror movie, what Ruth doesn't know is how happy I was to see her.

Ruth is doubled up on my couch, crying, her back to me, thinking she's the clumsiest piece of shit ever. I get the flashlight from under the sink, walk over to the couch. I touch her on the shoulder. Just a touch at first, then lay my palm down flat there.

"Come with me," I say. "Walk with me. I want to show you something."

RUTH TAKES A long time in the bathroom. When she comes out her face is fresh. A bit of lipstick. She tries to smile but it's not really a smile. Outside it's not raining. At least for now it's not raining. I show Ruth where the tent tarp is on the back porch and we walk, Ruth and I. Ruth with the bundle of tarp and me with the flashlight. I still don't know how to walk so good. So I'm holding on to Ruth's arm real tight. The night is partly cloudy. Partly clear. Stars over the city center. Dark clouds over Mount Hood. What a place of sky Portlandia city is. A new moon. Just a little slipper of a moon. Fresh air off the ocean dries the tears and mellows the Paxil buzz.

Pioneer Cemetery is surrounded by a cyclone fence with barbed wire at the top. I know a place though. At least I think I do. At the gate between a stone pillar and the cyclone fence, there's a spot so skinny they figure no body could make it through. Believe me, I've tried. But that was before I was walking skin and bones.

I shut the flashlight off. Put it in my back pocket. There's enough light to see. Ruth steps into the palm of my hand, by that time we're laughing like hell, and I lift with all my might. Ruth's a powerhouse, a fucking athlete the way she climbs up the pillar and a little scream when she jumps down. Then me, I slide through the skinny spot with an inch to spare.

We walk in the dark. We're giggling and we're kids, and it feels good to be walking in the place of the dead. I show Ruth where to spread the tarp. I lie down first and then Ruth lies down beside me. At first we lie there strict and straight as corpses. We don't touch. I take a deep breath and finally:

"This is my spot," I say.

I don't tell Ruth how much that spot really is mine. That I've bought that spot and right in that spot one day my ashes will be under us right where we are lying.

Tony Escobar. I start to tell Ruth about Tony Escobar. Tony lying right over there, no farther than two shovel lengths away. But I let the dead be.

Instead, I start talking about Hank Christian. Over the years, Ruth's heard so much about Hank Christian. He is to her, like he is to me, a Magician, a Titan, a constellation in the sky. The Beloved.

"Have you heard from him lately?" Ruth asks.

"I call," I say, "but he don't answer. Fucking Barry Hannah, man."

"Fucking Barry fucking asshole Hannah," Ruth says.

And we're laughing again, Ruth and I.

Ruth's breath comes out her mouth a little spirit. Her body is warm. She puts her hand around my arm, her cheek against my shoulder. And we lie there on the tarp looking up at the stars and the tiny moon. I'm just talking away. Spouting off shit. Really, I'm trying to get to what I really want to say but my body, the Paxil, I'm like some meth freak who can't think straight and I'm trying to get to the point but when I get to the point, the point isn't a point it's a spiral.

I raise up my head and Ruth puts her arm under my head. When my head rests down against her arm, the Paxil buzz stops, for a moment, two moments, the buzzing stops. A part of me wants to close my eyes and just let go forever.

Instead, I sit up, turn around, sit cross-legged. On the tarp, Ruth is a piece of night with silver edges, lying on the black.

"Ruth," I say.

My lips are doing that strange rubbery thing. I'm glad it's dark. But then I realize my face has got moon on it and Ruth can see my face. Where is Big Ben when you really need him?

"I don't know if I love you the way you want me to love you," I say, "but you gotta know what pleasure and solace you give me. Really I owe you my life. Plus the way you fucking make me laugh, man."

Ruth's hand reaches up, touches my forehead.

"I'm a gay man," I say, "with some long-ago exceptions. And the only way it's possible that you and I could work is if we're completely honest. I can't promise you anything except that I'll be honest."

Ruth's fingers along my cheek, down to my chin. Somewhere in there I realize she's tracing the shadows on my face, the moonlight.

"I don't want you any other way," Ruth says. "I love you, Ben, and I'll always love you no matter what."

"I promise," Ruth says.

The way Ruth is earnest, fervent. Such abandon in her voice. So much hope. Moments of intimacy and passion how easy it is to promise. I remember smiling to myself. So many times I've gone back to that moment when Ruth said *I love you, Ben, I promise* and I remember smiling. At her innocence. At how much I needed to hear I wasn't alone, that someone was there. *Ruth* was there, was promising love.

I'd told Evie that I loved her. Promised to marry her and married her. I told Bette, too. I love you Bette. And Tony. I love you so fucking much, Tony Escobar. Never did tell Hank.

And there in that moment, it's as true as ever I've ever said it.

"I love you too, Ruth," I say.

And we kiss.

THAT FUCKING KISS. So many times over all the years I didn't speak to Hank or Ruth, and now the years after Hank has died, I think about that kiss. How that kiss ended in so much heartache.

That night in the Pioneer Cemetery, I kissed Ruth the way a man kisses his lover. Destiny, fate, fucking fortune, whatever, I've run it through a million times. But what I come up with is always the same. All I can do is blame it on Big Ben.

Ruth loved me in all the ways a person can love. She was just there and full of love and ready to jump into the mess. But I didn't love her that way. I mean *all* the way, head-over-heels-in-love love. I mean, after all, I *was* a gay man. I could have kept a boundary. Kept it platonic.

After all these years, I've had all kinds of insights as to the nature, the motivation behind that kiss. But to tell the truth, that night I didn't have a fucking clue as to why I folded her up in my arms and kissed her with all my heart. I didn't kiss her with my dick, but I was half dead and didn't have a dick yet and I guess I figured the dick would come along because I loved this woman Ruth and it was the love that was important. Heterosexual, homosexual, bisexual, omnisexual, what the fuck. Where the heart goes, the dick goes too, don't it? The truth was Ruth was the centerpiece of my world. I couldn't imagine living without her. She meant life to me. Without her I'd die. I was sure of it. And so I kiss her.

And something else. When I kissed Ruth, for her it was the fairytale prince and the princess. Everything she'd ever wanted with that kiss came true. The way that promise fulfilled made

Ruth glow, made me want to glow, too. She was intoxicating. So full of life and passion. I wanted that passion. And so I kiss her.

And something else. I wanted to give it back. Give life back to her the way she'd given life to me. I'd loved other women. I could love a woman again.

And so I kiss her.

IN THE MOONLIGHT on the tarp in Pioneer Cemetery on my spot that is my grave, we kiss. But the way Ruth kisses me is like our first kiss. She just pulls her lips flat against her face.

The Greatest Sin Ever, I feel like I'm forcing myself on her. So I pull away and look at her. I don't know really what to say or how. Just two shovel lengths away, over there, Tony Escobar is sitting on his grave. The way yogis sit. He's naked and he's smiling. I don't look over, though. I just go ahead on and try to look into Ruth's eyes, but her eyes are her big plastic glasses and all I can see is the shadow reflection of the big cedar tree and maybe myself with moonlight on my face trying to look in to see if I can see in her eyes.

"Ruth," I say, "is this too fast? Am I being too aggressive?"

"Not at all," Ruth says.

The only thing left I can figure is either she's scared of getting AIDS or this girl don't know how to kiss.

"Are you freaked about AIDS? " I say. "Kissing is safe."

"I'm not freaked," Ruth says.

We kiss again and her lips are still flat.

Then: "No, silly," I say. "Like this."

I take Ruth's mouth in my hand and pucker up her lips.

"You know," I say, "smoochy."

And I hold her lips like that, pursed up, and put my lips on them. Our smoochy lips kiss.

"Better," I say. "Much better."

BACK IN THE house, Ruth and I are cold and wet. I'm shivering. Chills like that when they start sometimes don't stop. I've got my

wet clothes off in no time and Ruth turns on the shower. I grab the
towel that hangs on my bedpost and wrap it around me. My
body is shaking pretty bad, and I wonder if the shower is a good
idea. But when I get in the bathroom, the hot water pouring
down in the shower and the steam feels good. Ruth wraps her arm
around me, pulls me into her.

"The water's nice and hot," she says. "I don't think it's too
hot."

I drop my towel. Ruth steps back and holds out her hand
and helps me step in. She pulls the clear plastic curtain closed
behind me. Under the hot water I'm all sharp bones and angles
shaking and shaking. Ruth asks me how I'm doing but my
shaking teeth can't talk. The hot water comes down and down
and I stand bent in with my arms wrapped around myself.
Ruth's just on the other side of the curtain. The shape of her body,
hazy through the plastic, the way Ruth's leaning in and listening,
she's Joan of Arc out there, my protector.

As soon as I can get my mouth working again I say:

"You're cold, too. Why don't you come and join me?"

The shower water on the cement shower floor, on the
curtain. Through the plastic, I can't see Ruth anymore. There's
such a long time that nothing happens I wonder if she's left.

Ruth pulls back the shower curtain and steps in. She
doesn't look at me. She has her arm over her breasts and her
eyes are looking down. Our bodies touch first at the thighs.
Ruth's thighs are voluptuous thighs. And a nice curve up to her
waist. I move back away from under the shower so she can
have some room. When Ruth lifts her face into the hot water I'm
amazed at what I see. Ruth without her plastic glasses, Ruth
without the bangs hanging in her face. The water on her long
heavy red hair even more red, pushing it back. The silhouette of
her face. Her broad forehead, high cheekbones, a fine long
straight nose, full lips. And the chin. The chin that makes Ruth's
face Ruth.

"Is your bandage okay?" she asks.

She's blinking water out of her eyes. I wonder what she sees without her glasses.

"There's shampoo on the shelf," I say. "Do you use soap?"
"I don't have a shower," she says. "Just my big old tub."

"Kiehl's," I say. "Moisturizing. Okay?"

I'm rubbing Kiehl's moisturizing soap across Ruth's back before she answers.

Ruth's shoulders are almost as broad as mine. The muscles of her back, strong. She's got a booty on her, too, the way her ass flares out. Beautiful skin. Rosy skin that's never seen a zit. Her legs are long and she's long in her torso. My feet next to hers at the bottom of the shower looks like a hobbit's feet.

"The soap smells great," she says. "Ben, you're so thin."

"Coriander," I say. "Turn around, let me get your front."

I can see her take a breath before she turns.

She turns and there it is, that flush of red across her chest, up her neck, her cheek. This woman is solid. And long. Long legs, long torso, lovely long arms. Nice muscle. Not Madonna muscle, but still firm. The soap goes on her clavicle first. One of the most beautiful places on a woman. Neck, shoulders, clavicle. And just below, the expanse of skin before the pendulous breasts. But really what I'm doing is not looking at her breasts. So I make myself look. Breasts. Wow. A nice slope to them. Full. Pink nipples that are hard. Surprisingly large. I soap down between her breasts, brush over each breasts lightly, avoid her nipples.

A true redhead, Ruth. The carpet matches the drapes. The tuft of red hair down there, wet, symmetrical like something woven.

Ruth wants her turn at soaping me, but the hot water goes. We're in a frenzy drying off, and in four or five great leaps I'm in bed first, then Ruth. The bed is cool but in no time at all we got it warm. *Queen Lowlighta*, all the low lights make my bedroom glow. Purple and yellow flowers in a mason jar on the nightstand.

It's been so long since another body has been in my bed.

And a female body. Ruth's lying on her back and I'm curled into her, my hand on her belly. I miss my body as I touch Ruth's body. She's so alive and full of smooth muscle and heft. My heart is pounding, Ruth's is pounding too. My dick feels full but it ain't hard. I've learned by now not to worry about it. The last time I was hard, I can't remember. I take a deep breath, try and be present. A Joni Mitchell line runs through my head. *Love is touching souls*. What I want to do is put my head between her thighs and chew on her clitoris.

Edith gives good.

But that ain't safe.

"Close your eyes," I say.

I reach over, turn the reading lamp on that's clamped to the bed rail.

"What are you doing?" Ruth asks.

"I want to look at you," I say.

I take Ruth's head in my hands, try and turn her head to the light. But she won't let me.

"Ruth," I say, "you're beautiful. You know you're really something."

"No," she says, "I can't do this."

"It's the same as writing," I say. "Like Hank always says. You got to go to where it hurts."

Her breath in through her nose is long and slow.

Slow, real slow, Ruth turns her face to the light.

17.
The way it is

THE NEXT YEAR IS THE YEAR OF DR. MARK HARDY, ANTI-depressants, and Ruth Dearden. Ruth might as well move in with all the time she spends at my house. She sleeps over or gets up in the middle of the night and drives home. We always stay at my house because I'm afraid to go to her house. The way she loves me I don't understand it. I'm a mess. Sleep is the problem. I've just forgotten how to sleep.

With my insurance and my hospital, I have no other choice but Dr. Mark Hardy. When the Paxil doesn't work, I have to let two weeks go by so that all the Paxil is out of my system. So then I can start on another drug, which I have to take for two weeks. Dr. Hardy says that often a patient will feel a *speedy rush* but almost always that rush stops when the body gets used to the drug.

My body never gets used to it. I go from Paxil to Serzone to Lexapro to Zoloft to Wellbutrin and a shitload of others, but the speedy rush never stops.

All those months I stonewalled AIDS, forcing my body to withstand something I was in total denial of has hurt my body. Maybe totally fucked up my endocrine system or whatever system it is that every once in a while lets you rest.

The year with Dr. Mark Hardy really is a year of taking a drug that feels like I'm taking acid laced with rat poison, then going off that drug for two weeks, then starting another drug that fucks me up a different, even more heinous way.

IT'S LATE SUMMER and Dr. Hardy is taking two weeks off. I'm just at the point of switching from Serzone to Lexapro or whatever the fuck drug it is, and somehow I misunderstand his direction and I don't wait long enough between the two drugs.

Usually, the way I get through the mornings is to go out on the sidewalk and practice my tai chi. But those two weeks, mornings are so bad that all I know what to do is sit in a chair and breathe. I try to wait until after lunch to start popping Xanax, but that week I start the Xanax as soon as I finish my scrambled eggs. It's summer and hot and so I set the chair in my basement and I sit in the chair and breathe. That specific kind of breathing where you bring the breath into your belly, then move the breath down to just above your dick, then to your perineum, then across your asshole to the middle of your back, then you bring the breath up your back to your neck, from your neck to the top of your head, then down to your forehead, and then you let the breath out of your mouth and nose.

That's all I do. I sit on a folding chair and concentrate on nothing else but moving my breath through my body this way.

All around me it's a horror. Ghosts and goblins and apparitions and animals and ancestors and spirits dance. Huck-a-buckin'. I know about apparitions. They aren't really there. I'm the one creating them. But that just makes things all the worse. The dead aunts and uncles, the Shetland pony, the fucking red devil with the pitchfork that huck-a-buck around me aren't nobody's fault but my own.

Outside, what is inside.

The Secret: you create your own reality.

It's October before I can get an appointment with Dr. Hardy. That morning, Ruth can't make it, so I drive my Volkswagen to the hospital. I don't know how in the hell I can drive but I drive. Looking back on it, it's an impossible thing for me to try to do. But those days just getting up in the morning is impossible. Walking into the kitchen, impossible. Opening the refrigerator door, impossible. Everything's impossible, so I drive across town.

At the hospital I can't bear the thought of getting on the elevator, so I walk the two flights of steps down to the narrow gray hallway, dark, that looks like a lobotomy movie. *Mental Health,* the sign above the reception desk. They've called my name and I'm standing with my toes just behind the line of bright yellow tape.

The guy in front of me has just asked to use the phone.

The receptionist, an African-American woman with a great smile that makes me wonder how on earth she can keep smiling in this gray basement that way, smiles at the guy in front of me and asks if it's a local call.

It's a local call and the receptionist hands the phone up to the guy.

The guy is just gray like everything else is gray. He's shorter than me, no piercings or tattoos. The kind of haircut in the Fifties we called *Boy's Regular*. Gray khaki pants and a blue winter parka. It's when he dials I can see the bandages on his wrist. I can't hear all that he says, but what I do hear:

Suicide, protease inhibitors, psych meds.

Dr. Mark Hardy is tanned. He gives me a big smile. I don't smile. He asks me how I've been doing. I don't tell him about the red devil with the pitchfork and the huck-a-buckin' Shetland pony and the dead aunts and uncles. Just smile. He tells me to sit down and I sit down and then he sits. He's going through my file. It's a manila envelope with AIDS stamped in black over my typewritten name. I'm about ready to tell Dr. Hardy there's no fucking way I can do this anymore when he makes the remark. It's an off-hand remark, as if he's speaking to himself. The way a scientist might speak aloud something of unusual interest. What he says is this is: *you know it is possible that Serzone combined with Lexapro could actually open up an avenue of fear in the brain.*

Avenue of fear is all Big Ben needs. I get up and walk out of Dr. Hardy's office.

I don't ever go back.

In the bathroom, on the way out, I take a leak. It's a gray

room with a fluorescent light, one urinal, one toilet stall. The
piss out of me is spraying down onto the holes in the bottom of
the urinal. The door behind me opens, and a guy walks into
the toilet stall and locks the latch. I don't ever see him but I can
hear him in there. Within seconds he is weeping. Huge deep
sobs. I press my hand against the toilet stall. Then lean my head
in. It's all the help I have to give.

ALL THE WHILE I'm writing. Big Ben won't have it any other
way. I write at night when I can't sleep. AIDS and New York.
All that death and fear. It's like taking acid so you can take acid.
Only now I'm not writing about other people in the past. I'm
writing about the virus that's in me that's trying to kill me. When
I've finished a chapter, I read my pages to Ruth. Her critique
is great. I always listen to what she has to say. Mostly though it's
important just to hear myself read aloud in front of her.

By March, I'm teaching once a week. But it's just too hard
to do alone, so Ruth steps up and Ruth and I start teaching
together. Most of my old students drop out. Ruth, who was once
their peer, is now their teacher. It just doesn't work. But the
new students, and there are still plenty of new students, accept
Ruth right off. Ruth really brings something new to class too.
The way she talks about conflict and tension so different from
how I usually talk about voice and character. And we share the
money 70-30.

Ruth is looking great. She's lost a lot of weight and her new
pair of nerdy girl glasses are just right for her, plus she's got a
new hairdo. I actually go into the Salon Vogue with Ruth and talk
to Nancy, Ruth's hairdresser, because Nancy won't ever listen to
Ruth when she tells her how she wants her hair cut. Nancy and I
have a little showdown when I give her the hair tip and tell her
to stop the shit with the bangs already. And highlights. Ruth's red
hair could use some highlights. Nancy is forty years old with
Farrah Fawcett hair and she's no match for Queen Lowlighta.

When Ruth walks out of Salon Vogue that day, her hair

brushed up off her face, she's finally got a fucking forehead. And that pair of erector-set plastic monstrosities she called glasses are gone. What's left is a face. Ruth Dearden finally looks like who she is. A fucking beautiful intelligent woman.

That day we go secondhand shopping and we buy Ruth a tacky polyester-leopardskin pants suit, a summer cocktail dress from the Fifties, and a red feathered boa. High heels. Mules when she walks, how the shoes flap against her feet.

Ruth just kept getting brighter and brighter. Almost like *My Fair Lady* with Ruth, watching her change, become more confident. Really, that year, that terrible year, those fucking sleepless fucking nights, Ruth was the only thing that saved me.

I KNOW, I know. What about sex with Ruth and me.

With the antidepressant war going on in my body, and anxiety levels off the charts, three and at the most four hours of sleep a night, I mean take it from a guy who knows what it's like not to have a dick. Those days before Viagra, with all those antidepressants coursing through me, I had no dick.

With death so close every day, though, a part of me did think my dick should rise up in hope against all the despair. And I figure if I was just dealing with death, then maybe I could've stepped up and pierced the darkness, so to speak, but, unlike in the old days, my dick not getting hard had nothing to do with me. Back in the old days, before the magic of Atlanta and Hank, my dick was buried alive gasping for breath. But with antidepressants, it was a totally different story. Especially with what they call the SSRIs. Which was all that Dr. Mark Hardy was prescribing for me. With SSRIs, man, there ain't no dick that's trying to breathe. Because there ain't no dick. It's chemical, man. The dick is dead.

Not that I cared. Just getting through a day, the fact I'd gained a pound and that my lungs were free to breathe again was something. So I wasn't really thinking about my dick. And neither was Ruth. Not at first.

So many nights, Ruth got out her geranium-scented oil and gave me a massage. Really, I don't know if I can tell you how important Ruth's touch was. My body actually became a body while she was touching me. There was no anxiety, there was no fear, there was no death. My body wasn't something that just stumbled through a world it had no connection to. The way Ruth touched me, my body went back to when it did more than carry around fear and depression. I felt solid, alive, grounded. The way Ruth touched me showed my body where it ended and where the world began. Not *the* world but *my* world, because the way Ruth touched me, she touched my soul.

Or whatever it was I used to believe in before I got AIDS.

Still, though, there was something that troubled me. I can only admit it now. Way down deep was a voice I didn't want to listen to. Ruth may have been touching my soul but she always missed that other place. What makes a touch erotic.

Those days, though, by the time I got through the day, I couldn't do anything but lie down and read or watch TV. When Ruth massaged me, all I did, all I could do really, was lie there and let her touch me. I didn't massage her, or return her touch. I mean living together as much as we did we were always touching. Holding hands, rubbing each other's shoulders. Often in bed at night we lay and held each other talking talking 'til one of us conked out, but I never really touched Ruth deep tissue the way she touched me. I didn't have the strength.

After some months, though, and I was getting stronger, I wanted to give something back to Ruth. But I had to be safe.

Then one day early July, it's so hot Ruth convinces me to get out of the house. It's a stretch for me, but we decide to go to the naked beach on Sauvie Island.

That day is a celebration. The following day, Monday, is Ruth's first day of her new class. There's a waiting list for my class, and when Ruth proposes that she take my waiting list students and teach a class of her own, I think it's a good idea. She'll be teaching at her house and she's freaked but she could use the money. Really, we're both excited. It's a little weird, Ruth starting on her own like that. But I'm all for it. And she'll still be teaching my class with me.

And something else. I've finished my book. What a fucking relief. But I need some help editing. Ruth says it would be an honor for her to help.

RUTH IS RIGHT. I've got to start getting out. So after lunch, Ruth and I pack up the sardines and the rice crackers and the baked chicken and the coleslaw and the water and the sunblock and the towels and the blanket and the toilet paper.

The door you got to walk through. It's my kitchen door, just a wooden door that you open and close and lock at night. But that afternoon, standing at the door, my sweaty hand around the door knob, my kitchen door is more than just a damn door. It is a portal into another world. The step you got to take. Fuck.

Under my feet, the ground is a waterbed. Deep in my ears, the place that makes balance is a hula hoop. The world, strange slantings and tilts.

INSIDE RUTH'S HONDA Civic, I'm glad I'm sitting down. Out through the windshield, over Ruth's feathers and sticks and flowers and leaves on the dashboard, past the bobbing Barbie's head, the Wonder Woman action figures, the *women and fish* sticker, I look at the red roof, the cedar shingles of my house. Big Ben can't believe I've become one of those people who's afraid to leave their house.

Agoraphobia. But it's not the marketplace I'm afraid of.

The windows are down and the wind feels good. Ruth has the music cranked up loud. Meshell Ndegeocello's "Leviticus." Sarah McLachlan's "Angel." The wind at my ears makes me feel like I'm not alone. I've actually forgotten how it is to feel to be outside and feel alive like this.

So weird to be so many ways at once. To be petrified and still enjoy the wind and the music, enjoy Ruth and her crazy car.

Which one of you is petrified? Which one enjoys the wind? Who is singing along to the music? Which one is obsessing about Ruth's tires. They look pretty bare. And the temp gauge on the dashboard. What if the car overheats?

It's as if my body went into danger mode and once the danger was past, the needle stayed in the red danger area and didn't go back to normal. Once you fear like that, and after fearing like that for so long, your body just expects fear.

Sauvie Island's parking lot is dusty and the sun is hot. We park close to a Honey Bucket. There are no cars around the Honey Bucket, because it stinks so bad.

Your body doesn't forget that you almost shit yourself to death. And the biggest side effect of the AIDS meds is diarrhea. When you go out, the first thing you do is find out where the nearest toilet is and if it's clean and if it's got a door you can lock. The days of venturing out into the world are over. You're on a leash. You can only go so far from a reliable toilet.

The Honey Bucket on Sauvie Island has a lock all right. But inside it's twenty degrees hotter and there's a huge shit smear across the seat of the toilet. Big black flies. Fight or flight. I figure if it comes down to it I'll dig a hole and shit in the tulies.

Ruth's got the cooler with the sardines and the crackers and the water and the fried chicken and the coleslaw.

What kind of food it is and at what time you have to eat it. There's no just going to lunch and having a sandwich anymore. The wheat thing and the protein thing are no joke. No sugar. No caffeine. Nothing with any kind of stimulation. Even peppermint tea is out. Really you're only as good as the last meal you've eaten.

I've got the blankets and the towels and the boombox and the sunblock. The beach is crowded. The sun on the sand makes my eyes hurt. The way my head, my whole body feels thick – going on a month now without any antidepressants – I can feel the thickness so much more here in this new place. Really, where can you run to when you are what you're running from?

Your adrenals or your pituitary gland or whatever the fuck that's been strained to the max, there's just some places now you just can't go. Inside that store or that restaurant it's too jammed with people and noise and activity. Forget the fucking mall. It's the strangest feeling. It's as if a force actually pushes against you when you walk in. Like this hot bright beach. Dizzy. Try walking in a world that bounces with each step. The way that upsets you. Dizzy ain't the word for it.

FINALLY, WE FIND a clump of willows and some shade, a place not too close to any other people. Ruth's never been naked in public before and with every piece of clothing she takes off, she gets more liberated, more excited. *I'm taking off my shorts! I'm taking off my shirt! I'm taking off my bra! I'm taking off my panties!* Really, being with Ruth sometimes, how everything could seem extraordinary.

Lying naked in the sun is a wonder. Big Ben gets up the gumption and I go out where the sand is hard and do *tai chi* on the beach. Ruth takes a thousand photos of me. When I finish my *tai chi*, I go back to our blanket and Ruth is sleeping. Just like that, she's sleeping.

Sleeping. Ordinary people, Ruth, can just lay their body down, rest their head on their arm, even on a blanket in the sand in the sun, and fall asleep.

Sleep man, fucking sleep.

There's a moment when the sun has gone gold and the shadows are long. Everything seems to get quiet. The lapping of the water on the beach. The seagulls. Off somewhere, a Jet Ski. I'm lying on my belly and the sun is on my back. I turn my head and Ruth's face is right there. She's awake and alive and so in heaven. On the boombox Ella Fitzgerald is singing *dream when you're feeling blue*. Ruth loves the sun and her body is in the sun and she's with me, her man, and the song is sweet and it's a beautiful summer day. I see it all in her blue eyes.

THAT NIGHT IN bed, after Ruth's massage, I feel so relaxed and in the world. I look down at my thumb and Big Ben reminds me. What are you so afraid of, Mr. Propinquity?

I pull myself up and lean my back against the bed. Ruth's blue eyes are deep blue almost purple. Sweat on the skin of her neck and chest. We kiss, I keep expecting that erotic pull in my balls, but there's nothing. Still if I can't feel pleasure, maybe Ruth can.

"Come here," I say. "And lean against me."

Ruth takes her glasses off, folds them, puts them on the nightstand. Slowly, her body settles in between my legs, her back to me. My arms come round to the front of her just under her arms. Surprising, my skinny arms are no bigger around than Ruth's. But there's something smaller around about her chest, the otherness of her, then her breasts, full and heavy, the way they hang. Nothing on my body like her breasts, their firmness and their jiggle. I reach my legs out and hook them around Ruth's legs, pull her legs open wide. My legs, more olive in the skin, hairy, around Ruth's smooth pink hairless legs. Ruth's head falls against my shoulder. Her thick red hair, silk against my face. A deep sound in her throat. Laughter. My heart's beating just behind her heart. I want to do this right. I reach down, rub my hands across her breasts. Full and round, the weight of them, how they are alive and move and bounce. Her nipples, ten times the size of my nipples. Hard nubs big as the end of my little finger. My tongue around and around the channels of Ruth's ear, my breath. The way our hearts are close. Ruth turns her head, her mouth to my ear. So quiet I barely hear:

"Ben."

I spit on my thumbs and index fingers, move my fingers around her nipples slow then pinch her nipples hard. The sound that comes out of Ruth could be a sound that comes out of me.

Between her legs, Ruth's hair is soft, not pubic hair wiry. Wet. My God, the mysteries of a cunt. The way it scares me how overwhelmingly deep and complex it is. How her cunt could swallow me up. Folds and folds. The wetter it gets the larger it becomes. Right there in the center, the ecstatic mound of flesh. I try and touch her the way I feel when she massages me. That's what I think as I touch her clit, how Ruth can stop the pain. And I put that intention, that heart strength into my hand, and my fingers pull up slow back and forth along the sides. I rub and pinch and stroke her clit with all my heart. It is a prayer. My chin on her shoulder, my legs curled over her legs clamping them down. My hand inside her is wet up to the wrist. The smell of peat moss burning. Ruth's arms are above us, pulling on my hair. Her back arches and arches. There's not a sound coming out of her.

When she comes, I mean really comes, she holds her arms up to the sky. Her long slender hands waving. I put my hand over her cunt, my fingers inside her. She pushes up against my hand and up and up. Screams so lovely, so long, the pain, the transcendence of pain. My other arm's around her holding her to earth. She comes like a rock.

It fucks me up the way she comes. The way she's alive and comes and comes. I get really sad and start to cry. And Ruth sees I'm crying and she thinks it's because I'm full of joy. But we promised to tell the truth, so I tell Ruth it isn't joy why I am crying. I'm just jealous, man. The way she is alive, I'm fucking jealous.

NOW THERE'S A moment. *The* moment, right there. Where things start to fall apart for Ruth and me. I mean not right off. It takes months and months. But for sure, that evening, Ruth waving her hands in the air screaming her delicious scream was when it all started. The worm had started to turn and face its asshole.

What I mean to say is, after all these years of trying to figure out Hank and Ruth and me, what happened and how and why it happened, that night that I felt jealous of Ruth, her orgasm, the lifeforce she had a hold of, was the first time. Before that night, as far as I can remember, Ruth and I got along just fine. I mean I wasn't sleeping and I was irritable and the fucking world felt like it was out to get me, but I never made it Ruth's fault. Of course, there were little things. Her long red hair in the bathtub. Her rocks and feathers and pieces of wood all over the place. Her crazy fucking car. But I didn't let it bother me. Ruth was always there, helping me out, and I was grateful.

Strange how quickly gratitude can turn.

For example, in September, I take a gig teaching a six-hour Saturday writing workshop at the Sitka Center. Lord knows I'm too fucked up to teach a class that long, but I really need the money. Ruth, of course, teaches with me, I mean how could I manage a class like that alone. And she could use the money, too. Plus we get a free hotel room in Cannon Beach to spend the night and we have the next day on the beach to relax. The prospect of the weekend makes Ruth crazy happy. Me, all I can think about is all the shit that can go wrong. Ruth drives us to the coast because I can't drive.

The class is eleven middle-aged women and one young man, a poet. Andy, Andy Gronik, I think. In a wood-paneled room with windows facing the Salmon River Estuary and the Pacific Ocean. Sitting in a circle of wooden chairs. The kind of chair you can pull the panel up from the side and make a writing desk.

Pretty much you can figure on at least one asshole in a class of twelve. But this class is great. As we're going around, introducing ourselves, each woman has a story to tell. Marriage, divorce, child-bearing. These women have been through the wars. All eleven of them, one after another, are hungry to talk. When it comes Andy's turn, I have to ask him to speak up because we can't hear him. All he can say is his name and how old he is, twenty-one, and that he likes poetry. I feel a kinship with him right off. Bad skin, curly hair he's pasted down. Thick black horn-rimmed glasses. Bitten fingernails. An old leather briefcase next to his feet on the floor. Pointy black shoes. Pink socks.

But what's important about the class that day is what

happened between Ruth and me. Three different things. Things that had never have happened before.

The first is sometime after lunch. We're on the fourth student, a woman named Edna. She's written a piece about being fat and how her husband has had an affair. It's during that discussion I notice it. Ruth is finishing my sentences. I stop and check myself to see if I'm just making this shit up, but I'm not. I start a sentence and Ruth finishes it. I mean not every time, but most of the time. Then I wonder if Ruth has always been finishing my sentences and I'd just never noticed it before. So I start speaking up so she'll stop speaking for me. But it ain't easy.

By the sixth or seventh student, Ruth and I are dueling banjoes. I say something, then Ruth says more, then I say more. Then she says more. This back and forth between us just won't stop. Unless I stop. It happens with three different women, three times in a row. Ruth has to have the last word.

At the afternoon break, two-thirty, Ruth goes out to stand on the deck. The bright sun brings out the highlights in her hair. Usually, when I see Ruth beautiful like this, I'd put my arm around her, or touch her hand, but I'm angry and don't understand why I'm angry, and I'm feeling like a shit because I'm angry. Just as I stand myself next to her, a gust of ocean wind blows back her hair. Ruth turns and gives me a smile. Still, I don't touch her. Just stand, lean up against the porch railing.

"What's going on?" I say.

"Doesn't the breeze feel great?" Ruth says.

"It feels weird today," I say. "Between you and me."

"It must be the long drive," Ruth says. "Why don't you rest for a while. I can take over."

"Take over?"

"You know, silly," Ruth says. "Take a little rest, then you can come back feeling refreshed."

The thing I promised Ruth, the only thing I promised, was that I would be truthful, so I take a deep breath, try and make my mouth move to say the hardest thing. When I speak, my voice is the high-pitched Catholic boy.

"Ruth," I say, "why is it that I feel that you're one-upping me?"

"What?"

"I feel like I'm competing with you to be heard."

"You mean now?"

"Here," I say. "*Now*, right in class, the last four students."

The flush of red up her throat and onto her chin. Ruth pushes her glasses up onto her nose, then covers her neck and chin with her hand. She looks straight ahead, out to the ocean.

"Ben!" Ruth says. "I don't know what to say."

The ocean wind on our faces, the sun, October and there's sun, Ruth and me leaning against the cedar rail, not touching. It's hard to keep my eyes on Ruth. They keep wanting to look away like she's looking away but I make myself look at her.

"It kind of makes me crazy to say it," I say, "but I just had to."

Ruth doesn't say anything for a long time. The flush has her whole face red. Pretty soon, her shoulders are shaking and her chest is going up and down. In a moment, one long tear streams out, tear duct to chin. Ruth turns, quick puts her arm around my neck, pulls me close in. Her stomach muscles tight, little bumps of sobs against my belly.

"I'm really really sorry, Ben," Ruth says. "I was only trying to help."

"I know," I say. "Maybe I'm just being a bitch."

"Do you have a tissue?"

I go back inside the classroom. How closed-in and stuffy the room feels. I grab a couple tissues from the Kleenex box in the middle of the circle, then close the sliding doors behind me. When Ruth takes the tissues from my hand, her fingers stay touching my hand for a moment.

"You're probably right," Ruth says. "I think I'm just used to handling my own class."

The wind in my ears. The wind in Ruth's hair is wild. The

way the wind has pitted the cedar railing. Ruth's blowing her nose. The end of her nose is scarlet red.

"I shouldn't have even said anything," I say.

Ruth cries and then stops crying then cries again. I'm pretty sure I'm crying too. We stand for a long time, holding on tight to each other. Waves crashing on the beach sound. It takes a prayer or two, and some deep deep breaths, but after a while our regular breath comes back. I take Ruth's face in my hands. Really look at her the way she lets me look at her now. Both of us are just so fucking relieved. Nose to runny nose, arms wrapped around arms. What I say next surprises even me.

"Loudmouth bitch," I say.

Then it's Ruth's chance to surprise herself.

"You men are all alike," she says.

Just like that we're laughing our asses off, Ruth and me, and the world that only minutes ago looked so dark and full of trouble now is bright, cloudless as the sky and fucking free.

"Thank you," Ruth says.

"For what?"

"Keeping your promise," she says.

THREE O'CLOCK, ON the deck that afternoon, after Ruth and I pull ourselves back together, when we go back inside the classroom, when we're the fourteen of us all in circle again, it's Andy's turn to read. Andy pulls a stack of paper from his old leather briefcase. Passes the pages around the room. It's a poem full of shit and romance.

When he finishes reading I could kick my ass for telling Ruth she talked too much. I look across the room at Ruth and her lips are puckered up like they've been glued together. She's got a fuck-you grin on.

It's tough to point out to a young man how his language is flowery and overwritten. But I used to be one of those flowery boys. The way I talk to Andy is how I wish a writing teacher would've talked to me. Kind, but still tough. Always giving examples when I throw something new at him. Andy keeps his head down. Those black pointy shoes, his pink socks. I keep at him, keep asking him how he's doing, trying to get him to look up. It takes a while, but Andy sits up, pulls his shoulders back, starts looking around. As if he's surprised there's other people in the room. Once, then once again, Andy takes the chance. Looks at me right in my eyes. That's a good sign. But after class I go looking for Andy just to make sure.

There's a path down to the beach, and along the path a bench. Tall grass all around sticking up out of the sand. Andy's sitting on the bench. His dark curly hair doesn't move at all in the wind. The old leather briefcase is sitting next to his pointy black shoes and pink socks. He's leaning over his notebook, writing like crazy.

"May I sit down?" I ask.

Andy's eyes are dark green. Kind of startling. And his stiff curly brown hair, something rust-colored about it. When I sit down, our knees touch, just for a moment. We both pull our knees away fast.

It's nice sitting with him. The sun is still out and there's still a couple hours of daylight left. I haven't noticed before Andy's ruby red lips, and full. Marco. Tony Escobar. I'm just talking talking, checking in with this young man. I'm happy to find out he's still in one piece. At some point I say *fuck* or something inappropriate and Andy laughs and it's great when he laughs. An all over laugh like Hank's.

That's when Andy, from out of the old briefcase, pulls out both my books.

"Mr. Grunewald," Andy says, "would you sign these books for me?"

"Ben," I say.

"Yeah," Andy says, "Ben."

There they are, my two novels, in plastic covers. In Andy's square hands, his chewed fingernails, he holds my novels as if they are the most precious things. My books handed to me by a young man who has made those books his own. Gets me in the throat, real fast. I can't really speak, so I put my hands on the books while Andy still holds on to them. When he lets go the books seem so heavy.

It's while I'm signing *All My Best, Ben Grunewald* onto the first page of my second book is when Andy tells me.

"Ever since the day I picked up your first book," Andy says. Those full ruby red lips. "Since your first sentence, really," he says. "I've loved you."

I stop writing. Look up into Andy's dark dark green eyes. I want him to take his glasses off and then I think of Ruth and her glasses and that's when the second thing happens. All of a sudden it is Ruth, walking up to the bench. She's behind Andy, though, and Andy doesn't see her and he just keeps talking.

"I mean," Andy says, "not *in* love but I love you that you can make me see and feel things, understand things I've never understood before."

Andy's hand is on his crotch. On his hard-on.

Even though she's so close and getting closer, the way the wind is off the ocean, I doubt if Ruth can hear.

Words are coming out of Andy's ruby red lips fast but I can't hear them either. The moment, the sunlight, the breathless voice of a young man, so intimate. Ruth walks right into that moment. Then somehow the moment is hers. Something I cherished that was mine is now hers. And there it is again. That feeling that's so awful to feel.

I finish signing the book and quick lay both books onto Andy's lap.

"Hey! Ruth!" I say too loud.

THE NEXT MORNING, when we wake up, sun again, what a miracle. Ruth and I drive to the Otis Cafe. It's 9:30 on a Sunday and there's a long line and I'm freaked because if I don't eat by ten the world goes fucked up Francis Bacon on me. I'm hanging on tight to Ruth's hand. While we're waiting, Ruth buys me a thick white mug that says *Otis Café* on it.

We get in at 10, order by 10:10, and have our food by 10:30. Things in the world are definitely bouncing around, but soon as I start eating I'm okay.

It's in the middle of my spinach and mushroom omelet. Ruth's on her second cup of coffee and she's chattering away about how we should spend the afternoon when I get this yearning: I want to walk on the beach. Just get away for a couple hours and find some place in the shadow of a big piece of driftwood and be with the sun and the ocean and the day. Alone.

Alone. I feel like an asshole.

The night before, Ruth surprised me with reservations at the Haystack Rock Restaurant. So strange to walk into a beauty of a restaurant with duck on the menu and lamb chops and fresh salmon. Waiters in black pants and white shirts, black ties. Big white aprons. Took me back to my restaurant days in New York. When I was a person. It had been so long since I'd enjoyed food. Celebrated it. And wine. I ended up ordering lamb chops and a half-glass of an *Haut Medoc* for Chrissakes. All the while praying I wouldn't have some shit disaster or maybe the food and the sips of wine would disturb my sleep. If what I was doing lying in bed at night you could call sleep.

That night, when we got back to our hotel, Ruth took two dozen beeswax candles out of her backpack and lit them on little tin stands all around. It was a cathedral in the room, the firelight and the smell of the beeswax. Queen Lowlighta loved it. Ruth brought her boombox too and made a CD of all my favorite songs.

The massage Ruth gave me that night was different from other massages. At first I thought it was the massage oil. Lavender, not geranium. But something else was different, too. She was massaging my cock and balls and she'd never really touched them that way before. I try to tell myself it's my own trip, all just old propinquity shit, but then she was coming. Up and down my legs, my whole body, really, sticky wet with her cum.

Breaks my heart when I think back on that night. How much Ruth wanted me. How far away I was from wanting her. But still I didn't get it. There was a piece to the puzzle that was Ruth that was missing. I mean the pieces were all there, I just hadn't put them together yet. Not yet.

That night, though, with Ruth in the cathedral room of candles and the beeswax and *"Ne Me Quitte Pas,"* really I would have done anything, anything, to touch Ruth the way she was touching me.

AFTER BREAKFAST, WHEN we get back to the hotel it's almost noon. I've got my turkey sandwiches with gluten-free bread all ready to eat by one o'clock. Ruth's on the bed. She's got the maps out for trails we can walk on, beaches to visit.

My promise to always tell the truth.

Fucking promises, man.

My heart's beating in my throat. My face feels flushed the way Ruth's face gets.

"Ruth," I say.

"We could hike down to Ecola Beach," Ruth says.

"I'd like to spend the afternoon alone," I say.

"We can swim naked if we stay to the south."

"Just for a couple hours," I say. "To clear my head."

"There's a public entrance to Ecola just down from the Minot House."

"Ruth."

In a moment, Ruth slams her fist down onto the map. All those neat map folds all fucked up.

"Christ, Ben," Ruth says. "We get one day away and you want to be alone?"

High-pitched, my voice. That fucking Catholic boy.

"That's right," I say. "You want me to lie?"

Ruth, right then, the way she looks at me. All that hurt.

Red rims under her blue eyes. Something so tired about her face. Maybe that's the moment for her.

"Fine," Ruth says.

When she walks out the door, she slams it behind her.

No matter how hard I try, that slam stays with me all day.

I PUT MY sardines and my rice crackers and a bottle of water in my backpack. Check myself out in the mirror in the bathroom before I go out. As if to remind myself I still am who I am. At the hotel room door, there's a moment I stop, just as my hand is about to turn the knob. It takes me a while to admit I'm afraid to walk out the door. Alone. I tell myself there are toilets and I've got my protein and I've got a napkin and I have water and a plastic fork and there's a public shitter that's clean not far from the beach. Toilet paper, just in case.

Fucking fear, man.

Outside, I walk fast through the tourists. There's a Christian gathering of some kind. Heterosexual Christians and their wailing children. Strollers as wide as the sidewalk. The world that day is eating sugar. Saltwater taffy, hotdogs, candy apples, cupcakes, doughnuts, ice cream. Everybody's fat. I'm down the cement steps and on the sand I take off my shoes and socks and put them in my backpack.

Cannon Beach is hard to beat for Pacific Ocean beauty. Those big old dark rocks sticking up out of the gray blue, crystal blue. Seagulls squawking. Thank God there's sun. Everyone on the beach seems to be screaming it out loud. *Thank God for the sun.* It's too cool to swim but the beach is full of little kids in the water. Goose flesh head to toe. Old folks barefoot in parkas and beat up sun hats. Sandcastles. Blue plastic buckets and little yellow shovels. Everybody's smiling. One old woman I walk by is slumped against a tree root, her butt dug into the sand. She's covered by a bright yellow African cloth, her bare feet out in the sun. A pink long-billed ballcap. She's reading Proust. *Sodom and Gomorrah.*

I'm totally fucking jealous. Of everything. Of the life that's going on that I can't feel. My body wants to throw itself into a big baby torpor. For missing out. For being outside of. The sensuality. The beauty.

But because it's not mine to have, because it is the sunlight and not *my* sunlight, and because I can't *feel* it, the ocean is just the ocean, I figure at least I can be aware that it is beautiful. Maybe *because* it isn't mine to feel, by default, I make it mine. By not feeling, I am hyperaware. The *idea* of beauty, even though the beauty cannot touch me.

My head likes these thoughts a lot. But my heart is sore.

Far away down on the beach, I'm hunkered into some deep hole somebody's dug. Almost like a grave. In an hour the tide will be in and my hole in the ground will be gone. Across the hole, above me, a lattice work of driftwood. The sand is wet. The shadows and sun of the driftwood. How it all looks when I squint my eyes. The ocean waves. Finally, I can't hear my ringing ears. The wind. The shifting sand. Distant voices. Seagulls. My deep deep breath. Ah.

THAT'S WHEN THE third thing happens. At first all I'm aware of is that something is blocking my sun.

"I thought maybe you forgot your sardines," Ruth says.

She jumps inside my hole, my solitary grave, lays her body against me. Smacks my ear with her elbow. She puts the can of Bumble Bee sardines, a stack of sesame seed crackers in a Ziploc bag, a white plastic fork, and a napkin on my lap.

"It's cool in here," she says. "Way cool. Are you sure you're warm enough?"

ON OUR DRIVE back to Portland, the clouds roll in. Big dramatic thunderheads. Sometimes Oregon is only about the sky. Ruth's crazy old car. Feathers and pieces of paper, flower petals and shit fly around inside because our windows are open. I haven't said anything, because I'm afraid if I say anything all I'll do is curse.

The CD of my favorite songs is playing loud. It's when Bonnie Raitt starts singing "I Can't Make You Love Me" that I turn the damn thing off.

"You need to get laid," I say. "I mean a proper lay. What you need is a good old-fashioned fuck."

I know. I know. Telling the woman you're angry at what she needs is not a good start. You're supposed to start with *I* sentences like: *I feel angry*, or *I feel like I'm not being heard*. But hell fuck, the truth of it is I was spoiling for a fight.

Ruth puts in the clutch, shifts from fourth to fifth gear.

"What do you mean?" Ruth says. "Sex isn't just about dick. We've talked about this a thousand times."

"No, no," I say. "For *you* it's about dick. A good stuffing would do you wonders."

Ruth's white skin is so pale it's blue. Some part of her wants to fight back. The way she holds her jaw. But she doesn't. Maybe it's because she's afraid she'll lose me. Maybe because bottom line I'm her teacher and you don't fuck with your teacher. Maybe I'm her perfect older brother Phillip she never stood up to. Maybe I'm just fucking Ben Grunewald, published author and popular writing teacher, the reason why she doesn't fight back. Love? Fuck if I know.

"You need to start seeing other men," I say. "If for no other reason, I need some space of my own."

"Ben," Ruth says. "Why are you doing this?"

Boom. Fucking anger, man. My fist hits her dashboard so hard the dust rises up. The rocks tumble. The Wonder Woman action figures go tits up. Just like that I'm all New York on her ass.

"*Because!*" I yell. "Yesterday during class I couldn't speak because you wouldn't shut up. And the five fucking minutes I wanted to be *alone*, Ruth Fucking Dearden plops her bones onto my precious solitary silence and smacks me in the ear. *Because* a young man back there was telling me he loved me and you blundered right in. That's why."

"You mean *Andy?*" Ruth says.

"Just like some clueless motherfucker," I say.

"Andy Gronik!" Ruth says.

"Just some time alone," I say. "That's all I ask."

"He's so young, those pimples," Ruth says. "And a terrible poet."

"Maybe we shouldn't see each other for a while," I say.

"But if you'd like, we could invite him over to the house," Ruth says. "We could cook. Get to know him a little better."

"You're a beautiful young woman," I say. "You're smart. You could get any man you wanted."

"Really all he needs is to get rid of his sentimental language," Ruth says.

"Maybe clear away the rocks and leaves and stuff on the dining room table," I say. "So I can start writing in my journal again."

"I'm sure he'd spend the night if you asked him," Ruth says.

"Who?" I say.

"Andy Gronik!"

"What the fuck you talking about?" I say, "He's a child!"

In Portland, when we pull up to my house, it's my turn to slam the door.

THAT NEXT WEEK I don't see Ruth until our Thursday night class. I wasn't sure I would see her at all. I told myself I didn't care if she showed up for class or not, but the truth is, I was afraid she wouldn't show. But bless her heart, there's Ruth pulling up in her Honda Civic, there's Ruth with her notebook covering her hair, and she runs toward the house through the rain, there's Ruth in the kitchen shaking off the rain. That night we're a little shy with each other. Overly polite. Ruth doesn't say much in class. Which isn't a surprise. I mean when you tell someone their mouth's too big what do you expect? Fuck, some of the things I said. The students all know something's up.

After class, Ruth asks if she can spend the night. I have to take a deep breath. I tell her no, but I'll take a rain check. That's when it starts, that night. All the many long nights that are to come with Ruth and me talking talking. Hashing it out. Running things through again and again and again. Trying to figure it all out.

What Ruth talks about is what it is she needs to do, what's wrong with her. Why she isn't enough. I don't know what to tell Ruth. It really isn't even about sex. I just know I've promised to tell the truth. Whatever that is. The darkness around me is deep.

Another week goes by and I don't see Ruth until Thursday class. Then that weekend she drops by on Saturday with a big bunch of yellow flowers to see how I've slept. Sunday night we watch *The Sopranos*.

I have to say, time away from Ruth felt good. I figured all I needed was room to breathe. After two weeks, then three, one morning when Ruth walked in the kitchen door, I don't know what she did, in fact she didn't *do* anything, she was just Ruth standing there talking, and the moment opened up as if it was an eternal moment, and I was laughing, the way I always used to laugh with Ruth, and believe me, it was a huge fucking relief because Big Ben, man, sometimes, when he decides some shit, there's no going back.

For Thanksgiving, I cook. A big old pot roast and quinoa and winter vegetables. We watch Ruth's favorite movie, *Living Out Loud*, and then my favorite movie, Bertolucci's *Besieged*. Ruth has baked a pumpkin pie and brought over one thin slice for me to try. With a tiny dollop of whipped cream. Man, I love eating that piece of pumpkin pie, could have eaten an entire fucking pumpkin pie, but even with that tiny slice, I pay for it. Hardly sleep at all that night.

Too many Brandy Alexanders back in the day.

But everybody I know from back in the day, everybody who didn't get AIDS, that is, are all still drinking their Brandy Alexanders.

Fucking AIDS, man.

Ruth doesn't want to talk that night. I'm surprised. She

goes out dancing with her girlfriend, Lucy. I feel like an old man on the porch that night when Ruth leaves, kissing his daughter goodnight, telling her, *be careful. Take care of yourself. Call, if you have any problems.*

ABOUT A MONTH later, it's around New Year's Eve and Ruth invites me to a party. Her yoga teacher is back from India. As you may know by now, I'm no longer the kind of guy who just goes out to a party. Let alone a New Year's Eve party. But Ruth is excited for me to meet this yoga guru guy. He's supposed to know everything about health and eating and exercise. Ruth thought maybe he could tell me how to start sleeping again.

So we get to this party and it's in this huge McMansion in the West Hills and there are only men, Indian men, boys really, dot not feather, at this party, and they are all tiny and skinny. Five foot two, these guys. And *haute couture*. Dressed to the nines in Ralph Lauren, Gucci, and Tommy Hilfiger. Their straight black hair cut short and spiked with lots of hair product. The perfume in that room is *heavy*. There's twenty or so of these men and they're speaking Hindi or whatever language they speak and they're drinking alcohol, and talking loud and laughing. The sitar music, mixed with a heavy drumming dance rhythm, is loud. For some reason, the yoga guru isn't there. He couldn't make it, or he arrived later, I never found out. Ruth and I are the only white people and Ruth is the only woman there. She's wearing the dress she bought at Buffalo Exchange, a red satin strapless evening gown.

It takes me a while to figure out that these men are all gay men. But a specific kind of gay man. These boys are all girls. I mean they aren't trannies. They're young men who are feminine. With attitude.

I have to be careful because it's easy for my own homophobia to step up here when it comes to describing these men, because men, or as in this case, these boys, who are acting like I think girls would act, can set something off in me. I mean my daddy was a cowboy and when I look for a man I usually find some guy like Hank Christian or Tony Escobar. So right off these young girlish fashion victims are pushing my buttons.

A guy who's spent most of his life trying to have a cock can easily be confused by a man who seems proud to act as if he doesn't even have one.

And what does acting like you have a cock actually look like? Fuck.

It's times like these, at least back when I was healthy, that I love the most. Something that's tripping shit off in me that I don't understand and I want to understand. Racism, sexism, homophobia, man. We're all guilty.

So I'm talking to these men, or trying to talk to them. One in particular. His name is Aadya. He's drinking a purple drink in a dramatic up glass and he smells like a gardenia. I'm drinking Perrier with lime. His dark eyes are lined with kohl. I think he's wearing lipstick. Stressed denim pants way too tight. A black shiny shirt with the tails out. Some kind of Oxford Italian boots. Aadya and I are sitting on the top steps of a circular stairway. He sits on the step with his legs curled under him. Whenever Aadya moves his hand, *limp wrist*, are the words that go off in my mind.

Across from us is a ridiculously huge chandelier and below us on the ground floor a kind of crimson ballroom. The music is loud and down there it's a big white Ruth, shoulders and décolletage, long white arms, in a gown that's just a shade brighter than the walls, with twenty tiny Indian men dancing around her.

Aadya has been studying yoga with the yoga guru guy for ten years. At one point I ask Aadya why everyone is drinking alcohol.

"Because we're young and have the chance," he says.

"What if your guru finds out?"

"He probably already knows."

That's when Aadya asks me a question that makes my breath go away.

"Why are you so tired?"

I almost cry that he isn't afraid to ask.

That's when we really get into it. In order to talk about how tired I am we have to talk about depression. Is it chemical? What is chemical? Stopping the mind. How to do that. What is there when you stop the mind. Pretty soon, Aadya's and my knees are touching, and it's not sex, it's intimacy that's going on. We're talking about everything. Life, love, death.

What's most interesting about this night, though, is what happens next. Aadya has just given me his Hermès handkerchief. I'm worried about getting snot on it. In a moment, I look down through the banisters at the dancers below. Something about what I see below me makes me a little crazy.

It's Marilyn Monroe and *Diamonds Are a Girl's Best Friend*, this scene. Against a crimson background, a red-haired Ruth, startling white shoulders and cleavage and arms, surrounded by men. But there's something about the way the young men are looking at her. Maybe it's just me. Like she's a doll or something that isn't real. I mean something that's not to honor. What I see them doing is making fun of the big tall white girl and her large breasts. I don't know how innocent this is, or if they are intentionally mean. Or if they are mean at all and I only interpreted it as meanness. Maybe she seems artificial to them and it's campy and they're simply enjoying her. And if they are making fun, so what, it feels harmless enough. Anyone could see the oddly stark juxtaposition. We humans all make fun of each other when there's a big difference and you're right up next to it.

The trouble, though, isn't the young men. It's Ruth. How Ruth, among these tiny brown-skinned skinny men, makes her body go clumsy and goofy. The way Ruth first did with me a blue moon ago when I first asked her to dance.

Ruth's no Shingli-shoozi.

Instead of Marilyn Monroe, Ruth's a clown.

AT THIS POINT, I'd like to step up and say I saw the humanity of it all. Saw in Ruth the buffoon *I* was and my own ridiculous quest to embody my sex. But I didn't. Something fried behind my eyes. And I didn't understand what it was. Not yet.

A WEEK LATER, I wake up with a name that keeps running around my head. *Buster Bangs*. Buster's a former student. Big Ben goes through my papers, finds his phone number. Buster's a massage therapist, but really he's a sex worker. I'm surprised when he answers. At first Buster thinks I want to talk about writing. Fuck, I talk so much about writing, but I let Buster talk for a while about his novel and what he's been doing since he left class. I don't know how else to say it, so I just say it. I tell Buster I want to pay for a massage, maybe the kind of massage with a special ending. We'll just have to see.

It's quiet for a moment on the other end of the line. Then: "For how long, Mr. Grunewald?"

"Call me Ben," I say.

Then: "No," I say, "call me Gruney."

"Gruney," Buster says.

"Two hours," I say.

"That's two hundred dollars," he says. "But for you I'll make it one fifty."

BUSTER'S RED, TOO, like Ruth, only he's rust-red and freckles all over. Short and stocky, he's an imp, this guy. The way he moves, he moves quick, then stops, then moves quick again. Like a stop-action camera. A red beard with braids in his beard and sometimes beads in the braids. Rust-red hair that sticks up in clumps all over his head. Hair you'd think could only look like that with lots of product. But Buster's not a product kind of guy.

As it turns out, Buster has that afternoon free. It's a Wednesday, Ruth's night of teaching class. One of those cold, gray, rainy January afternoons. Buster shows up just after sardines at four at the back door in an orange windbreaker with a beaded leather bag over his shoulder. He's wearing sandals and carrying a massage table. When he first looks at me, there's a way he has to stop and take a breath. I don't look at all the way I used to look.

Then Buster's big smile. One tooth missing, same one as Silvio's.

"Beautiful day, ain't it, Mr. Grunewald?"

"It is, Buster," I say. "Come in! Come in!"

THE FURNACE IS on and I'm lying face down on Buster's massage table on top of a purple paisley sheet. The way my face lies in the headrest for a moment I don't think I can breathe, so I sit up quick. Buster is naked, too. That rust-red hair across his chest. The carpet matches the drapes with Buster, too. Thick arms and legs. The nub of his cock sticking out the hair that's darker between his legs.

Buster's lighting a stick of incense. He puts the incense stick into a gold chalice he's brought that's full of sand.

"Hey, Mr. Grunewald, man," Buster says, "it's cool."

"Gruney," I say.

"Mr. Gruney," he says.

Buster lays his hand on my shoulder. The pad of his hand is thick and his hand is especially warm. It's the first hand that's touched me besides Ruth's since I've been home from the hospital.

"I'm sorry," I say. "I have this thing about breathing. The cover on the headrest, there isn't much room for air."

Buster's over at the headrest in a quick flash, fiddling with the cover. Then that quick he's back looking at me. Strange blue eyes a little off kilter, as if he is looking just over my shoulder.

"Breath is important," Buster says. "Why don't you try it again."

I lie down again, put my face into the headrest opening, take a deep breath.

"Much better," I say. "Thank you."

Then: "Mr. Grunewald? I mean Gruney?"

"Yeah?"

"I'm going to put a CD on my boombox here," he says. "It's my sex magic CD. I hope you like the music. I made it myself. If you don't, we could put on some classical music or music you'd rather hear."

Through the headrest, Buster's bare feet are still tanned in the pattern of his sandals.

"I'm sure your music will be fine," I say.

"I'm going to pray a little," Buster says. "And when I pray I make a sound with my lips, so don't let that freak you out, okay?"

"Okay."

"And I'm going to touch your head first," Buster says. "I usually touch the ass first, but with you my spirits tell me to touch your head."

THE MUSIC IS a flute, soft. Something lonely. When Buster touches my head it's like the soft music is in my head. Buster's hands are hot like he's got a fever. He works my muscles much harder than Ruth's massages. He uses his elbows, his legs, his whole body. Really, I'm in some other dimension. At one point he's sitting on my ass and pulling my arms straight back. The way his ass feels. Bare ass against bare ass. I remember as a child under the front steps I played a game called *kissing bums* with a boy named Kelly.

"Hey, Gruney," Buster whispers in my ear, "you can turn over now."

When I turn over, Buster takes the headrest off and stands at the head of the table. The flute music is in my body now and it ain't the flute that's lonely. My poor lonely body. I feel it welling up, the big lonely weep. But I've had enough fucking tears, what I want to do is come. Come the way Ruth came. That's when Buster steps up closer, lays his balls, his dick onto my face.

"I'm HIV," I say.

"Aren't we all," he says.

My nose against Buster's rusty ass, my mouth around his

balls, my dick is, praise the fucking Buster Spirits, hard hard hard.
The way I come is one huge breath breathed in with a fast slap.
I'm breathing like a racehorse, crying like a baby. But Buster's
balls are in my mouth. In no time at all, I'm off the table and in a
paisley heap with Buster. We're laughing our asses off.

BUSTER STAYS FOR dinner. Nothing fancy, he's a vegan, so I boil
up some carrots and potatoes, sautée some spinach. Pour some
yeast seasoning and Bragg Liquid Aminos on the vegetables.
Buster's impressed that I know how to cook hippy. For my dinner,
I add a piece of Ruth's homemade meatloaf. Lots of ketchup.

Buster and I are sitting at the kitchen table. We've got our
clothes back on and Buster's massage table is folded up. The
paisley sheet inside his leather bag.

I'm hoping Buster will stay a while. Buster's just told me
his spirits had just told him that I live too much in my head. That
I need to get out and be in nature and breathe some mountain air.

Big Ben is the guy who says it: "Maybe you could spend
the night?" I say. "I could make a fire in the fireplace."

Buster is across the table from me. His smile. That missing
tooth like Silvio's.

His hand, that warm hand that had touched me, that got
me hard, that jerked me off, made me come, is lying next to his
fork. My hand goes down as if in slow motion and I lay my hand
on top of Buster's hand.

Buster's face is a lot of things right then. His off-kilter
blue eyes go a bit more south. Later on, he'll tell me how he was
perplexed. He never mixed business with pleasure and already
he'd accepted my invitation to dinner. Another rule was he didn't
date the guys he did his sex work with. Then there was the fact
that I was Ben Grunewald, his former writing teacher that he'd
always had a crush on. Plus, I was kind of famous. A Gay Icon.
Plus he hadn't kissed me and he wanted to kiss me.

"You're not going to fall in love with me, are you?" Buster
says. "Lots of guys fall in love with their sex worker."

I fold my hand into Buster's. His hand is like a portable heater and my hands are always freezing.

"I don't think I have any falling in love left in me," I say. "I'd just like the company."

"Would you read to me from your new novel?" Buster says.

"Twist my arm," I say.

That's when Buster takes what he wants. His blue eyes go a little wonky and he tilts his head. Before I know it, Buster Bangs is kissing the Gay Icon. Garlic big time on his breath. My tongue against his broken tooth.

Buster and I have just leaned away from our embrace. I've let go his hand and am just standing to get him another helping of carrots and potatoes when Ruth walks in. Ruth doesn't knock, she never knocks, why should she? She's been walking in like that since the first day.

Something about Ruth that is so left over from the New Year's Eve party. The way her face sticks out from the hoodie, wet red hair smashed against her forehead. Her nerdy girl glasses are crooked. As soon as she sees that I am regarding her, that flush of red on her cheek. I'm sure my face is just as red.

"Class ended early," Ruth says.

THAT THING BEHIND my eyes that fries, deep fries to a crisp. All I know what to feel is embarrassed and all I know what to do is try and cover it up. I guess what I feel is guilt. Sex with Buster. Old Catholic stuff but still, even though Ruth and I have never promised sexual fidelity, the way Ruth and I have been operating as one unit, it feels like an infidelity.

But so much more is going on inside me. A fucking maelstrom, man. But I won't feel it. It's like that class with Jeske when he asked me to tell the scariest thing about myself. I knew what the scariest thing was. I mean looking back on it now I know I knew. But in that moment, at that point in my life, there was no way I could have accessed that kind of truth telling. It would take me twenty years to tell that kind of truth.

Same way with that night in my kitchen with Buster and Ruth. Looking back on it now. All that I knew. But there was no way I was going there.

It won't be long, though, and it's all going to explode.

Ruth is surprised to see another body in the house. She stops, takes off her glasses, pulls the hoodie over her head, shakes out her hair. In the winter light, her thick red hair seems almost dark brown. The way the windows are steamed over, there's no way Ruth has seen Buster and me kiss or that our hands were touching.

Ruth wipes off the lenses with her sweatshirt. When Ruth puts her glasses back on, she recognizes the man in my kitchen is Buster. She drops her sweatshirt and opens up her arms to her old classmate.

"Buster! Hi!" she says. "Weren't you in Santa Fe?"

"Ruth!" Buster says. "Wow! You're looking awesome!"

Ruth and Buster throw their arms around each other. She's a head taller than him. My God all that red hair.

"Zuni Mountain," Buster says.

"What are you doing here?" Ruth says.

Buster's rolling his shoulders, moving his arms. Always in movement this guy. His fingers move like he's playing a piano.

"I just gave Gruney a massage."

"Gruney?"

"Mr. Grunewald," Buster says. "Never run into shoulders that tight."

"Gruney," Ruth says.

Ruth's look over at me is slow. I can't tell you for sure how I react but I'm pretty sure all I do is smile. I know Ruth so well. She's wondering about this massage and why I never told her about it. She's wondering what kind of massage it was and what the massage *meant*. But Ruth sees me smile, so she puts it away for something that she and I will talk about later. Then Ruth does what she always does. She takes over. First, though, she gives me a smooch on the cheek, then starts cleaning up our dinner dishes. When Ruth kisses me, I look over at Buster. There's no doubt about it. Buster's haywire eyes are trying to figure out that kiss.

I tell Ruth, *no I can do that, you sit down*. But Ruth helps me anyway. We clear the dishes and then she's got the refrigerator open and she's got the canned peaches out, and the frozen blueberries, and the bananas, and the yogurt. She's pouring warm water on the frozen blueberries. She's popping the lid to the peaches. She's peeling the bananas. She's got bowls out for all of us. For me, it's just plain yogurt. Ruth boils water and makes tea, *Midnight in Missoula*. All the while Ruth is talking talking. She and Buster are back and forth, a couple of busy bees, those two. They're talking about Zuni Mountain and Wolf Creek and the Radical Færies and about magic and spells and how before anything you have to believe in magic before it will work. Really, I try a couple times to stop Ruth, to stop Buster. This pleasant back and forth, the way Ruth goes on and on, if Ruth knew it was post-handjob, and pre-coitus, this conversation would probably be a whole lot different. Buster's clueless. The handjob isn't an issue. That's his job. Still, I can see him wonder how many former students of mine are kissing me.

No matter what, I can't get a word in edgewise. At one point, I scream bloody murder, but it's only after, when nobody's heard me scream, that I realize I haven't opened my mouth. Really, we spend the rest of the evening that way. Two or three hours at least, the two votive candles lit on the table, the blue one and the green one, the tall beeswax candle left over from Cannon Beach, the drips down onto its tin holder, onto the table, those two talking like they were best friends and hadn't seen each other in months. Ruth tells Buster about her new class, ten students, all women. How much she already loves these women. Buster is real interested in Ruth's class, so Ruth gets a piece of paper and a pen and she writes down her phone number and address and the date of the class and the time. They're both excited that he'll be the only man.

Ten-thirty or eleven, Buster pats the top of my hand with his. The flames of the candles move. It all happens in a moment.

Buster says, "I'd better be going."

I say, "Can't you stay?"

My hand goes for his hand, but it's already gone.

Ruth says, "You're not biking in this weather are you?"

Buster says, "No, I got a car now."

Ruth says, "What kind?'

Buster says, "An old Datsun."

Ruth says, "I saw it parked out there, red right?"

Buster says, "Yeah, red."

I say, "Buster."

His right eye's fine. It's Buster's left eye that looks like he's looking at something behind you. In the candlelight, it takes me a moment to get that I'm the one in Buster's gaze.

Buster says, "Sorry, Mr. Grunewald, it's late."

To Ruth he says, "I'll see you in class on Wednesday."

Ruth says, "Can't wait!"

Then Buster's putting on his orange windbreaker. The way he moves about so quick. His beaded bag is over his shoulder. He and Ruth bear hug like old war buddies. When Buster steps toward me, he kisses me on the cheek. Then the other cheek, like in Europe. When he smiles, his crooked tooth.

"I'll twist your arm another night," he says.

RUTH AND ME alone in the kitchen. Rain against the window. The votive candles, the blue one and the green one, thin lines of smoke. The Cannon Beach candle is a low flame in a pool of wax. How the low flame jumps. Ruth is sitting across from me, her long arm, her elbow, on the table. The candlelight on her arm. She is a statue, a dark statue in shadow, some long-suffering female Catholic saint. Women who wait.

On the chair where Buster sat, the darkest shadow.

Talking. All that stuff that happens in me just before I tell the truth is happening. The antidepressant buzz in my ears is

two octaves higher, I'm sweating, my heart is beating fast and
I'm trying to speak but I can't speak because there's no breath.
The desire to move, get out, run. When I finally speak I'm not
looking at Ruth, I'm looking down at my hand.

"Tonight," I say. "Buster's massage."

My thumb moves to the knuckle, to the no-fear place.

"I got hard," I say. "And he jerked me off and I came."

My thumb presses down hard. When I make myself look
up, Ruth has moved her face into the light. She's got that smile.
Big Nurse or maybe the principal.

"I suppose you're going to do it again," she says.

Suddenly I'm in a battle of life and death and I really want
to hurt her. When I speak again, the rage surprises me.

"He was going to spend the night," I say. "But then you
bust in and fill up the room."

Ruth's fist slams down onto the table. The dishes jump.
The Cannon Beach candle goes all the way out. Ruth gets up
from the table and switches on the fluorescence of the overhead
kitchen light. Just like that she's in my face.

"You mean this whole time you two were." Ruth stops.

"Yes," I say. "We *were*."

"And you don't tell me this very important detail earlier in
the evening," Ruth says, "because I'm a larger than life loudmouth bitch?"

"Something like that," I say.

The flush of red on her neck, up the side of her face. Eyes
as blue as ice. Her fist comes in a round house that I grab with
my fist and stop. For a long moment Ruth and I are grunts and
groans, Hank Christian and Barry Hannah armwrestling.

No doubt about it, she could kick my ass. Maybe I should
let her. I'm the asshole man and I deserve it. But still my fist
stays around her wrist.

Everything above is bright bright and on the floor black
shadows suck up and stick onto the underneath of things.
Ruth's hair ain't red, it's pink cotton candy. Her face, the skin of

her arms and hands, as if the red blood inside her has turned to lemonade. A black shadow sucked up and stuck under her chin.

"You're hurting my wrist," she says.

"Then stop trying to hit me," I say.

Ruth steps back, I let go, Ruth holds her wrist with her other hand. Under her brows, her eyes are black round bruises.

"Ben," she says, "Fucking Ben Grunewald. How humiliating."

I have to cover my eyes. The kitchen is small and with the table the only place to stand is between the sink and the table right next to Ruth. I don't know what to do. Maybe try and touch her, but I don't want to touch her. I end up just standing in a bright room with my hands over my eyes. *I'm sorry I'm sorry I'm sorry* is what's going round in my head. But Big Ben ain't sorry. He loved getting hard and he loved coming. What's there to be sorry for. And he's pissed that he even has to explain.

Stomping. It's easy to stomp in my house because it's old and there's no insulation and the fir flooring sets right on the floor joists. And Ruth is a big girl and she's stomping. Shakes the whole house. She stomps into the dining room and turns on the overhead light. Then into the living room. Ruth turns on the overhead light in there. Then the bedroom, and the bathroom. Stomping. It ain't long and all the bright overhead lights in the whole house are on.

Fucking bright overhead lights, man. Queen Lowlighta in a meltdown.

"You need to bring some light into this fucking place," Ruth says. "Maybe you could see something."

Before I know it, Ruth's grabbed her hoodie and she's out the kitchen door. The slam that rattles the dishes. Outside, Ruth turns on the bright porch light. I open the kitchen door, follow Ruth out the door, into the rain. Through the gate, out into the street, I stand by her Honda Civic as she starts the car. Her door is locked. I'm knocking on the window.

"Please, Ruth," I say.

For a moment, Ruth looks up from behind her window.

The lights of the dashboard gold and amber onto her face. Terrifying, really, how beautiful she is. I think maybe she will stop. She will roll down the window and we'll. I don't know. But just then the music goes loud inside the car. "Rock Lobster." Ruth lets up on the emergency brake. Leaves a patch of rubber just inches from my toes. Ruth's silver Honda Civic is a roar down the street, then red brake lights, a turn signal, and she's gone.

My house, every light's on in the place, and through the rain and fog, my house looks haunted.

It is haunted.

My wet socks on the wet asphalt. My clothes are soaked through. The wet feels good on my hot skin. I could lay down right there and never get up.

And that's just what I do. Lie down in the fucking street.

It ain't five minutes and Ruth's Honda Civic screeches back around the corner. Headlights straight for me. I think maybe she's going to run me down like a dog. But she doesn't. Really, I'm disappointed.

Pretty soon it's Ruth's body lying next to me on the asphalt. Close but not touching. On the shiny black pavement of SE Morrison. Rain coming down in buckets. Like we're in a shower stall, the way the rain comes down. Hard rain on our faces, pounding our chests, our legs, smashing our clothes onto our skin. Fuck it. What's a little rain when you're half-dead and you haven't slept a decent night's sleep since forever.

Fucking rain, man.

When the squall has passed and the rain is coming down light, when I finally have stopped crying, Ruth lays her head on my arm and clears her throat.

"So tell me," Ruth says, "isn't *Gruney* what Hank Christian used to call you?"

THAT NIGHT WE stay up, Ruth and me, sitting across from each other at the kitchen table, under the bright overhead kitchen light. In the house, all the overhead lights on bright. *Midnight in Missoula* talking talking.

I don't know what to tell Ruth. All I can say is *I'm sorry, Ruth.* Shit, I sound like every other guy in the world trying to explain why he can't keep his dick in his pants.

Later on, on the couch in front of the fireplace, I'm sitting up and Ruth's lying down with her head in my lap. I'm staring into the fire and it comes to me.

"It's like in your favorite movie, *Living Out Loud,*" I say. "The part where Holly Hunter tells Danny DeVito that she loves him but not like he loves her."

In no time at all, Ruth's up from the couch and she's got her coat.

"What?" I say.

"*I'm* Danny DeVito?" she says.

Ruth starts crying so hard she gets the hiccups. When Ruth slams the kitchen door this time, she slams the door so hard, a water glass falls out of the drying rack and breaks on the floor.

THEN COMES THE night. The night. Ruth's class and my class, twenty writers in all, decide to get together on a Saturday night and have a dinner at a restaurant three blocks from my house. When I corner Ruth, she swears she didn't have a thing to do with the party. But I don't believe her. It's Ruth's favorite restaurant. And it's close to my house.

I, of course, don't want to go. My days of drinking too much white wine, baked Vienna sausage hors d'oeuvres, talking about writing, and Chicken Kiev and wild rice for dinner, are over.

But I go.

It's summer, almost, May, I think, and the evening is warm. Sunlight comes through the leaves of the maple in front of my house. Sunlight and the shadows of the leaves shake around on the faux Persian carpet on the living room floor. I've put on a clean white shirt and my khaki pants. The black belt I bought a dozen years ago on St. Mark's, I've had to punch a new hole in to hold my pants up. Right there at the button on the top, my pants bunch together like khaki drapery folds. I slip on my black loafers. I decide to go sockless, like I always used to do. Back in the day, I'd roll my pants up and show off my tanned ankles and my beautiful feet. I step out the back door, though, and look down. My ankles are not tanned and they're skinny and old. My beautiful feet are cold because of the neuropathy. Two of my ten toenails are ugly with fungus. I go back inside, pull on a pair of dark socks, load my pockets up with enough Xanax to kill a regular customer. That's when the phone rings. It's probably Ruth. Ruth is the only person who calls me.

That voice. I'll never forget that voice.

"Hey, Gruney!"

Fuck me, I can't believe it. Hank Christian.

Something in my heart, a sudden flame, a fire in my heart I didn't even know was out.

"My God Hank," I say. "Where are you? How are you? I've fucking missed you so much, man. Are you a doctor yet?"

"Tough times, Gruney Babe," Hank says. "Real tough times."

"Are you all right?"

"The big C, man," Hank says. "Cancer."

"What?!"

"I just got back from the doc today. They say it's in remission. So I thought I'd come see you."

"I got AIDS, Hank," I say.

Three thousand miles of wire between us. I can hear every wire.

"*Porca Miseria*," Hank says. "I heard."

There are no right words so I just say something.

"Are you all right?" I say. "I mean in your heart."

"Yeah, Darlin'," Hank says. "Thanks for asking."

Then: "Let's talk about all this when I get there."

THE RESTAURANT WHERE the writers are meeting is the same restaurant where a year later Ruth and Hank will have their wedding reception that I'll not be invited to.

Walking the three blocks that evening, I'm thick and dead. I feel so shocked, the world outside pushed even further away. Fucking cancer, man. The evening air is charged with doom. Yet at the same time, I'm so fucking high. And in the doom like never before, there's a hope. In August, the month that's too hot to be in Florida, Hank Christian will come and stay with me. Really, I'm not walking, I'm floating down the street.

Just before I walk in the door of the restaurant I pop two Xanax. Open the door. Old grease smell from the kitchen only people who've worked in restaurants as long as I did can smell. The toilets right there at the entrance. The women's door is propped open with a yellow cone. The smell of hair product and ammonia and something else. In the dining room proper, only three high windows, windows you can't open. Bad art on the walls. Lots of bad art. Two more Xanax.

Ruth's got everything prepared. Two tables of eight and a table of six in a special roped-off section of the dining room.

I'm early, of course. The bartender is a young man in a white shirt and black tie. He is so young and fresh-faced I want to cry. His collar is soiled and his black tie has a stain on it. But that's all right. The restaurant is dark and soon the sun will be down. His smile makes up for it all. I ask for a large soda water with a little ice and no lime. He pours my soda water, sticks a straw in it. Puts a wedge of lime on the rim. I tip him a dollar anyway.

Above each place setting there's a folded card with a name on it. I'm in the middle table. Ruth's name is right next to mine. *Buster Bangs's* folded name card is all the way across the room behind me. I sit down in my chair, prepare my strategy to get through the evening. Stay in my seat, don't move around. If someone wants to talk they'll have to come over to me. The person's name on the card on the other side of me I don't know. It's a woman. Jan or Jane or Janet Something. Another Xanax, just the thought of talking to somebody I don't know.

NINE O'CLOCK, THE evening and the dinner is in full swing. All the writers are a little tipsy, loud. So much laughter. But I'm not laughing. It's one of the things I do these days, stay sober and watch other people get drunk. Really it's like they're taking stupid pills. But there's another part of me. Slug down a shot of tequila is what he wants to do, and roll a Drum, and start getting real, getting down to the down low.

Ruth is wearing a new dress she bought at the Deseret. It's a sleeveless mint green summer shift. She's pulled her hair up with combs in the back. I've never seen her neck so long and graceful. She's wearing her new contacts, tinted blue contacts that make her eyes unreal blue. That night, her face is flushed. Ruth's never more than a one glass of wine girl. Tonight, though, she's on her second. She's touching my hand, my arm, she's touching my leg a lot.

I am miserable. I mean there I am in a room full of people who love me, respect me, all of them a little drunk, happy, showing off, flirting, full of emotion. Such a lovely way to enjoy yourself being human. But it's not for me. The being human part, enjoying it. Not yet. It will be three of four more years before I can be present enough to enjoy a moment again. Believe me, I'd tried.

And that night I tried too. Just fuck it, so what if it feels like there's not enough air in the room, so what if Janet next to me wears too much Shalimar and has asked three times now, each time in a more particular way, why I never write in the third person. *Ben sat at the table, perplexed, head reeling, wondering how he should answer the persistent Janet.* So what if the salad with blue cheese, the knife and fork in my hands are so far away from my mouth. So what if the world wobbles every time the fucking table wobbles when somebody leans an elbow on it. So what if the room keeps tilting hard to the left. So what if the ringing in my ears sounds like a far off radio station. So what if my stomach feels that any minute it's going to come blowing out my ass.

Just fucking relax. Remember to smile. Breathe.

Just as the dinners are being served – our choice of either meatless lasagna or braised chicken breast – the door opens. Cool air hits the back of my neck. It's Buster and he's high as a kite. Must be a speed freak the way he moves. His hair is full of gold glitter and so's his beard. A red polka dot bow tie clipped onto the collar of his shiny green paisley shirt. A roar goes up from the women in Ruth's class. Everyone else turns to see what the commotion is.

Buster Bangs, standing there, trying to stand there. A grin so big on his face, there's no doubt about it, you *definitely* want to do whatever he's been doing.

Buster tries to take a step but backs up two. The wall and the bad art on the wall is what's holding him up. The roar and the laughter has stopped and everybody gets quiet. Ruth quick grabs the sleeve of my shirt then lets go.

When Buster sees where I'm sitting, he makes his way over. Funny, when he seems to know where he's going he can go just fine. When he gets to me, he leans his face down. Just like that, Buster kisses me full on the mouth. I start to pull away, then don't. Ruth grabs a hold of my hand, then as the kiss goes on, her hand disappears. Buster's heavy marijuana smell, his garlic vegetarian breath. As we kiss, my chin goes up and up and Buster's lips press hard.

In all the world all there is, is Buster's scratchy mustache and beard, his soft lips, marijuana, garlic, his tongue, and his broken tooth, The kiss goes on forever. For me it does, anyway. Really, I don't want the kiss to stop because of what will happen after.

When Buster pulls his lips away, gold glitter falls from is hair and beard. My lap, my arms, my hands, my shirt are covered in gold glitter. Buster kneels down on one knee. His blue eyes, I

mean the right one, is looking deep into my eyes. His other eye
looks like he's looking at Ruth. When he speaks, his voice is low,
raspy from too much pot, and fucking sexy.

"Hey, Gruney," Buster says, "you should come with me."

I start to say something. Some shit I don't know. But
Buster stops me.

"It's really best for everybody," Buster says.

I look down at my glittery gold thumb. Big Ben moves my
thumb to the glittery gold no-fear place. For some reason, I'm
thinking about my kitchen. The refrigerator that's full of food that
Ruth has cooked. A roast chicken, sprouted wheat bread she's
baked, a big pot of kale because kale is good for you. Protein
drinks without sugar. On the refrigerator, the magnetized words
that Ruth bought that Ruth has constructed into strange sentences. *He touched her implacably in the moist middle. My heart is
a can of sweet grass honey. Cornucopia of green earth, your
insidious armpits. Fluid, she makes of the day the milky way.* The
kitchen table that's set with the turquoise cloth napkins that
match the turquoise elephant in the pattern of the tablecloth that
Ruth bought on sale at Pier 1 Imports.

In fact, there is nothing in my house that doesn't have something of Ruth about it. The butcher knife and knife sharpener
she bought because mine was shit. The salt and pepper shakers
that looks like chickens. The hot pads that look like watermelons.
The little dish that says *non parlare, baciami* on it on the stove
top so you can lay down your dripping spoon. The big colorful
Mexican plates. In the living room, the velvet faux-leopardskin
throw on the couch. The camelskin lamp she bought because
I'm Queen Lowlighta. The glass prism sculpture that reflects the
light. Her Danskin leotard and her running shoes by the bedroom door. In the bathroom, the Lady Speed Stick and the toothbrush and the plate with her silver jewelry in it. The CDs from
her car, and the feathers and the rocks and the sticks of wood on
top of the refrigerator, on top of the coffee table, on the bedstand
by the bed. Her computer on the dining room table.

And that night, there in the restaurant, my name *Ben Grune-wald* on the name card, right next to *Ruth Dearden*.

A sudden rage. Big Ben rage. Ruth and I are suddenly married and Ruth is my wife the way Evie was my wife, that fucking weird heterosexual sick pairing of opposite sexes that means I can't breathe or be myself, not a person anymore who can do as he feels, go where he wants, have autonomy. *Married fucking married*. Seven years married, spiritually dead is right there again, right in my face, ready to devour me again. No longer a line around me that says this is me, this is my space, and you have to acknowledge this space because it's sacred and that line has to be there because it took my whole life to set up that line and without it I cannot exist.

And there I am sitting next to Ruth in her favorite restaurant with a grilled piece of stringy chicken breast covered *au beurre noir*. The mint green freshness of the summer shift against her skin. And I'm every man that I've ever hated that fucks over his woman. That I'm even in the position to fuck over *my woman* pisses me off. Since my wife Evie, since my sister, since my mother, I've been fucking diligent to keep my ass out of this crack.

And what a laugh to feel that my fucking sacred autonomy has been compromised. When you're fucking sick to death and so alone, Christ, you'll sell your soul for comfort.

Truth. I thought if I could keep telling the truth I'd be okay. You go along, talk about your feelings, trying to say the hard stuff, and you think it's okay. But really you don't have a clue. The real truth comes only years and years later, after therapy, after writing, and finally one day your body feels safe enough to feel it.

Either that or truth descends like the hand of an angry god and rips your heart out. Bam, there it is, truth, from out of nowhere, there you are one day getting a massage and then you've got his balls in your mouth and in a flash you're hard and you're coming and it is suddenly. Surprisingly. Brutally true.

Fucking truth, man.

There's a price you pay when you help someone the way

Ruth helped me. That deep life and death kind of help. Both of you have to pay. What the heroine expects from the man whose life she's saved. Ruth thinks she's loved you pure and simple and true, no strings attached until that moment that May night 1999 in her favorite restaurant in front of everybody when you get up from your chair and Buster Bangs leads you out of the restaurant. Finally, she finally realizes you won't love her back the way she wants you to and no matter how honest and giving a person she is, no matter that she's promised to love you no matter what, her indignation is righteous and overwhelming.

And Ruth has seen you weak, half-dead, trembling, afraid to come out from under the bed. You end up hating her because you've needed her so much.

Fucking resentment, man.

Ruth's glorious red hair piled high. Her ultra-blue eyes looking into mine. How sad they are. How much she loves me. How long she's suffered for her love. That lock of red hair hanging behind her ear. How did she get so beautiful. So skinny. Such a presence.

This movie ain't *My Fair Lady*. This movie is *All About Eve*. This movie is Stephen King's *Misery*.

Ruth.

Who I see is my mother. Who named me after the priest with soft hands. Me, her boyfriend she dressed in girl's clothes and had tea with in the afternoon. I was her redemption, the one who would save her.

Who I see is my sister Margaret. The sister who used tell me *jump* and I'd say *how high*. The sister, like my mother, who I danced with, cheered up, made myself into the one someone in the world she could love so the world could be a place that she could live in. The photo of Margaret and me on the cement steps. She's holding me and saying, *he's mine*. I'm holding her and saying, *I'm all she has*. The ugly sister. Not Marilyn Monroe but the clown.

Fuck. The Cockless Man at the Bottom of Hell I thought I

was rid of is back again. The Most Miserable Clown of All. A new version of my own fucking self-hatred for the twenty-first century. He's looking back at me through the eyes of Ruth. Ruth herself, I couldn't see.

It's weird. With Hank, with Tony Escobar, the more I loved them, the more I was myself. I guess I thought I could do that with Ruth as well. But Ruth wasn't a guy. Ruth was a girl and that meant Ruth was my mother, my sister.

My mother, my sister. My mother, my sister.

Fuck me, Dr. Freud.

And with all her loving soulful touch, Ruth could not open the door to my ecstasy.

But a garlic-soaked, rusty-haired hippy could.

Because he was a man.

It's fucked. I know. Totally fucked. But that's just the way it is.

18.

Hope

RUTH WASN'T THE ONLY ONE WHO NEEDED TO GET fucked. It had been so long I thought it wasn't possible anymore. But Praise the Lord, Buster Bangs fucked me good.

As soon as he comes, though, Buster passes out. For a while it feels as if maybe I'm going to return to the world. I lie on his futon, my lungs full of fresh breath, my hand around Buster's foot. But it doesn't take long and things are back to being fucked up. Dizzy. Plus Buster's snoring away.

There's no way I'm going to spend the night in a strange house with a bull moose who eats garlic for breakfast on a lumpy hard hippy futon.

I'm out of there. Thirty blocks maybe to my house. It's cool out, so I borrow Buster Bangs's red wool sweater. My ass is sore, but it feels good to walk.

The moment I unlock my back door I can tell things are different. I turn on the overhead light in the kitchen. It takes my eyes a while to see what it is. All of Ruth's things are gone. I mean everything, the rocks and sticks and feathers, the tablecloth and the matching napkins, the salt and pepper shakers, the hot pads, the magnetic words on the refrigerator, the big colorful Mexican plates.

In the bathroom, I turn the overhead light on. Her Lady Speed Stick is gone and her soaps and the dish with her silver jewelry. Her shampoo and soft brush in the shower. Her running shoes and leotard by the bedroom door. In the bedroom, I turn the overhead light on. On the nightstand, her sticks and rocks and feathers are gone. Her fancy Indian bedspread, her foam rubber pillow, the green and blue sheets with the high thread count. Gone. In the dining room, I turn the overhead light on. Her computer gone from the dining room table. In the living room, I turn the overhead light on. The faux-leopardskin throw, the camelskin lamp, gone. In the whole house. Everything. Right down to the roast chicken and the bowl of kale in the refrigerator, gone.

Damn, in that moment there's so much to feel I don't think I can feel it all. Such a strange sensation. In that space between the crack my arms make with my chest and just above my nipples, where I might have wings, the spirit in me starts to rise up and out, and when I lift my arms that spirit soars up high to the heavens. For a moment, there's a heaven above. It's so clear there's a heaven above, because what's coming out from under my armpits is connected to it.

My tired old body jumps up and I kick my heels and I yell out a loud *Whoop!* Find my Paul Simon CD.

> Get out of the pen, Ben.
> Just get loony, Gruney.
> And get yourself free.

I dance and I twirl and kick up and shake my ass, a full-on dance marathon through the bright rooms. Dance and dance and don't stop dancing. I fall down more than sit onto the kitchen chair. Turn off the boombox. I'm breathing hard and I lean my elbows on the bare wood of the table.

It's in that silence I begin to feel something else. In the dish rack by the sink, one blue plate, one fork, the glass with the yellow balloons, the thick white cup with Otis Café on it. My house looks like somebody's house who doesn't really live in it.

I turn off all the overhead lights and turn on my lava lamp, my illuminated world globe, my faux Tiffany lamp. Make a fire in the fireplace. Grab a blanket that's still left on the bed. Something smells of garlic. Buster's red sweater. I pull the sweater over my head and throw it in the corner. On the couch, I curl up under the warm blanket. The pitch in the firewood makes the fire pop and spit.

In the middle of the night, I wake up. The fire is out and I make it into bed. Feels good, alone in bed and I stretch out. But there's something along the edge of the bed. Something old. I know what it is but I won't admit it. Three hours of sleep.

The next day, Sunday. Rainy, cold, and dark, early June, Portland. About three in the afternoon I call Buster. I get is his voicemail. I don't leave a message.

My long clawfoot bathtub is the only place. Hot bath and boombox the only place left to go. My only CD I'm not sick of listening to is the CD of my favorite songs Ruth made. I don't know if the CD's a good idea, but I put it on.

In the tub, surrounded by hot water and bubbles, Jane Siberry's "The Gospel According to Darkness." I wonder if I've ever cried so hard.

Monday morning, Hank calls again. His voice is what I need to hear. His news ain't good, though. He can't make it in August. The doctor has told him he shouldn't travel so soon. Airplane air. *Maybe I can make it for Christmas*, Hank says.

A couple hours later that same day, another phone call. As soon as the phone rings, I know it's death.

It's my ex-wife, Evie. I'm not sure at all what to say. How to make my voice sound. Finally, it's the Catholic boy with the big apology. I mean me trying to cover that voice up:

"Hi, Evie," I say. "What's up?"

The silence before Evie speaks. All the years, all that we never talked about.

"I just wondered if you'd heard," Evie says.

"Heard what?"

"The Atlanta Boys," Evie says. "Gary died last week. AIDS."

My breath goes away, but still I speak.

"I didn't even know he was sick."

"You're not the best one to keep in touch," she says. "The

only way I got this number was I remembered your sister's married name."

Then: "And you know about Reuben and Sal," she says.

I pull the kitchen chair over, sit down on it real slow.

"In April," Evie says, "their Jeep Wagoneer sideswiped a logger truck. They went over the side fifty feet into the spring runoff. They died on impact."

That's what I do, too, fall fifty feet into freezing water.

"Why didn't anybody call me?"

"That *anybody* would be me," Evie says. "And I know you've been sick. And I'm calling you now."

THE KITCHEN CHAIR has no cushion, just my boney ass against the wood. My right leg crossed over my left. Outside the gray light, inside the house, dark. There's no way I could get on an airplane. Even an hour flight to Boise. I can't even get up off the chair. I sit there so long that when I finally get up my legs won't work.

When I turn on the light in the kitchen, in the dish rack, the one blue plate, the one fork, the glass with the yellow balloons, the thick white cup, Otis Café.

At the sternum, right in the middle of my chest, the lightbulb. The filament flickering flickering.

I call Hank. *You know what you got to do.*

I call Ephraim, but Ephraim's not home.

That night, I do my deep breathing exercises, listen to my self-hypnosis tape. Babbling brooks and wind in the pines. Popping Xanax. But the Xanax doesn't work. Every time I look at the clock ten minutes have passed. Outside the window it's black. All I can see is my ghost self in the window in the room with low lights. At 3:30 I turn the clock around. I keep my eyes closed tight. Then the morning birds begin to sing. I open my eyes and outside the window it's blue-gray.

Buster Bangs's answering machine goes like this: *I'm off to Tennessee. Travel mode's the key.*

I cancel class on Thursday and spend the next ten days and nights not sleeping. So easy to say now, that there was a time in my life, eleven days and nights in my life, that I didn't sleep.

After the third night it becomes a challenge. Sooner or later the fear will relent and nature will take its course and I will fall and there will be a place for me when I fall and someone or something will lay me down.

The photo on my calendar is of Princess Diana sitting on a yacht at sunset in the Mediterranean with Dodi Fayed. All that peace and calm. Nobody is safe. I mark off the days with big dramatic black grease pen Xs.

Your body just does things. I leave the television on day and night. Then on the third or fourth day, I shut the television off, unplug it, turn the screen around. I play all my old CDs. Look through photos of Hank and me from New York. That one of us especially, on the Brooklyn Bridge. We're laughing hard at our joke. Instead of *cheese*, Hank has just said the thing Jeske always said, *Got to go pal.*

But soon music is only noise. I pile my CDs in a pile behind the armchair where I can't see them. Unplug the stereo. It's the electric buzz. On my bed in the light of the lamp on the bed rail, I reread my first novel, my second. Sit down to write at the computer on my third book, but I cannot get past the first sentence.

Finally, I turn my computer off, unplug it, set it in a pile behind the armchair next to the CDs. Unplug my clock. Set it back there, too. Unplug my phone. Unplug the lamp on the bed rail.

By the sixth day the Xanax is gone. I don't find out until later that the Xanax I think I've been taking isn't Xanax at all. There are so many pills in my medicine chest. I can't close the door on my medicine chest, there are so many pills. It's steroids I've been taking, testosterone, that just looked like the Xanax.

The following Thursday there's a knock at my back door. Through the living room window, I can see the back porch. It's filled with people for my writing class. No Ruth, though. I quick lie down on the floor, barely breathe. They sit out there on the porch and laugh and talk easy, the way people do. After an hour, they all leave.

My bed is a corner of hell. Your body just does things. I move my bed so it faces the door. Sweep under the bed. Tidy everything up. That starts me on the rest of the house. Four in the morning, I'm cleaning out the vegetable bins in my refrigerator and I know I'm crazy.

I forget what I eat. I know that I eat but I don't know how I buy the food or how I cook it. In the last of the days at night in that dark I walk through my rooms, pushing my body against it. Darkness that I can actually lean against. I look into the abyss and the fucker looks back. At least there is something else that is there.

It feels like God. God is too bright and full and is pushing me down.

That night I don't lie down, because if I lie down maybe I won't be able to lift my head back up again. So I sit on the edge of the bed and do the deep breathing thing. All around me it's a horror. Ghosts and goblins and apparitions. Avenues of fear. Dead aunts and uncles, the Shetland pony, the fucking red devil with the pitchfork. Huck-a-buckin'.

The next morning, in the kitchen, I'm trying to make my protein fiber and oatmeal, my chamomile tea, but the way my neck is stiff, the way my eyes hurt, the brightness, the buzz the buzz, the ringing in my ears, I can't stop shaking. I take my cup, the thick white coffee mug from the Otis Café, and throw it against the door. I'm yelling *Fuck God Fuck Fuck Fuck!*

Out the window, my neighbor is raking up muddy leaves in his backyard. I see that he's heard the loud crash, he's heard me yelling. He flips open one of those new cell phones. Dials a number.

As I watch him, he calls the police and tells the police he's heard a gunshot.

Of course, I have no idea.

I SWEEP UP the broken pieces from the mug, pour them into the garbage can. It's while I'm washing up my breakfast dishes that I think about my neighbor. That I've startled him and I should go and apologize. I think maybe I should change my clothes first. Clean up a little bit. But I leave on my Ugg slippers, my Levi's that won't stay up, my green plaid pajama top.

When I step out the kitchen door, just as I'm locking the door, I hear a loud voice. Right off, I know it's God.

"Step away from the door and put your hands behind your head!"

A high-pitched homosexual scream comes out my mouth and I drop my keys. When I finally get myself together, I turn around and I'm not exaggerating. There are twenty guns pointed at me. The closest is a cop on my back porch, a young guy, not even twenty, his arms stuck out in a crouch position with a pistol. There's another cop behind him, a woman. She's young, too, prom queen beautiful, hair in a flip. She's crouching and pointing a pistol, too. Down the steps, under the grape arbor, the wide-swinging gate is open and there are three, maybe four cops with rifles or some kind of big guns that look more complicated than rifles. Pointed at me.

All these cops are wearing the same outfit. Dark blue almost black dungarees with big white lettering across the chest. SWAT. To the west, over the side of the cedar fence, there's a guy who looks like Rocky Balboa in wraparound sunglasses. He's pointing something like a bazooka at me. Or maybe it's a flame-thrower. The guy with the bullhorn is General Douglas MacArthur and he's standing just under the guy with the flame-thrower.

Down the brick steps and in the garden, there are two more cops in the same outfit, crouched down, arms out, with guns, just pistols, pointed at me. And these are only the cops I can *see*. Children. They're all children.

I step away from the door and put my hands behind my head. It's then I realize the ringing in my ears has stopped. The fried place behind my eyes isn't frying. No neuropathy in my feet or legs. No complaints from my stomach. No shit fears. Not one ache or pain in my body. The world isn't dizzy. In fact, the world is fucking solid.

General MacArthur shouts out:

"Keep your hands against the back of your head. Walk to the porch steps, descend the steps slowly, and walk toward me. Any quick movement or unnecessary gesture will be taken as threatening behavior and you will be shot."

It takes me a while to speak, but I know I have to, and when I speak I speak loud enough so General MacArthur will hear.

"My pants are going to fall down!"

"Hands behind your head! Walk!"

I wonder what pair of shorts I'm wearing. Either a stretched-out pair of Hanes briefs, the red bikinis, or the black seamless mesh briefs Ruth bought me.

The two young cops in a crouch back up slow as I walk along the porch. At the stairs, I pass by them and just as I pass by them, they make a sound with their guns. Like in cowboy shows, that click that means they're serious. Three steps down, I take the steps slow. With every step my Levi's sink lower down my hips. The way the morning air hits my back, and the way it all feels down there, it's then I remember. I'm not wearing underwear at all.

Below me, my feet in my Uggs walk slow toward General MacArthur. I'm trying not to lift my feet, trying to keep my knees together as I walk. General MacArthur is holding the bullhorn and still speaking through the bullhorn even though I'm right there in front of him.

"Don't move your hands. Keep your hands behind your head. No quick and unnecessary gestures. Turn around slowly."

General MacArthur is about seven feet tall. Those kind of General Douglas MacArthur glasses. The bullhorn is the same color as his outfit. The same color as the other outfits.

I turn around. It's fast and rough the way they push me, grab my hands, my arms. In nothing flat, I'm handcuffed, my hands behind me. Still no panic. The way they frisk me, I damn near lose my Levi's. But quick as I can I hold my hands against my butt and my Levi's stay up.

"Proceed down the brick steps and into the clearing. When you reach the center of the clearing, stop, turn around slowly with your back to the house."

Down the six brick steps, I'm walking real slow. I'm pressing my handcuffed hands into the butt of my Levi's. Still my Levi's are slipping. On the northwest corner of the house, there are three more cops in outfits, one with a rifle and two with guns that look like *Star Wars*. Across in my neighbor's yard, more cops. One in particular leaning against the fig tree. This one's the real Spaghetti Western. Square-jawed and crewcut hair, tanned, his sunglasses are mirrored. His face is a fuck-you staredown. His huge complicated rifle bazooka thing has a telescope on top of it.

That telescope is pointing a red dot of light right in the middle of my chest. That place, right at my sternum, a little lightbulb that you can see the red filament flashing.

You create your own reality.

Portland's version of Clint Eastwood has got the Running Boy in his sights. Exactly in that place in the middle of my chest. His little red filament right there just itching to blow open a bloody hole. As soon as I look down and see that red filament just to the right of my heart, that quick I'm the Running Boy's and I got to run.

Right then's when Big Ben decides he's had enough. He's tired of being in this old body who can't sleep. Tired of being sick and sober and anxious and dizzy and no longer in control. Tired of AIDS.

On the third brick step, I stop walking. From my armpit, one slow drop of sweat rolls all the way down to my hip. A quick hot gust of wind in the bamboo. My body feels surprisingly free. Through the leaves of the fig tree, the Clint Clone, the guy I've always hated, envied, lusted after. Finally, finally, after all these years I stop. I take a breath and stare him back right in the eye.

Over my heart, the red dot of flickering light, the way it's searching.

My whole life I've been waiting for this moment. A wave of my hand, a jump, or even a sneeze and my sick, fucked, anxious life will be over.

Big Ben's handcuffed hands lift away from the butt of my Levi's.

That quick, my Levi's fall down around my ankles

The sound of the beginning of World War Three. Military artillery clatter on alert. Safeties off, all those guns being cocked, hammers pulled back, rotating cylinders, pumps of the shotgun.

Death By Cop.

You wait for the blow to kingdom come.

INSTEAD, HANDCUFFED IN my garden, my back to the house, I stand with my shoulders up around my ears, my eyes squeezed shut. My pajama top is long, but not long enough. It's just me and my old pope and my skinny AIDS ass hanging out. All that artillery still pointed at me, as the SWAT team goes through my house, my drawers, my closets, my cupboards. I think about the marijuana in the top drawer of my nightstand.

After a while and a lot of talking back and forth on the walkie talkie, General MacArthur walks down the brick steps and stands next to me. He doesn't say anything, just stands there. I take it as a sign that I'm allowed to talk.

"Look," I say, "I have AIDS and I'm being treated for depression. This morning was especially bad and I yelled and broke a cup. I saw my neighbor make the call on his cell phone."

"Where are the pieces to the cup?" General MacArthur asks.

"Under the sink," I say. "In the garbage can."

General MacArthur gets on his walkie talkie.

"Check under the sink in the garbage can for a broken cup."

That static sound. Above and behind me, I can hear the squeak of the cupboard door opening to under the sink.

Static sound again. Something over the walkie talkie.

"What color is the cup?" General MacArthur asks me.

"White," I say. "With an Otis Café logo on it."

From behind and above me, I hear:

"Check on that white Otis Café cup, sir. There are broken pieces in the garbage can."

"At ease!" General MacArthur says.

The clatter of guns and rifles and *Star Wars* weapons, the entire SWAT team puts their safeties on. Cops relax, start moving around, talking to each other.

"Routine maneuver when a firearm is reported."

That's what General MacArthur says over my shoulder as he takes off my handcuffs. He hangs the handcuffs on his leather belt.

Efficient, silent, quick. The way the SWAT arrived, they leave.

I pull up my pants.

IT'S RAINING CATS and dogs, cougars and wolves, in the Pioneer Cemetery. Tony Escobar is still naked but he's wearing a Chinese hat and sitting under a colorful umbrella in a lounge chair with a cocktail in his hand. The big hairy chest of him. I sit on my grave, he sits on his. The world is spinning and my body hurts all over.

Fear and trembling, man.

Fuck the rain, Tony and I, we go through it all over and over about the fascist SWAT team and what America is turning into and who the fuck are they to handcuff me and let me stand naked and what the fuck is Bill Clinton up to allowing fascist shit like this in our country and civil rights and human rights and bullies with guns and the quality of life and what it is life and death dreams and waking nightmares and what is fear and why do I fear so much. Did AIDS get to my adrenals? What is AIDS dementia and how do you know you have it? Is it my pituitary gland, the Catholic Church, or my mother or my father or my sister the school bully, whatever the fuck that's been stressed to the max, where is there comfort, even the Portland cops are after me.

Tony tells me to hold on. Tony tells me to call my doctor.

FOR DAYS AFTERWARD, a Portland City cop car keeps driving up and down past my house. It's the Clint Clone. One day, out on the sidewalk, the whole time I'm doing my tai chi, he just sits in his cop car there on the corner of Morrison, the engine running.

FINALLY, I GET a hold of my nurse practitioner, Madelena Papas. I haven't seen her in months. *Seven and a half months*, she says. I try and sound like I'm not crazy. She prescribes me more Xanax, but I can't drive to pick it up. I tell her I have no car and the buses freak me out.

"I'll have it delivered," she says.

"Today?"

"Are you still having trouble sleeping?"

"Yes."

"Are you still seeing Dr. Hardy?" Madelena asks.

"Avenue of fear," I say.

"What?"

"He opened an avenue of fear," I say. "He's a bullshit doctor and I won't go back to him."

"Ben," Madelena says, "that was over a year ago. You promised you'd go back. Are you seeing another doctor?"

"No."

"Are you taking your antidepressants?"

"They're like taking speed. Do you know any other doctors?"

"Your health insurance won't cover anyone else," she says. "Have you been sleeping?"

"But what if I pay?"

There's a moment of silence on the line. I mean not silence, all the wires the way my ears always sound.

"Give me just a minute," Madelena says.

Then: "Do you have a pen and paper?"

I uncap my black grease pen.

"Her name is Dr. Shelley Roth," Madalena says. "She's a psychopharmacologist and has her own practice. "

Across the Mediterranean sunset, across Princess Diana and Dodi Fayed, in black grease pen I write: *Dr. Shelley Roth*. And her phone number.

"Ben?" Madalena says, "I know Shelley. I'll call her myself."

ON THE PHONE, Dr. Shelley Roth can hear it in my voice. She gives me her address and tells me to come the next day at one o'clock. I ask her how much she'll charge and Dr. Roth tells me we'll talk about payment after she sees me.

The next day is another gray day, cold, but that's June for you. I'm in my kitchen, showered, shaved, in my pressed white shirt. *My good white shirt,* as Hank Christian would say. At my waist, my pants bunch up khaki drape folds under my black belt. My black loafers spit-shined and dark socks. My shiny blue suit jacket that fits a 42 long. I'm swimming in it. Hair product in the gray fuzz that used to be my hair. In my wallet, I've got one hundred-dollar bill left. Two twenties, a ten, three fives, and a bunch of ones. I'm waiting for the Radio Cab to honk outside.

There's a knock on my door. I cuss that I didn't hear the cabbie honk, open the door. There on my porch stands Ruth. We both put our hands up to our throats.

Beautiful, according to Hitchcock, skinnier than ever. Her hair is pulled off her face into a bun. Strands of blonde in the red. Those ultra blue contact blue eyes I never got used to looking into. No drag that day, no feather boa, no leopardskin, no vintage. Just her sweater. Pearls on the breast of her creamy white sweater. A flowered cotton skirt, no underslip. Red ballet slippers.

"My God, Ben," Ruth says, "you look horrible."

"I'm waiting for a cab," I say.

"I'm your cab today," Ruth says. "We're going to the psycho-pharmacologist."

"How'd you know?"

"You put me down as next of kin," Ruth says. "Madalena Papas called me and asked me to drive you."

"No," I say. "No, the cab will be here any minute. It's best I go with a cab."

Ruth reaches out, puts her hand on the shoulder of my shiny blue jacket. Ruth's biting her lip and her eyes are starting to tear. Her touch makes me jump.

"Ruth," I say, "we can't keep doing this."

"I totally agree," Ruth says. "Believe me. All I'm doing this afternoon is taking a sick friend to the doctor."

"Ruth," I say, "you've helped enough."

"You'll never be able to repay me," Ruth says. "Now hurry up. We've only got ten minutes."

"Don't tell me to hurry up, Ruth," I say.

The standoff on the porch. Ruth's got a red Chinese clutch bag she's holding in front of her. My hands are folded over my crotch.

Ruth could be Doris Day, Tippi Hedren, Kim Novak, Grace Kelly.

"Come on, Ben," Ruth says. "You need some help. Please."

DR. SHELLEY ROTH'S office is in a yellow Victorian house in Southwest, just off First Avenue. Ruth and I sit in a small area under the stairway that maybe used to be the pantry. Some designer has tried to make it look like a waiting room. Matching small overstuffed burgundy chairs. Matching burgundy pillows. Burgundy panels on the window. A round spindly wood table with magazines. Old *People* magazines. Monica Lewinsky. Madonna on tour. Weird Michael Jackson.

It isn't long, though, and a door opens. Footsteps down the hallway.

Dr. Shelley Roth is a small woman, looks like Frida Kahlo, only Jewish. Her brown hair is long and going gray, pulled back in a barrette. I'm thinking about the last Jewish doctor I went to on 83rd Street. But there's something about the way Dr. Roth moves. The way her clothes fit her. Like she's really comfortable in them.

Then she smiles. Wrinkles around her eyes and mouth. It's a face that has smiled a lot. My heart stops beating so hard. I take a long deep breath.

"Good afternoon," Dr. Roth says. "I'm Dr. Shelley Roth, and I presume you are Benjamin Grunewald."

I smile, start to say something, but Dr. Roth has already turned.

"Please follow me to my office," she says.

I know Ruth too well. No way she's not going in. I give her the go-ahead nod and Ruth and I follow Dr. Roth down the hallway, past the stairway, and into the front office. The office was once the front parlor of the house. Behind Dr. Roth's desk, a shiny new wall where once there was probably a sliding pocket door. A painting on the shiny wall. Just a big black rectangle framed behind a glass. Maybe a Richard Serra. Shelves and shelves of books, and books piled up on her desk, piles of papers. Ruth and I sit down on the loveseat in the bay window. There's room enough on the seat that we don't have to touch. Sunlight coming through the clouds right then. My God, sunlight.

"This is my friend," I say, "Ruth Dearden."

"Hello, Ruth," Dr. Roth says. "Thanks for driving Ben here today."

Ruth and I give each other a look.

"Ms. Papas told me she called you, Ruth," Dr. Roth says. "I've been expecting you."

Dr. Roth opens a manila envelope, puts on a pair of tortoise shell glasses, reads for a while, then sits down.

"So, Benjamin Grunewald, tell me something about yourself."

I MEAN, WHERE do you start? I don't know, so I look at that big black painting and I start talking. I start with my mother and my father and my sister and Catholicism, Idaho. Go straight to being homosexual, New York City, AIDS, sleeplessness. Dr. Mark Hardy, SSRIs and his Avenue of Fear. I talk for a long time. A couple things I say I can tell Ruth's never heard. She doesn't know about my mother, or my sister. Not really. She's totally surprised when I tell Dr. Roth that I haven't slept in eleven days. I keep talking for a while longer but then I stop. Feels like I'm babbling and I'm afraid Dr. Roth will think I'm crazy. Have me committed.

There's a long time in Dr. Roth's office that nobody speaks. It's as if the three of us forgot how to breathe. Ruth uncrosses, then recrosses her legs. Her red ballet slippers. The sun goes behind the clouds, comes back out again. We're just reflections on the glass of the big black rectangle.

Dr. Roth gets up from behind her desk. From where I'm sitting, she looks much taller. Small bones, tiny wrists and ankles. She walks around her desk and sits in the chair closest to me. Her knee pops when she sits. She takes off her glasses and looks straight at me. When Dr. Roth finally speaks, her voice is low. And there's a hitch in it. A warbly sound the way when some women sing.

"Benjamin," she says, "according to your records, from talking to Madalena, and from what you've told me here, I can tell you with all candor that I have never met anyone who has been so deeply anxious for so long who has lived through it. Most people's bodies would have simply failed them. Then there is suicide. I must tell you, the suicide rate for anxiety like yours is phenomenal. I don't know how you have managed to stay alive."

My body, in that moment. I'm so proud of my body – Big Ben, Little Ben, The Running Boy. And something else. When Dr. Roth stops speaking, I know for sure. That's the closest I'll ever feel what it's like to have a mother.

DR. ROTH STARTS writing prescriptions.

"Take as many Xanax as you need to stop the anxiety," Dr. Roth says. "Whatever you do, stop the anxiety. You're used to the Xanax, so you might try the Valium. It's the strongest of the benzodiazepines, just be aware of that. For sleeping you should try the Klonopin. It doesn't peak so quickly. The trazodone will keep you asleep. Before you go to sleep, start off with one milligram of Klonopin and fifty miligrams of trazodone. If you aren't sleeping eight hours a night within a week, increase the dosage by a half. I'm putting you on an antidepressant that's just come out. It's had a lot of success. It's not an SSRI and its side effect is sleep."

When Ruth and I get up to go, there's a long back and forth between Dr. Roth and me. Finally she accepts my hundred-dollar bill.

AT THE DRUGSTORE, it takes about an hour, but I get all the prescriptions. It's in Ruth's car in crosstown traffic that I open the container of Xanax. As soon as I see the pills, I know in an instant. Fuck. That all along I've been taking fucking steroids. As fast as I can, I pour four white pills out into my hand and put them in my mouth.

Instant relief. The world is a little bit more *my* world, twenty minutes tops.

In front of my house, so many dramatic scenes in front of my house, Ruth and me. Ruth stops the car and pulls up on the hand brake. I gather up my bags full of drugs. It takes a while for my big body to get out of Ruth's little car. Just before I close the door, we grab each other's hands quick, then let go.

10:30 that night. I lay the three yellow antidepressant pills in a pile on the kitchen counter alongside the one green Klonopin and the white trazodone. All my searching for an answer, for meaning to it all, has come down to this. Life and death in a pile of pills.

I stare at those three little yellow pills for a long long time. I won't let myself think about it. What will happen if this antidepressant doesn't work.

The glass with the yellow balloons, I fill it up with tap water. I hold the pills in my hand. That moment.

AN HOUR LATER maybe, I'm sitting on the couch in front of the fire, a blanket over me, my head resting on a pillow. I don't need the TV or music. In those moments, just the fire and being alive is all that matters. The phone rings and it's Ruth.

"I just wanted you to know," Ruth says, "that it was only today in Dr. Roth's office that I realized something."

Ruth clears her throat. She's crying but so I can't hear.

"That whole time we were together," Ruth says, "there was a part of me that thought – the depression, the anxiety – that you were just making it all up."

It's at that moment, or soon after, I drop the phone and fall asleep. A deep sleep I don't wake up from 'til ten hours later.

Book Two
Hank & Ruth

19.
The spiderweb

LOOK AT HIM. BEN GRUNEWALD SPRAWLED OUT ON HIS couch, in front of the fireplace, sleeping like a baby. When he wakes, it will be a new world.

The AIDS cocktail. It doesn't feel like it, but the AIDS cocktail, with some adjustments, is working. Men are starting to live and not just die.

Plus now Ben has an antidepressant that works.

Well, *works* isn't quite the right word, and we'll talk about that later, but now, I mean just look at him. At least he's sleeping. And a couple years down the line, Viagra will come along. There's so much hope in a hard-on.

All he'll need to do is take his meds, eat right, exercise, and keep a good attitude. A good attitude. Like the famous guy who, when he was told he had cancer, locked himself up in a room, watched a shitload of funny movies and laughed so hard he cured himself.

Or Shirley MacLaine when she won the Academy Award. How she made such a rousing speech: if you really and truly want something with all your heart and soul you can make it come true.

And Shirley was absolutely right. You want proof, it's right there on your TV. She's the bitch on the stage holding the golden statue.

A good attitude. That's the secret. With a good attitude there's nothing that can stop you. Fucking people can be so stupid. Still I'd give my left nut that it were true.

That this story would have a happy ending.

DECEMBER 24, 1999. Hank Christian is flying into Portland, Oregon. It's Hank's forty-first birthday. Hank and Jesus Christ. Maybe that's how Jesus got his middle initial.

Jesus Hank Christ.

SO MUCH HAS happened in the last four months I don't know where to start. I'm teaching my class again. Alone. And so far the class is full. I run out of energy all the time but *arbeit macht frei*. I'm taking a yoga class twice a week. Hot Yoga. Sometimes I think I'm going to melt in there. My viral load is way down and I have 148 T-cells. Sleeping eight hours. I'm back up to 176 pounds. The way the weight's coming back on my body, though, is totally fucked. I still have no ass, and my legs and arms are skinny, which leaves my belly. The AIDS belly.

Oh, and I'm developing a pendulous left tit. Somehow the AIDS meds fuck with your DNA and so you start developing breasts. Or rather one breast. The doctors don't call my left tit pendulous, though. They don't even mention the area or that the area is under my left nipple. They just call it the fatty tissue deposit.

The day I went in to have my fatty tissue deposit checked out, it was at the same hospital where I was treated for AIDS. A sprawling piece of architecture that looks like an old yellow brick university campus that huge space-age sculptures of steel and glass have suddenly erupted out of.

When I finally found the clinic, the word above the desk was *Mammography*.

I've been to a lot of clinics at this hospital. The otologist who checked out my tinnitus. The optometrist who checked out my CMV. The specialist who checked out my positive test for tuberculosis. The neuropathic doctor. The gastroenterologist for the colonoscopy. The dietician. And a shitload more ologists I can't even tell you. All the clinics had spacious waiting areas, with big windows, plenty of natural light. I never had to wait longer than twenty minutes.

This clinic, *Mammography*, the clinic that deals almost exclusively with women was the worst. Well, not the worst. *Mental Health* was the worst.

In the *Mammography* waiting room it wasn't pretty. Fifty women were jammed into a small room. No windows. Crying children. All the women looked stressed-out, hollow-eyed, and going through it.

Maybe it was just the day, but sitting in the *Mammography* waiting room, it was so clear to me that women really are treated different.

The woman I sat next to, middle aged with dyed-black hair, designer labels, and Gucci glasses, brought her own magazines to read. *Vogue, Wallpaper.* Her Chanel No. 5 could not conceal her fear.

My appointment was at one o'clock and at three-thirty they still hadn't called my name. I hadn't brought my sardines. I asked the nurse for something to eat and she gave me a saltine cracker.

Finally, in a small square bright room with two doctors, men, I took my shirt off. One was an older guy, five or six comb-over strands, thick glasses. Full of language I couldn't understand. The younger doctor had thick black hair. I remember the hair because of the bright room and the white.

Without warning, no local anesthesia, no Valium, nothing. The black-haired doctor stuck a long needle two or three inches just under my nipple. The pain was so sharp and instant I couldn't speak. When the doctor pulled on the syringe, it felt like my heart was coming out through the needle. That's when I started cussing.

Then I sat in that white room alone for over an hour with the door closed, holding my tit, fucking staring at a fucking bright white fucking wall wondering if I was the one fucking man in the world with fucking breast cancer, when finally a nurse came in with the test results on her clip board.

"Benign tumor," she said, "Mr. Greenblatt. Good news."

That's the only time a doctor or a nurse ever called what was under my pendulous left breast anything but a fatty tissue deposit. A benign tumor. *Of a kind and beneficial disposition.*

I wish to God that had been Hank's kind of tumor.

AT FOUR IN the afternoon, Christmas Eve, there's a knock on my kitchen door. Four o'clock December in Portland is already dark. Of course it's raining. It's been a downpour all day and it's not going to let up. Thank God it's not freezing. When I hear the knock, I flutter. Everything about me flutters – my hands, my fingers, the breath in my chest. I take a deep breath, run into the bathroom and look in the mirror, check what's left of my hair, look myself in my eyes and mark the moment. *Hank Christian is knocking on my kitchen door.* I suck in my belly.

The light on the porch is out. When I turned that light on at 3:30 it was working. I flip the fucking switch on and off but nothing. The doorknob smells of Windex. I've been cleaning house all week. I swing the door open and the rain is loud, big drips falling from the gutter. A gust of wind blows the rain in. The smell of rain and wet cedar boards and earth, the compost heap. Just then the porch light flashes on and I blink and blink and raise my hand to block out the bright, then the light goes out again. Hank in his black rain gear is a mass of shiny wet inside the black rainy night. I go to speak, but suddenly Hank's hand pokes out of the darkness and into the overhead fluorescence of the kitchen right at me. It is the hand of Tarkovsky's *Andrei Rublev* and appears as if out of another dimension. I look and look and look at the hand, then grab it, Hank's hand, and I pull him in as if Hank out there was drowning in dark water. *The Maroni.* Both Hank and I laugh a little the way I've hauled him in. When I catch a look from Hank's eyes, I quick pull my hand out of Hank's, and my hand falls down against my leg, fluttering.

There's a way my body is in shock to see my beloved friend right in front of me. All that the eleven-and-a-half years have done to him.

Hank's in shock, too. Both of us just stand and stare. The door still open, the wind banging the door against the wall, rain blowing in. We get the whole big *gestalt* of each other, no details really. My eyes go right to Hank's black eyes. We say some shit like *hey buddy* or *how's it going man*. In no time at all we're front to front in a big embrace, no bicycle in between us like the last time. At first it's proper bear hug, man to man, back slapping, no crotch. But the embrace doesn't stop. Our bodies get closer and pretty soon we're a full on frontal. New red potatoes in a shovelful of earth. After a while we both have to admit it. We are the one holding the other one up. Those kind of tears that just roll out your eyes one endless stream without any sobbing sounds. For me that's how it is. Hank is sobbing big sobs, his belly bouncing against mine.

"Fucking Gruney, man," Hank says. "I never cried once through the whole cancer thing. Now just look at me."

Hank pulls away, his hands holding on tight to my shoulders. He pushes out and raises up his chest, pulls his chin down – that bit of cleft, pulls his shoulders down, too, flexes his biceps. Fucking Hank Christian, man. Hasn't changed a bit. That's when I see his right eye, how the old right eye is gone, and the new glass eye has replaced it. Still real tears, not glass tears coming out that eye. Under that eye, something deep under the skin that's yellow and dark blue. The scar that makes a dent there. His neck is thicker, his face rounder. Still the efficient line of Roman nose. Hank's sweet smiling lips. Rain dripping from his black baseball cap. I can't see his hair because of the hoodie and the ballcap. I can tell it's clipped short but I can't tell the color. Not yet. Just for Men, how the light when it shines through his hair makes his hair look purple.

What I see Hank see. Where I've lived the last twelve years. The overhead bright fluorescence of the kitchen light. The square wooden table in the middle of the kitchen and the four unmatched wooden chairs. The wooden tabletop, scratched and stressed with circles where I've set down pots that were too hot. Globs of candle wax I've tried to scrape off. A big blue candle scented with lavender in the middle of the table. Three votive candles in red glass. The yellowish refrigerator and matching yellowish stove. The cupboards that look like real wood with a fucked-up fancy design but are made out of particle board. On the counter, my new set of glasses with red and yellow balloons I just washed. Four new big white plates I bought after Ruth left. The ugly linoleum on the floor with yellowish squares with some kind of blue triangle in them. Above the sink, a painting Ephraim did of tipis in the snow. Then there's the smell. The Windex and lemony ammonia smell from mopping the floor.

I close the door. Turn the overhead light off. I light the big blue candle, and then three votives in the red glass.

"It's like a church in here," Hank says.

"There are some hooks on the wall behind you," I say, "where you can hang up your things."

Just beyond the candlelight, Hank is black in the shadows, taking off his coat, his sweatshirt, hanging up his ballcap. The candlelight on Hank's face. The night in Pennsylvania with Olga when Hank danced to Billie Holiday's "April in Paris."

"What about my boots," he asks. "They're soaking wet."

"You're standing in the mud room," I say. "Just leave them there."

I'm standing between the stove and the table. Fluttering, my hands. I don't know what to do with them.

"It's just like on East Fifth Street in here," Hank says, "only a little bigger."

Strange to hear Hank's voice in the rooms of my house. I put my fingers around the top on the wood of the chair and look around, at the voice of him in there. My hand flutters up and covers my pendulous tit.

"I've got a big old couch in front of the fireplace," I say. "That's where you'll be sleeping."

"You need some food?" I say, "I've got chicken soup."

"No thanks, Gruney," Hank says. "I'll be hungry later, though. We'll go out and get a burger."

Hank doesn't know I don't go out. I mean not like going out used to be. And that I can't eat hamburgers. When he asked if I could pick him up at the airport I told him my driver's license had expired.

"We could go to our old hangout on Columbus Circle," Hank says. "Silvio would be so happy to see us."

"Silvio's dead," I say.

From out of the dark: "Oh."

Then: "Did you hear about Olga?"

"No."

"Double mastectomy, man," Hank says. "Fucking cancer."

"Fucking AIDS," I say.

"*Porca Miseria*," Hank says.

I MAKE TEA and we sit on the couch. Lemon Zinger for Hank, chamomile for me. Our days of Budweisers and cocktails and doobies are over. The fire's really going. Still, that batch of wood with all the pitch. Hank loves how the fire cracks and spits. There's a couple times I have to lean down to keep the fire screen closed.

The Christmas tree ain't big, maybe four foot, a spruce. It's behind the couch. I bought the tree that day for two dollars. It was the only one of three trees left on the lot. The guy just wanted to give it to me.

In the basement, when I opened the box marked *Christmas Stuff*, all the ornaments were from the two years with Ruth. The Rudolph ornament. The Cinderella ornament. The red balls, the blue balls, the green balls with snowmen on them Ruth bought at Fred Meyer. The smaller bell-shaped lavender ones. The garlands, the tinsel. The ball Ruth made with a photo of me on it naked doing *tai chi* that day we went to Sauvie Island.

All that Christmas shit, all the memories. Ruth had been what made Christmas, Christmas. I threw the whole box in the garbage. That's when I saw it. Just the black hairy legs.

Tony Escobar's Fairy Drag Queen. The Ken doll as Christmas Angel Barbie. Her lopsided halo you can plug in. I pick up the Fairy Drag Queen, lift up her dress. The red jock strap, the wired connector on his asshole so he can sit, a proper star, on the very top tip of the tree.

No wonder everybody hates Christmas. Fucking memories, man.

TWO HOURS LATER, after scrambled eggs and sprouted wheat toast, Hank's in my living room on the couch, sitting close to the wall. Another cup of tea. The firelight on the bruised, dented face of my friend. Me all the way on the other side of the couch with my cup. Hands still fluttering. Just over my left shoulder, Hank's right shoulder, at eye level, the tip of the Christmas tree up his ass, the Fairy Drag Queen pokes himself up over the couch, his flowing robe, his lopsided halo, his wings spread, his arms out. Measuring the years, all that space, on the couch between us.

Silences at first. Just the crackling fire. Not bad silences, but Big Ben knows something's going on. Little Ben thinks the silences are my fault. And they partly are, I mean at this point I'm still a pretty fucked up guy. But what's really going on, what's heavy in those silences between me and Hank – besides the grief of years and hellacious suffering, is that there's something Hank ain't saying. A grief so big in his heart it won't be until the next day, after Hank's on his third or fourth cup of coffee, that he'll finally be able to speak it.

It takes us a while, that night by the fire, but finally Hank and I do relax some and we get to talking talking. Just like in the old days, it seems, when there was an actual place in the world that existed only because we existed. In a space together, Hank and me, inside something. Under a miracle umbrella.

"Hell, Gruney," Hank says. "What the fuck's happened to us?"

"Fucked, ain't it?" I say.

"It's the kind of cancer usually only people with blue eyes get," Hank says.

"The Jewish doctor on 83rd," I say, "said *you're HIV positive so you're going to get sick, so you're going to die.*"

"You knew in New York?" Hank says. "Why didn't you tell me?"

Chamomile tea smells like when I used to bale hay. Tastes like baled hay, too.

"You were so excited about Florida and Barry Hannah," I say. "It was such a downer."

"Why didn't you tell *me*?" I say. "It's been more than five years, man, since we've talked."

Silence. The sense there's something hidden or missing. I feel it in my throat, in my breath. I think it is my soul.

"I just didn't know how to do it," Hank says. "Hi, Gruney, I have cancer."

Outside, Christmas carolers somewhere out there sing "Silent Night." In Hank's new eye, there's a flame. An actual fire. It takes me a moment to figure. In his glass eye, the fire is a reflection.

The carolers' "Silent Night" gets louder, walks past us on Morrison just outside the window, turns south down the street. On the corner there, the carolers stop and laugh and talk. The winter night in their voices. After several tries, it's another night, "O Holy Night." Hank and I sit so still. We are every Christmas we have lived.

"How long ago was that?" Hank asks.

"What?"

"The last time in New York," Hank says, "when we stood in front of Auden's poem."

"Going on twelve years," I say.

"Holy fuck," Hank says. "Twelve years."

"That poem's a part of me," I say.

"Just one fucking line," Hank says, "but it rips your heart out."

"It's a line from a larger poem," I say.

"Someday," Hank says, "let's you and I go back and read that poem again."

Another life, another world, so far away, so impossible that Hank and I could stand together one more time at #77 St. Mark's Place.

Regret, man, fucking regret.

"I was in denial big time," I say. "Wouldn't accept that HIV had anything to do with AIDS."

"Did you ever get your doctorate?" I ask.

"I've just got my dissertation to finish," Hank says. "They've given me an extension."

"I called a bunch of times," I say. "Got your voicemail at first. Then nothing."

"When did you go into the hospital?" Hank asks.

"December first '96," I say.

"Man, in '96 I was lying in a quarantined room," Hank says. "There was so much fucking radiation they delivered my food through a slot in the door."

"Chemo, too?" I ask.

"Threw my guts up," Hank says.

"I've never thrown up," I say, "All these years, not once. Almost shit myself to death, though. I was down to like 160 pounds."

"Shitting, man," Hank says. "You think you ain't ever going to stop. I got down to 140."

"My asshole was so sore," I say, "I couldn't use paper anymore. Had to shower after I shit."

"Gave me some honking hemorrhoids," Hank says.

"I named my hemorrhoid after the homeopathic doctor who told me the cure was to drink more milk," I say.

"Julie O'Connor," I say. "I call my hemorrhoid Julie O'Connor."

It's something to see, Hank Christian's laugh. That big burst from down deep in him shaking him around. I'd almost forgot how overwhelmed he gets. Just like that, Hank is down on the floor on his hands knees, laughing. Trying to get his breath. I'm happy that Hank is laughing. The strange silence has gone and Hank is laughing. Even more, I'm happy I am still a guy who can make him laugh like that. Of course him laughing makes me laugh too.

Weird. Laughter in my body. As I'm laughing I say to myself *this is laughing*. After all the suffering and the horror now *laughter*. I mean, what the fuck is it. I'm coughing and my belly hurts and I can't breathe, it's so intense.

Hank pulls out a handkerchief and blows his nose. *Porca fucking Miseria,* Hank says and leans against the couch. His arm touches my leg and he knows his arm is touching my leg and he keeps his arm there.

Silence again. The heaviness of it. I figure it's just the depression, me over here, trying to get over there.

Hank, all in black, is stretched out in front of the firelight. That's when I first notice all the weight he's gained. I'm a little shocked. But only for a moment. That quick, Hank's body, to me, is perfect again. Weird, though. Hank's extra weight makes me feel better about my gut and pendulous breast.

Rain beating down on the tin roof of the porch. Me on the couch, Hank on the floor, his arm against my leg. Behind us, the Fairy Drag Queen's outstretched arms.

Hank's bare feet right up against the fire. So fragile and smooth, his feet, as if they're made out of porcelain. Our two empty cups of tea with the string and the labels hanging over the lips, setting on the hearth. The pitch and the spitting fire.

Long long moments just staring at the fire. Finally, the silence makes me too too crazy. I just blurt it out:

"Bye bye, Mr. Chemotherapy!"

Hank's down for the count.

Fucking laughter, man.

THE COUCH IS long and soft and wide and I give Hank a big fluffy pillow and a duvet. Hank's in the bathroom first, brushing his teeth. Gargling. Pouring out his pills. When I'm finished in the bathroom, I turn off all the lights. Unplug the Christmas tree. Get into bed. Like always, I've forgotten to turn down the heat. The thermostat's in the living room right by the couch. I'm just in my T-shirt and underwear. Years ago, I'd have secretly wanted Hank to see me undressed like that. But with the AIDS belly and the pendulous breast, I'm thankful it's dark and I'm covered.

In the living room, just an arm length from Hank on the couch, I'm punching down the digital thermostat.

"Sweet dreams, sweetheart," Hank says.

"Happy Birthday," I say.

"Merry Christmas," Hank says.

I'm almost back to my bedroom when Hank asks:

"Idaho was really something, wasn't it?"

My heart starts beating so loud. Reuben and Sal and Gary. I don't know if I can speak that they are dead out loud. I clear my throat, try my best to make my voice sound normal, which makes my voice sound weird.

"Idaho was a miracle," I say.

"How *are* those guys? Is Ephraim doing all right?"

This next silence is mine, all mine. I sit down on my bed. The years I hardly slept, the eleven days I didn't sleep at all. Those nights are still on my bed, a ghost story that's a fog that lies across the bedspread. There's no doubt about it. To tell Hank about Reuben and Sal and Gary is going to kill me.

"He's still smoking a pack of More Menthols a day," I say.

My breath. I wait for Hank's next question. And wait.

From the living room comes an old familiar sound.

Hank Christian is snoring.

MORNINGS SUCK. MORNINGS have always sucked, but since I was diagnosed they really suck. Then the seven months I was dying and in denial – big-time suck. Then AIDS. Every morning I woke up I had AIDS. I was forty-eight and my health was gone, piles of pills and shitting my brains out. Fucked up, man. Then the antidepressants didn't work, and the mornings, fucking horrific. Almost two years of mornings sucking hard like that. Just put your feet on the floor, stand up, and keep going no matter what. Ruth never even *tried* to talk to me until after lunch. Then the eleven days without sleep. Those days there weren't *any* mornings because it was always morning. Now there's a huck-a-bucking fucking hellacious suck for you. No way to tell you how bad. Then the antidepressant that worked and the sleep meds and four months later, it's not a hell of a lot different. You open up your eyes, you get out of bed, look around the room, drugged zombie fuck.

Fucking mornings, man.

That morning waking up with Hank in my house is no different. I'd bought all the stuff for a healthy breakfast. Eggs, if Hank wanted them, pancake mix and real maple syrup if Hank wanted those. A bunch of different kinds of healthy cereals. Cheerios, Corn Flakes just in case. Bacon, ham, Italian roast for my French press. Toast. Tea, herbal and Earl Gray. Milk, sugar. Vegetables. I had it all.

The problem, though, isn't breakfast. It's that the host, the guy who's supposed to make breakfast – me, because breakfast comes in the fucking morning, is nowhere to be found. I mean, yeah, my body's there and I'm walking around and talking and doing things to make breakfast, but the human being named Ben Grunewald is in another dimension. The suck dimension. I mean, it's *morning* for Chrissakes.

The problem is how to tell Hank that I'm not really there, that actually I am in hell. You can't tell anybody what hell is like unless they've been there themselves. And Hank ain't been there. Not this hell. His cancer didn't get his spirit the way AIDS got mine. Obviously. Hank's up at seven-thirty, showering, whistling in the shower, puttering around the house. Happy to be alive in a brand-new day.

Fucking Maroni, man. Wish I was made out of the same stuff as him.

Nine o'clock, I'm sitting at the table eating my five eggs, only two yokes, my bowl of kale and half a papaya. Hank says *I'll have what you're having,* so that's his breakfast, too.

"Hell, Gruney," Hank says, "you got your nutrition shit together, man. This breakfast is *healthy*."

Me, I can't tell the difference between the kale, the papaya, or the scrambled egg. I'm just eating food. I know I should say something back to Hank but that's the thing about depression and this new antidepressant. I know that if I were a regular person I'd be saying this or that. I mean, my response is in my head, but my body just won't let me say it. Other times it isn't even that lucid. I just look over at Hank. I know he's just said something that I should say something back to, but I've forgotten what he's said. Or if what he's just said to a normal person the say back is easy but there doesn't seem to be any point in answering.

"How about those Trailblazers?"

I wouldn't even know what to say to that if I was still normal.

Here's the real deal:

You've been running a jackhammer all night for years and doing speed but you need to sleep so you take a downer. You sleep because of the downer not because your body knows it needs sleep. When your body wakes up, the jackhammer's still going all through your body. Especially in the arms and shoulders. And the neck. The neck is real bad. No bright overhead lights. Bright overhead lights can shut the entire system down. The thought of food makes you feel sick but you eat food because you know you have to. *Healthy* food, but it might as well be sawdust. The ringing in your right ear has taken over your head. Don't get up too fast or you'll fall over. Forget about bending down.

But most of all, more than anything, is that a part of you is well enough to know how fucked up this is. But that well-enough part is bound and gagged, and all that's left of you, the filament flickering flickering, is really really afraid for any fucking reason you can possibly find. This morning it's because there's another body in the room next to you. Even though it's Hank's body. Fuck. How when his body moves what your body does. *Donnie Darko* is two years down the line. But that *Darko* shit is happening right there in your kitchen that morning. I mean every morning.

So you take a deep breath. You take a bite of egg, or kale, or papaya. Whale blubber. Whatever it is. You really hate Hank for his fucking cup of fucking coffee.

IT WILL BE three years before this gets any better. One day in 2002, maybe 2003, you're walking down the street and it's spring and you see a tree, a pink blossoming plum, and your charcoaled soul actually sees the tree and remarkably the tree sees you. In that moment, you bless the moment and in the blessing there is a transformation.

Bam, just like that, you start to come back to life.

BUT NOT YET. Not this morning with Hank.

"Gruney, man," Hank says. "Gruney, you all right?"

"I've got yoga class at eleven," I say. "You want to come?"

"What kind of yoga?"

"Hot yoga."

"On Christmas Day?"

"They're not Christian."

"Nah," Hank says. "The doc says nix on that."

AFTER YOGA CLASS, I'm back in my body as much as I can be. I'm in the shower at Bikram's when suddenly it becomes real that my best fucking friend Hank is at my house. I hightail it home and when I open my kitchen door I really do wonder if I haven't scared Hank off altogether.

Hank's right there, though, in the living room in the big

chair under the window. Sunshine. Of course it's sunshine, Hank
Christian is here and he's writing in his leather notebook in
the sunshine. The sun through his hair and Just for Men. Purple.

When I speak, my voice is way too cheery.

"Hey, Hank," I say. "How about a sandwich?"

TUNA SALAD SANDWICHES for the both of us. I'm just putting
the sprouted wheat bread in the toaster, just mixing in the
mayonnaise into the canned tuna, when I say:

"Hank, I'm sorry if I weirded you out this morning."

Hank has that half-smile of his on, like on the back cover
of his book. He's dressed all in black again. The same clothes as
far as I can tell.

"It's the depression," I say. "It's hard to explain."

In the daylight, Hank's eye looks like he's been punched.
And the punch left a scratch that hasn't quite healed. One
crooked line down from the middle of his eye. Like a blood tear.

"I've been a little depressed myself," Hank says. "And I
came all this way just to tell you about it."

The fucking silences, man, what was in them. Hank finally
lays his cards down on the table.

THE ENIGMA OF Hank Christian. He's peeled back his top layer
of black sweatshirt. Just two more layers of black and it's Hank's
white skin. I'm on one side of the table, he's on the other. A tuna
salad sandwich on a big white plate in front of Hank, his matching white coffee mug. A tuna salad sandwich on a big white plate
in front of me, my glass with red and yellow balloons filled with
sparkling water. The stove's behind me and I'm looking at Hank
with the window light behind him. He's on his second cup of
coffee, maybe his third, black, no sugar. The way he starts talking,
I remember what caffeine does to you. The words gather up and
crowd his throat, each one trying to get out first.

"Her name was Maria," Hank says. "We met at Hal Taylor's
wedding. Up in Connecticut. You remember Hal, don't you?"

"He thought you and I were having an affair," I say.

"Hal's an asshole," Hank says. "Married him a rich Connecticut girl. What a mess that turned out to be. *The Great Gatsby: The Miniseries*," Hank says. "'Course I'm not one to talk. Look how my marriage turned out."

"Hank!" I say. "You married this Maria?"

"Not really." Hank says."I mean I did. We got married at the Justice of the Peace on Staten Island. But it wasn't two days I found out she was still married to her first husband."

"What the fuck?"

"I should've known soon as I seen her," Hank says. "Had to be something wrong with a woman that perfect. Tall, olive skin, green eyes. Crazy the way her brown hair could go from blonde to auburn with the light."

"She ever get the divorce?" I ask.

"Right after I found out about her husband," Hank says. "I met her son, Boomer."

Hank takes another swig of coffee, picks up his tuna salad sandwich then lays it back down. Hank looks at the sandwich, as if he's studying it, but really he's not looking at the sandwich.

"I loved that kid, Gruney," Hanks says. "You should've seen him. Sturdy little guy, full of piss. More than I ever loved *her*. You'd have loved him, too. At seven years old, he already had a heart like yours. Smart as a whip. He came to stay with us for a couple of days and never left. His father didn't want him back."

Hank's black eyes look over the table at me. The sorrow of a son whose father doesn't want him. The way the light comes through the kitchen window, you can see Hank's glass eye rolls a little. Not like Buster's, but just enough to notice.

"There's no doubt in my mind," Hank says, "I was that boy's true father and he was my true son. We even look alike. We had this thing where he was Spider-Man and no matter where he went, our spiderweb was always connected. Heart to heart. The crazier his mother got, the more he needed me. Broke my fucking heart."

"Crazy?"

"Cocaine," Hank says. "Did it every chance she'd get. And other drugs, pills. All kinds of pills. Course I didn't figure that out until our second year together in Florida.

"*Porca Miseria*," Hank says. "Of course the sex was out of this world.

"But she kept coming up with these weird reasons why she had to fly back to New York. Most of them had to do with business, but the one that topped them all was *I'm going to die if I don't have a cappuccino.*"

Hank pushes the big white plate away from him. It smacks into his coffee cup. I hold on to my new glass, the red and yellow balloons.

"*Crap*pucino," Hank says.

"That's all right, though," Hank says. "Boomer and I didn't miss her at all. Saturdays we'd head out to the beach and spend the whole day there."

My mouth is full of tuna salad sandwich but I can't wait to speak.

"But was she totally addicted?" I say. "I mean like a junkie?"

"The drugs were just frosting," Hank says.

"Then I got the first cancer scare with the tumors on my dick and all," Hank says. "And all of a sudden this weird-ass woman starts acting like a human being. I mean she was still on the drugs then. I didn't find out about the drugs for a long time. But for some reason, when I got sick, Maria completely changed. She came home from work every night, cooked dinner, even wore different clothes and tied her hair back. Like all of a sudden she was the Maria in *For Whom the Bell Tolls*. *Ave* Maria. Fucking crazy bitch. She was even considering becoming a Catholic."

"You said *business*?" I say. "Did Maria have a job?"

"Maria's a fucking lawyer, man," Hank says. "Corporate. Found a job in Gainesville the first day she went out. Didn't put a thing on her body that wasn't designer."

"So she supported you?"

"She supported herself," Hanks says. "And her habits."

"All the while," Hank says, "I'm trying to keep my little family together and my health together and go to school. Take good care of my boy. I'm working for the college library. Didn't make much, couldn't make the rent on the fucking lavish apartment Maria insisted we live in for fuck's sake, but I bought the groceries."

"All in all though, I'd say," Hank says, "we stayed together a pretty good family for two years. By that time Boomer and I were blood. Then I found the rock of cocaine and her stash of pills."

"In one of her designer purses," Hank says. "Gucci. A huge leather purse filled with bottles of pills, all different shapes and sizes, blue and pink and white capsules. Smiling faces on some of them. And the rock of cocaine. It's what they call an eight ball, man.

"When I showed her the cocaine and the bottles I'd found," Hank says, "Maria went ballistic. She called my dean at the college and told him I was sexually abusing Boomer."

Hank, those sweet smiling lips, the way his lips flatten, push tight together.

His black eyes staring straight into my eyes. Not *staring*, really, *searching*, the glass eye just off enough. The scar under it, a crooked blood tear. As if in my eyes there was a secret and Hank had to know this secret.

"Gruney?" Hank says, "Can you fucking believe that shit?"

"Then she called up every person in the department with wild stories of how I was a sex addict and that I was taking drugs and assaulting her and her son. Really it was fucking nuts."

"So what did the dean say?" I ask.

"Oh, everybody at the university was cool," Hank says. "They could see what I couldn't. One day I come home and there's a note. She's moved back to New York and if I ever want to see Boomer again, I'd better not come after them."

"She took my *son*, Gruney," Hank says. "Stole Boomer and left me alone in the night without my son."

Hank's fist hits the table. The salt shaker tips over, the pepper too. I gulp down the last bite of tuna salad sandwich, quick reach over, hold the water glass.

"Three months later," Hank says, "she's crying to me on the phone, telling me she can't live without me and how much Boomer misses me and she's not doing drugs. So they came back. They gave her her old job back."

I pick up the salt shaker. Take a pinch of the spilled salt, throw it over my left shoulder.

"First thing Boomer does when he sees me," Hank says, "the Little Shit, green devil eyes just like his mom. He's Spider-Man, see, the web between our hearts. You should have seen it. He leapt clean across the room right into my arms."

At my kitchen table, Hank Christian has his empty arms out and is waving his arms around his head.

"Two weeks in the house all together," Hank says, "shit started up again. The cocaine, the pills, the phone calls, the allegations of abuse."

"There was this one day," Hank says. "It was the last day Boomer and I were together. We both knew there wasn't much time. I took him to his favorite place, Back Yard Burgers, and I tell you, Gruney, it was just like that one time with you and me and Silvio on Columbus Circle – that boy and me sitting in the booth in a diner. I asked him right out please to not cry because if he did cry I'd start too. That's what kind of boy he was. He didn't cry so he could protect me."

"And of course *that*," Hank says, "makes me start crying. Fuck. For some reason, both of us are holding onto the Heinz ketchup bottle, a grown man and a boy, crying our eyes out."

Under Hank's new eye, the scar that makes a yellow and blue dent there, the crooked blood tear, a bolt of lightning.

"The next day when I get home from work, she and Boomer are gone," Hank says. "No note, nothing. That was just two days after they'd found the tumor behind my eye. Fucking things never looked so bad."

Hank snuffs up, wipes his good eye. In a moment, he pulls the hood of his sweatshirt up to his new eye, holds the fabric there. Soft, the way you'd touch something brand new, or a baby. The trembling in Hank's big hand.

"By Christmas, though, she was back on the phone. Crying. Telling me how much she and Boomer missed me, begging me to take them back. I was just starting radiation."

Hank pulls the hoodie away from his eye. That's when Hank stops. Everything. As if before my eyes he's turning to stone. I wonder if he's breathing. I wonder if this is how he does it. Pulls his cards close into his vest. Shuts it all down.

The coffee in him keeps going, though. Jet propulsion. I pull my chair across the ugly yellow linoleum with purple triangles, around the table next to him, sit down close enough that our shoulders touch. Hank's chest is up, his shoulders down. He doesn't move, just stays wound up like that. His shoulder and his arm muscle, man, as if I were touching stone.

"That's when I did it," Hank says. "I moved to a studio apartment closer to the university, changed my phone number, and made it unlisted."

My tuna salad sandwich is a bunch of crumbs on my big white plate. The big white plates I bought so Hank and I could have something to eat off of. On Hank's big white plate, his tuna sandwich looks like a hurricane had hit.

Hank's bottom teeth come out, bite his upper lip. Chest so full, he's going to burst. That's when Hank turns his head, locks his eyes into mine. One eye looking at my soul, the other eye staring into nothing.

"The crazier his mother got, Gruney," Hank says, "the more that boy needed me."

I put my arm up around Hank's granite shoulder, lay my open palm against the back of his neck.

"I fucking left him, Gruney," Hank says. "Boomer."

"I left my son when he needed me the most."

"And that's why I came here," Hank says. "To you. I knew

you'd know what to say. I've been so fucked up. Gruney? Do you think I did the right thing?"

SO MANY THINGS happen in that moment. Portland, Oregon, Southeast Morrison, in my yellow house, in my kitchen, sitting in one of my wooden kitchen chairs. Christmas Day. All that goes away. There is only one place where I exist. Inside Hank's eyes, the place in there he's made for me. The eye he can see through and the eye that he can't.

A gaze that fucks me up because it's looking for an answer.

And Little Ben is an oracle without a clue.

Big Ben is going wild on advice: sometimes when you lose things you can find them again. Sometimes you can't. Sometimes when you find them you can fix them. Sometimes you can't. Sometimes things are just gone and there's no coming back no matter what you do.

But the longer I sit in Hank's gaze, I figure Hank didn't fly three thousand miles for advice.

Guys, real guys, don't want advice. Hank came to me because he had a story he had to tell. A story he'd never told before, even to himself. A story so heavy it was getting him down. And there was no one else to tell it to.

The place where you scribble down your prayer to God, lay it in a chink of stone, bury it in the sand, whisper it into a crook of broken tree limb, then cover it with mud. The altar where you lay your burden down.

That's when I really finally get it. Hank wants to know if I've got his back. That's the only thing Hank wants to hear.

From a guy who's never understood guy things, right then I think hard about what to say and how to say it. With authority, but not like I'm trying to have authority. And then when I say it, how I should touch him. There's got to be a touch, but it's definitely got to be a guy touch.

And this time I think I get it right. I make my hand into a fist, not hard, just close my fingers in, pull my thumb around. I take my not-hard clenched fist and pop Hank one, a blow of love, right in the middle of his chest. When I speak, my voice ain't Catholic-boy high. It's my voice, deep and clear and smooth.

"With you and Boomer," I say, "how solid was it? The web between your hearts?"

The scar under Hank's eye that makes the yellow and blue dent there. Inside Hank's gaze, in his good eye, right then something changes. Light from down deep, and out of the black there's color. His breath comes back. Mine too. I'm back in the chair at my kitchen table. My arm around Hank, my open palm against the back of his neck. On the table, the big white plates. On my plate, tuna crumbs. On Hank's plate, a tornado tuna salad sandwich. Across the room, outside the kitchen window, it starts to snow.

Never ceased to startle me, the way Hank and I could look at each other. So many times Hank Christian has turned his black eyes on me. But none of those times were this look. Never seen him so fragile, so close to busting open the seams. Vulnerability like that, only being close to death can make you feel. In your bones the way you fret. Hank's good eye is looking at my question. Looking at the spiderweb that connects his heart to his son's heart.

Like a tree falling in the forest, there's no sound, there's a crash, fuck, I don't remember. All's I know is Hank and I are on the kitchen floor, lying on the ugly linoleum, his head in my lap, and he's curled himself up into a ball.

20.
Stink eye

RUTH HAS FINISHED THE EDITS ON THE LAST CHAPTER of my novel, so that next morning Hank and I drive to Ruth's house.

That's what I told myself for a long time. That the reason I introduced Hank to Ruth was because he just happened to be there the day I picked up the final edits.

FINAL EDITS. I know you've got it by now the relationship between Ruth and me was complicated. She saved my life and she was a pain in my ass and every fucking possible nuanced psychological aspect in between.

There's one specific part of our relationship, though, that I haven't really stepped up to talk about.

As a writer, your editor is the only person in the world you allow in. Where what is invisible through your breath becomes structured. Where you exist the best and are the most vulnerable. The only place that is holy. Where you tell your truth from. How the words rise up out of you, in there in between your soul and its utterance. Your ecstasy.

Your editor. Your fucking editor, man.

Ruth Dearden is your editor.

THAT AFTERNOON, HANK puts his sunglasses on before we go out. The glass is so dark it's black.

"Never leave the house without them in the daylight," Hank says.

It's two in the afternoon and it's already getting dark.

"You call this daylight?"

"Ultraviolet," Hank says, "is my enemy."

In my driveway, my green Volkswagen was covered with a canvas and at least two years of leaves. I hadn't driven that car in months. No idea if it would start. In fact, it didn't. Had to push it out from the driveway and get it pointed down the hill. Hank and I pushed, then I jumped in and popped the clutch. Never fails on a Volkswagen. Unless the generator's bad. Hank didn't ask me no questions about my expired driver's license. He just got in the car, slammed the door. Drizzling rain. Crazy fucking windshield wipers moving like paraplegics. Cigarette butts in the ashtray from years back. No heat. The exhaust backfiring. The driver's door won't stay shut and I have to hold it closed with my armpit. Hank and me driving up Hawthorne Blvd., Hawthorne to S E 60th, then onto Pine. Thank God they're both left turns or I'd have lost the door completely. Plus I'd forgotten. The horn honks whenever you make a right turn and more times than not, the horn got stuck.

Quite an adventure getting to Ruth's house. To meet our destiny.

Ruth's brick house is on a hill and it's just as I pull up in front and pull the emergency brake that I realize I've never driven myself to Ruth's house before. It's always been in Ruth's Honda Civic, Ruth who drove.

So the only time I drive to Ruth's house is the only time I have Hank with me.

Years later now, of course, I can see what I couldn't see then. I dusted off my old Volkswagen, pushed it down the hill, jumpstarted it, then drove across town illegally, in the rain, the windshield wipers not working, the windshield covered in steam, holding the door closed with my armpit because of some pages Ruth could have sent me in the mail? And this from a guy who was still afraid to leave his house.

The truth is I wanted Hank and Ruth to meet. For a bunch

of reasons I didn't have a clue about. I mean, really, no doubt about it, Ruth and I had gone through the wringer. Over two years of trying to make sense of what was going on between us, we'd fucked each other up pretty good. And by that time we were only speaking when we had to talk about the edits. Still, no matter what I say about her, I have to admit it. Ruth was the one who went through the wars with me. Day by day, man. Nobody else, family or friends, had made that kind of commitment. Yeah, there was Ephraim, but he was seven hundred miles away.

So I guess I wanted Hank to meet the only other person who was still alive I had a strong connection with. Even if that strong connection was full of shit and resentment.

Then, too, I knew how much Ruth wanted to meet Hank. Like with all my students, the way I'd talked up Hank Christian over the years, Hank was a literary John Lennon to her. The truth is, I wanted to be there, in the moment, when I presented my hero, my beloved, to Ruth, in the flesh. It was a way of proving that it wasn't all talk, that I really knew the famous Hank Christian, and here he is and ain't I cool.

And something else that was more difficult to see. Took me years. Ruth's care for me had been a mother's care. Most men with women get past the mother thing and miraculously somehow turn it around and then want to fuck the mother. I'll never understand how they do it, but that's how it goes.

The truth is, deep down, the way Hank was suffering, some part of me wanted to introduce him to a woman he could trust, a woman with the healing powers of a mother, Ruth Dearden, the woman who had saved my life.

And Ruth: the man I couldn't be for her, had just arrived in the flesh.

I didn't even call first to see if Ruth was home. Just all of a sudden knew in my heart it was right and Hank and I were out the door.

RUTH'S FRONT DOOR was locked but we could hear the music. The soundtrack from *Living Out Loud*. The key was usually under the *bienvenue* mat in the alcove, but when I looked under the mat, the key wasn't there.

Hank and I walk around to the back of the house. Nobody walks along the side much, so it's overgrown with ivy. Tall dead flowers. That's where Hank steps in the dog shit. Only we don't know it. Ruth's back door has a glass window and it's painted white. Something scrapes at the bottom when I open it. I don't for a minute think about that door, what it means that I am opening it.

Inside, I call out to Ruth. The music's way too loud, so Hank and I let ourselves in. We walk through Ruth's white kitchen, Hank's dog shit shoes across Ruth's white tiled floors, into her Craftsman dining room with the wood paneling. Two six-top banquet tables side to side take up almost the whole room. I remember thinking: *this is where Ruth teaches her class*.

On the table, a manila envelope with the last pages of my novel in it. Ruth's black cat, Maupassant, walks right up to me, slides her body against my leg.

"A fucking cat," Hank says.

But Maupassant doesn't want anything to do with Hank. That cat ain't dumb. Hank's shoe is covered in dog shit.

The music is coming from the back bedroom. Ruth's banging around in there with Queen Latifah. As I knock on the bedroom door, Queen Latifah is in the middle of "Lush Life."

Ruth opens the door with a paint roller in one hand, cornflower blue dripping off it. The floor of the room is covered with newspaper. She's got a red bandana pulling back her red hair and she's not wearing a blouse. She's just in her bra and Levi's. A pink bra same color as her pink skin.

Those too-blue eyes of Ruth's, her pink lingeried breasts, her thin waist, her full hips, the voluptuosity, her red hair pulled back off her forehead, strands of blonde in the red, luminous her white skin, the thick blue paint dripping down, the smell of the room, cornflower blue and sweat, Queen Latifah: *and there I'll be while I rot with the rest/of those whose lives are/lonely too.* Hank Christian didn't know what the fuck hit him.

Ruth's startled, suddenly modest, goes to cover up her breasts, then not modest. She pulls her arms back and sucks in her breath. Her breasts get even larger.

"Ben?" she says.

"Ruth," I say, "this is."

"Who stepped in dog shit?" Ruth says.

"Hank," I say.

HANK LEAVES HIS dark glasses on and his shoes outside. They're those kind of tennis shoes with traction and the dog shit is imbedded. Ruth pulls on a paint-stained large old Columbia T-shirt of mine and, for the longest time, she and Hank do a dance trying to see who can get the dog shit up on the floor first so the other doesn't have to clean it up.

Tea. Ruth always has rose hip tea. Hank and I sit on the loveseat under the big dining room windows. Gray rain hitting the glass behind us. On the end table, Ruth's deco lamp of a woman bending backwards, holding up a globe. Ruth's taken off the red handkerchief from her hair. Her hair is that perfect tousled look, the strands of blonde. She sits at the table in her teacher chair. Two heads higher than Hank and me. The way we're sitting, Hank and I are schoolboys. Ruth is Mother Superior. Hank loves every minute of it.

I. Fucking. Hate. It.

What was I thinking. I can't wait to get out of there. The manila envelope is in my lap and I'm slurping my rose hips like mad. Hank hasn't even touched the cup to his lips. That's when Ruth starts in. Does that thing she always does. You know, takes over. In nothing flat, she and Hank are deep into it. Writing, William Faulkner, Denis Johnson, Ray Carver, Jeske, Padgett Powell, Cynthia Ozick, Cormac McCarthy. When Hank tells Ruth he studied with Barry Hannah, that moment, just so only I can see, Ruth's too blue eyes give me a look.

"Barry Hannah!" Ruth says, "Awesome!"

Then fuck, Hank's just got to say it.

"Yeah, Barry and I used to armwrestle," Hank says. "Beat him two times out of three."

"Really?" Ruth says. "Barry Fucking Hannah."

I can't help it. I spit rose hip tea across the two banquet tables. Splashes of rose hip tea onto the manila envelope. Fucking Ruth Dearden, man. After all the shit we've been through, still she can make me laugh.

Of course, then Hank thinks we're laughing at him. I don't know what else to do, so I fess up. I tell Hank about the Barry *Fucking* Hannah joke Ruth and I have going.

"I was stink eye," I say. "There's no other excuse. I was jealous that you went all the way to Florida for this Barry Hannah guy."

"I didn't go to Florida for Barry Hannah," Hank says. "Well, not *just* for him. They gave me a scholarship."

What I figure is coming next is some straight guy talk that wants to stay away from anything to do with affection between men. But then Hank surprises me. He takes his dark glasses off, folds them, puts them in the pocket of his hoodie.

"You're the one who's in my heart," Hank says. "You know that. From the very beginning."

Ruth's face right then. Hank's face. Mine. With Hank's sunglasses off, it's the first time that each one of us is present, and we all actually see each other.

Ruth has folded her long legs up into her big teacher chair. She's in heaven, you can tell, to be in the rarified air between Hank Christian and Ben Grunewald. And in that moment, she's smiling way too big. Hank's taken his sunglasses off and she can see Hank's black eyes and the intimacy in Hank's voice has just knocked the breath out of her.

Hank's pulling his shoulders down, straightening his neck, pulling his chest up and out, flexing his biceps. His sweet lips are a matter-of-fact flat line under his Roman nose. The cleft in his chin. It's pride what he's filling himself up with, and the way his right eye rolls out a bit, his feelings are hurt.

Who knows what my face looks like. *You're the one in my heart* went straight to my heart and my heart went right up into my throat. So I probably look a lot like Ruth. Trying to find breath. My big face red as a beet, my Catholic-boy smile.

Such a long long moment. In Ruth's dining room, the day after Christmas. Hank in his black pants, T-shirt, and black hoodie, his knee against my knee on the loveseat. Our cups of rose hip tea. Ruth above us in the large blue and red Columbia T-shirt, just one of her long legs away from Hank, curled up in her teacher chair.

Sit. We just sit. The rain on the windows, the smell of paint. Rose hip tea on my tongue and throat. The manila envelope rose hip wet I've tried to wipe off. Before that moment, it was the two of us, Hank and me. The two of us, Ruth and me. Now after, all of us are different.

We're three. Then we're two again.

If three doesn't find four, then three goes back to two.

Hank and Ruth.

The moment Hank saw Ruth in her pink bra, the smell of paint and sweat, dripping cornflower blue and that red hair, "Lush Life": Hank was in love.

The moment of Hank's voice, how simple and clear he'd spoken: *you're the one who's in my heart*: from a straight man to a gay man, from Hank Christian to Ben Grunewald, Ruth was in love.

Of course, it would be a while before we all know this. I mean it's like that Jeske thing. We knew but couldn't quite yet know that we knew. But the way that moment lasted long and long, there's no doubt about it. We all got it. Something real, so real it was going to fuck us up, had just happened.

Ruth, of course, is the one who saves us.

"So, Hank," Ruth says, "Ben says you might come teach writing classes with us here in Portland."

Just like that, Hank's black eyes go far away and Hank Christian leaves the planet. I sit there and watch the phenomenon. The way Hank pulls his cards in, holds his cards close to his chest. He reaches into his pocket, pulls out his sunglasses. I think for sure he's going to put them on, but he doesn't.

"Hard to make any plans these days," Hank says. "But let's keep talking about it. I'd love to teach with you and Gruney."

That's when Maupassant decides to jump up on the loveseat, right onto Hank's lap. That fucking cat knew. Hank never had any intention of living where the sun don't shine, teaching something that wasn't tenure track and involving a university. You got to remember, Hank's a Capricorn. Who needed a health plan.

Still, though, it got my hopes up, Hank and me teaching together again.

Hank jumps up and out of the loveseat like a man on fire. Maupassant goes screaming. Hank's all the way across the room and his sunglasses are back on before he speaks.

"Fucking cats, man. Sorry," Hank says. "Ever since the cancer I've been allergic."

TWO NIGHTS LATER, I'm trying to make a dream come true. The two young men Hank and I were in Manhattan, Wednesday nights, after the West Side Y, sitting in our booth at the café on Columbus Circle, our buddy Silvio waiting on us, Hank and me eating our hamburgers, our French fries and ketchup, dreaming our dreams. That our words would be true and because they were true, and the voice that spoke them so unusual, so full of character, our words would go straight to the reader's heart, and our books would go down in history.

The way I was proud to introduce Hank to Ruth, I wanted to expand that pride, expand the glory, the adulation, and introduce Hank to all the writing students with a big bang in Portland's finest Italian restaurant.

The table is a feast. Anything Italian you can imagine. Big loaves of ciabatta and focaccia, saucers of olive oil, plates of fettuccini, rigatoni, oven-baked pizza. Lamb roast, veal chops, pan-fried oysters, *prosciutto y meloni*, smoked salmon, fresh halibut, sand dabs. So many savory smells: roasted garlic, fresh tomatoes, baked pizza crust, basil and oregano. The table is lined with bottles of wine – Frascati, Amarone, Barbaresco, Montepulciano d'Abruzzo.

All around us, people talking talking. It's too loud for my whanged-out ears, but fuck it. There's a wonderful sense of celebration. Even I can feel it. The writing students at the table, almost twenty of them, are drunk and happy and they all want a piece of him. The legendary Hank Christian sitting at the head of the table.

Believe me, it took everything I had to get this gig together. And a lot of Xanax. But I did it without Ruth.

There's a moment. One of those moments I'll keep forever. Nothing really happens, I'm just sitting there adjacent to Hank, my starched white napkin folded in my lap, the heavy shiny silverware, my hand around a fluted glass filled with Prosecco. Yeah, I'm sipping the sparkly. I'm wearing my vintage tweed suit, the new tie I bought and the white shirt I had washed and starched at the laundry. In my glass, the way the light hits the bubbles, how the bubbles stay in my throat, the solid way my heart is in my chest. And my butt, how it's sitting in the chair. There's no place else in the world I want to be. I'm so full of pride for Hank. I'm proud of my students too.

All around me the room is spinning. Sounds like dogs barking. Just at that moment, under the table, Hank's knee pushes against my knee. So I look over. Hank's black corduroy shirt is buttoned at the top button. His face is rosy with wine and yeah his hair is purple. He's sitting in a saffron, ornately upholstered Italian chair. Behind him a heavy, wine-red brocade curtain. Hank's sweet smiling lips.

Hank lifts his glass, I lift mine. The little sound of two fluted glasses touching. That smile is exactly what I wanted. Hadn't seen Hank smile like that since the olden days. That smile says *look around, Gruney, I told you all our dreams would come true.*

Hank's black glass eye, the glass eye they replaced his real eye with, because from behind his real eye, they had to remove a tumor the size of plum. The tumor, the hole in his head it made, the ruined eye. Lying in a hospital room on fire with radiation. Hank alone with his cancer and his radiation and his chemo-therapy thinking about his lost son and crazy girlfriend, did he do the right thing.

Human suffering, man, fucks you up.

Fluted glass to fluted glass I know exactly what to say and say it out loud with Hank at the same moment he says it.

Porca Miseria, man.

Porca fucking *miseria.*

IT'S WHEN I tap my fluted glass with my knife, and stand up. Before I speak, I do that thing in my throat I always do in a public place to make myself be heard. Suddenly, everybody watching me. It's when I'm trying with all my might to make my lips move the way I want them to move. *I won't cry. I won't cry.* It's just as I say *There's a great man among us* that Ruth Dearden walks in.

I'm not surprised to see her. She always seems to pop up at moments like this. Besides, I invited her myself. Hank made sure I did. Ruth's blue contacts and her too-blue eyes look right at me. Her red hair is down and it's long again, to her shoulders. A pearl barrette pulls the hair off her forehead. Ruth's dress is tiny with a scooped neck and its black velvet. A string of pearls around her neck. The flush of red on her throat.

When the students at the table see Ruth, those of them who know her get real quiet. Ruth's is a dramatic entrance and every group has its drama. Especially this group when it's Ruth Dearden. The *woman* their gay teacher had an affair with.

Fucking *affair*, man. That word. If people only knew.

Ruth is aware of the dish that's going to fly. The first thing

I think is how much courage it's taken for Ruth to show up. But then Ruth has never been lacking in courage. And you know, come on, it's *Hank Christian*.

I go on with my little speech. Talk about the young men Hank and I were in Manhattan. How Hank has always been my friend, my writing teacher, my companion. At the other end of the table, someone is pouring Ruth a glass. When we all stand and raise our glasses to Hank, Ruth's is full of prosecco.

"Welcome to Portland," I say.

"Welcome to Portland, Hank," everybody says together. Because we all got the email.

LOVELY AND A little decadent how the evening progresses. I hang in there. One fucking glass of bubbly and I'm totally drunk. So I just sit and enjoy alcoholism while it lasts. Don't think about the bad night's sleep coming up. Because it's all perfect. I'm sitting next to Hank Christian and he's at the head of the table in his saffron Italian throne and Ruth's still at the other end of the table and it's all just perfect.

After dessert and espressos, people walk outside to have a smoke. I want to go outside and smoke and smoke, too. But I don't. I just sit in my starched white shirt and new tie and my tweed suit trying to look like Jimmy Joyce, or Billy Faulkner. I think on it for a while and decide I look more like Faulkner than Joyce. Nothing Irish about me. Ruth's pulled her hair behind her ear, that one long strand of blonde. A single pearl earring. We've all pitched in and paid the bill and I've made sure we've over-tipped.

One more glass of Montepulciano and Hank's got his sunglasses on. The restaurant lights are up high and they've turned the music up. Hank's favorites. John Coltrane, Miles Davis, Stan Getz, Charlie Parker, Oscar Peterson, Terence Blanchard. Billie Holiday comes on, and it's when I recognize the song she's singing is "April in Paris" that I lean into Hank. Hank may be sitting right next to me, but he ain't there. Those black eyes behind his dark glasses are looking only at one thing. Down the table at the red haired woman with the pearl barrette and pearl necklace and pearl earring in the little black velvet dress.

"It's our song," I say.

"What?" Hank says.

Hank looks at me as if I'm nuts. I mean with his dark glasses on, when he looks at me, that's what I think.

Then: "Oh yeah, man, Billie Holiday."

I don't say anything more. About the night Hank shook his ass in a cornflower blue turban in the candlelight at Esther's house in Pennsylvania. *The Maroni*, how his bare chest looked in the candlelight.

Hank goes back to the vision behind his sunglasses. Still no movement as yet. Ruth still at the other end of the table. Hank still next to me in the saffron throne. I'm betting on Hank to be the one who moves first.

I'm the one who moves first. It just makes things easier. And I really got to pee.

OUTSIDE THE RESTAURANT, the night is way too cold for Portland. The air so frozen I can feel the air in my lungs. My old overcoat is more Dashiell Hammett than Faulkner or Joyce. My breath comes out of me in clouds. My hands deep into the overcoat's pockets.

Ruth's silver Honda Civic is parked next to my Volkswagen. Hank walks out the door of the restaurant next to Ruth. She's wearing her grandmother's unborn baby lamb coat and matching hat. Hank in his dark glasses is one of the Blues Brothers. Ruth with the hat is Jane Fonda in *Julia*.

Look at us. The three of us, Hank Christian, Ruth Dearden, Ben Grunewald, standing between Ruth's car and mine. We're all freezing, all of us a little enchanted with the cold, still night. When Hank embraces me it's a full-on frontal. Hank's breath against my neck below my ear starts a chill that that goes all the way down my back.

"Got to go, pal," Hank whispers.

We laugh at our old joke. I push at Hank's shoulders. He pushes back. A mock battle between men. The next time we share that joke it will be in the got to go pal letter and Hank and I won't ever talk to each other again.

"I'll call you tomorrow, okay?" Hank says.

Then Ruth. We look in each other's eyes for only a moment, then lean in for a quick embrace.

"Thanks for inviting me, Ben," she says.

My battery's been charged so my VW starts right up. Both headlights are working. I roll down the window and hold the door with my armpit. Ruth still hasn't started her car. I figure it's best not to look over, though, so I don't wait to see if her car is going to start.

When I pull out of the parking lot, my headlights flash over the silver Honda Civic. For an instant the light flashes onto Ruth's face. It's shocking really, the way Ruth looks. I recognize the look right off. But I haven't seen it in a long long time.

At the beginning, that first night in the cemetery, it's the way Ruth used to look at me.

A child at Christmas. A woman in love.

THE NEXT DAY, I'm like a kid who has a secret nobody else knows. I can't stop thinking about Hank and Ruth. But Wednesday's one of my big writing days and I'm busy all day on my rewrites. Plus it's the holidays and there's no class Thursday and I got the whole week to write. Really, it's not until that night when I get into bed that I realize Hank hasn't called. I'm worried for a moment, then feel a little hurt he hasn't checked in like he said he would, but then figure, what the hell. Later on in bed, trying to get to sleep, I get to thinking about the two of them fucking and I have to put the pillow over my head.

Thursday, still nothing from Hank. All day I stay focused on writing. I think I'm doing fine but I'm not. Ruth's little editing messages on my pages – smiling faces on my pages, her stars.

Her penmanship I can't make heads or tails of. Somewhere in between, in my concentration, in the maze of virtual and hard copy, going back over sentences then back over sentences, over and over, somehow some other me balloons up just above me and behind me with a big realization that I live my life more on the page than in my body.

If you can't live in here then live out there. It's pure and simple.

Fucking bliss, man. You don't follow it because you want to. It's survival.

That afternoon, Hank calls and I'm not in my body, so the answering machine takes the message.

"Hey, Gruney," Hank says, "we're grooving here, buddy. Talk to you soon."

When I go to call back, it's weird dialing *Ruth's* number. So I can talk to *Hank*. But I keep dialing. In my buzzing right ear, that familiar ring. It's Ruth's ring, even though it's no different from any other ring, still that ring is Ruth's. Five of those rings and I get Ruth's message. The fucking message I've heard way too many times. Her sing-songy voice. I almost hang up.

"Hank," I say, "call me back."

Friday morning, while I'm brushing my teeth, there's Hank's L.L.Bean toiletry bag. I know it sounds silly, but I'm suddenly worried for Hank that he doesn't have his green toothbrush and his Crest and his razor and Barbasol shaving cream and his Mennen stick deodorant. I almost call him up to remind him he's left his toiletries here, but then I realize how dumb that is. Of course Hank knows he doesn't have his toothbrush. And he knows it's New Year's Eve. Besides I can't just call up Hank. I have to talk to Ruth first. And I don't want to talk to Ruth. So I figure what the hell, ten dollars at the Walgreens will put the Maroni back in business.

Friday afternoon, right after I get back from yoga, I'm at my kitchen table when the phone rings. It's Hank, and in the background I can hear Ruth laughing. Hank doesn't say hello or anything to me because he's laughing, too. He covers up the phone with his hand and Hank is with Ruth in Ruth's house and I'm across town in my kitchen mixing mayonnaise into tuna in my white bowl and they're laughing and I'm standing on my ugly yellow linoleum with purple triangles and I listen to them laugh.

I fucking swear, to be jealous of Hank and Ruth is the last thing in the world I'll do. Whatever they have, what they do, how they laugh on the phone, will all be cool with me. I learned a long time ago not to get between Hank and his woman. Then *Ruth is Hank's woman* starts to freak me out. But I compose myself and I do it quick. This shit is not going to fuck me up.

"Hey, Gruney," Hank finally says, "I can't talk right now. Call you later. Ruth's got moths."

What's going on that I don't know about is Ruth has just opened an old package of pancake flour and a bunch of moths have flown out into her kitchen. Ruth is freaked and the way Ruth is freaked is making Hank laugh and because Hank is laughing, Ruth starts laughing too.

But in the moment, on the phone New Year's Eve afternoon, I don't know about the moths. In fact, when I hang up the phone, I won't admit it. Despite the swearing and all the decisions and the promises I've made, really what I think they're laughing at is me.

About an hour later, the phone rings again. I'm mid-sentence and think I won't answer. But I answer. Hank apologizes right off then tells me the whole moth story.

"Fucking funny, man," Hank says. "When anything starts flying around her head, birds or bugs, man. Totally freaks Ruth out."

All of a sudden, it's that silence that opens up and it's my turn to talk. I don't say anything, though. Don't know where to start.

"Of course," Hank says, "you probably already know that."

"When does your plane leave?" I ask.

"Sunday afternoon," Hank says.

"What you doing tonight?" I ask.

"It's New Year's Eve, man," Hank says. "That's why I'm calling. Ruth wants to cook. Would you like to come over?"

21.

The end, my friend

MORE THAN LIKELY, YOU'RE LIKE ME AND THINK THAT something like this could never happen to you. That you could love a man, then love a woman – two extraordinary people, two unique ways of loving, from different decades, on different ends of the continent, and what happens is something you could never in a million years have planned. There you are the three of you, dancing the ancient dance whose only rule is with three add one, if not, subtract. If three doesn't find four, three goes back to two.

I mean this shit is *mythical*. With three you go directly back to the father and the mother and the child. Or this: a parent and two children. In either case, you're back to what's most fundamental about you: who has the love and who's going to get it.

From the time I hang up the phone on New Year's Eve day until nine months later when I sit down and write Hank the *Got to go pal* letter, I just got to cop to it. I'm no longer reliable. This time, this book, no matter how hard I try, I can't be one of the big-spirited, redeemed men who's gone through it all, seen the light at the end of the tunnel, and from that high place of awareness, narrates the story.

I keep falling into fits and rages.

Pain like this is too old, too irrational, too hard to bear.

Pain like this has to be somebody else's fault.

NEW YEAR'S EVE, 1999, as I'm talking to Hank on the phone,

there's no doubt about it, I'd rather suck a hemorrhoid than spend New Year's Eve at Ruth's house. But then out of nowhere it's one of those moments. I can't believe the words coming out of my mouth. *Sure, I'll be right over.*

As soon as I hang up the phone I have to quick sit down on a kitchen chair and hold my gut. That old fear of leaving my house. Alone. Plus there's a rainstorm coming and my car is out of gas. Even *with* gas, my car can't possibly make it one more time across town. New Year's Eve, everybody driving drunk. The expired license tags.

But none of these things, really, are what I'm afraid of.

On the stove, the meatloaf I'd cooked and the brown rice and broccoli. For Hank and me. A couple of long-necked Budweisers for Hank. On the kitchen table, the videos I'd rented. New Year's Eve, what could be more perfect than Hank and me and a fire in the fireplace and *Shakespeare in Love*, Scully and Mulder, *The X-Files*.

Fucking Ruth Dearden, man.

On the ride over to Ruth's, it's raining buckets. Crazy fucking windshield wipers like paraplegics. No heat. I'm ignoring the gas gauge. There's always the reserve tank. With one hand I'm rubbing a hole in the steam. My other hand is freezing to death. My other hand is outside trying to hold the door closed. At Belmont and 39th, the engine backfires so loud, a drunk at the crosswalk in a Santa suit thinks I've shot him. Through the static, some guy on the radio's going on about computers, the new century, and the fucking apocalypse. On 50th I hit a speed bump too fast and the horn starts honking and won't stop, even after I'm parked in front of Ruth's. Silent night, holy night, I kick that car in the ass so hard it makes my leg hurt. But the horn stops.

A holiday evening with Hank and Ruth. Happy Fucking Y2K, man.

Ruth's front door is an arched alcove, a small porch you can step into out of the rain. On the flagstones, a fiber mat, *bienvenue*. Above, a Craftsman lamp hanging down. A Christmas

wreath on the dark wood door. Ruth's front door, just a damn
door, but that night another portal. The step you got to take.

The doorbell that sounds like Beethoven's Fifth. As soon
as Hank answers the door it's weird. First of all, it's *Hank Christian*, my old friend of so many years and twelve years we'd been
apart. He's been three days at Ruth's and my eyes are happy all
over again just to see him. But Hank is opening *Ruth Dearden's*
door. A door I hardly ever walked through because Ruth always
came to my house, because my house was the only place that
felt safe, and when I did go to Ruth's, no matter how hard I tried
it always freaked me out and now that's all I can remember about
it. Freaking. And there I am standing in her doorway already the
second time in one week.

Both Hank and Ruth are smiling way too big, trying to be
extra nice. I'm dad come home from work and found the kids
playing doctor. Really, they're both kind of bobbing and bowing
as if I'm the Dalai Lama or something. The way Hank takes my
coat. The way Ruth folds it gently on her arm and carries it to the
bedroom.

In *Ruth's* fireplace, not *my* fireplace, there's a fire and *Ruth's*
Christmas tree goes all the way to the ceiling with those bubbly
lights and Laura Ashley homemade cookie ornaments and shit.
Fuck, it's the coolest Christmas tree ever. Hank's in a new soft
brown bulky knit sweater, pajama bottoms, and soft wool socks.
Ruth's wearing the exact same thing. They could switch outfits
and nobody could tell the difference. Ruth, of course, is more
beautiful than ever. Hair pulled back off her face. Her hair's long
enough to be pulled into a barrette at the back of her neck. The
blonde strands shining gold. Must have lost two pounds since I
last saw her. She looks so relaxed.

I *told her* what she needed was some serious dick.

Something else about Ruth, though. Maybe it's just me,
but I keep getting the feeling she's staring at me. That night, that
very first night, I think *that* early on, she gets it. That I could be
a serious threat to her and Hank. I know for sure she's surprised.

For Hank it was no big deal I drove across town. But Ruth knows different. That I've left my house at night and driven all the way across town alone. In all the years, Ruth's *never* known me to do that.

Where I can really tell, though, is with the food. Ruth's made one of her wacky chef salads. That woman could put the strangest things together and call it a salad. That night it's carrots sliced too thick, iceberg lettuce, purple grapes, tomatoes, green pepper, sliced chicken breasts, walnuts, and pickles with too much creamy vinaigrette.

As far as Ruth's salads go, this New Year's Eve salad is not *that* unusual. But it's when the three of us sit down at Ruth's oversized dining room table, me at the head of the table, Ruth to my left, Hank on the right – when I look down at the extra boiled eggs she's cooked for me. At first I think it's cool Ruth has con-sidered that the salad didn't have enough protein for me. I start staring at them eggs, though, and then I look around at the chicken in our bowls. I stare at the chicken. There's no more than *two* chicken breasts worth of chicken meat for *three* of us. Back and forth I'm staring, the chicken, the eggs. Then I'm sure of it. Ruth wasn't at all planning on having Mr. Protein for dinner. She thought for sure I wasn't going to come. At the last minute, she had to quick come up with more fucking protein and all she had was three fucking eggs. An afterthought. Didn't even have the time to cook them all the way hard.

When I finally look up from my three extra not fully boiled eggs, I look straight at Ruth. Her beautiful long red hair, those too-blue eyes. She has that looked-at look only beautiful people have. Ruth for sure knows I'm scrutinizing her and her protein *faux pas*. And sure enough, there it is. The tell-tale scarlet flush up her neck, onto her chin. The way she's trying to cover it with her hand. She knows damn well her neck is giving her away. But she's ignoring me. Her eyes suddenly all transfixed, staring into Hank's. Hank's staring back at her. His eyes beholding her. As if she is something newly formed, precious. His breath breathing life into her.

Hank's making a toast.

They're having prosecco.

I'm having water.

Hank's black eyes, the right eye shiny, rolling a little south. Hank's doing that thing he does when he's trying to express something inside him that's big – as if his body is literally trying to push the thought or the feeling that's inside him, out. Chest raised up and out, his chin pulled down, shoulders down, flexing his biceps.

"Here's to old friends, new friends, and a new century!" Hank says.

Not a one of us that night, when we clinked our glasses, Hank or Ruth or me, had any idea, not yet, not really, about the new century and the huge load of horseshit it was going to bring.

But looking back on it, it's like that Jeske thing. You know but you don't know you know.

Maybe Hank didn't know it yet.

But Ruth knew.

And I knew it too.

SUNDAY MORNING HANK rolls into my kitchen door about ten-fifteen. His airplane leaves at one. Hank's back all in black, his jacket, his baseball cap, the hood of his sweatshirt up. His dark black sunglasses. I'm eating my five scrambled eggs with two yokes when he walks in. We give each other a big bear hug in the mudroom. When I put my chin on Hank's shoulder, I can smell lavender from those scented square pieces that Ruth throws into her dryer.

"How'd you get here?" I ask.

"Ruth drove me."

"She coming in?"

"Nah," Hank says. "She's got some shopping to do."

"How you getting to the airport?"

"Ruth," Hank says. "She'll be by about noon."

"You better be careful," I say. "She's always late."

Hank lays his big hand on my shoulder, squeezes my shoulder. Stares his big black eyes into mine. We both take a breath. I can't help it. That shiny black glass eye of his makes me love him all the more.

"*Porca Miseria*, Gruney," Hank says. "What a fucking ten days it's been!"

The brooding dark Hank that stepped out of the darkness Christmas Eve was gone and now there he is, right in front of me, his hand on my shoulder. The Maroni once again. Bright as a star. Freshly fucked, gorgeous. And why can't I just blow it off and be happy for him.

There's so much I want to say to Hank right then. But it's not one of my better moments. It's morning all right, but it's more than a drug hangover and the time of day. I'm ashamed. That I could be so petty. I mean now that I look back on it. The stink eye, man. There's not a worse feeling in the world. Like you've been slimed. And that Sunday morning in the mudroom, believe me right then, I don't want to be anywhere near my tiny Catholic heart.

Hank takes off his coat and his dark glasses, his black baseball cap, and unzips his sweatshirt. Pulls down the hood. He sees my eggs and I can tell he's hungry. Ruth never did get it how much a man can eat. So Hank sits down and I crack a bunch of eggs into a bowl and all the while Hank is talking talking. I smile and act like I'm listening while I'm scrambling eggs, but I'm not listening. Hank's talking about Ruth. Ruth this and Ruth that.

What I'm really paying attention to, what I start obsessing about, is the time. I've got yoga at eleven o'clock and I still have to get my shit together. I mean, what the fuck. Hank's come back over to my house, an hour early, without Ruth, to catch up with me. And I could easily blow off yoga for one day. But why should I interrupt my schedule because it's convenient for him. He knows I go to yoga every day at eleven. And during the past five days he's had all the time in the world to drop by and chat. Or even call just to check in.

So instead of being thankful that I can see and talk with my dear friend for a whole blessed hour long, all I can think is that if his L.L.Bean toiletry bag and his green toothbrush and his Crest and his razor and Barbasol shaving cream and his Mennen stick deodorant weren't hanging in my bathroom, he'd probably be calling me from the airport.

So when I turn around, dump the scrambled eggs on his plate, I tell him:

"Sorry, Hank," I say. "Don't have the time to talk right now. Yoga's at eleven and I got to get there early to get a good spot."

"You all right?" Hank asks.

"Yeah, I'm fine," I say. "Leave the door unlocked. Call me when you get back to Florida. We'll have some real time to talk."

We hug once again, before I leave. Hank's eyes, Christ, he's got so much to say. But I'm late and I waited for him so now he can wait for me.

After yoga, about twelve-twenty, I'm walking up a side street when Hank and Ruth drive by on Morrison. I quick duck into a bush so they don't see me. Late as always, Ruth's shifting into second. She's got the silver Honda Civic floored. They don't look like they're stressed, though, Hank and Ruth. Both of them big smiles. And the damndest thing.

Ruth's wearing dark glasses. Just like Hank's.

TWO DAYS LATER, two phone calls. The first one's from Hank. He knows what time to call exactly. Pacific time after yoga and my shower and after my tuna salad sandwich on my special bread. One-fifteen. Hank's doing good. He's rested and feeling strong. Me too. My stink eye's nowhere around and it's like we're back to being Hank and Gruney again. Just talking as if we'd never stopped.

In a moment, Hank takes a deep breath I can hear all the way across the United States. His voice gets lower and full of all that Hank love. He thanks me for listening about Boomer. What a good friend I am and how much he loves that I was there for him.

I don't know what to say, but I know Hank would do the same for me, and so I tell him that. Then Hank asks a question. And when he asks the question it's as if everything we'd been talking about so far was just a prelude.

"So tell me about you and Ruth," Hank says. "The two of you had a thing going for a while there, didn't you?"

Ruth Dearden and I, a *thing*. All that I want to say to Hank, beloved Hank, about Ruth, fucked up beloved Ruth. I try, really I do, to come up with some shit that means something not just some bullshit. But I can't. I mean, what can I say about Ruth Dearden and me, the thing we had, on the phone on a cloud-covered January day in the middle of the afternoon. Fuck.

"Yeah," I say, "we had a thing."

"It's over now, right?" Hank says. "I don't want to be stepping on any toes."

"All Ruth and I have left," I say, "is one more session with my novel."

"That's what Ruth said," Hank says, "that she's editing your book for you."

Fucked up the way Hank saying *editing your book* makes me want to scream. Like Ruth is all of a sudden the Grand Chooser or something. What pisses me off is not what she says about my writing. It's that I've given her the power to say it. This time it's my deep breath all the way across the United States.

"Yeah," I say, "she's helping me out."

"So tell your old Hankster buddy about her," Hank says. "What's the scoop? Anything I don't know? Something I should watch out for?"

Don't dump her then introduce her to your best friend.

"Be careful," I say. "She's strong and she's clumsy. She's damn near knocked me out three times now."

Hank Christian, man. The way that man can laugh.

THE SECOND PHONE call is from Ruth. I'm surprised it's Ruth and at first I don't know what to say. Her voice is upbeat, cheery. Hello. How you feeling. New Year's Eve was nice. Are you sleeping. What did you think about the edits I made? Is your computer all right?

"My computer?" I say.

"You know," Ruth says, "the Y2K thing."

My computer. Ruth just spent four days fucking my best friend and what she wants to talk about is my computer. But don't get me wrong. I'm not saying Ruth was a conniving evil bitch trying to manipulate me. To tell the truth at this point, I don't really know what Ruth's motivations are. She probably doesn't know either. But really that day on the phone, she just sounded like the old Ruth I knew and she wanted to talk and the something she wanted to talk about wasn't easy for her.

"Looks like you got Hank to the airport on time," I say.

Ruth never could hide a thing from me. As soon as I mention Hank, there's quiet that's too long, then her laugh like a little girl.

"Traffic was a nightmare," she says.

Then: "Ben?" she says. "Are you okay with this? I mean Hank and me?"

All the things I could've said. And that day, all I really knew was Hank loved redheads and Ruth got to fuck a rock star. My own jealousy and feelings of being passed over? Same as with Hank. Where do I start.

The maze of three, man. Fuck.

What I say surprises even me.

"Well, he sure as hell ain't me," I say. "If that's what you're looking for."

Quiet that's too long again.

"I know he's not you," Ruth says. "But what's he like? I mean is there something I should watch out for?"

"If you catch him writing fuck poems to a woman he works with," I say, "throw all his stuff out the window."

Ruth's laugh isn't a little girl's anymore. It's Ruth and she's really laughing. Maybe too hard.

"You know, Ben," Ruth says, "Hank said you've really changed a lot. From the old days."

Then something new in Ruth's voice. The first time I ever hear it.

"He said he doesn't feel as close to you," Ruth says. "How *were* you in the old days?"

My mother. My sister.

Ruth Fucking Dearden, man.

THREE MONTHS AND one more run through, alone, on the novel later, Ruth calls me on the phone. She's been to Florida to visit Hank. That's all I ever find out about it. That Ruth flew down to Florida and for one week Ruth visited Hank. No news about where Hank lives, his friends. Nothing about the weather, or a good crayfish restaurant they ate at. How different the cultures are, Northwest and Southeast. No alligator stories or how a four-night fuck fest has turned into a cross-country love affair. Nothing. From Ruth or from Hank. Oh yeah, Ruth fucking loved the sun. That's it.

But Ruth does have a surprise. She and Hank have come up with an idea. At least Ruth says Hank was in on the idea. When Hank comes to visit in the spring, the three of us should teach a weekend workshop together.

It was the first I'd heard of Hank's spring visit and it felt weird Hank hadn't called to talk to me about teaching together. I didn't know it then, but this was how it was going to be. Hank would talk to Ruth and then Ruth would talk to me. I bought into it, though. To teach with Hank again. The chance to hang out and talk about writing. I'd have done anything. Then there was the extra money. Hank was finishing up his dissertation and he was having trouble finding a job, and I was barely scraping by and, now that I look back on it, that's about the time Ruth's alimony started to run out.

So the second week in April, on the weekend Ruth has scheduled the class, a bright warm spring day, probably the only bright warm spring day Portland's ever had, I load up on Xanax. My old Volkswagen and I make it one more time over to Ruth's.

At Ruth's front door, in the arched alcove, I'm standing on the *bienvenue* mat. On the other side of the dark wood door, the sound of people. Ruth's front door, just a damn door. The Running Boy wants to bolt. I pop a Xanax, then another one. The doorbell that sounds like Beethoven's Fifth. The step you got to take.

HANK'S BEEN IN Portland for over a week and I had no idea.

They make it like a surprise. I come walking into the crowd of people in Ruth's living room and *ta da!* Hank jumps out from behind the dining room door and everybody laughs.

Really, that moment, the way Hank just jumped out like that. The guy that told *Ruth*, the guy that didn't tell *me* he doesn't feel close to me like he used to. Ruth's visit to Florida, and now he's a whole fucking week in town. How that might make me feel. That's the moment right there I got it. The three of us, the fucking endless nuanced painful maze it was. A bull in my china shop, man. Hank Christian didn't have a clue.

Hank grabs a hold of me and actually picks me up in his arms and holds me the way Mary held Jesus. I only weigh maybe a hundred seventy-five pounds, still it's weird, a grown man, being held like a child. Hank makes a big deal about kissing me on the lips in front of everybody.

I felt like a gay circus ride.

The day is so warm, Ruth wants to have the class outside. I don't care how warm it is, I'm always freezing, but I don't say anything. Hank and Ruth and me, everything feels so delicate, so I just go along with the plan. On the picnic tables in Ruth's backyard, the sun shining down through the dogwood branches, there's chips and dip and dried fruit and pasta salad and three bean salad, coleslaw, three stinky cheeses and dill pickles.

1

5

34 | TOM SPANBAUER

Paper plates and plastic forks and decorated napkins. A decanter of French press and assorted coffee cups.

Hank and Ruth and I sit at one end of the picnic tables. Ruth's on one side of me, Hank on the other. Hank's still heavy, trying to slim down, all in black. Ruth's skinnier than ever. Her hair so long she can pull it into a rope and tie it up on top of her head. She's wearing the blue taffeta vintage dress I bought her years ago, the pink sweater with the pearls on it.

Look at us. The three of us. Hank and Ruth and me and ten students sitting around two picnic tables in the springtime in the sun. Above us, pink dogwood blooms. Hank's got his dark black sunglasses on. Ruth's sunglasses are white, and the glass is dark too, like Hank's. Ruth is talking. She has to talk loud because her voice is small in the big bright day. The flush up her neck, onto her cheek. Old friends, new friends of the new millennium. Behind my back, Ruth's hand and Hank's hand are clasped together. In the middle of my back I can feel Ruth holding on tight to Hank. Along the side of my leg, it's Ruth's black cat, Maupassant. Sun. A warm sunny spring day in April. I'm wearing my winter coat and stocking cap. When I close my eyes and look at the sun, on the backs of the lids of my eyes, all I see is red.

THE CLASS WAS a success and the money was good, so Ruth comes up with another idea. In the summer, we'd schedule another workshop. Hank would be finished with his dissertation by July and the class would be a good excuse for him to get away from the Florida summer. Hank's all for it. I'm not so sure. In that point of time, the Hank Ruth Ben dance, I was confused to say the least, and all I wanted was for everything to work out. One thing for sure was we could all use the money. So we schedule the class. On one condition, we hold the class at my house.

But in June, there's some problem with Hank's dissertation, and Hank has to cancel.

You'd think I'd have a lot of memories about that weekend. Ruth in my house again, sitting across the table from her again, the dueling banjos. The rich history of shit between Ruth and me and all the new shit that was going down with her and Hank. But there's only two things I remember. I mean two things I'll never forget.

It was nothing new for Ruth and me, teaching the workshop. It was during the afternoon break on the last day. All the students were away from the table. Ruth had just sat down in her chair with a fresh cup of hot tea. More than likely, I was eating my sardines. It was the way she said it and how it came out of nowhere:

"You know," Ruth said, "I've got twelve people in my regular Thursday class and not one of them have any idea who Ben Grunewald is."

I looked over at Ruth. She was still wearing her dark sunglasses. Her hair down past her shoulders. Hank Christian loved long hair on women. Maybe it was because the light from the floor lamp was behind her, or maybe it was my tired eyes. Whatever it was, even though I knew Ruth Dearden was the person sitting right across the table from me, except for the scarlet flush on her neck and up her chin, I never would've recognized her.

The other thing happened later that afternoon at the end of class. Five o'clock and the students were gone. The lights were out, the paper recycled, and I'd just locked the basement door.

Back in the old days, that last day, after Ruth and I'd finished teaching, we always gave ourselves a little time and space to talk to each other about the class. That afternoon, as I was walking up the stairs, I remember looking forward to checking in with Ruth.

Upstairs, Ruth was on the phone. In my kitchen, at my kitchen table, on my telephone, in front of me. Ruth was laughing and talking all about the class she'd just taught.

To Hank.

For a moment, I think she'll hand the phone over to me. But then she hangs up.

EARLY SEPTEMBER. HANK calls me from Florida and leaves a message that he'll be in Portland for a month. *It's been too long, Dear Heart,* Hank says, *We'll get to spend some quality time together, man. I promise.*

In my kitchen that day, after my shower, making up my tuna salad sandwich, I'm standing with a piece of toast in my hand. My special wheatless bread toast. On the table, the bowl of tuna salad, the lettuce, my glass of sparkling water. One-fifteen, I'm listening to Hank's voice on my voicemail.

He'd called when he knew I'd be in yoga.

Still, I was surprised. *Dear Heart* and *I promise.* Fucking Hank Christian, man. Really, it was great to hear his voice again.

Since the *ta da!* moment last April when he stepped out from behind Ruth's dining room door – for about a month after that, when he got back to Florida, Hank had called me a bunch of times. But I didn't call him back. The truth is, I can fold up my cards, too, and disappear. It's survival, man.

So that day of the voice message, after hearing Hank's voice, I get to thinking. Since Ruth and I'd finished up the edits, for several months now, we hadn't talked at all. And Hank and I weren't talking. Everything had got so confused. And I think what the fuck. Really, things didn't seem they could get much worse. All that weird silence. I was so far away from Hank, and it was pretty clear I wasn't going to get any of Hank without Ruth, so I figured it was time I held up a white flag. I mean the shit was piling up in me.

It's almost Ruth's birthday, so I call Ruth up and ask her out to lunch.

"Out to lunch?!" Ruth says. "Ben, are you all right?"

Ruth knows me pretty well, too. Lunch to me is a nightmare. Lunch is about bread and bread is about wheat. Or lunch is about salad and salad is about not enough protein. Lunch for me is either the expensive fish dish at the bottom of the menu, or it's some kind of fucking grilled chicken breast. And fuck me, if I never eat another fucking grilled chicken breast again, I'll be just fine.

"For your birthday," I say. "Let's go down the street to your favorite restaurant."

THAT NEXT WEDNESDAY, Ruth and I meet in the restaurant just three blocks from me. Ruth's favorite restaurant where the following September Ruth and Hank will get married and I won't be invited to the wedding.

Ruth is late. She breezes in the restaurant with her sunglasses on in an off-white summer dress. As she walks toward me through the tables, the sun's behind her. I can see the silhouette of her naked legs. Her sandals have a low heel and no strap on the back. The sandals snap against the bottom of her feet. She's carrying a shopping bag from Nordstrom's.

But the most amazing thing. Ruth has done something to her hair. Her hair and all of its unruly thick curls is totally straight. It hangs down almost to the middle of her back. The incredible weight of it, the shine. The blonde highlights are gone and the red of her hair is almost copper. She sets the Nordstrom's bag down, tucks her dress in, and sits down on the chair across the table. She takes off her sunglasses, folds them, and puts them in a case, and puts the case in her purse, one of those new huge designer leather purses, puke green.

Really, I don't think I've ever seen Ruth look so beautiful. For a moment I think she's had some face work done. Then I realize she's so thin, the shape of her face has changed. She now has major cheekbones. And there's something new about her makeup, around her eyes. Mascara, eyeliner, dyed eyelashes, I can't figure. I'm looking close but can't look too close. Ruth is watching me look at her. Her too-blue eyes jump out at me like never before.

Ruth pulls her chair closer to the table. Then she does what I've seen so many beautiful women do. She moves her head, lifting her chin, so her mass of copper hair swings to behind her shoulder. She sits up, lifts her chest, her new Wonderbra, checks the bra strap and the scooped neckline of her dress with her fingers. She brings both hands up to her forehead, and with her fingers along her hairline, pulls her new straight hair behind her ears. Gold hooped earrings. Her long thin white arms. On her right wrist an expandable gold bracelet with dangly gold charms.

Hank always did love his women, gold and silver on their arms.

Gorgeous. Ruth is fucking gorgeous. But there's something, I don't know, something so *done* about her. A way a lot of women were beginning to look those days. Polished, finished. Sleek. Ready to get down to business.

The waiter comes to the table, stocky, clean-shaven, blonde. He's shiny, too, like Ruth. Straight white teeth, gay. He doesn't look at me. He's staring at Ruth's hair. He says *good afternoon,* puts the water glasses down, gives us each a menu, walks off.

Ruth pays no attention to him. Since she's sat down, her too-blue eyes, that new thing about her eyes, that gaze right into me.

"Happy Birthday," I say.

What Ruth says next, how she says it, is a challenge. Right off, a fuck you Ben Grunewald.

"I just read my horoscope," Ruth says. "According to what it says about being born on this day, a year from now you won't even recognize me."

It takes my breath away, really, her power. *I'm beautiful and young and healthy and you aren't. Daddy loves me more than you.*

I almost throw my glass of water in her face. But I take a breath. Really, if we could just get to the bottom of all this. If we could start talking about what was really going on, maybe there would be a chance.

I take the chance. The only way I know how. I start talking about my feelings. After I broke it off with Ruth, all those hundreds of hours I sat and listened to her, how she was hurt, how she wasn't good enough, what could she do to change so that I would love her. I figured now it was my turn to talk, Ruth's turn to listen.

The Catholic boy with a big apology, my voice is high at first, but then I settle in. I'm just at the part where I'm telling Ruth how left out I feel, just about to mention the last time Hank was in Portland, the whole week he was here and how I didn't even know about it, when Ruth, the slender arm with the expandable gold bracelet with dangly gold charms, waves her hand and that arm and the dangly gold in between us, eye level. It's a gesture the way a mother shuts up her child or the principal when she catches you daydreaming, or when your sister lorded it over you that she was the only thing that stood between you and your crazy mother and your fucked up father.

It's right then I realize Ruth and I are sitting only one table away from where we sat the night in that very same restaurant, how long ago was it now, that Buster Bangs came in high and kissed me. And I'd left with him, leaving Ruth alone in front of everybody.

"For Chrissakes, Ben," Ruth says, "let's be sensible."

And with that, all those hundreds of hours of Ruth talking my ear off, the payback I think I deserve, all goes down the drain. This time, I'm the fool. And I fucking hate it. I look for the flush of scarlet up her neck, but there is no flush of scarlet. When I throw my menu down, I knock my water glass over. I don't stop to see the damage I've done.

As Big Ben walks out the door, he's got only one thing to say to Ruth. Well, two.

"Fuck you, Ruth."

"*And* your fucking hair."

HANK FLIES INTO town that night. After the lovely birthday lunch with Ruth, I don't expect to see him. But that night I get a call. It's from Ruth. But I don't want to talk to Ruth and I ask for Hank and Ruth tells me Hank's too angry to talk. I tell Ruth to tell Hank I'm tired of talking to him through his beautiful corporate assistant and if he don't want to talk to me personally then he ain't going to talk to me at all. Hank tells Ruth that I should get my fucking ass over there to Ruth's fucking house. I tell Ruth to tell Hank to get fucked and he's got to haul his sorry fucking ass over to my house if he wants to talk so bad.

Four days later we meet at the restaurant three blocks down from me. The restaurant where in three months Hank and Ruth will get married and I won't be invited to the wedding. You know, *that* fucking restaurant. I know. I know. Don't ask me why I kept going back to that damn place.

Look at us, the three of us, two of us with dark sunglasses on, sitting in a triangle around a square table covered in white butcher paper. Hank's got a Florida tan and Ruth and I are frog-belly white. It's early and we're the only people in the restaurant. This time it's the same *exact* spot in the restaurant where Billy Bangs kissed me, where Hank and Ruth and me sit.

Somehow or another, it's got into Hank's head that Ruth and I are still in love and we're having an affair behind his back and we're hiding the truth from him. How the hell he came to that is beyond me, so I ask him.

"How did you come to that fucking conclusion?"

As soon as those words are out of my mouth, I realize it's the first time I've ever talked to Hank that way. Challenging him. With anger in my voice.

He's talked to *me* that way. That day in Pennsylvania with the flowers and the cop when I stepped between him and Olga. And that night after the Spike when Hank threw up in the street. All of a sudden, that night how Hank turned into a smoldering piece of rage I didn't know how the fuck to deal with. Wasn't until I figured out he was scaring me like my father scared me, that I kept on talking to him. And after that night he disappeared for months.

The three of us, a triangle at a square table, butcher paper. Hank and Ruth and me, four days after Ruth's birthday, Hank tanned, Ruth and me frog bellies, sitting right there in *that* fucking place, the restaurant, *that* fucking restaurant.

As soon as those words come out of my mouth, Hank's face. Like he can erase any feeling from it, his eyes go cold and far away and all of a sudden he's a big slab of marble staring you down. Zeus is pissed and something big is going to blow. God the Father's going to kick some ass. The Pennsylvania working class straight guy, the brother who hunts down his sister and beats up her boyfriend and hauls his sis back to mom. All that macho Italian Maroni shit. A nuclear blast coming off Hank and he's not moving a muscle.

There's no breath. All those big mean men I've been afraid of and now Hank's one of them. All I want to do is run.

Frank's First Call Boiler and Repair. My white Key West shrimper boots. There was no going back. Nobody is ever going to scare me like that again.

My voice is clear and clean and smooth.

"Hank," I say, "Hank, look at me."

But Hank won't do it. He's afraid, too, of the Raging Bull going on in him.

"I'm the guy who's in your heart, remember?" I say. "Gruney. And I'd never lie to you. And Ruth won't either."

Hank slams his fist down hard on the table. Ruth jumps out of her skin. I jump too, but fuck it.

"Then why are you guys fighting with each other the way you are?" Hank says. "Only people still in love fight with each other like that."

The chef, a heavyset guy with pit stains, pushes open the swinging door of the kitchen.

I look over at Ruth. Ruth looks back at me. Believe me, between us there ain't no hidden love nowhere. And, if I may speak, once, for both Ruth and me, if we could have comprehended all the levels and nuances of shit that was going on between us, we both would've stepped forward and spoke the truth out loud to Hank, to the whole fucking world to hear. But we didn't know.

You know that Jeske thing. We knew but we just couldn't bear that we were capable of such darkness.

"I'm not in love with Ruth," I say.

"I'm not in love with Ben," Ruth says.

"Then what the fuck is going on with you two?" Hank says.

Hank's good eye is bloodshot, weary, full of fury. His glass eye rolls out a bit, staring out at nothing.

Ruth lifts her chin, turns her head, her mass of straight copper hair swings to behind her shoulder. She reaches over, puts her hand on Hank's arm, rubs his arm.

"We both love you," Ruth says.

When I say it, there's got to be a touch, but it's definitely got to be a guy touch. Hank's pissed and I have to be careful. I make my hand into a fist, not hard, just close my fingers in, pull my thumb around. I take my not-hard clenched fist and pop Hank one, a blow of love, right in the middle of his chest.

"*Porca Miseria*," I say.

A COUPLE DAYS later, ten o'clock at night, my phone rings. It's Hank and he wants me to come pick up him up.

"Maupassant," Hank says. "The cat hair is driving me nuts. Can I spend the night with you?"

I fill my pocket with Xanax, get in my Volkswagen, drive one more time across town. When I get to Ruth's house, Hank is sitting on the front steps. The sky is clear and it's a warm night for June. Hank's wearing a white T-shirt and cutoffs, white socks and white tennis shoes. New shiny white tennis shoes that glow in the dark. Pretty much the same thing he wore that first night in Manhattan when we started arguing at Night Birds about who should walk through the door first.

As ever, my Volkswagen is making a lot of racket. When I turn the corner, the horn honks but Hank just sits there on the cement steps holding his head in his hands. The headlight shine on the top of his head. Hank's thinning hair. Purple.

I shut the car off, pull up the emergency brake, and get out of the car. The horn's still honking, then I kick the fender.

That's when I hear it, inside the house. Dishes breaking, big thuds, crashes, all sorts of hell breaking loose.

Hank looks up his black eyes at me. In the night his right eye is a dark star.

"Hey, Gruney," Hank says.

Inside the house it sounds like the roof's caving in.

"What's going on?" I say.

Hank, that half-smile of his. Part bewildered, part amused. The expression on his face the same as the photo on the back of his book.

"It's Ruth," Hank says. "As soon as I called you, she started going apeshit."

"She all right?"

"What am I supposed to do?" Hank says. "That fucking cat, man."

Just then the lamp on Ruth's nightstand goes sailing through her bedroom window. Loud breaking glass. The lamp and the lampshade land on the ground and roll out into the front yard.

"What the fuck, Gruney!" Hank says. "I couldn't breathe."

As soon as we get to my house, Hank says he ain't feeling so good. That's Hank's way of telling me he doesn't want to talk. So I make up the couch for him and as soon as Hank hits that couch he's asleep.

In my bedroom, I lie on my bed listening to Hank Christian snore. Ruth's broken bedroom window and her broken lamp, and the lamp shade, man. Rolling out into the front yard like that. I start laughing and can't stop. Really really laughing. That kind of laughing where you look down at your belly because it's jumping around without you doing anything. I have to put the pillow over my face to keep from waking up Hank.

Ruth Dearden.

You've come a long way, baby.

That next morning at breakfast, Hank and I are sitting at the kitchen table. The batch of eggs I've scrambled up are sitting in a bowl next to Hank. Hank's on his second cup of coffee when he starts to talk.

"I guess I'll just never figure women out," Hank says.

My special bread toast pops up out of the toaster. One for Hank, one for me. I start buttering.

"I mean it's just for one night," Hank says. "Why she have to go get all bent out of shape?"

I ain't saying *nothing*. I stack Hank's piece of bread on top of my piece of bread, slice them on the diagonal.

"Seriously, Gruney," Hank says, "I'm asking. Why do women act that way?"

Straight men are from Mars, man.

I look into Hank's black eyes. Even with his one good eye, Hank can't see worth shit.

"Pass the eggs," I say.

PASS THE EGGS. The message I saved on my voicemail for years and years.

That message only existed because of a letter I wrote to Hank. When Hank was back in Florida. Not the *Got to go pal* letter. A long, long letter I wrote before the *Got to go pal* letter, explaining to Hank something he'd asked me once. About the *thing* Ruth and I'd had.

In that letter, I told Hank the whole long story, every sordid detail of Ruth and me, from that first night she was dancing alone in the moonlight 'til Buster Bangs kissed me in the restaurant and I walked out on her. Didn't leave a thing out. Nothing. Even the way we did, or didn't, have sex.

It was a last-ditch attempt. To make sure Hank didn't have just one version of Ruth and me.

For years, so many times, when I picked up my phone, and the automated voice of the woman on the line would tell me I had too many saved messages, I'd have to go through each saved message and listen to it and then decide if I was going to keep holding on or just let go. I mean how else do you remember your life? Every time I'd come to Hank's message, I got to listen to Hank, beloved Hank Christian, once again, even after he was dead, his voice on that day right after he'd got my long letter. Funny and a little weirded out by all the detail. Still full of love.

"I don't know," Hank's voice says. "I sure don't have the answer."

Then it's Hank's laugh, the way it rises up in him, shakes him all around.

"As a wise man once told me," Hank's voice says, "when I asked him how to figure out women. This is what he told me: *pass the eggs*."

Hank Christian. That laugh of his, man. I'll never forget it.

AND NOW ONE more last event in the long tragic story, the maze of three, of Hank and Ruth and me.

An afternoon, early October. For some damn reason or another, Hank and Ruth are supposed to be at my house at one o'clock. I think it was a Sunday and the three of us were going to go to the movies. I'm pretty sure it was the movies. I didn't go many other places besides the movies, and toward the end there, Hank and Ruth and I, we never did things together, except once in a while go to the movies. Hank and I love movies.

Wherever the hell we're going, they're late. Hank and Ruth that morning had gone on a hike and with Ruth, even with her new hair and her new *her*, on a hike you just never could tell. She'd get lost in the beauty of a fucking flower or the wind on her face or whatever and they'd be gone all day.

Two hours late. *Nothing* pisses me off more than having to wait. Especially for those two. And that summer, by the end of July, toward the end there, the tension, man. You never could tell, any little thing could set any one of us off. Usually me.

At three o'clock, I get in my Volkswagen and figure what the fuck I'll just drive for a while until the cops pick me up. Just as I pull out onto Southeast 30th, in my rearview I see Ruth's silver Honda Civic pull up to my back door on Morrison Street. I pull over, shut my car off. Watch in my rearview as Hank runs to the back door of my house and knocks. And knocks and knocks. Even as far away as I am, looking through a mirror, I can tell. Hank's upset.

Hank walks back to the car, gets in. Ruth drives off. I follow them. At 39th Avenue, rain starts pouring down in buckets. My fucking windshield wipers. But nothing's going to stop me. As loud as my car is, they have no clue I'm behind them. Maybe it's the hellacious downpour of rain. When Ruth parks in front of her house, both Hank and Ruth stay in the car. I park right behind them. I can see Ruth lean over and embrace Hank. Later on, I'll find out Hank's crying because he thinks for sure this time, he's lost my friendship.

A flat tire. Up on Powell Butte, Ruth had a flat tire and even though a year from now I'll supposedly never be able to recognize her, today she's still fucking Ruth. No spare.

I open the door to the Honda Civic on Ruth's side. Ruth quick turns around and Hank looks over. I squat down square, framed in the doorway, so the both of them can see all of me. Two sets of dark glasses stare back at me. They're both in the same outfit. Wilderness Backpackers. I pull my shoulders back, my arms down, make my hands, fists. I'm already soaked to the skin.

"Who wants to go the first round," I say, "the fucking Amazon or the fucking Maroni."

Porca Miseria. We're all screaming and yelling, cussing, slamming doors, running around from car to car. Fucking rain, man, is pouring down on us. We all end up on Ruth's front yard. Squishy grass. Hank pulls his shirt off and so I do too and we square off, dukes up. Ruth's running around Hank and me, pounding on us, yelling at us to stop. Her long copper hair is frizzing up and her dark glasses are hanging off one ear. She's yelling, but we're all yelling, and with my ringing ears I can't hear a fucking thing.

That moment squared off, the macho moment that has always freaked me out. Now this time I'm squaring off, it's with Hank. It's fight or flight, and I've promised myself I'd never again flight.

Such a long sad moment standing with my fists up in the rain. I don't know what to do. My head's telling me to stop, but something about Hank's dark glasses, his Beat Generation cool dark glasses, and that he's wearing them, even in a fistfight in the fucking rain, pisses me off.

Hank and I are circling circling. Finally, I can't stand it no more. I throw a punch, but just as I'm throwing the punch, I think of Hank's eye, so mid-swing I change my mind and aim low. Hank jumps back and I go sailing and land on my back on the wet grass under a shrub.

The grass is so wet it's mud. Can't keep my eyes open for the rain. I jump up fast and run at Hank. Hit him hard.

Hank and I, we're front to front.

New red potatoes in a shovelful of earth. Hank's cool dude fucking glasses go flying. We're stumbling around, slipping in the wet grass, we're smacking each other on the back. We fall together, a thud of air out of the both of us, then Hank and I are rolling around in the mud. I call him a *fat fuck*. He calls me a *crazy asshole*. Ruth is yelling *stupid fucking men*.

Hank and I have rolled out to the corner of the lawn, just at the cement embankment. If one of us falls over, we'll fall almost six feet. About that time, suddenly Ruth's right there, and while she's trying to pull us apart, her big hiking boot steps on my right hand. Grinds my fingers into the concrete. I'm yelling so loud Hank gets up.

Ruth kneels down over me, her knees in the mud. One of the dark lenses is busted out of her glasses. That one too-blue eye. Hank's looking over her shoulder. Ruth's frizzy hair, Hank's thin purple hairs sticking up. A bad hair day for the both of them. Don't ask me what I looked like. Then I don't know how it happens, but as Ruth is helping me up, she elbows Hank in the mouth. Instant blood mixed with rain flowing down Hank's chin. Fuck. The Keystone Cops, man. We all end up on Ruth's front yard in a heap. Hank on one side of me, Ruth on the other. On top. Me on the bottom.

Hank and Ruth and me.

The three of us.

Crying too hard, big sobs and snot.

In the front yard in the mud in the rain.

WISH I COULD say Hank and Ruth and me cried so hard we started to laugh.

That our tears miraculously turned into rain.

Fucking wishes, man, regret.

October 12, 2000. *Got to go pal*. All day I sit with that letter. Silver morning light, late afternoon sun, the Portland sky evening blue, the street light on the sugar maple making the leaves glow fiery red and yellow. Wondering if I should make it sound so final and forever, or fuck it, just take the risk and say something more, something ridiculous at such a ridiculous time to say it: if I should tell Hank to stop using that Just for Men hair color, because the light through his hair made his thin hair look purple.

When you say goodbye to someone you love, maybe if you say something crazy, something true, maybe he won't stop loving you.

I end up not giving Hank the hair tip. How many times have I regretted it, thought I should've gone for it, said the hair thing right after *Got to go pal*. Maybe it would've changed the way things turned out.

If nothing else, it would have made him laugh.

Then those last words on the page, man, that I wrote in at the last moment.

That old litany in this strange new place. How it made my heart stop.

Got to go pal.

I can hurt you, and because I know I can, I will.

22.
The more loving one

JUNE 19, 2008. THE STUMPTOWN COFFEE SHOP ON BEL-
mont. A sunny day in Portlandia and people are sitting outside
on the chairs along the painted red brick wall in the sun. Coffee
and dreadlocks and tattoos and piercings and bicycles and dogs.
There are no chairs left outside, so I sit down on the curb with
my peppermint tea. Just like in the olden days in Manhattan in
front of One Fifth Avenue. The sun on the curb is warm on my
ass. It's taken me seven years to sit in the sun like this again.

The tea is very hot. I try for a slurp but even the cup is too
hot to hold. That's what I'm doing, setting my cup on the curb.
When somebody sits down next to me. Close, on my left. Death
comes from the left. The sun's in my eyes and I have to put my
hand over my eyes. He's a student of mine, Dab.

"Sorry to hear about your friend," Dab says.

Dab's a guy a little younger than me. Long silver gray hair.
Lives in his SUV with his cat, Eggsy. AA's what brought Dab to my
writing class.

"My friend?"

Dab knows right off he's stepped in shit. He pushes his John
Lennon glasses up onto his nose, looks at the gutter, like there's
something important to look at in the gutter, then he raises his
eyes up. Dark eyes but not black like Hank's.

Dab knows somebody who knows somebody who knows
Ruth. He puts his hand on my shoulder.

"Yesterday," Dab says, "Hank Christian died of liver cancer."

THE NIGHT BEFORE I get on the airplane, I visit Tony Escobar in the Pioneer Cemetery. It's raining and I'm in my raincoat and waterproof pants, lying on my grave talking away. Tony's always been a good listener. That night, he's wearing a flight captain's uniform and when he speaks it sounds like he's talking through a microphone.

Just have the huevos rancheros *at Café Orlin*, he says, *and you'll be fine*.

Where Hank is buried, I'll probably never know.

There's only one choice. Big Ben and I agree.

Manhattan.

FOURTEEN YEARS SINCE I've been on an airplane. And I'm traveling alone. Since 9/11, just the words *security check* can start a cold sweat. Dizziness. The ringing in my right ear. Even after all these years, HIV is still a sure ticket you're going to shit spray in public. The humiliation, man. Plus I still have to eat special food at regular intervals. And airplane food isn't even airplane food anymore. It's a tiny bag of pretzels and Coke.

So I have to pack my breakfast, my lunch, my afternoon sardine snack, and just in case, a couple of pieces of chicken for dinner and some coleslaw. And all that food has to fit into a container that fits under the seat in front of me.

Just getting up early in the morning, after all the drugs I've taken the night before to get me to sleep, and having the presence of mind to gather all my shit together and walk out the door and then get into a cab that will take me to the airport, that will lead me to the security check, what you can have in your carry-on bag, what you can't, then to the right gate. All those announcements over the intercom and I can't hear anymore. I need my glasses too. Then my other glasses to read the monitors. Then I'm afraid I'm going to lose my glasses. Where is my wallet, where is my ticket. Where are my glasses. I'm cramped into a flying tin can packed in with hundreds people jammed in together thousands of miles above the earth in a middle seat, airplane air for six-

and-a-half hours, then get off the plane. The airport's too bright
and at baggage claim I try and find my bag. I've put a red ribbon
on my black bag, but so has everybody else. Not just my right
ear, both ears totally fucked up. Where is my wallet, where is my
baggage claim, where are my glasses. Then get a cab and drive
the nighttime collision course into Manhattan, try and act like I
can hear what the Afghan cabby is saying to me, then try and
find my glasses so I can see my wallet and figure out a twenty percent tip. Then into the hotel, the reservations for the hotel.
Where is my wallet, where are my glasses, where is the reservation for the hotel, where is the credit card. The host is Chinese
and she may as well be speaking Chinese because my ears are
still over Kansas someplace. And then I got to face the elevator.

THE COOPER SQUARE Hotel. On the corner of Fifth and Bowery.
Where the old wood Sinclair station used to stand. I slide the
card into the lock of Room 19-3. Thank God the green light goes
off and I'm opening the door and then the door is closing behind
me and I lean up against the door. Drop my bags. Take deep
breaths. Thank Big Ben for his big decision. Thank Little Ben for
getting my ass here.

The room is big, floor to ceiling windows, white curtains.
Heavy gray shades for the morning sun. It's sweltering outside,
but inside it's cool. Almost chilly. But it's the nineteenth floor
and none of the windows open. Jet lag, man, and I'm dizzy. The
room is gray and taupe, spotlessly clean. The queen bed is firm,
a white duvet and big white pillows you can fluff up. The room is
small, but this is Manhattan and for four hundred and thirty
dollars a night, what do you expect.

The bathroom is black and white with designer amenities.
Next to the sink, I lay out my meds – they take up almost the
whole white marble counter.

On the floor in front of the big window facing east, on a
double napkin, I spread out my pieces of chicken, fried in
Portlandia. I have no idea if it's time I should eat. I'm not hungry

but to be safe I'd better eat, so I eat. And better to start out in a new place with food that I know. Sitting cross-legged on the floor, crumbs of fried chicken fall onto the perfect silver-gray carpet. The coleslaw is limp and watery. I forgot the fork and my fingers get all greasy. The hand towel in the bathroom is so white and clean I decide not to use it.

After a long, very hot shower, the white flannel bathrobe feels good on my body. I pull the chair in front of the big window facing east. Below me, the city lights, what an incredible sight. Really, I have to take a breath. A landscape like no other. Out of the black tar roofs of the red brick tenements, strange sleek towers, like the one I'm sitting in, rise up and out, shiny bright, nouveau riche. Looks like spaceships that have landed.

East Fifth below me, the mercury vapor street lights. Right *there*, just two tenements to the east, the roof of my old home. And the tops of all the buildings I was the super for. *Up on the roof.* Only place to get away and get out and get some air.

Midnight on a Friday night in Manhattan. It's nine o'clock to me. I put on my baggy striped bermudas, my blue chambray shirt, roll the sleeves up to the elbow. Sal's old red ballcap from Atlanta, Idaho. White cotton socks. New tennis shoes, the same brand Hank always wore, only black. I have to slide in the foam rubber sole supports. Then it's my knee brace.

My hand's around the doorknob. The door you got to walk through. The damn door. The portal. After the portal opens, after it closes, everything is different. My Xanax is in my left pocket. The plastic card that is the key to Room 19-3 in my right. My reading glasses, my wallet. And one more thing, a wad of toilet paper.

The step I must take. Where I must go. Where that is. What it looks like. How to get there exactly. I'm not sure. All I know what to do is to walk, and keep on walking.

IN THE HALLWAY, under my new tennis shoes, the carpet is a waterbed. Strange slantings and tilts of the hallway walls. The elevator doors slide open and deep in my ears, the place that

makes balance, the fucking hula hoop. Propinquity. I'm in a
small box with Muzak that hauls you down by a bunch of cables.
Nineteen floors, man.

Through the lobby, over the hardwood and slate floors,
swinging out the big glass doors, I'm out in it. Manhattan. The
humidity and the heat. Instantly, my body remembers my old
home. The Lower East Side. My new black tennis shoes are standing on the sidewalk and the street right in front of me is Third
Avenue. The Bowery.

Freakin' wild the way the city feels on a summer Friday
night. The deep breath I take is a sigh, really. East coast heat,
man, the humidity, and Manhattan's own version of it. My skin is
immediately oily and slick. I take a couple steps and turn the
corner.

All those thousand days and nights I swept this stretch of
concrete. In the winter, shoveled snow. Summer, I sprayed it
all down with a rubber hose. The way a blind man knows braille,
I knew every crack and every bump of that sidewalk.

Before I know it, my body's standing in that hallowed place.
My old home. 211 East Fifth Street. In front of that old smooth
cast iron stoop Hank and I used to sit on. But the damndest thing.
The stoop isn't cast iron anymore.

Look at me. Sixty years old, dizzy, sweating my ass off, a
length of toilet paper folded in my back pocket, just in case.
Standing there as if maybe if I stand in front of them steps long
enough, something will happen and time will go back and the
stoop will change. But no matter how hard I try, there's no curving
balustrades, shiny rubbed smooth steps, no cast iron newel
caps. Just painted shiny red steel with diamond tread covering.

There's a guy sitting on the shiny red steel stoop, smoking
a cigarette. Gnarly brown hair. A V-neck T-shirt with a pen
clipped in the V. I walk up the stairs, sit on the shiny red diamond
tread one step down from him, start talking. Behind his greasy
glasses, his eyes are blue. Fuck-you blue. He takes a drag, blows
cigarette smoke into my face. I'm just another crazy to him, but

that doesn't stop me. I tell him about the night Hank on those steps told me about his old girlfriend Mythrixis. How it was over between them. How I had to turn and look up at Hank, the porch light right there so I had to put my hand up to shield my eyes. The song that was playing on the boombox. *Every time you go away, you take a piece of me with you.* Hank's black eyes. They were kind of misty, his eyes, as if the whole Mythryxis thing was a whole lot tougher than he'd ever let on.

It's all sad, Gruney. If we let ourselves know how sad it really is, there wouldn't be anything left of us.

THE GUY ON the stoop walks off New York Drop Dead Fuck You. I'm walking too. It isn't long before I know it. A ghost in this place. That's what I am. Or I'm real and Manhattan is a dream.

Fish Bar. When I open Fish Bar's stained wood door and go to step inside, my body just won't let me go in. Too crowded. Barely room to walk in there. But maybe inside, that's the place where I must go. To find what I need to find, so I can feel what I must feel. Grief and panic, man. My body has never known the difference.

I press my face against the window, making my eyes see everything. On the jukebox, "Soul Makossa" is playing. At *my* spot at the bar, in the corner next to the wall, on the same stool my ass used to sit in drinking dirty Bombay martinis up, there's a young man sitting there alone drinking from an up glass. Fourteen years ago, he could be me. Fourteen years ago, in the bathroom on the right, on the aqua blue wall, the piece of graffiti that used to be just above the toilet: *AIDS Schmaids – just shoot that cum all over me.*

Walking. Second Avenue is still Second Avenue, I mean most of the buildings are the same. But it's different. Love Saves the Day is gone. The Greek diner on the corner of Second and Fifth – turkey sandwiches on Thanksgiving Day, gone. Optimo Cigars, gone. Le Culot. Café 113, gone.

Night Birds, *you go first, no, you go* — gone gone gone.

Schacht's Delicatessen, man.

An hallucination of bright fluorescence. The smell of old wood, weird cheese, and chicken soup. Hum of refrigeration. At the back aisle cooler, Hank opens the cooler door and all that cold air comes rushing out. Hank swings the door back and forth making a breeze. It's a miracle night, all right, and the miracle is taking in the whole world.

Schacht's is fucking gone.

WALKING. TOMPKINS SQUARE Park. Now that place is a *trip*. All duded up. You wouldn't even know it was the same place. Respectable manicured lawns, authentic lighting, wrought iron fences and shit – at one o'clock in the morning jogging yuppies talking on their cell phones. Man, we used to call this park *Dog Shit Park*.

On the corner of Seventh and A, it takes me a while to figure, but after careful consideration I'm sure it's in the exact same spot. The skinhead dude with the red, white, and blue mohawk is standing up, his back to me and Hank, waving his arms. He's yelling, trying to get the attention of his twenty skinhead cowboy dudes. That loud loud music.

You need to watch out who you're calling a Republican.

That night, the night I'm a ghost, not a mohawk in sight. Pyramid Club's open, though. Recently made into a *Drag Landmark*. Now there's progress for you.

The Lower East Side. Everywhere I look, everyone seems rich, young. I mean, not just because I'm not rich and not young. When I lived here, a stoned white teenage girl in low-slung tight pants and ass crack just would've made it across the street. It's safer all right. But safe from what.

HOUR AFTER HOUR, that night, early into the morning, I'm walking. Back and forth on every street from Tenth to Houston, between Third Avenue and Avenue C. Same way Hank and I walked that night, walking side by side, back and forth up and down, under a miracle umbrella, through the Lower East Side. When things have gone bad, when things have gone good, when things have dumped shit on your head, when you're in the stars, when you're fucked up, when it's too hot, when your ass is freezing, when you're old and sick and your lungs are sore, when you're heart's beating too fast, when your ears are some kind of fire alarm, when you're sweating like a pig, when your knee hurts, just walk. Keep on walking.

Maybe now that Hank is dead, I don't have to go through Ruth to get to him.

ON EAST FIRST Street, Dixon Place, the whole damn block is gone. I just stand and stand. Maybe a new muscle will develop in me, or my whole body will become a new muscle with super computer powers that if you just hit *save* I can soak in everything, how things smell, the muggy air against my skin, the sweat running down the inside of my arms. Store every detail in one forever accessible file that never changes.

The dark heat of the night, the six-story walkups, every window open. I stop in a bright Korean market, buy a fucking bottle of water for three dollars. It's the first time I've thought of my body. Me, Mr. Hypersensitive about my body. But I'm a ghost. A ghost haunted by a dream. As if I'm on acid, this night, even at three a.m., in a part of the world that fourteen years ago was only night and dark, the world is bright and loud and full.

Walking. My lungs feel like when I used to smoke. My body, one big crotch rot. On the stoops, swarms of pierced and tattooed kids. Every now and then a big muscle guy in a stretched-out T-shirt, standing in front of a velvet rope. Some black dude loud inside rapping away *mother fucker mother fucker*.

Walking. At 39 East Seventh Street, its shit flood basement, on the bottom step, where I left my white Key West shrimper boots, the entire building is gone. The mimosa tree, gone.

Walking. Every once in a while, a restaurant with gold stars and black limos parked out front. On top of the street smell –

exhaust and garbage, sweaty bodies – the thick smell of *marihoo-chi*. And a new smell. Never a part of my New York. The designer smell of money.

The narrow streets crowded with cars, honking taxis, loud hip-hop music I'll never know. The later the night gets, the earlier the morning, the more it's humid. I'm out of breath. My chambray shirt, my baggy striped bermudas, my underwear, my ballcap, even my new black tennis shoes are soaking wet.

I'll buy you a soda.

A BLISTER ON my right heel. My knees. My hips. But where I must go I haven't found it yet.

On the cab ride across town, to the West Side Highway, the cab driver is from India. Hindu. On the dashboard, the incense, the plastic flowers around a statue of Ganesha. I ask him if he knows the Spike.

"On Eleventh Avenue," I say. "Somewhere in the Twenties. Next to the river."

Napalm. Behind us, the bar back with its bottles, glowing green, glowing blue, clear, amber, glowing Wild Turkey dark brown. From underneath the bar, Judy lights from down low so the bartenders can see. In front of us, three men deep. Beyond, the bar is dark. Smoky dark. A foggy night, an ocean of men, dark waves. The tall guy with his balls thumbtacked to the bar.

In front of all of Homosexual Heaven I tell Hank about getting fucked in the ass. Hank, that fucking guy, man. I don't see Hank for over three months. Whenever he wanted to, that mother-fucker could totally disappear.

"You mean the Life Saver Lofts?" the cab driver says. "In West Chelsea?"

When the cab driver drives past the Spike, out the window of the cab, out of the old Plutonian darkness, the napalm cloud opens. From out of the bones of the building that used to be the Spike, a strange new sleek tower has risen up and out, shiny bright. Another spaceship that's set its ass smack down on my history. Aliens from the spaceships, man. The Life Saver Lofts. Twelve million dollars for the penthouse apartment.

You know all those crazy fuckers who used to walk down the streets talking to themselves? Now they have cell phones.

THE CAB RIDE up to Columbia, 116th and Broadway. If I can stand in that doorway of the classroom where Jeske taught, the place where I first really looked at Hank, Saint Hank Christian, Guardian of the Portal, maybe I can finally find it, feel it.

Hank Christian is dead.

But the iron gates are locked. Of course they'd be locked. But still I stand at the gate, my hands around the wrought iron. Dodge Hall, the corner of it, just right there. I'm shaking the gate, cussing. I guess I'm screaming too. The cabbie thinks he's got a real crazy and starts honking and yelling in Hindi. A lot of really strange fast words and every other word is fuck.

DRIVING FAST IN the dark. My hand's in the plastic handle above the window. I'm hanging on. For dear life. Bright lights flash by. The city that never sleeps. The night sky is no longer black. Light, just barely. *Entre loup et chien.*

Columbus Circle. Wednesday nights, after teaching at the West Side Y, that goddamned burger joint and Silvio. Cheeseburgers and all that hope. In that booth where Hank and I dreamed our writer dreams, another strange sleek tower. A gigantic glass and steel spaceship. The ass on my history on this corner is concave. Bloomberg. Aliens, man. Billionaire aliens.

"SAINT PATRICK'S CATHEDRAL," I say.

The cabbie rips a quick left around Christopher Columbus. He hardly lets up on the gas. Four in the morning, we're the only yellow Plymouth screeching through. Destiny, fate, fucking fortune, the way the earth is spinning spins the cab. Just me and a Hindu man. I'm in the back seat, sweat soaked and smashed against the back door, hanging onto a plastic handle. On the dashboard, incense, pink and white plastic flowers, his beloved elephant god. It ain't long and we're driving down the most expensive street in the world. St. Patrick's smack in the middle of it.

Hell is your Virgin Mother got inside you. The thing you dreaded most, the fucking worst way to fuck up, you fucked up. You got fucked in the ass and you were banished from the world of men.

The man who doesn't know he's a man, is hiding from men because he's afraid of men, because men are his father who he hates, and all he knows, what's left to do, is weep in the dark as an infant weeps.

The weeping and the gnashing of teeth. The epidemic of fear, the purple sores, the wasting, the dementia. All of heaven pointing at you, laughing.

God's special little bitch.

AIDS.

And yet I am still alive.

Really alive. I mean look at me. I'm sixty years old and it's four in the morning and I've been HIV positive for over twenty-two years. Hope. The worst thing isn't that you can't find it. It's that you'll stop. And I'm roaring down Broadway in a cab in Manhattan, the hot wind through the open window blowing against my arm, my face, and I am not dead.

When you get close to the vein that's pulsing truth, when you open that vein, you can scrub your soul clean with the blood.

Years ago, in the hospital in Portland, *Mental Health*, the security guard who told you to stay behind the yellow line like all the others. You were nobody special.

No connection to a special intimacy.

It was just me, only me, down there in the dark lobotomy basement on the Avenue of Fear.

With everybody else.

I never thought I'd say it.

Thank God I got AIDS.

Made me like everybody else.

Human.

THE CLOCK ON Cooper Union. 4:55. The acid clarity of the night has turned to speed and even though I'm a ghost my body's shaking. I find my glasses. Pay the cabbie his fare. Tip him extra. Leave a dollar bill on the dashboard for Ganesha, Patron of Letters, Remover of Obstacles.

I'm ready to call it a night. Maybe tomorrow I'll find it, the next day. Room 19-3 and my firm four-hundred-and-thirty-dollar bed waits for me.

But I'm hungry. At a time when I'm not supposed to be hungry. Then when was the last time in Portlandia I was up at two o'clock in the morning?

Café Orlin on St. Mark's Place. That's the ticket. Tony's *huevos rancheros* at Café Orlin.

ON THE CURB in Portlandia, by the sun on the red brick wall of Stumptown Coffee, after the day Dab told me Hank was dead, all the calls I got, the condolences. Lucy, Ruth's good friend called me, and we hadn't really talked since Ruth left, so we were catching up. Then in a moment, Lucy, her voice suddenly soft, in almost a whisper, she said: "You know Ben, Ruth was there for Hank until the very end."

We all have a right to love and the real prayer is that each of us will find it. Hank found it. I hope Ruth did too. And on his deathbed, beloved Hank was in the best of hands. Ruth's hands.

WALKING OUT OF Café Orlin, three steps up to the sidewalk of St. Mark's Place. The *huevos rancheros* were, as Tony promised, delicious.

The sun is rising. Through the smog, a bizarre peach and violet sky. Light that doesn't shine, it glows. The buildings to the south in shadows that are navy blue. The air, almost cool on my skin.

My belly is full and I'm no longer a ghost. My body is right here and my awareness is here and so is my spirit. It's been a long time since the three of them have been altogether at the same time. My thumb is in the no-fear place.

I'm walking.

And my body knows exactly where to go.

#77 ST. MARK'S Place. When I get to that piece of sidewalk, I'm just about to look up, when it hits me. How very perfect that poem is. True the way truth can make you wince, make you cry, bring you to your knees. I'm on my knee, a genuflection, then both knees, then my elbows too. My upper body rolling out repeated bows. Wystan Hugh Auden. His slum apartment *was so cold that the toilet no longer functioned and he had to use the toilet in the liquor store on the corner.*

The first time.

#77 St. Mark's Place. Night Birds. Hank's and my first date. We'd walked all over the Lower East Side. It was early morning like it is now, only twenty-four years ago. I read Hank out loud the line of poetry on the plaque under the second-story window. Hank and I stood there for a long time. Closer than most men would stand, but not touching. I was trying not to cry. But Hank was crying too.

A big old smooch right on the lips, Hank Christian's sweet lips on mine. He walked away and waved without turning around, the same way we'd walked away from the skinhead dude. Just move your legs and walk. Into a brand-new world. It was that easy.

The second time.

A year and a half later. A Sunday morning early, after our night at the Spike, at #77 St. Mark's Place, a proud gay man at the Gates of Homosexual Heaven, I was standing half-dead from exposure to ice and cold before the poem that breaks my heart. Breaks it open. My friend, My "April in Paris" Friend, *what have you done to my heart* Hank, was standing next to me. He'd just asked the second question after the first question, *homosexual?* that follows sooner or later: *do you take it up the ass? And do you like it?* This was right after maybe only an hour before he'd said: *Assholes are feminine. That's why guys say I got your back.*

Most of me wanted to run. But mostly always I ran, then fell, stumbled, tripped, cracked, broke, then tried to get up again, tried to put it back together. That morning, though, that plaque, the line of poetry, I was staring at my homosexual history and all the brave men and women who have gone before.

The third time.

Really, it was third time.

Because it was the last time and because it was after the sweat lodge and after Alturas Bar, the rock rolling down and down over the century and a half, the tiny splash into the deep dark blue-green pool, the sun on the water in the porcelain pans, bye bye Mr. Chocolate Chip Cookies, Hank's Hercules, my Fair Adonis, the wedding ring bed.

Atlanta, Idaho. Where Hank and I were most alive.

May 5, 1989. #77 St. Mark's Place. It was the first time Hank and I had been together since Atlanta. It was my last day in Manhattan and Hank was in town from Florida to get his shit out of storage. We were staring up at the line of poetry Wystan Hugh Auden wrote on the plaque under the second-story window. We'd been standing there for I don't know how long. It was just past noon on a day that was sunny but still cold. Hank was in his gray hooded sweatshirt and Levi's. Still wearing the straw cowboy hat Gary'd given him. His new white tennis shoes. His hair was cut short and his beard shows gray. The Eighties were about over and my head's a buzzcut. Still with a mustache. I was wearing the green coat Gary gave me with Idaho Dairy Association on it. Levi's, my Red Wing boots. Sal's red baseball cap. In fact, I know everything about what we're wearing, everything about how we look, how blue the sky is, the gusts of chilly wind down the street. Because this was the last day ever that Hank will be this Hank and I will be this Ben and we will be together.

It will take us twelve years to see each other again. A Christmas Eve night in Portlandia.

Auden's poem. How very perfect that poem is. True the way truth can make you wince, make you cry, make you proud.

I'd brought an old bike along somebody'd left in one of my basements. Hank said he could use it in Florida. It was one of those stripped-down bikes with ten gears and knobby tires that's good for dodging through traffic. Hank was standing on one side of the bike, me on the other. I gave Hank a quick rundown on the gears and the clutch. How you have to watch the rear brake because it sticks. I let the bike go and it stood alone for a moment, then fell into Hank.

Hank's body, my body came together, front to front. It was a quick embrace with a bicycle between and I wondered why the bicycle was between and we slapped each other on the back. Five seconds tops we touched. And then we parted. A couple of guys, so cavalier. We had no idea the darkness that lay ahead. Hank was moving to Florida. I was leaving for Portland. Like all youth, we couldn't know yet just how far away a person can go. Auden is smiling. Auden is weeping. All of Homosexual Heaven turns away. *How everything turns away from the disaster.*

I went to say it, but Hank said it first:

"Got to go, pal," Hank said.

The way Hank Christian can laugh. He rolled his right pant up to just below the knee. So white and fragile, glass-looking, his calf muscle flexed, pushing down on the bike pedal. Hank crunched the straw cowboy hat down onto his ears, and then he was off on the bike, clowning around like he was going to crash. Halfway down the block he waved without turning around. I waved back. Wasn't long and Hank was just a little dot, a straw cowboy hat, the sun on the brim of it, a gust of wind and he was gone.

Up the stoop, below the second-story window, the plaque and the line of Auden's poem.

If equal affection cannot be, let the more loving one be me.

In front of #77 St. Mark's Place, alone at the gates of Homosexual Heaven that day, May 5, 1985, I cried the way women in
the Mediterranean all in black cry. Cried so hard I had to sit down
right there on the sidewalk. It took me forever, but when I got
myself together, I snuffed up and looked and on the asphalt right
in front of me there were Hank's new white tennis shoes.

And there he was again, Hank Christian, straddling the
bike, holding his body the way he does. Red potatoes in a shovelful of earth. His deep set eyes – eyes with his complexion you'd
think would be blue, but aren't, are black. Under the efficient
line of Roman nose, above the square jaw a bit of cleft, Hank's
sweet smiling lips.

Never ceased to startle me, the way Hank and I could look
at each other.

Hank made a point of looking his eyes full on into mine.
Too long he looked. Somebody who does that. Reveals you to
yourself. I didn't look away. The look was long because he was
trying to express something inside him that's big. That half-
smile of his, part bewildered, part amused, wasn't a smile at all,
was Hank just trying to make his mouth work right.

Took him a while but he did it. So perfect, so true to who
he is. Right out loud he said it:

"I loved you more."

Acknowledgements

A BIG SHOUT OUT OF THANKS TO RHONDA HUGHES AND Hawthorne Books for loving my novel. Also at Hawthorne Books, thank you to Liz Crain, Adam O'Connor Rodriguez, and Adam McIsaac.

Always my thanks to Neil Olson of Donadio and Olson Literary Representatives, NYC. And to you, too, Carrie Howland. And in LA, thanks to Judi Farkas Management LLC.

Thank you, Grey Wolfe. *Muchas gracias*, Johnny Dynell. Also: How old Mendy Graves. Thank you, my dearest Clyde Hall. Cole Coshow, and Frankie, you've always been there for me.

Many thanks to Hunter Morrison, Sam McConnell, Julie Christeas, Schuyler Weiss, Greg Sirota, Justin Vivian Bond, John Cameron Mitchell, Paul and PJ, Susan Anderson, Evelyn Newham and Mick Newham, Morgan Persons, Queen Mae Butters, Jicama, Chaser Rue, Judi Reeves, Frank di Palermo, Scott Ehrlich, Elle Covan, Steve Dearden, Sheena Dearden, and Ella Mae Dearden, Danny Broderick, David Peterson, Alexandra Cadell, Thomasina and Isolde, Martin Mueller, Janice Halteman, Bill Crane, David Young, David Zakon, Woody at Crush, Walker Kozik, Travis Coloma, Paul Ann Peterson, Monica Drake, Kassten Alonso, Chuck Palahniuk, Suzi Vitello, Aaron Scott, Thomas Lauderdale and Philip Iosca, David Weissman, Stevee Postman and Padme, The Esalen Institute, Grandma Ruby, Robert Vasquez, Joe Wheat, Kerry Moosman, Andy Mingo and Miles Mingo.

Thank you to my nurse practitioner, Maria Kozmetatos,

Sheila Walty, LC SW, and Tim Irwin of Studio X. The Naraya dancers at Wolf Creek.

Big love to all the Dangerous Writers, especially Colin Farstad and Kevin Meyer. Thanks to Domi for the Burnt Tongue Readings. Thanks also to Judith Waring.

And in loving memory:

Howard Wasco

Bob Waring

Kay Oswald

Tom Trusky

Bjorn Millom

James Lord.

And to you, my beloved Michael Sage Ricci. None of this would be possible without you. The very thought of you, my beautiful friend, and I forget to do. Lots and lots and forever and forever.